THE MEANING OF LOVE

CONNECTED TO LADY OSBALDESTONE'S CHRISTMAS CHRONICLES

STEPHANIE LAURENS

ABOUT THE MEANING OF LOVE

#1 New York Times *bestselling author Stephanie Laurens explores the strength of a fated love, one that was left in abeyance when the protagonists were too young, but that roars back to life when, as adults, they meet again.*

A lady ready and waiting to be deemed on the shelf has her transition into spinsterhood disrupted when the nobleman she'd once thought she loved returns to London and fate and circumstance conspire to force them to discover what love truly is and what it means to them.

What happens when a love left behind doesn't die?

Melissa North had assumed that after eight years of not setting eyes on each other, her youthful attraction to—or was it infatuation with?—Julian Delamere, once Viscount Dagenham and now Earl of Carsely, would have faded to nothing and gasped its last. Unfortunately, during the intervening years, she's failed to find any suitable suitor who measures up to her mark and is resigned to ending her days an old maid.

Then she sees Julian across a crowded ballroom, and he sees her, and the intensity of their connection shocks her. She seizes the first chance that offers to flee, only to discover she's jumped from the frying pan into the fire.

Within twenty-four hours, she and Julian are the newly engaged toast of the ton.

Julian has never forgotten Melissa. Now, having inherited the earldom, he must marry and is determined to choose his own bride. He'd assumed that by now, Melissa would be married to someone else, but apparently not. Consequently, he's not averse to the path Fate seems to be steering them down.

And, indeed, as they discover, enforced separation has made their hearts grow fonder, and the attraction between them flares even more intensely.

However, it's soon apparent that someone is intent on ensuring their married life is cut short in deadly fashion. Through a whirlwind courtship, a massive ton wedding, and finally, blissful country peace, they fend off increasingly dangerous, potentially lethal threats, until, together, they unravel the conspiracy that's dogged their heels and expose the villain behind it all.

A classic historical romance laced with murderous intrigue. A novel arising from the Lady Osbaldestone's Christmas Chronicles. A full-length historical romance of 127,000 words.

OTHER TITLES BY STEPHANIE LAURENS

A Fine Passion

To Distraction

Beyond Seduction

The Edge of Desire

Mastered by Love

Black Cobra Quartet

The Untamed Bride

The Elusive Bride

The Brazen Bride

The Reckless Bride

The Adventurers Quartet

The Lady's Command

A Buccaneer at Heart

The Daredevil Snared

Lord of the Privateers

The Cavanaughs

The Designs of Lord Randolph Cavanaugh

The Pursuits of Lord Kit Cavanaugh

The Beguilement of Lady Eustacia Cavanaugh

The Obsessions of Lord Godfrey Cavanaugh

Other Novels

The Lady Risks All

The Legend of Nimway Hall – 1750: Jacqueline

Medieval (As M.S.Laurens)

Desire's Prize

Novellas

Melting Ice – from the anthologies *Rough Around the Edges* and *Scandalous Brides*

Rose in Bloom – from the anthology *Scottish Brides*

Scandalous Lord Dere – from the anthology *Secrets of a Perfect Night*

Lost and Found – from the anthology *Hero, Come Back*

The Fall of Rogue Gerrard – from the anthology *It Happened One Night*

The Seduction of Sebastian Trantor – from the anthology *It Happened One Season*

Short Stories

The Wedding Planner – from the anthology *Royal Weddings*

A Return Engagement – from the anthology *Royal Bridesmaids*

UK-Style Regency Romances

Tangled Reins

Four in Hand

Impetuous Innocent

Fair Juno

The Reasons for Marriage

A Lady of Expectations An Unwilling Conquest

A Comfortable Wife

THE MEANING OF LOVE

THE MEANING OF LOVE

Copyright © 2021 by Savdek Management Proprietary Limited

ISBN: 978-1-925559-50-7

Cover design by Savdek Management Pty. Ltd.

Cover couple photography by Period Images © 2021

First print publication: October, 2021

Savdek Management Proprietary Limited, Melbourne, Australia.

www.stephanielaurens.com

Email: admin@stephanielaurens.com

❀ Created with Vellum

CHAPTER 1

MARCH 4, 1821. CARSINGTON CASTLE, DERBYSHIRE.

*J*ulian Delamere, seventh Earl of Carsely, drew rein on the rise where the bridle path emerged from the woods to the west of his home and looked down on the sprawling pile that was Carsington Castle.

The sight was as familiar as his own face. Built of local stone in a mix of colors from pale cream to toffee gold, despite its substantial walls, crenellated battlements, and twin towers, his home exuded a warmth that beckoned, particularly on such a cold gray day. Originally a fortified manor house, the castle had been added to over the centuries and remodeled and enlarged several times. As all projects had continued to use the local stone, the end result was both visually pleasing as well as reasonably practical. He and his four siblings had grown up there, and each of them knew every inch of the house, grounds, and surrounding woods.

Scanning from right to left, he took in the fields waiting to be sown and the herds of cows and sheep lazily grazing. Spring had yet to show its face in Derbyshire, but a group of red deer had emerged from the woods north of the castle to nibble on the emerging grass.

All was as it should be—as it needed to be. He'd spent the past year picking up the reins of the far-flung estates he'd inherited on the unexpected death of his father. He hadn't thought it would take that long, but it had. He didn't begrudge the time; he'd always accepted that, along with the title, would come that responsibility—and others.

The heavy hunter beneath him shifted and settled, perfectly content to wait while his rider wasted time. Julian patted the gray's neck. Regis had been his father's mount. It still puzzled Julian that, although Regis was the least flighty or temperamental horse he'd ever known, it was from Regis's back that his father had been thrown.

He still couldn't reconcile that.

At the time, he'd been in Ireland, with the Home Office, as right-hand man to the Under-Secretary for Ireland in Dublin Castle. The news of his father's death had come as a bolt from the blue; as far as he'd known, his father had been in excellent health. Although he'd rushed to get back, he'd barely been in time for the funeral—far too late to investigate anything. Now, a year later, he still felt unsettled over what they assumed must have occurred, uneasy over simply not knowing—not being sure. His father had been an accomplished rider who had ridden to hounds all his life, yet he'd apparently been unseated by a jump over a perfectly ordinary three-barred gate, one Regis would have taken with ease. The horse had sustained no injury, but his father's neck had been broken.

Fatal riding accidents weren't unknown in those parts, yet...

After several moments of staring unseeing at the castle, Julian shook aside the unsettling uncertainty and refocused on his next inevitable step in assuming the mantle of the Earl of Carsely. The management of the estate was firmly in his hands, with the necessary adjustments in place to ensure that all continued running smoothly subsequent to the execution of his father's will. All was done and complete, and there was no reason to further delay facing the next issue he needed to address.

He shook the reins. It was time to get on with his life and take charge of shaping his own future.

～

Julian reached the stable yard, dismounted, and led Regis toward the open stable door.

Hockey, the grizzled stable master, emerged from the depths of the large building and met Julian at the door. "Just as well you took the old man out." His expression grim, Hockey reached for Regis's reins.

Julian met Hockey's gaze. "Why?"

"Because Regis is the size he is, you had to use your father's saddle rather than your own, and when Mitchell went to put your saddle back in the tack room"—Hockey tipped his head toward the far end of the stable

—"he noticed the inner seam was split and a wicked big thorn had been tucked inside."

Julian stared at Hockey. He'd intended to ride his own mount, Argus, a flighty Arab, that morning, but neither he nor Hockey had liked the way Argus had been favoring his right front hoof. Consequently, he'd opted to take Regis; the big hunter hadn't been ridden as much as he was accustomed to since Julian's father's death. "Any idea how the thorn got there?"

His lips compressed, Hockey shook his head. "But I do know that the way it was set, it would likely have worked its way out while you rode and, at some point, would have given Argus a nasty jab, perhaps more than one, and he wouldn't have liked that one bit." Hockey's gaze grew concerned. "Who knows if you'd've been able to hold on? And with your father—"

Julian gripped Hockey's arm. "That wasn't your fault." He couldn't bring himself to state that it had been an accident; he still wasn't convinced it had been.

Hockey humphed and looked away.

Julian understood Hockey's sensitivity. A few days after his father's death, his father's groom, Campbell, had hung himself in the tack room. No one knew whether the suicide had been prompted by misplaced guilt —which, given how long Campbell had been his father's groom and how devoted to the late earl Campbell had been, was a definite possibility—or if there'd been more to it and, for reasons unknown, Campbell had somehow contributed to whatever had caused the late earl to be thrown.

Although none of them could imagine the latter, the thought lingered in the backs of many minds.

Julian released Hockey. "Nevertheless, that's…disturbing."

"Aye, it's that, all right." Hockey looked deeper into the stable. "I'm thinking of locking the stable and carriage barn when we're not around. At least for a time."

Julian nodded. "That's a sound idea." At least until he could figure out what was going on.

He met Hockey's eyes, nodded in dismissal, and strode toward the house.

His saddle was newish and in excellent condition; the seam couldn't have split by itself. It was even less likely that a large thorn would have found its way into the gap—not without assistance. But assistance from whom? The stable had a large staff of grooms and stablemen. Other than

Mitchell, who was relatively new, the rest had been employed at the castle for years if not decades, and most were from families who lived on the estate.

Julian crossed the drive and walked up the gravel path that led to one of the castle's side terraces. He was climbing the terrace steps when the sound of footsteps on the flagstones above had him looking up. His brother Felix appeared at the top of the steep steps.

Felix saw him, smiled, and halted. "How was the ride?"

Julian stepped onto the terrace and grunted. "Relaxing. What wasn't so relaxing was discovering that someone had stuck a thorn under the saddle I was going to use but, by sheer luck, didn't."

Consternation swamped Felix's expression. "What?" He fell in beside Julian as he continued toward the side door.

Succinctly, Julian relayed what Hockey had told him.

"I suppose there's no easy way to find out who did it?"

His expression as grim as Hockey's had been, Julian shook his head.

After a second, Felix ventured, "After what happened with Papa—"

"Exactly. But sadly, neither you nor I was here at the time, and for all we know, that was an accident."

"A thorn in your new saddle's seam isn't any accident," Felix countered.

"No, it's not." They'd reached the terrace door. Julian gripped the handle and paused. "But no more than I can reconcile that Papa was simply thrown can I make sense of it. I've been largely absent for more than a decade. I was in Ireland for eight years before returning, and as far as I know, I've made no enemies, before or since. Why anyone would arrange to have me thrown…I have absolutely no idea."

Worry was written all over Felix's face. "So what will you do?"

Julian arched his brows. "As far as I can see, there's nothing—at least nothing useful—I can do. Too many people, including someone sneaking in from outside, could have gained access to the saddle. The stable hasn't been locked."

Felix grimaced.

"So"—Julian opened the door—"I'm going to carry on as I'd intended." He led the way inside. "I'm going to London. I've decided it's time to plunge into the fray and look for a wife who will suit me. A preemptive strike, as it were."

Felix's "Really?" rang with stunned surprise.

Cynically, Julian smiled. "Far better that I choose my own wife than have the grandes dames foist their preferred candidate on me." He glanced at Felix. "You know they will."

"Well, yes, but…this seems a mite precipitous."

"Not at all. It's the start of the Season, and I'm hoping no one will expect me, that they won't anticipate me being proactive. I'm counting on having the element of surprise, at least long enough to look over the field without interference." He'd long ago learned that in any negotiation, acting unpredictably never hurt.

The man who had arranged for the thorn to be placed in the Earl of Carsely's saddle closed the door to his sitting room, then crossed to an armchair angled before the hearth and sank into its comfort. He smiled to himself. He felt entirely confident that no one would ever suspect him of having designs on Carsely's life.

He drew out the letter with the Wirksworth postmark that he'd picked up from the salver in the front hall earlier in the day. Now that his landlady, as he thought of her, had taken herself off to some ball, he could peruse the missive in peace. Eagerly, he broke the plain seal, spread the single sheet, and read.

"Damn it!" The oath exploded from him, and his expression, which had been radiating eager expectation, contorted into one of petulant anger. He muttered another oath, then crumpled the note, flung it into the fire, and watched it burn.

He stared at the flames.

Gradually, his expression eased. "It was a long shot," he reminded himself. "An opportunity worth seizing, but in no way guaranteed."

After a moment, he went on, "At least it seems that the attempt hasn't harmed his usefulness. In fact, it might have consolidated his position, and that can only help. Another opportunity—a more certain opportunity —will come his way soon enough, and when it does…"

He had his agents in place, primed to take advantage.

"Steady and sure will win this race, and in this case, time is very much on my side."

This was a complex mission—one far more challenging than any of his previous advances—and he prided himself on being patient in pursuit of long-term gains.

~

Melissa North stood by the side of Lady Connaught's ballroom and wished she could have remained at home. For years, she'd been able to use her much prettier sister, Mandy, as a social shield. Where Melissa was tall and willowy, with straight sable-brown hair, very pale fair skin, dark-blue eyes, and a naturally reserved manner, Mandy had bright golden curls, sparkling light-blue eyes, and a peaches-and-cream complexion, and she'd always bubbled with an enthusiasm for life that had guaranteed every gentleman's eye had fixed on her.

Mandy and Melissa, less than a year apart in age, had made their come-outs together. Mandy, the elder, had insisted on that, and Melissa had been happy to agree. While outwardly, Mandy was socially confident, in reality, it was Melissa who was the calm, collected one able to deal with any drama, and thus it had always been. Mandy was the bright light while Melissa was the anchor.

The sisters had made a pact that they would not make any matrimonial choices during their first Season, when they'd been just nineteen and eighteen respectively. They'd held to that and, instead, had enjoyed themselves learning society's ropes. Unsurprisingly, in their second Season, Mandy had caught the eye of Rufus, Lord Sedon. Unfortunately, due to the death of their paternal grandmother, they'd missed the subsequent Season entirely, so it was only two Seasons ago that Mandy and Rufus had been able to announce their engagement.

And then Melissa had had two beautiful people to hide behind, which had suited her very well.

Inevitably, however, toward the end of the previous Season, Mandy and Rufus had wed. Consequently, this Season, Mandy, expecting their first child and rather large, wasn't around to act as a distraction.

That left Melissa having to fend off those gentlemen who, finally, had noticed her.

She didn't want to be noticed.

The musicians put bow to string, and irritatingly, two gentlemen determinedly approached. A yard away, they saw each other, halted, and eyed each other discouragingly.

Lord Cargill's son blinked first, and with a triumphant smile, Lord Hopgood advanced, beaming winningly at Melissa. "My dear Miss North, might I request the pleasure of this dance?"

Summoning a weak smile, Melissa met his brown eyes and flicked open the fan she carried for such moments. Fanning her face, in a timid, almost faltering voice, she replied, "I fear, sir, that I'm feeling rather faint. Perhaps…later."

The thought of a female swooning in their arms was usually enough to make gentlemen rethink the wisdom of pursuing her company, and so it proved, although to give Hopgood his due, he did solicitously inquire as to whether she wished to be escorted to her mother's side.

Heaven forbid. Melissa's mother would never believe such a tale of her robustly healthy daughter. "No, thank you. I would rather remain here, out of the way." Melissa smiled more genuinely and released Hopgood to find some other partner. Cargill had already taken himself off. Having successfully avoided yet another dance, Melissa folded her fan and kept her eyes on it, her gaze directed downward so as not to invite further attention.

By ton standards, she was definitely not in Mandy's league in terms of visual beauty, and she had to admit that the gentlemen's attentions, genuine enough, were flattering in a way, yet senselessly encouraging any gentleman formed no part of her forward planning.

Slowly, she allowed her gaze to rise again, until she was contemplating the couples whirling about the dance floor. Idly scanning, she noted the bright, hopeful expressions on the faces of many of the year's debutantes. Despite her intended direction, she could appreciate the emotions behind those starry-eyed expressions. Once, she, too, had hoped to find a gentleman with whom to spend the rest of her life. The right gentleman—the one she could marry with a glad and whole heart—with whom, hand in hand, she could establish a home and a family of her own. Given her background and her family, such a desire was ingrained, yet despite applying herself diligently to searching for said gentleman, she'd never found him. In the years since her come-out, she'd met no man she could even remotely imagine spending the rest of her life beside.

Within her first two Seasons, she'd established that either the gentleman for her didn't exist, or she was too picky. Or both.

Then during the year of their missed Season, while the family was in mourning, she'd discovered other interests. Interests society deemed acceptable for a lady, even an unmarried one, to pursue.

On returning to the ton and finding it and her prejudices unchanged, she'd formulated a plan for her future life. Unfortunately, a necessary prerequisite—at least as far as her parents and maternal grandmother were concerned—was attendance at all suitable social events through to the end of this Season.

Only then would her "looking for the right gentleman" ordeal be declared at an end.

She'd badgered her parents into accepting that, come June this year, she would be beyond the age of mixing with debutantes. Although they'd yet to acquiesce to her describing herself as being formally "on the shelf," they'd agreed that, instead of attending the balls and parties of the social whirl, she could devote her time to improving the welfare of orphaned children up and down the country. That was her aim, and once she reached the end of this Season and had appeased her elders, she was determined to strike out and fashion a satisfying life of enlightened spinsterhood.

She couldn't wait for the Season to end.

Predictably, the grandes dames were in no way amused by her direction, which they'd learned of from her grandmother and her bosom-bows. Having a grandmother who ranked among the grandest of the grandes dames wasn't always an advantage. Indeed, several grandes dames had demanded that she describe her "right gentleman," something she'd found well-nigh impossible to do. It was difficult to explain that some finely honed instinct simply knew—with absolute and unwavering certainty— that none of the gentlemen who had appeared before her was the right one for her.

The grandes dames had not been impressed by her vague replies. She was fairly certain several were combing through their acquaintances, searching for whom they might, in desperation, thrust into her path over the coming months.

The music faded, and the dance ended. As the couples drifted from the floor and conversational groups formed, she wished she could fade into the paneling. Avoiding dancing was one thing. Avoiding conversational interaction was rather more difficult.

Apparently idly, she scanned the room, noting several determined gentlemen who were looking her way, then her gaze snagged on a particular dark head directly across the crowded room.

Curious as to why he, whoever he was, had snared her attention, she focused on his profile, all she could presently see as he spoke with several ladies. He was tall, dark-haired, with upward-angled dark brows and thick black lashes, chiseled cheekbones, a clean-cut jawline, and patrician nose. Something about him seemed familiar...

Her eyes widened. "Good Lord," she muttered. "It's Dagenham."

No, not Dagenham—he's the Earl of Carsely now.

"What the devil's he doing here?" She frowned. "He's likely to be mobbed."

That was not a facetious prediction. She'd known he'd gone into the Home Office and, subsequently, been sent to Ireland. During her first Season, she'd wondered and, ultimately, had surreptitiously checked and learned that he had still been on the other side of the Irish Sea and had not been expected to make an appearance in London any time soon.

And he hadn't.

Then last year, his father had unexpectedly died, cutting short Julian's Home Office career and, presumably, bringing him back to England, but he hadn't returned to London. Given that, courtesy of succeeding to the title, he'd shot to the very top of the eligible bachelor stakes, she'd considered that a very wise decision.

As far as she'd heard, he hadn't been sighted in the capital—until tonight.

She continued to frown. He had to know that he'd become a prime target for every matchmaker in the ton. To come strolling into Lady Connaught's ballroom... Cynically, she arched her brows. "Perhaps he *wants* to be mobbed."

She hadn't spoken with Julian—Viscount Dagenham as he'd been—for over eight years, and even then, their interactions had spanned only a matter of weeks. She'd been fifteen and he twenty-one when they'd agreed that their budding juvenile romance was a connection neither could see any viable way to pursue. They'd both been too young; either asking the other to wait for three to four years hadn't been in their cards.

They'd parted and gone their separate ways.

To say that, in the years since, she hadn't thought of him and of what might have been would be untrue, but equally, not knowing how he'd changed over the years—as he most certainly would have; by her calculation, he was thirty now—she hadn't felt she'd known him well enough to pine for something that might never have eventuated.

Besides, given he'd been stationed in Dublin and she'd heard that the social round was much the same there, at least in intent, she'd assumed that some enterprising young lady would have caught his eye by now.

Yet there he was, with no enterprising lady hanging on his arm, and for some benighted reason, she couldn't seem to tear her eyes away from him.

The crowd between them shifted, groups rearranging, and she had a clear line of sight.

She stared, and as if sensing her regard, he turned his head and looked her way.

Their gazes collided.

And locked.

She felt it as a physical connection—a stunning blow, then being seized and held.

His gray gaze captured her; his presence commanded her awareness and consumed her every sense.

She couldn't move. She couldn't breathe as she fell into his gaze—and he fell into hers.

She couldn't look away, and neither, it seemed, could he. Neither moved or signaled any awareness of the world around them.

The wordless connection held and swelled and gained intensity and weight.

Neither wanted to be the one to break it.

At the edge of her vision, she saw the ladies he'd been conversing with trying to regain his attention, in vain.

Yet he and she couldn't simply stand there, trapped by memories in a snare of unrequited longing. At any second, people would see and realize...

She sensed movement to her right; someone was approaching.

With a massive effort, she hauled in a huge breath and swung her gaze that way. It landed on the complacent features of Gordon Delamere.

Melissa inwardly groaned, but she was too desperate for something—anything—to counter Julian's grip on her senses to send Gordon off.

"Good evening, Miss North." Gordon halted beside her, bowed, and reached for her hand.

Reacting by rote, she turned to him, murmured a greeting, and surrendered her fingers. To her horror, she felt giddy, her wits still whirling and her thoughts consumed by Carsely.

Good Lord! I need to find my feet!

Gordon was only a year or so older than she, yet since the start of the Season, he'd been assiduous in his attentions and annoyingly persistent despite her admittedly subtle discouragements.

Subtlety, one had to conclude, was wasted on Gordon.

True to form, he attempted to engage her in a conversation that might have been appropriate had she been eighteen. At twenty-three, she was past the age of even pretending an interest in a gentleman's driving exploits, and with her senses still skittering after the impact of locking eyes with Carsely and her thoughts in disarray, she didn't pay any attention to what Gordon was saying.

Unable to stop herself, from the corner of her eye, she glanced across the room. Her heart leapt as she found Julian—Carsely—still staring at her, but now, he was frowning.

What he was frowning about, she couldn't guess, but doubted it boded well.

"I say, are you feeling quite the thing?"

She refocused on Gordon and found him peering rather concernedly at her face.

"You're looking a trifle pale, and if you don't mind me mentioning it, you seem a bit dazed." Gordon glanced at the windows beside them. "Perhaps a turn on the terrace might help?"

Her heart was thumping uncomfortably, and she could barely form a coherent thought; cold fresh air on her face and a little time in a quieter space sounded divine. She gripped Gordon's sleeve. "Yes—you're right. I'm not feeling a hundred percent and could do with some air."

She all but pushed him toward the French door that gave onto the terrace running alongside the ballroom.

"Allow me." Pointedly, Gordon opened the door, lifted her hand from his sleeve, and ushered her through, onto the terrace.

Biting back an acid comment about fragile male egos, she allowed him to lead her along the terrace as if they were strolling in the cool night air. No other couple had yet sought the relative privacy of the flagstone expanse, but the ball was barely halfway through, and there was a chilly breeze blowing.

Surreptitiously, she glanced through the windows into the ballroom— and saw Julian, his expression grim, cutting through the intervening guests, making a beeline for the terrace door.

Her senses—along with her stupid heart—leapt again; why, she couldn't have said, but the reaction held a large dose of panic, and the instinct to flee surged.

Abruptly, she turned to Gordon. "I've always wanted to examine her ladyship's gardens by moonlight." Thankfully, the moon was shining from a largely cloudless sky. "Would you mind if we strolled a little? If we take that path"—she pointed to the gravel path leading away from the bottom of the terrace steps—"we can circle through the gardens."

She leaned closer and all but batted her lashes. "You don't mind, do you?"

Gordon blinked, then smiled in transparently genuine delight. "Not at all—happy to oblige." They'd reached the top of the steps, and he waved downward. "Shall we?"

After a fleeting glance at the ballroom—confirming that Julian was still some way from gaining the terrace—Melissa smiled equally sincerely. "Indeed—let's."

She matched Gordon as he went swiftly down the steps, then ensured he kept up the pace as they strode swiftly along the path that, she knew, led to a small gazebo.

When the shadows cast by the trees swallowed them, she breathed a touch easier.

~

Julian bit his tongue against the urge to tell those who insisted on waylaying him to go to the devil. Instead, he forced himself to pause each time he was hailed, acknowledge whoever spoke, and exchange a modicum of civilized conversation before excusing himself and moving on.

He needed to go after Gordon and Melissa, but for her sake, he shouldn't draw attention to his mission.

As matters stood, Gordon, who was a cousin twice removed, couldn't be trusted with any marriageable young lady who commanded a decent dowry, which Melissa, being one of Lord North's daughters, presumably did. Gordon was in severe financial straits and, apparently, was looking for a well-dowered wife to help him come about. Julian's mother had informed him of that, and he didn't doubt she had it right; she rarely made mention of such things, but when she brought something of that nature to his attention, it was because it was true, and she expected that he, as the head of the Delamere family, would at some point have to deal with some less-than-satisfactory development.

Julian had hoped that Melissa would have heard of Gordon's situation, but it seemed the news was not yet widespread.

The possibility that she did know, but nevertheless, had chosen to go apart with Gordon...

Julian stuffed that notion into a mental compartment labeled Surely Not.

To his abiding surprise, it appeared Melissa was still unmarried. For years, he'd assumed that, while he'd been stuck in Ireland, she would have had her Seasons, and some clod would have snapped her up, but apparently not. She wore no cap or other ornament in her dark hair to signal she was a matron, and if she was married or even promised to another, Gordon wouldn't be wasting his charm on her.

Regardless of that charm, regardless of what Melissa herself thought, of one thing Julian was absolutely certain. Melissa North was not for the likes of Gordon.

While he smiled and chatted, his mind remained wholly focused on rescuing Melissa. Operating on two levels simultaneously was a skill he'd perfected over the past years; being able to do so was essential when dealing with Dublin's elite. Analyzing his reactions had also become second nature, yet while he recognized that the intensity of the compulsion to rescue Melissa from Gordon's clutches bordered on the irrational, he didn't consider resisting, much less questioning the near-overwhelming impulse.

Finally, he reached the terrace door, opened it, stepped swiftly through, and closed the door behind him.

He'd expected to discover the pair on the terrace—possibly in the shadows that draped the far end—but one searching glance confirmed they weren't anywhere in sight.

His compulsion ratcheted up several notches along with his temper. "Damn!" *Where are they?* Surely Melissa knew better than to go into a dark garden with a man like Gordon!

Julian eyed the path that stretched away from either end of the terrace, leading into the night-shrouded gardens. Which way would they have gone?

His hands on his hips, he stared at the path, then closed his eyes. He'd been in this garden years ago; the Connaughts' son had been a chum at Eton, and one summer, they'd spent several afternoons smoking cheroots—

"In the gazebo." He opened his eyes and swore.

Without further hesitation, he strode for the steps at the terrace's farther end. He went quickly down. The instant he hit gravel, he started to run.

∾

From inside the gazebo, which was wreathed in helpful shadows, Melissa kept watch on the path from the terrace.

She hated feeling panicky, but until she was sure Julian hadn't followed them, her nerves weren't going to settle enough to think of anything else.

The breeze sighed through the branches of the conifers that overhung the hexagonal gazebo; she hadn't realized the interior would be quite so gloomy. She shifted and peered in the opposite direction; if Julian followed, he could approach from either side.

Behind her, Gordon cleared his throat. "I say, Miss North—Melissa, if I may?"

"You may not." That didn't require thought.

He made a strangled sound. "Look here, you're out here, alone with me, in the gardens, and you were the one who wanted to come into the gazebo—you chose to come here."

"Hmm." She looked the other way, narrowing her eyes in an effort to pierce the shifting shadows.

"See here." Gordon was growing belligerent. "The least you can do is pay attention to me."

Why? "Tell me about your horses." Gentlemen always wanted to talk about their horses.

"I already have! I use hired hacks—I mentioned that before."

Now, he sounded petulant.

She squinted. Was that movement on the path?

"Look, I know we haven't had time to learn much about each other, but I'm sincere when I say"—Gordon's large hands closed about Melissa's shoulders, and he forcibly turned her to face him—"that—*Ow!*"

She'd stamped hard on his foot; as she was wearing hard-soled dance shoes, that had hurt enough to be effective. Her features set, she shoved his hands off her shoulders, stepped into him, and thrust a warning finger in his face. "Don't you ever—*ever*—presume to lay hands on me or any other young lady!"

Her nerves were stretched taut, her senses skittish, her wits fragmented. The compulsion to keep her eyes trained on the path was a physical thing—and now, she had to deal with Gordon!

"*Presume?*" He limped a little as he backed away. "But why did you come out here with me if not to"—he gestured between them—"further our acquaintance?"

Her temper ignited. "I have no interest whatsoever in furthering my acquaintance with you! I came outside—thinking to claim your protection as a gentleman—because I needed to get out of the ballroom and get some fresh air!"

His expression turned ugly. "Well, damn it, we're here now." He lunged for her.

She hadn't expected that, but her brother, Christopher, was only a year younger than she, and years of wrestling with him had taught her a few tricks.

Slamming her elbow into Gordon's sternum gave him pause and stopped him from hauling her completely into his arms. She kept her head back so that he couldn't kiss her, narrowed her eyes and trapped his gaze, and in a tone vibrating with fury, succinctly stated, "Let. Go. Of. Me."

He froze, but didn't immediately obey.

She smiled chillingly. "If you don't—if you do not instantly behave in an appropriately gentlemanly manner—on my return to the ballroom, the first people I will speak with are your mother, my mother, my grandmother, and my godmother, Lady Connaught. I will describe your puerile behavior in detail. I'm reasonably certain you will then find that you are persona non grata in all the best ballrooms for the rest of the Season at least—and just think of how your peers will laugh when that news gets around."

He paled. Then his grip eased, and his expression aggrieved and somewhat puzzled, he released her and stepped back.

"An excellent decision." The minor triumph was a welcome distraction from her earlier panic.

Frowning, he complained, "You're supposed to be biddable."

Incredulous, she all but spluttered, "*Biddable?* Who told you that?"

"You're always quiet. Quiet girls do what they're told, don't they?"

She stared at him. "Gordon, you're delusional. For your information, quiet often means stubborn and, most likely, thinking of other things. You've met my mother and my grandmother. In what universe would I be *biddable?*" Her voice had risen. For some reason, she found the suggestion deeply insulting.

Even in the poor light, she saw Gordon blush. "Well," he said, jaw setting, "we'll just have to manage this regardless."

To her surprise, he started determinedly toward her. But then his gaze went past her, and he halted. All color drained from his face. "Carsely." Shock wreathed Gordon's features. "What are you doing in London?"

"At this moment, I'm saving Miss North from you."

Melissa closed her eyes and bit back an oath; thanks to Gordon, she'd taken her eyes off the path. Julian's voice was deeper, more resonant, than she remembered it; the sound strummed across her taut nerves and set them twanging. Her awareness and every one of her senses flared.

Gordon blustered, "I don't know what you're talking about."

She blinked, then stepped sideways and turned. Julian was standing, loose-limbed and taller than she remembered him, just inside the gazebo. She hadn't heard him approach and climb the steps; the sight of him sent frissons dancing over her skin and down her spine.

He'd matured since last she'd seen him; then again, so had she. The man who stood two yards away was a far cry from the lanky young nobleman he'd been; this version was plainly a force to be reckoned with.

His dark, almost-black hair was elegantly cut and fashionably windswept, a style that suited his Byronesque handsomeness. His evening clothes were the height of elegance and fitted his broad-shouldered, lean, and rangy frame to perfection. The impression he projected was one of calm, contained, and controlled power, of flexible, effortless strength of both body and mind. His intelligence was evident, directing every movement and every word.

With his gaze locked on Gordon, he walked forward and halted a few feet from her. "I'm referring to your notion of repairing your financial situation by marrying a well-dowered lady—not, of itself, a disreputable aim—but how you go about it, that, dear cuz, does concern me and all the rest of the family."

The penny dropped, and she realized that Julian, as the earl, was now the head of his family, and apparently, that family was the Delameres. She hadn't previously heard his last name. He'd always been Dagenham or, more recently, Carsely to her, and in the years since they'd parted, she'd been extremely careful not to evince too much interest in him.

But Julian was still speaking, wielding words like a whip as he laid into Gordon over the younger man's dissolute habits and profligate ways, which, unsurprisingly, had led to his currently precarious pecuniary state.

Gordon grew surly but, other than tossing Julian dark looks, didn't even attempt to defend himself, leaving her to conclude that all that Julian so succinctly and clinically laid bare was true.

That Gordon Delamere had set out that evening to somehow force her into marriage gradually sank in.

If she hadn't been distracted by Julian's appearance—hadn't been sent fleeing by the impact of that shared glance—she would never have accepted Gordon's escort onto the terrace, let alone to the secluded gazebo. She recalled how pleased Gordon had been at her suggestion they go outside; he'd caught her at a weak moment, and she'd fallen like a ripe plum into his hands.

If Julian hadn't come after her...

That didn't bear thinking about.

Her temper surged anew, but as Julian was doing such an excellent job of ripping strips off his cousin, she wrestled her temper into submission and let him have the field.

By the time Julian dismissed Gordon with a harshly condemnatory look and a pointed recommendation to rethink his strategy, she almost felt sorry for Gordon.

Almost.

With his lips compressed, after fleetingly glancing at her, with a careful, wary look at Julian, Gordon stepped past him and left.

Julian turned and watched his cousin go and fought to rein in his raging temper. He'd long ago learned not to lose it—he couldn't remember the last time he had—but at that moment, bombarded by feelings on so many fronts, he was struggling to harness his fury.

He wasn't even sure who he was angrier with—Gordon or...

The instant Gordon was out of sight, Julian swung to face Melissa. He looked into her face—a moonlight-pale oval surrounded by the frame of her dark hair. His gaze roved her features, hungrily committing each to renewed memory, overwriting the vision he'd carried of her; her finely arched black brows, large dark-blue eyes, and lips the color of a pale blush rose, their lines drawn by a master, seared into his conscious mind. Important—so important.

Something in him had always known that.

He tried, truly tried, but couldn't stop his anger from spilling forth. "Don't you have the sense you were born with? What the devil possessed you to come out here with such an obvious if pretty cad like Gordon?"

Her eyes narrowed, and her lovely lips compressed. After a second, she responded, "He's not that pretty, and why I chose to accompany him outside is none of your business."

"Really?" He couldn't stop himself; he shifted closer, looming over her. "And how did you imagine you were going to manage once he got his hands on you?"

Her eyes all but sparked. "For your information, he'd already tried that and had discovered I'm not some helpless biddable female." She tipped up her chin. "I didn't require any rescue. I'm not the young girl you used to know."

"That's half right"—she certainly wasn't the slip of a thing, retiring and reserved, he'd been so attracted to all those years ago—"but trust me when I say Gordon wasn't about to stand down. He is that desperate." The notion she would have been able to subdue his cousin was nonsensical. She was slender, sleekly curved, and a lightweight, and Gordon was almost as large and strong as he was.

She wouldn't have stood a chance.

The realization of how close she'd come to... His temper surged. He gritted his teeth, thrust his face closer to hers so their eyes bored into each other's, and bit off, "Regardless of your, likely misplaced, confidence in your fighting skills, gentlemen like Gordon are not for you."

Toe to toe with the man she still occasionally dreamt of, with her temper in the ascendant, Melissa felt not a single qualm in meeting his gray eyes, full of silver fire, and quietly, evenly, and categorically stating, "You have no right whatsoever to dictate with whom I choose to associate."

She glared into his eyes and saw silver deepen to pewter. His temper was a tangible thing, beating against her own. She sensed more than saw the tension in him waver, as if he teetered on the knife-edge of a decision.

Then he moved.

His hands rose and framed her cheeks, and he drew her to her toes, bent his head, and crushed her lips beneath his in a hard, fiery, passionate kiss.

CHAPTER 2

*S*hocked, stunned, Melissa stood stock-still for a heartbeat, then her hands rose, fisted in his lapels, and she hauled him to her and kissed him back.

A ragged sound escaped him. One of his hands cupped her nape, and crowding closer, he changed the angle of the exchange.

Instinctively, she parted her lips and was shocked anew—beyond thrilled—when he thrust his tongue into her mouth and claimed.

This. Oh yes. This.

This was what she'd craved for over eight years. What she'd dreamed of experiencing, times beyond counting.

Others had kissed her, and she'd felt nothing—none of this fizzing and sparking, nothing remotely like this rising hunger.

She followed his lead, mimicked his actions, and sensed his ardor rise to meet hers. Giddy, beyond breathless, she held him to her and savored.

~

His hands shoved into his pockets, his gaze on the gravel, Gordon trudged along the path toward the terrace.

"Damn it all," he muttered. "Why couldn't Carsely mind his own business?"

Two paces later, he grumbled, "Anyway, what's it to him if I persuade Miss North to accept my proposal?"

No answers came.

Disgruntled, aggravated, and still stinging from some of Julian's all-too-perceptive rebukes, Gordon was halfway to the house when, abruptly, he halted and raised his head. Drawing his hands from his pockets, he frowned. "Should I call off the troops?" He tipped his head. "Or not?"

He debated for several seconds, but the image of his exalted cousin having to explain himself after being found alone with Miss North—a sharp-tongued shrew if there ever was one—decided him.

"Serve Julian right. Let him talk his way out of that."

Gordon grinned and, in a much better mood, continued to the house.

Inside the gazebo, Julian broke from the kiss purely to haul in a much-needed breath.

Dazed, his wits reeling, his arms trapping Melissa's slender form against his harder frame, he focused on her Madonna-like face, lit by the faint, filtered moonlight.

Her long lashes fluttered, then rose to reveal dark eyes shining like stars.

"I've waited eight years for that." He barely recognized his own voice, so gravelly and deep had it become—how affected.

Her lightly swollen lips faintly curved. "So have I." Deliberately, with clear intent, she slid her hands to his nape and drew him inexorably to her.

His gaze fixed on her lips—soft, succulent, parted, and oh-so-tempting—and on a groan, he complied and dove back into the kiss, desperately craving more of the magic.

He couldn't get enough.

Like a man who'd been starved for decades and more, who'd hungered every day for this unknown sweetness, now he'd tasted her and savored the glory of her response, he couldn't force himself to stop.

Through the increasingly heated exchange, they communed; there was no other word for it. She welcomed him, encouraged him, lured him deeper, until they were spiraling through layers of sensation, lost to the moment, to the building passion.

All that he felt, she felt, too; that much reached him clearly. That much he registered and relished.

She—*this*—was more than just the appeasement of a craving. She was who he needed; he'd known that eight years ago and, patently, nothing had changed.

Need—his and hers—thrummed in the heat of the engagement.

Tittering—*tittering?*—jerked him to awareness, back to the gazebo in Lady Connaught's garden.

Melissa had heard it, too. As their lips parted and he raised his head, her eyes sprang open, the same consternation that he felt flooding her expression.

Even before he turned, he suspected what he would find. No one tittered quite like a certain breed of older lady.

Sure enough, three of the species were clustered in a knot just inside the gazebo. He couldn't imagine what had brought them out there, but as he straightened and the weak light fell on his face, he saw surprise light their features, and suspicion bloomed. He set it aside for now; he had more urgent matters to deal with.

Beneath her breath, so quietly only he would hear, Melissa murmured, "Naturally, we have to be found by three of the biggest gossips in the *ton*."

Without conscious thought, his hand had found and closed about one of hers. Surreptitiously, he squeezed her fingers in warning, then summoning a suitably delighted smile, he raised her hand, pressed a kiss to her fingertips, then lowered them and announced, "Ladies, you're the first to learn our news. Miss North has just done me the honor of agreeing to be my countess."

The three ladies gasped, genuinely startled.

To Melissa, he murmured, "Smile as if you truly want to be the Countess of Carsely."

He felt the touch of her gaze on his face, then she stepped out of his shadow and positively beamed at the three avidly inquisitive ladies. "Isn't that the most wonderful news? I'm thrilled!"

"Oh—oh yes!" The ladies broke into gushing expressions of delight and tripped over themselves to offer their felicitations.

From Melissa's point of view, what followed was a random mix of moments of sheer nightmare, challenging charade, and unexpected amusement.

The nightmare was the effort of clinging to their necessary façade in the face of quite scarifying attention. She'd had no idea, and plainly Julian hadn't had, either, that so many of the grandes dames would take such a close and immediate interest in them. That they'd originally come to know each other while under her grandmother's eye in Little Moseley was the single element in their concocted tale that rendered it acceptable to such observers.

Knowing they stood on such shaky ground made both of them exceedingly careful.

Projecting a believable image of a couple delightedly acknowledging a surprise betrothal was a charade well within their social skills; they knew what was expected and played their parts with convincing ease. Their way was smoothed by having seized the moment when Julian returned her to her mother's side to whisperingly hint at the truth, enough to alert her mother to the real situation. Her mother had focused briefly on Melissa's lips—presumably slightly swollen—then her mother had glanced at Julian and taken charge. As Melissa could have predicted, Henrietta, Lady North, responded faultlessly, acting the delighted mother-of-the-bride-to-be to the hilt.

Although she stood on deeply familiar ground, Melissa nevertheless felt unsure of her footing, a feeling she ascribed to being forced into close proximity with Julian combined with the shock of being declared the next Countess of Carsely.

He seemed to take the situation in his stride, artfully replying to the more inquisitive of their well-wishers without actually revealing anything. Home Office training, she supposed. Certainly, his adroitness in steering the exchanges led to her mother being ever more accommodating regarding his directions.

Melissa would have sniffed disparagingly if he hadn't proved so usefully adept at preserving their fiction. She felt certain that other than her mother, not one of those present realized their supposed engagement was a sham.

In truth, she didn't want to think of that herself; how to resolve their faux engagement was a matter best left for later. She couldn't afford to lower her guard, and plainly, she and Julian were not going to be given any moments to discuss anything in private during the rest of the evening.

At one point in the proceedings, he murmured sotto voce, "Just how many grandes dames are there? It seems like fully half of them are here."

She considered, then, still smiling serenely, conceded, "About half, yes." She caught the startled look he sent her. "Lady Connaught is one of the premier hostesses."

His brows faintly rose. "I didn't realize. She wasn't the last time I was in town."

The comment alerted her to his difficulty in operating on superseded knowledge. Thereafter, as more couples and groups queued to tender felicitations at their happy news, she made a point of mentioning those whose situations had changed.

No one in the ballroom wished to be behindhand, and Lady Connaught was in alt.

After their hostess swooped in and patted them both delightedly and commended them for standing and receiving for so long—thus ensuring they continued—Julian murmured, "I suspect we've made her evening."

"Her week," Melissa corrected. "As a hostess gift, having an elusive earl declare a surprise betrothal at one's event rather takes the cake."

He huffed a laugh, then had to smother it as the next lady and her disappointed daughters came up to congratulate them.

It was wearying, but had to be endured, something neither of them questioned.

But eventually, a slight frown in his eyes, Julian whispered, "I had no idea people would be so keen to see us wed."

She'd noted the same thing. "They've clearly taken the notion to heart." She grasped the chance to add, "I'm fairly certain Gordon arranged for those ladies to turn up at the gazebo. All three are friends of his mother."

"Helen?"

Smile unfaltering as another group of guests approached, Melissa nodded.

Under his breath, Julian murmured, "That was why they were so stunned. They were expecting to find him, not me."

Through her smile, she replied, "Exactly."

They dealt with the latest crop of well-wishers. As the group moved on, Melissa seized the moment to murmur, "If I had to be caught in such a situation, I admit I would rather it was with you than with your cousin."

She felt Julian's gaze on the side of her face. After a moment, he dryly replied, "That's comforting."

She wasn't sure how to respond to that, but didn't get a chance as Lady Hamilton and her daughter-in-law came up to offer their congratulations.

As the Hamilton ladies glided away, Melissa, inwardly frowning, said, "I'm rather surprised. The vast majority of those congratulating us have been entirely sincere."

After a moment, Julian asked, "Why does that surprise you?"

Somewhat patronizingly, she pointed out, "Because as far as they know, I've just snared London's most eligible noble bachelor before most of the ton even knew you were in town. I've taken you off the matchmakers' lists, and I can't fathom why so many seem genuinely happy about that."

He grunted.

More people descended, intent on wishing them well.

It was a considerable time later before she managed to murmur, "So how are we going to reverse this without causing a scandal?"

He didn't reply for some time but, eventually, chose a moment between well-wishers to suggest, "After a suitable time, you can simply cry off." He cast her a swift, unreadable glance. "Can't you?"

She forced her lips to remain relaxed. "Theoretically, yes. But given what we've weathered tonight, I foresee a potential problem with that."

Julian forced himself to shrug. "We'll work it out."

Although he'd been the one to suggest she cry off—standard procedure in such cases—he was already thinking about how to convince her to choose the other option.

The constant stream of guests fetching up before them meant he couldn't pursue that line of thought all that far.

Finally, Lady North declared they could leave, and their ordeal was at an end. He accompanied Melissa and her mother into the Connaughts' front hall and took Melissa's midnight-blue velvet cloak from the butler. As he draped it about her shoulders, he murmured, "I'll call on you tomorrow morning at...is it Mount Street?"

"Yes, North House."

"And we can discuss what to do."

She threw him a speaking glance, one he interpreted as *"We most certainly will."* But all she said was, "Indeed."

He kept his grin to himself. He'd already had it borne in on him that this Melissa was a significantly more forceful young lady than the Melissa he'd known long ago. What had surprised him was the realization that the Melissa of now was far more to his liking and spoke far more to his needs, those of the man he now was, than that girl of long ago.

They'd both matured and changed, their personalities and characters growing more definite and defined, yet instead of growing apart... After having stood by her side for just a few short hours during which they'd interacted with what had seemed like half the ton, he firmly believed that the pair of them had independently evolved into the person the other most needed now.

He glanced at her. He already saw her as his most appropriate partner, his best choice of wife. He hoped that in the same way, she would come to see him as the best husband for her.

He wouldn't have labeled himself an impulsive man, but in this... given he'd known her for so long, deciding that she was the right wife for him didn't seem impulsive at all.

He dutifully escorted her and her mother to their carriage, handed Lady North up, then took Melissa's hand.

He captured her gaze, raised her hand to his lips, and kissed the backs of her gloved fingers. Straightening, he said, "I'll call at eleven tomorrow."

A hint of wariness had entered her gaze, but her lips firmed, and she nodded, and he handed her up the steps.

The footman shut the door—looking curiously at Julian as he did—then the carriage jerked and rattled off.

Julian watched it go, then set off walking to Carsely House. His gaze fixed ahead, he strolled with nonchalant ease. He knew he should be thinking about the situation—about the meeting tomorrow and how best to manage it and her—yet all his mind and senses wanted to dwell on was that utterly amazing kiss.

The following morning, Julian sat at the breakfast table, remembering the kiss in all its glory and dwelling on its revelations.

The arrival of his brothers, Felix and Damian, put an end to that pleasant exercise. They'd been out the previous evening; this was the first he'd seen of them since he'd returned to the house.

They bade him good morning with their usual grunts.

He polished off his kippers, set his napkin aside, and waited until they'd helped themselves at the sideboard and had taken their seats before announcing, "Last night, at Lady Connaught's ball, I effectively offered for Melissa North's hand, and she more or less accepted."

Cutlery fell clattering from both Felix's and Damian's hands. Both stared at him in unmitigated surprise.

Damian shook off the shock first. "That was fast! Felix said you'd only decided to look about you the day before you left the castle."

Julian inclined his head. "Matters came to a head rather more quickly than I'd anticipated."

Felix was still staring. "More or less? What does that mean?"

He hadn't made up his mind how much to reveal, but he'd always been close to Felix, and he knew he could count on Damian's support come hell or high water. "I first met Melissa North just over nine years ago, on one of those Christmas holidays I spent in Hampshire with Henry Fitzgibbon at Little Moseley. Melissa's grandmama, Lady Osbaldestone, has a house down there, and Melissa was holidaying there as well. We met there again the following year and...although we felt we'd formed a bond, she was only fifteen at the time, and I was about to be sent to Ireland, so we parted ways. Then, last night, I caught up with her again. Unfortunately, Gordon had his eye on her as well."

"Gordon?" Damian looked nonplussed. "Our cousin Gordon?"

Julian nodded. "And yes, I would have been surprised to see him in a ballroom, but Mama had dropped a word in my ear that she'd heard from one of the aunts that Gordon was in dire straits and his latest tack, so they'd heard, was to find himself a well-dowered young lady. Unfortunately for Gordon, he fixed his eye on Miss North and arranged to compromise her in the Connaughts' gazebo. Miss North was unimpressed, and he didn't get far with his scheme. However, even more unfortunately for Gordon, I'd seen them leave the ballroom and, knowing his intentions, followed them and sent him off with a flea in his ear."

He paused, then went on, "Miss North and I renewed our acquaintance, but neither of us realized until it was too late that Gordon had organized witnesses to make sure of his plan."

When he didn't say more, Felix, who'd been hanging on his every word, incredulously asked, "And those witnesses caught you? You and Miss North?"

Julian nodded. "I, of course, did the honorable thing and informed the three ladies, who Miss North informed me are the biggest gossips in the ton, that I'd offered for Miss North's hand and she'd accepted, and subsequently, Miss North and I made that stick."

"Well, of course, she was only too happy to go along with it." Damian leaned back in his chair. "You are one of the biggest catches, if not the biggest, on the Marriage Mart."

Faintly smiling, Julian shook his head. "Be that as it may, at this juncture, there is no guarantee any marriage will take place." He met Felix's gaze. "That's what I meant by 'more or less.' At this point, our putative betrothal is just that—something that might lead to something more or might not. I'll be meeting with Melissa and her parents later this morning and hope to have some better understanding of how matters might progress after that."

Felix had been studying his face. "You want to marry her."

Not a question but a simple statement. Julian dipped his head in acknowledgment. "I thought we would suit way back then, and now, having met her again, I'm even more convinced of it."

"Given your interests," Felix mused, "as Lord North's daughter, she'd likely have a much more appropriate background than the average chit."

Julian nodded. "Indeed. Although we've only spent a few hours getting to know each other again, it certainly seems that way."

Damian slowly shook his head. "I still can't take it in. Only you could come to London with the intention of finding a wife and land a bride you actually want within hours of venturing into the ton."

Julian grunted noncommittally.

"So what," Felix asked, "do you propose to do next?"

Julian arched his brows. "That rather depends on her."

At eleven o'clock that morning, Melissa led Julian into the back parlor of her family's home in Mount Street. She'd persuaded her parents to allow her to meet him when he arrived and speak with him alone.

In the carriage from Connaught House, she'd explained to her mother what had actually happened—why she'd felt compelled to take refuge in the gazebo and what had occurred while she'd been there. All of it. Complete disclosure, except for the details of the kiss.

To her surprise, her mother hadn't been as upset, disapproving, or censorious as she'd expected. She'd chosen to speak in the carriage, knowing the shadows would hide her blushes; unfortunately, those same shadows had made her mother's expression impossible to decipher.

When they'd entered the house and she'd finally been able to see her mother's face, all she'd discerned was a sense of wondering complacency, as if having a daughter embroiled in a faux engagement to shield her reputation was nothing to get overly excited about and more along the lines of what her mother and her cronies would describe as "an interesting development."

She'd left her mother to break the news to her father. She'd encountered her sire over the breakfast table that morning, and he, too, had seemed entirely unperturbed. Then again, he was exceedingly high in the Foreign Office; to him, dealing with high-stakes disasters and emergencies was routine.

Still, she'd expected something a little harsher than "Well, my girl—a bit of excitement, what?"

While she'd expected her parents' support, their easy acceptance of the situation left her floundering. She'd assumed their reaction would give her a clue as to what her reaction should rightly be.

She'd spent a restless night, bedeviled by memories of that kiss and thoughts of Julian, both as he was now and as he had been, and what they'd got themselves into—and that kiss.

Now that the moment of facing him and discussing the situation was upon her, she was more than a trifle on edge.

She walked straight to the wide windows and halted as if surveying the rear garden.

He followed her into the room and closed the door.

The instant she heard the latch click, she drew in a breath and swung to face him. "So, what do we do now?"

Julian took his time crossing the room to join her, using the moments to study her face and try to read her expression and her eyes. He was accustomed to negotiations and wanted to know where she stood—what she was thinking and how she felt about the situation. He wanted to know if she saw it as he did—as an unlooked-for opportunity—and if not, figure out what he could do to nudge her in that direction.

Her dark-blue gaze was guarded, her expression controlled, but he sensed a certain wariness—not of him, but of what might transpire.

So, then...

He halted before her and, entirely unaggressively, held her gaze. "You know the ton's ways better than I do, but I assume we'll need to play the part of affianced couple for several weeks at least."

She humphed dismissively. "More like several months—all the way to the end of the Season. The ton won't stop watching us until then, until the major families retire to the country."

He inclined his head. "Until the end of the Season, then." That suited him to the ground. The more time he had to convince her of the desirability of the prospect he envisioned the better.

She was studying him curiously, almost suspiciously. "You seem remarkably amenable to a constraint you couldn't possibly have foreseen."

He lightly shrugged. "Why do you think I came to London?" When she frowned, he supplied, "To find a suitable wife."

Her frown deepened. "You're only, what...thirty?"

He inclined his head. "But I'm not of a mind to wait and allow the grandes dames to meddle in my life."

She tipped her head in acknowledgment. "I can understand that."

He forced himself to ask, "Will participating in our faux engagement interfere with any plans you had?" He hoped the question would distract her from the track her mind had been following, and he needed to know if there was any other gentleman in her life—specifically one from whom she might have had hopes of receiving an offer.

He hadn't had time to research her current life, and the only person he could viably ask was her terrifying grandmother, and if at all possible, he would prefer to avoid having to explain their present situation, much less his thoughts on how it might be resolved, to Lady Osbaldestone. She might be moved to support him, or she might not. At this point, he wasn't keen to risk it.

Melissa's expression clouded, and her gaze fell from his face. He found himself holding his breath, but then she shook her head. "Not really." She glanced up and met his eyes. "If you must know, my plan for this Season was to see it out, then sue to be left in peace, socially speaking."

He frowned, then rather carefully admitted, "I'm not quite sure of the logic there, but regardless, as matters stand, if we wait out the Season, then once everyone's retreated to the country for summer, you can cry off, citing irreconcilable incompatibilities or whatever the latest acceptable phrasing is."

Melissa studied him, then said, "While I agree that such a sequence of events would normally be accepted without much more than a passing remark, I suspect that, in our case, we're going to run into difficulties."

He was genuinely puzzled. "Such as?"

"Such as everyone in the ton declaring ours to be"—she surrendered to impulse and spread her arms dramatically—"the perfect match!" Lowering her arms, she crossed them and met his gaze. "On top of the fulsome congratulations we received last night, this morning brought a host of congratulatory missives from the other half of the ton who were not present at Lady Connaught's event."

He looked taken aback. "That was quick!"

"Indeed. Apparently, your august lineage taken together with my family's standing and connections throughout the ton, coupled with my family's prominence in the Foreign Office and your association with the Home Office, plus, well, every other possible consideration make it so!" She huffed. "The grandes dames are in alt."

He frowned. "I wouldn't have thought they'd be so keen to marry me off."

She all but growled, "Not you—me! They've been trying to marry me off for years!"

"Ah." Julian sternly suppressed a smile. Apparently, Fate was looking kindly on him; even the grandes dames were on his side.

He watched Melissa swing about and scowl disgruntledly at the view outside, then deliberately stated, "And then there's that kiss."

She glanced at him.

He caught her gaze and arched a brow, inviting her response.

As he'd hoped, she didn't back down. Her lips thinned, then she nodded tersely. "Indeed. There's that." She returned her gaze to the winter-brown lawn.

His voice quiet, his tone undemanding, he asked, "So what are we going to do about that?"

He waited, knowing she would understand that he wasn't talking of the kiss per se but of what it portended, the underlying connection evidenced by all they'd experienced during the exchange.

There were times in any negotiation when patience was the order of the day. He felt vindicated when, after a lengthy silence, she stirred and asked, "What do you suggest?"

He moved to stand beside her, shoulder to shoulder as if examining the garden outside. This was the tricky part; for half the night, he'd worked on formulating what amounted to a proposal. "You know our past as well as I do—in parting as we did eight years ago, we left a great deal between us unresolved. We had feelings for each other, a connection, albeit youthful and half formed, yet it was there, and we left it lying in abeyance when, given our respective ages, we did what we had to and walked away." He lightly shrugged. "We couldn't have done otherwise at that point. No one could have predicted how our lives would play out, much less what would become of such a youthful connection. Regardless, we both know that what existed between us then amounted to a romance that never got a chance to bloom."

He waited, and after a moment, she tipped her head his way. "That's our past—not our present."

"True. But that kiss suggests that, for good or ill, something of our long-ago feelings for each other remains extant, alive and surprisingly strong. What exactly that attachment might be—what it might amount to, how strong it might prove—at this point, neither you nor I can guess."

He drew in a measured breath and continued, "Yet here we are, and apparently, in however many Seasons, you haven't found any other gentleman who suits you, and I haven't any other candidate in mind for the position of my wife. Others wiser than us might say that perhaps some influence of our past connection lingers, affecting our thoughts and keeping us from forming suitable links with others. Perhaps that's true. Or perhaps the romance that seeded between us all those years ago is the one we, together, should pursue. Either way—whether to lay our past to rest once and for all so that we can move on to find other partners or to allow our nascent romance to bloom and grow—I believe we should take the opportunity this unexpected situation has handed us and use the rest of the Season, the necessary time we'll need to spend pretending to be an affianced couple, to give whatever existed between us eight years ago a chance to rekindle, develop, and grow or, alternatively, to fade away."

She'd turned to watch his face as he'd spoken.

He met her eyes. "We turned our backs on what might have been once. Given the opportunity that's fallen our way, we would be less than wise to do so again."

She searched his eyes, then said, "In Ireland, were you by any chance a negotiator?"

He blinked. That was what she took from his carefully prepared speech? "As a matter of fact, I was."

She nodded. "It shows."

He looked at her, noting her self-confidence, the assurance she hadn't possessed back then. "Well? As far as I can see, testing the waters will cost us nothing but time, time both of us are committed to spending together regardless." Inspired, he added, "Are you up for the challenge of putting what was between us to the test and learning what could be?"

Melissa softly snorted. She recognized his strategy, but she couldn't fault his tactics. No more than he could she walk away from the prospect of learning, once and for all, what could have evolved between them. She'd harbored so many dreams back then, ones in which he'd featured; might they—could they—come true?

He was correct in that they hadn't planned this, yet Fate had thrust the chance upon them, and they'd be fools not to seize it.

That said, she saw the risks clearly, chief among those the risk to her heart. Yet there was simply no overlooking the fact that she interacted with him in a wholly different way than she interacted with any other gentleman. There was some sort of direct connection she shared with him and no one else. She'd recognized that link and appreciated its uniqueness eight years ago, and not only was it still there, but like them, it seemed to have matured.

At this point, she trusted in that—in the existence of that link—more than she trusted in much else.

Could she walk away from learning what it meant?

She drew in a breath and raised her head. "Perhaps it's wooing the wrong way around—after the betrothal rather than before—but yes, I agree." She looked up and met his gaze. "Let's take the time, give ourselves the chance, and see what eventuates."

She saw satisfaction leap, a flash of silver in his gray eyes. "However"—narrowing her eyes, she held his gaze—"if our connection doesn't live up to expectations, I will cry off in May. June at the latest."

Unable to hold back his smile, Julian promptly agreed. "It's the first week of March. Let's give ourselves until the first week of May before revisiting the question and deciding yea or nay."

She nodded. "That will leave us time to plan the necessary steps for dissolving our engagement."

"If that's what we decide."

"Indeed."

He held out his hand, and after a fleeting hesitation, she placed her fingers in his. He raised them to his lips and, capturing her gaze, pressed a lingering kiss on her knuckles.

Her eyes widened a touch.

He wanted nothing more than to draw her to him and kiss her witless, but...forcing himself to lower her hand, he said, "I'd better go and see your father. I take it he's expecting me?"

Retrieving her hand, she threw him a reproving look and turned toward the door. "*We'll* go and see him. Believe me when I say he'll be expecting both of us."

He grinned at her back and, wryly amused, dutifully followed her from the room.

~

Later that afternoon, at the height of the fashionable hour, with Melissa beside him, Julian tooled his curricle through the Grosvenor Gate and into Hyde Park.

On seeing the carriages lining the avenue some way ahead, he murmured, "I had no idea an outing such as this was mandatory for recently engaged couples."

Melissa threw him a cynical look. "This is the ton, after all."

He snorted. He was in two minds over the events of the past hours; he wasn't entirely sure he understood all the currents at play.

On following Melissa into her father's study, with Lady North sweeping in on their heels, he'd discovered Melissa had given her parents a full accounting of what had occurred the previous evening, omitting only the intensity of their argument and any meaningful description of their kiss.

He hadn't anticipated her being that forthcoming and had been ready to support whatever version of events she'd offered, yet he had to admit that the truth was easier to deal with, especially as the Norths seemed remarkably unperturbed by what had occurred.

The one point she'd failed to explain, at least in his hearing, was why she'd chosen to go to the gazebo with Gordon in the first place. He was more than curious about that. His memory insisted she hadn't been seeking fresh air until after they'd noticed each other; if so, her sudden attack of breathlessness was rather revealing.

Regardless, he knew better than to press her for her reason. However, he had made plain why, knowing Gordon's ambition, he'd followed the pair to ensure nothing untoward took place, and Melissa had agreed that, in light of the subsequent exchanges between her and his cousin before he'd arrived, that had been just as well; Gordon's designs on her had been blatant and evident to all.

Lady North had supported Melissa's hypothesis that Gordon had arranged for the three older ladies to discover him and Melissa in a compromising situation, but as it transpired, it was Julian who had been with her at the time.

Lord North had listened to everyone's report without interrupting.

When they'd fallen silent, he'd remarked, "I have to say that, as two people unwittingly trapped in a tangled plot not of your own making, the pair of you are handling the situation with commendable sense. I could wish certain of my junior staff would react with such calm composure."

Lady North, Melissa, and Julian had stared at his lordship for a moment, then Lady North had explained that Melissa and Julian had known each other from weeks spent in Little Moseley years before. That, apparently, had answered his lordship's unvoiced question; he'd nodded sagely as if entirely satisfied.

After sharing a quick glance with Melissa, Julian had seized the opening to connect their past with their current plan to use the situation foisted upon them to see if, after all, they might suit. He'd admitted he'd come to London in search of a bride, adding that, after his long absence from the ton, he'd assumed Melissa already wed.

Lord North had exchanged a look with his lady, then concisely stated, "So—through you, Carsely, rescuing Melissa from a matrimonial snare engineered by your cousin, the pair of you have been trapped into declaring an engagement, but due to your past association and your present individual situations, you are proposing to exploit the situation to determine if, in fact, you might marry." He'd looked from Julian to Melissa. "Have I got that right?"

He and she had assured his lordship that he had.

Melissa had added the caveat that they had agreed to review their situation in early May, and if they'd discovered that they would not suit, she would cry off later that month or in early June.

Over that, Lord and Lady North had communed without words, then his lordship had declared that they were willing to support that plan.

While that had been a relief, he was still somewhat flummoxed by the Norths' ready acquiescence; he'd anticipated more difficulties.

Subsequently, with the help of both ladies, he and Lord North had drafted separate notices for *The Gazette* and duly dispatched them to be run in the following day's edition.

Then he'd been invited to stay for luncheon, and her parents and younger brother, Christopher, whom he hadn't previously met, had been charming and pleasant throughout.

Thereafter, the sense of unreality had deepened, with Lady North dispatching him to fetch his curricle and return to take Melissa up for this apparently compulsory jaunt in the park. While at Carsely House, he'd seized a moment to dash off a missive to his mother and send it with a groom to go north on the night mail. His mother would never forgive him were she to hear of his supposed engagement from the papers or, worse, from some delighted friend.

Then he'd driven his matched bays to Mount Street, found Melissa waiting, and here they were.

The avenue was crowded, and they'd been inching along. As they approached the first of the carriages drawn up on the verge, he murmured, "At least being engaged allows us to drive without a chaperone."

Melissa looked at him, then turned her head farther to glance at his tiger, perched behind them.

Julian smiled. "Trust me. Kieran's ears might be flapping, but he's too well trained to utter a peep about anything he hears."

"Not sure I'd understand all them big words, anyways," Kieran piped.

Melissa glanced at him again. "You're Irish?"

Julian assumed Kieran nodded.

Melissa faced forward, then murmured, "How old is he?"

"I know he looks ten, but he's actually sixteen. I found him on the streets of Dublin."

She cocked a brow at him. "Another of your rescues?"

He smiled. "So to speak. But he's a dab hand with horses, so my motives weren't entirely altruistic." They'd reached the first carriage, which contained an ancient lady and her companion; the lady peered haughtily at them through a lorgnette. "You'll need to direct me," he said. "How do we manage this?"

"Just continue driving slowly along, and if anyone waves at us to stop, ask me before you do."

"I place myself unreservedly in your hands."

He quickly realized his effective surrender of the reins had been wise; Melissa knew everyone there, at least by name and association, and almost every lady present and several strolling gentlemen wanted to offer their congratulations. Every time they pulled into the verge, they were mobbed.

It didn't take him long to decipher the ton's message, underscored as it was by pointed comments from every major hostess and grande dame who set eyes on them. He was given to understand that their nuptials were universally approved and were viewed as beyond appropriate—indeed, as highly desirable.

As they continued their slow circuit, Melissa muttered, "I cannot believe how many matrons with daughters to settle have so peaceably and apparently sincerely put aside all hopes of snaring you. I know the hostesses and grandes dames viewed my lack of a suitor as a personal affront, but I wouldn't have thought the likes of Lady Hammond, Lady Davenport, and the Duchess of Lewes would be so pleased to hear of our engagement."

"Pending engagement—the notices won't have run in *The Gazette* yet."

"Precisely! Obviously, the grapevine has been running hot. Everyone knows of our engagement already, and they're *pleased.*"

He glanced at her, unsure whether to be amused or concerned. "Is that a bad thing?"

"If we decide we don't suit, it will make disabusing them of the notion that we are, in fact, the perfect match that much harder."

"Ah."

Melissa hid her gritted teeth behind a suitably delighted expression. If she'd harbored any doubts over her prediction that dissolving their engagement wouldn't be straightforward or easily accomplished, the afternoon had laid them to rest. Yet even she hadn't foreseen such universal approbation.

When they drew away from yet another grande dame who had graciously bestowed her blessing, she muttered, "Her granddaughter is in her second Season, a beauty, well dowered and well connected—quite the catch. Yet she's happy—actually happy—to see me waltz off on your arm, so to speak. It's"—she flung up her hands—"inexplicable!"

It was beginning to be alarming.

That said, she couldn't see any alternative but to continue along the path they'd plotted.

While Julian was charming, distracting, and diverting, it fell to her to deflect the often subtle but sometimes not-so-subtle interrogations of the more inquisitive grandes dames.

Eventually, it dawned on her that any difficulties arising from how the ton saw them would apply only if they decided they wouldn't suit. What if, instead, they agreed they did—if they agreed to make their faux engagement real and go forward and marry?

If they were the perfect match...

For the past three years, she hadn't truly considered marriage, other than as "not for me." She'd had her years of hopes and dreams, but those had faded. Now... She glanced at Julian. Now, she was going to have to seriously consider marriage, specifically marriage to him. That might once have been her dream, but it had remained vague, unformed. Yet there was nothing nebulous about him or their situation. She had no option but to deal with both.

Facing forward, she decided she shouldn't try to prescribe their future; she didn't know him well enough to guess what might be, and after all, that was the point of their back-to-front betrothal.

Seated in a carriage just ahead, Lady Hornthwaite waved at them.

Melissa would have pretended not to see, but Julian muttered, "She's a connection," and drew his horses up so the carriages were side by side.

After delivering her beaming congratulations, Lady Hornthwaite fixed Melissa with a sharply inquisitive gaze. "I wasn't aware you were acquainted with Carsely, my dear."

Melissa cast a smiling glance at Julian and couldn't think of any way to avoid responding; for a wonder, no other lady had inquired how they'd come to know each other. "As it happens, we met many years ago, at my grandmother's house in the country."

"I used to holiday with friends in the same village," Julian added.

"I see." Lady Hornthwaite's eyes gleamed. "So you had previously met over only a few weeks?"

Melissa's smile felt tight. "Indeed."

Lady Hornthwaite clasped her hands to her ample bosom. "My dears, that's so romantic!"

Melissa kept her smile in place and excused them as quickly as she could.

As Julian drove on, she groaned.

Amused, he asked, "What?"

"Now, she's going to blab it all over that our meeting again was *so romantic*—regardless of whether it was or not! We will no longer be dubbed 'the perfect match' but 'the most romantic perfect match'!"

"Ah, I see."

"No, you don't!" She swatted his arm. "What you haven't yet seen is that we're going to be expected to live up to that ideal!"

Julian tried to smother a chuckle and failed.

He looked at her and found her narrowing her eyes at him. His smile growing wider, he faced forward and mildly said, "I'm not averse to dancing to their tune." He chanced another glance her way. "As I have to marry, why not marry you in the most romantic perfect match?"

The sound she made was rudely dismissive.

He couldn't stop smiling. The more he thought of his words, the more the sentiment rang true. He'd come to London to find the right wife, and it seemed Fate and Gordon had conspired to hand him just that.

As he turned his bored horses out of the avenue and finally allowed the poor beasts to come up to a trot, Melissa asked, "Have you told your family yet?"

"I saw my brothers this morning, and I've sent a letter to my mother, who's at Carsington." Dryly, he added, "I'm sure I can leave it to her to inform the wider family."

Melissa stirred and sat straighter. "How many brothers do you have?"

"Two. Felix is the closest in age, only a year younger, and Damian is the youngest of the brood at twenty-three."

"Sisters?"

"Constance and Eleanor, between Felix and Damian in age, and both married. Constance is in Scotland—she's Lady Maclachlan—and Eleanor is Lady Dalrymple and lives in Northumberland."

"I vaguely remember Eleanor."

"I've met Christopher and Amanda—do you have any other siblings?"

"No, but I have cousins galore on both sides."

"How are Jamie, George, and Lottie?"

"The last I heard, they were thriving. Jamie has started at Oxford, and George is in his last year at Eton. Lottie, I believe, is due to come to London soon, so you might see her shortly."

"I'll look forward to it." He glanced at Melissa. "I enjoyed their company back in Little Moseley."

"I have to admit those three are my favorite cousins. I warn you, their younger sister, Emma, looks angelic, but is a spoilt brat."

"I'll keep that in mind." He guided his pair out of the Grosvenor Gate; they'd completed a full circuit of the avenue.

Soon, he was drawing rein outside North House. Kieran jumped to the pavement and raced to proudly hold the bays' heads. Julian smiled, stepped down, and tossed him the reins, then turned and gave Melissa his hand.

He gripped her fingers, helped her down, and kept hold of her hand as he escorted her up the steps to the door.

She shot him a warning glance.

Undeterred, after halting on the porch, he grinned and raised her fingers to his lips and kissed her knuckles.

Her lips compressed, and with her free hand, she tugged the bell chain.

He lowered her hand and, running his thumb over the spot his lips had touched, confirmed, "Eight o'clock?"

She nodded. "We'll need to leave about that time."

He released her as the butler opened the door.

She inclined her head. "Until then, my lord."

Still smiling, he saluted her. Once she'd crossed the threshold, he turned and went quickly down the steps and heard the door close behind him.

As soon as he'd climbed up, retaken the reins, and started the horses trotting again, Kieran, proving his hearing was acute, asked, "Are we going out again, then, guvnor?"

"Not the bays, so not you, either."

From the corner of his eye, he saw Kieran's puzzled frown. "I've been commanded to accompany Lady North and Miss North to the theater." Wryly, he added, "I've been given to understand that such duties are the lot of an affianced gentleman."

Kieran's nonverbal response suggested he was unimpressed.

Julian rather agreed.

CHAPTER 3

*A*t the front of the North box in the Theatre Royal, Julian sat beside Melissa and, as the performance commenced, pretended to be unaware of the lingering stares and the rabid interest displayed by a good portion of the crowd. Some in the boxes were even hanging over the front walls, the better to observe him and Melissa.

Even though the curtain had risen, the whispering and staring continued.

From the gloom beside him, Melissa murmured, "I hope we're nothing more than a seven-day wonder—pray God, the fevered attention wanes soon."

"Amen." After a second, he added, "And hopefully much sooner than in seven days."

The sound she made suggested he was dreaming.

The farce on the stage wasn't particularly engaging, but then they'd come more to be seen than to see. After a few minutes enduring the increasingly tepid performance, keeping his eyes on the stage, he murmured, "Your experience of the ton is greater than mine. Do engagements such as ours always garner such attention?"

She shifted but, like him, kept her gaze trained forward. "Yes and no. Yes in the sense the ton are quick to notice and pass judgment, and no in the sense that the attention is usually far less intense." She paused, then went on, "It's not really our engagement per se that's fueling the avid interest—our proposed union is hardly strange or in any way abnormal.

It's the 'romantic perfect match' that's responsible for much of it—the ton's utterly captivated by the idea."

"The concept rather than the reality?"

She dipped her head. "Indeed."

A moment later, she softly snorted and, in an undertone, stated, "That's ridiculous—no woman would react in that way."

Having thought much the same of the labored plot being enacted before them, he replied, "As far as I can tell, none of these characters' dialogue or actions bears any resemblance to reality."

They continued exchanging sotto voce comments as the short farce, the prelude to the main drama, rolled on. The farce's plot, or lack thereof, offered plenty of fodder, and their comments and quips confirmed that they both possessed sharp eyes for the ludicrous as well as similarly dry senses of humor.

The instant the farce ended and the curtains swished closed, Melissa turned to Julian. "Brace yourself—the intermission is going to try our tempers."

He arched his brows, but merely uncrossed his long legs, rose, and drew back her chair. She and he stood side by side, their backs to the front of the box, and did their best to greet and suitably respond to all those who squeezed into the limited space to offer their felicitations.

Most of the visitors were also hopeful of slipping in a question or two and learning more, but their numbers defeated them; each group barely had time to shake hands or press fingers and deliver their congratulations before the next group were there, pressing forward and all but shuffling the earlier group aside.

Melissa's mother and aunts, Margaret and Catherine, did their best to manage the incoming stream, but the situation quickly devolved to something resembling a rabid reception line.

At one point, Julian dipped his head and murmured by her ear, "They're like mechanical dolls on a revolving belt—one comes up, speaks, then turns away, and the next shifts into place."

She threw him a speaking glance. Mechanical dolls. After that, she was hard put to keep a straight face, especially once he started to predict —correctly—what words would come out of the next group's mouths.

At last the theater's bells rang, and as her mother steered the last visitor to the door, Melissa could finally lower her guard. She glanced at Julian. "Thanks to your commentary, that was less of an ordeal than it might have been."

He lightly shrugged and reset her chair for her. "I've lived through countless similar civic events—the only way to relieve the boredom is by recognizing the inherent ridiculousness of the exercise."

She laughed softly and sat.

After seeing her mother and her aunts to their chairs, set in a row behind his and hers, he reclaimed the chair beside her.

The lights started to dim. Idly glancing at the crowd in the pit, Melissa noticed a man staring their way; his pale face, turned upward, had caught the fading light and her eye. He had curly dark hair and wore a dark coat, and as the seconds ticked by, he continued staring.

Melissa reached out and tweaked Julian's sleeve. When he glanced at her, she nodded toward the pit. "There's a man down there, staring at us." She paused, then amended, "Or at least, I thought it was us, but it might just be you. Do you know him?"

Julian scanned the masses and saw the man, still staring up at the North box. "Dark curly hair, dark suit?"

"That's him."

He squinted, but in the increasing gloom, couldn't make out the man's features. "From this distance, I can't be sure, but I don't think so. I don't recognize him."

At that moment, the lights snuffed out and the curtains swept back, and the bright lights on the stage cast the pit into Stygian darkness.

Julian pretended to follow the action on the stage, but most of his mind was wondering about the man. Whether the man's attention had been on Melissa and Julian or just Julian, there'd been an intensity in his unwavering regard that suggested something more than mere interest. Julian trawled through his memories, but couldn't place the fellow.

He waited for his eyes to adjust to the gloom and, during a well-lit scene when the stage lights cast a glow over the pit, searched for the man, but his dark head was no longer where it had been. As far as Julian could see, the fellow had gone.

Hmm.

Melissa shifted on the chair beside him. "At least this is more believable."

He returned his gaze to the stage, where a lady of dubious virtue was creeping toward a window beyond which a gentleman was about to be murdered. After two seconds of watching the actress inch forward, he murmured back. "In real life, creeping along bent over like that, she'd probably trip on her hem and crash forward, and our putative murder victim and the would-be murderer would come rushing to the window to see."

She smothered a laugh. "That would certainly rewrite the plot."

"Well, if the shoe fits." In a barely breathed exchange, he and she proceeded to do just that; as their inventiveness knew few bounds, they entertained themselves very well.

The play finally ended, and the curtain came down. As the applause faded and the lights came up, he turned to Melissa. "I have to admit I enjoyed the play far more than it deserved."

She returned his smile. "I confess I did, too. I've never tried reinterpreting like that before—it was certainly more engaging."

Julian helped all four ladies don their cloaks, then gave Melissa his arm, and they followed Lady North and Melissa's aunts—Catherine, Lady Osbaldestone and Margaret, Mrs. Osbaldestone—from the box.

"Keep close behind Mama," Melissa warned, "or we'll be besieged."

By dint of remaining tightly within the older ladies' wake, they managed to descend the stairs, cross the foyer, and pass through the doors and onto the theater's raised porch without being detained for more than a few seconds at a time. They halted on the porch and waited for the carriages to roll up; the queue of carriages along the front of the theater was moving very slowly.

Julian glanced at Melissa. "What's next on our schedule?"

She hesitated, then said, "As the notice of our engagement will appear in *The Gazette* tomorrow, I absolutely have to go into Surrey to see Mandy and her husband, Rufus Sedon, and explain the situation to them. If I don't, I'll never hear the end of it."

"I'm surprised Mandy isn't in town."

"She normally would be, but she's expecting their first child in a month or so, so is confined to Sedon Hall."

"Ah, I see. Where in Surrey is Sedon Hall?"

"Not far from Farleigh. The fastest way is via Croydon."

"If you like, I'll drive you down." He caught her eyes as she looked up at him. "We should go down together, shouldn't we? Especially as it's Mandy."

She smiled in clear relief. "I didn't know if you would have the time."

"As an affianced gentleman, I'll make the time." He smiled back. "At what hour should I call for you?"

They settled on half past ten the following morning.

Catherine's carriage drew up, and Catherine and Margaret said their goodbyes and departed.

Melissa turned to her mother and filled her in on their plans for the next day.

Lady North nodded approvingly. "An excellent notion. Aside from all else, that will save you from the heightened attention bound to be running rabid in the park tomorrow."

Heightened attention?

Julian caught Melissa's eyes as she glanced at him. She widened her eyes slightly; she hadn't thought of that, either, but like him, was grateful they would avoid it.

"Where is our carriage?" Lady North peered along the row of carriages.

Julian and Melissa, both taller, looked along the line.

A figure across the street caught Julian's attention.

The man who'd been staring at them in the theater was standing beneath a lamp post and, once again, staring their way.

Melissa swayed back, nudging Julian. "Do you see him?" she murmured.

"Yes. Be damned if I know who he is."

"There's Felsham." Lady North waved to her coachman. "At last!"

Julian glanced at the oncoming coach, then looked across the street in time to see the man step back and fade into the shadows.

Melissa glanced questioningly at Julian.

Hiding a frown, he nodded at her mother's carriage and urged her toward it.

He helped both ladies up the carriage steps, then followed and shut the door. He looked out of the window into the darkness, but there was nothing to see, and he was left with absolutely no idea as to who their mystery man might be.

Late the following morning, Melissa sat beside Julian in his curricle, enjoying the feel of the breeze in her face. As they bowled into Croydon along the Brighton Road, she directed him onto the side road that would take them to Selsdon and Farleigh and, eventually, to Sedon Hall.

She'd seen him manage his high-stepping bays in the park, but there, the carriage had been barely rolling along. Today, once they'd left the bustle of the capital behind and fields and orchards had started to border the road, he'd eased his hold on the ribbons, and the horses had lengthened their strides until they'd been fairly bowling down the macadam. She'd been relieved when he'd checked the beasts at the first bend and been further reassured by his constant monitoring of the pair and the road ahead.

She'd relaxed and enjoyed the sights, the sounds, and his company. He hadn't brought his tiger today, so there'd been no restriction on the topics they could broach. They'd started by swapping dry observations about their experience at the theater, then she'd expanded on the various events at which she suspected they would have to appear over the upcoming week. His questions had underscored how out of touch he was with the ton's ways, and when she'd asked, he'd described the more limited social round in Dublin.

"Because I only came home twice a year—at Christmastime and around midsummer—I effectively spent no time in London, either during the Season or through the rest of the year."

"I see." She made a mental note to remain aware, as they continued parading through the ton's ballrooms in support of their faux engagement, that he might not be as experienced in ton machinations as she. The notion of acting as his protector in a sphere in which she was supremely confident made her smile; eight years ago, he'd been so much more worldly and experienced than she.

The thought gave her pause. As they bowled along the country lane, deeper into the green fields of Surrey, she reflected that her view of him was still largely that of the man he'd been, which—experience of the ton being one example—was not necessarily the man who sat beside her.

The man she'd agreed to consider marrying.

Hmm.

After they'd rounded the next curve, she asked, "Is it normal for those in the administration in Ireland to remain in the country so consistently?"

"Not usually." He glanced her way. "Gregory—he's the Under-Secretary for Ireland, the head of the civil service over there—liked the way I approached negotiations with the Irish, and he ended up wanting to keep me close in case of need."

"What was it about your way of doing things that was so impressive?"

"I don't know about being impressive—effective might be nearer the mark." He guided his team around a tight bend, then went on, "I always thought it was because I can talk to just about anybody." His lips lifted in a fleeting smile. "One of the benefits of my years as Dagenham and rubbing shoulders with villagers in Little Moseley and others of that ilk."

"Do you still keep in touch with Henry Fitzgibbon?"

He nodded. "And Thomas, George, and Roger as well." Briefly, he met her eyes. "Back then, we were all, relatively speaking, untitled, and during our shared holidays while at Eton and later Oxford, we used to visit each other's homes, and there, we'd just be like any local lads."

"So through that, you learned how to deal with ordinary people?"

He thought, then shrugged. "More that I learned not to judge people by their rank or to make assumptions about honesty and integrity based on wealth or standing or lack thereof."

They rattled into Selsdon, then took the lane to Farleigh. Once they were bowling along again, she asked, "You mentioned that your mother lives at Carsington—that's your principal seat, I take it?"

He nodded. "Carsington Castle, home of the Earls of Carsington since they were barons under Charles the Second."

"It's that old?"

"Parts of it." Without further prompting, he sketched a word picture of a rather large castle-cum-mansion. "Mama lives in rooms in one wing, as does my uncle Frederick."

"Her brother?"

"No, my father's youngest brother. There were four brothers. The other two—Harold and Claude—died some years ago. Their wives—my aunts by marriage—occasionally visit, but live with their married daughters."

She made a mental note to pick her mother's and grandmother's brains regarding his family. "Is Frederick married?"

"No, he's a bachelor. I understand that, as the fourth son, he never felt the need, even though both Harold and Claude only sired daughters."

"Well, you do have two brothers." Sure she now had the succession at least clear, she turned to other matters. "I assume there are acres attached to the castle?"

His voice warmed. "Yes, of course." He launched into a description of the estate, and she needed no interpreter to tell her that he loved the place. It seemed that he knew every tree in his woods, every dip and hollow and field and farm.

By the time they reached the gates of Sedon Hall, she'd gained some understanding of the scale of his holdings, but it was clear that his heart lay at what he called "the castle" and not at any of his lesser properties, even though several were closer to London.

Julian held his bays to a steady trot as he guided them up the drive of Sedon Hall. The avenue was lined with trees, presently leafless. As they approached the house, he saw a couple standing on the lawn bordering the forecourt, shading their eyes as they peered at the curricle.

"That's Mandy and Rufus!" Melissa waved.

Julian slowed his horses, halting them by the edge of the lawn. Without waiting for any assistance, Melissa jumped down from the curricle and rushed to Mandy, whose face lit with delight. Mandy held her arms wide, and the sisters embraced, rather awkwardly, over the large bump of Mandy's pregnancy. To Julian's eye, educated by his sisters' confinements, Mandy looked ready to, as his brothers-in-law had always termed it, pop.

Melissa, a trifle taller, had to lean forward over the bump to kiss Mandy's cheek.

A groom appeared, and Julian stepped down to the gravel and handed over the reins.

After releasing Melissa, as Melissa straightened, Mandy fixed widening eyes on her sister's face. "But what's brought you here?" She tried to peer past Melissa.

Melissa shifted so Mandy could better see Julian and waved to him as he walked up. "You remember Julian from Little Moseley? Dagenham, as he was then."

Mandy's eyes found his face and lit with recognition. "Of course! How delightful to meet you again." She looked from him to Melissa, then back again, curiosity infusing her gaze. "But what's brought you both here?"

Melissa patted Mandy's hand, which was clutching hers. "In a moment." She smiled at the tall, sandy-haired gentleman standing patiently by. "Rufus—it's lovely to see you."

Rufus, Lord Sedon, rounded his wife and bent to kiss Melissa's cheek. "It's a pleasure to see you down here, my dear." Sedon's gaze shifted to Julian. "Do introduce me."

Melissa complied. "Julian, Earl of Carsely, allow me to present Rufus, Lord Sedon, Mandy's husband."

Sedon's face lit with interest, and he held out his hand. "Carsely. I heard you'd succeeded your father. Are you intending to join us in the Lords?"

Julian gripped the proffered hand. "I hope to become more active in the future, but as to exactly when, that depends on several issues." He looked at Melissa.

"There's quite a lot to tell you." Melissa smiled brightly at Mandy. "Perhaps we should go inside."

"Of course." Mandy gripped the hand Sedon offered and started waddling toward the house. "I came out for some air, and we were just returning indoors." She glanced rather woefully at Julian. "In my present condition, I can only amble a short distance before I run out of steam."

He smiled easily. "My sisters were the same."

He noticed that both Melissa and Mandy took note of his implied experience.

With Melissa flanking Sedon, Julian walked beside Mandy as Sedon, rather overly solicitously, helped his wife up the steps and into the house.

It was a neat manor house, airy and charmingly cozy. With Melissa, Julian followed Mandy and Sedon into a sunny drawing room.

They sat in comfortable, well-padded chairs, and Melissa immediately launched into an explanation of the reason for their visit. *The Gazette* hadn't yet reached the house, and Mandy and Rufus were, at first, stunned, then agog.

Julian noted that, while Melissa explained how their unexpected engagement had come about and that they'd agreed to allow the situation to stand, this time, she made no mention of her crying off if it proved they did not suit.

The picture she painted was of a somewhat precipitate but otherwise normal betrothal; entirely content, he made no move to amend that view.

Bright eyes wide, Mandy looked from Melissa to him. "But that's wonderful! Even at Grandmama's dower house all those years ago, I thought you two would suit, and now"—she spread plump hands—"given both your backgrounds, yours is well-nigh a perfect match all around!"

Julian grinned and glanced at Melissa, catching her flash of chagrin over Mandy echoing the ton's verdict.

Immediately, Mandy rattled on, seconded by Rufus, and if their eager questions were any indication, both were genuinely thrilled at the news and entirely supportive.

Julian relaxed even further.

Then a spasm of discomfort crossed Mandy's face. Waving off Rufus's concern and his offer to help her up the stairs, Mandy claimed

Melissa's arm instead, and the sisters went off, heads dipping together as Mandy continued her interrogation.

Julian, who had come to his feet as the ladies rose, took in the besotted look on Rufus's face and inwardly smiled. The man was transparently in love with his wife.

When the ladies disappeared into the hall, Rufus turned back to him, and they sat again.

"Are your estates near London?" Rufus asked.

"Derbyshire," Julian replied. When he married Melissa, Rufus would be his brother-in-law, and given how close Melissa and Mandy clearly still were, it would behoove him to find common ground. "As we drove in, I noticed your orchards. What crops do you grow hereabouts?"

Through the ensuing discussion, both he and Rufus discovered that, in managing large agricultural estates, they shared many concerns and, in fact, had a great deal in common.

"I'm anxious to see whether the corn price will stabilize," Rufus admitted. "We do a lot of barley, and that always fetches a solid price, but the corn is very up and down."

Julian agreed. "Not that we have much to sell from Carsington, being that our farms there primarily run sheep and cattle, but my holdings in Somerset and Hampshire have quite decent acreages under corn. It's hard to plan when one simply doesn't know what the return will be. I'm hoping with Liverpool as Prime Minister, the push for the Bank to return to the gold standard will move forward—that should help even things out."

"True."

Increasingly easy in each other's company, they continued exchanging views and opinions.

~

In Mandy's bedchamber, Melissa had resigned herself to answering the barrage of questions Mandy had waited only until she'd relieved herself and was comfortable again to ask.

Finally, Mandy fixed her with a very direct look. "The one thing you haven't even hinted at is what you truly feel about this. Do you *want* to go ahead and marry Carsely? Do you love him?"

The bald question put Melissa on the spot. She knew Mandy wouldn't allow any slinking around on the subject; her sister was the sort to face everything head-on. "Well..."

What did she feel? What did she truly want?

Do I love Julian?

"Long ago, I thought I was in love with him, and yes, back then, I would have married him without a qualm. Now..."

When she didn't go on, Mandy, seated in an armchair facing the window seat on which Melissa perched, huffed. "That was then. This is now. So what's changed?"

"Us, of course." She met Mandy's eyes. "Both of us."

"In the sense of maturing, yes—you're both older and, one would hope, wiser—but fundamentally, people don't change all that much. A person's bedrock doesn't change, and if I've learned anything through falling in love with Rufus, it's that those things, the elements that make each person who they are, are the essential foundation on which love grows."

Melissa let those words sink in, then arched a brow at Mandy. "So you think if I was in love with him once..."

"That it's very likely you'll fall in love with him again." Mandy huffed. "In fact, in your case, it's more like your love was placed in hibernation, and you've finally allowed it out into the sun."

The image made Melissa smile. After a moment, she said, "Be that as it may—and I admit that more and more I'm inclined to want to go ahead and marry Julian—there's still a lot he and I have yet to learn about each other."

Mandy humphed, but didn't argue. She pushed up from the chair, and Melissa rose and went to help her.

Once Mandy was fully on her feet, she linked her arm in Melissa's and steered her toward the door. "Just remember what I said—you already know the important things about him, even if you think you don't. Even years ago, your heart would never have settled so definitely on him if that wasn't so. All those other things you think you need to know are incidental, superficial, and unimportant in terms of love."

Melissa merely said, "We'll see."

But Mandy wasn't finished. She halted at the top of the stairs and fixed Melissa with a firm look. "Just promise me that in making up your mind, you'll do so with open eyes and an open heart."

Melissa smiled lightly, but Mandy wasn't about to be gainsaid. "Promise?"

When Melissa didn't immediately do so, Mandy made her eyes huge and added, "As I'm about to make you an aunt for the first time, it's the least you can do."

Melissa laughed and capitulated. "All right—I'll do as you say and employ open eyes and an open heart."

Satisfied, Mandy beamed.

They returned to the drawing room to discover Rufus and Julian as thick as thieves over some parliamentary bill. The gentlemen came to their feet and set that topic aside as they repaired to the dining room and settled to consume the luncheon Mandy had arranged.

The exchanges over the table were far more relaxed than Melissa had anticipated; it was patently obvious that in the short time they'd been left alone, Julian and Rufus had struck up a friendship. Rufus was four years older than Julian, so they hadn't rubbed shoulders before, but it quickly became apparent that they shared any number of interests.

Finally, after returning to the drawing room for a cup of tea and scones and jam, it was time for Melissa and Julian to head back to London.

"I have three events I can't avoid appearing at tonight," Melissa told Mandy as the four of them walked out onto the porch.

"Oh? Which hostesses?" Mandy rubbed her distended belly. "At times, I think I miss the social round, but then I remember all the rush and fuss"—she threw a smiling glance at Rufus—"and realize I don't truly miss it at all."

Melissa softly snorted. "You're starting to sound like me. But to answer your question, Lady Haverford, Mrs. Quincy, and Lady Enderby." She caught Julian's resigned expression and smiled commiseratingly. "Luckily, all three events are soirées, and none is likely to be a major crush."

After she and Mandy traded hugs and kisses and the gentlemen made their farewells, Julian handed her into his curricle, and they were off, rolling briskly down the drive.

Once they'd turned onto the lane, retracing their route from the capital, she asked, "How did you and Rufus get on?"

"Remarkably well." Julian slanted her a glance. "It transpires we have much in common."

Smiling rather smugly, she admitted, "I thought that would prove to be the case."

"And what did Mandy have to say about our engagement?"

She pondered how best to answer and, eventually, vouchsafed, "She approved and was hopeful of a positive outcome."

His gaze on his horses, he murmured, "Good to know."

All in all, Julian felt heartened by how well the day had gone. Indeed, he felt reassured by how easily many individual elements seemed to be falling into the right position to support his push to make their engagement real.

Their conversation on the way home revolved about sights they saw along the way. When, eventually, they reached Mayfair and he was forced to slow his horses to a walk, he glanced at Melissa. "The Haverford, Quincy, and Enderby soirées."

She met his eyes. "You don't have to accompany me."

He managed not to clench his jaw. "But as we're a very recently affianced couple, people will notice and comment if I don't." Later, perhaps, he might acceptably leave her to waltz through the ton alone. Then again… "What time should I call?"

He felt her amused gaze on his face. "You don't sound very enthusiastic."

"You can't possibly expect enthusiasm over attending not one, not two, but three haut ton soirées in one night!"

She laughed, then as he turned his horses onto Mount Street, said, "Very well. I accept your sacrifice. Shall we say eight o'clock?"

He agreed and felt contentment steal over him; indeed, he felt content with the entire day.

~

The gentleman intending to remove the current Earl of Carsely settled comfortably in the armchair in his sitting room, stretched out his legs, crossed his ankles, and flicked open *The Gazette*.

He focused on the listing of court appointments, checking the names in case anyone he knew had been favored with a lucrative post, then idly skimmed the notices of births, deaths, engagements, and marriages.

He scanned past the crucial entry before the names registered, then his gaze jerked back to it, and he read the words, barely able to credit their meaning.

Not just one formal notice but two!

Abruptly, he sat upright, rigid in the chair. He stared at the notices, then swore. Violently.

How could this happen without me having even an inkling it was on the cards?

Obviously, his source of intelligence was deficient.

He grunted. He'd known that for some time.

So where did that leave his plans?

The more he thought of it, the more curious he found it that he hadn't heard even a whisper of an impending engagement, much less of any wedding in the offing. Surely unions at that level never occurred willy-nilly.

"I didn't even know they were acquainted, and he's only just come back to town."

So where and how did they meet, much less form an attachment of sufficiently long standing to give rise to a betrothal?

He read both notices again and wondered if, perhaps, the reason he hadn't heard of the association before was because there hadn't been anything to know. If so, this betrothal was suspiciously sudden. "Out of nowhere, as it were."

Unexpected and precipitous betrothals often didn't lead to weddings. He could attest to that himself, several times over.

After mulling the possibilities, he decided that until he learned for certain that a wedding had been announced, there was no need to rejig his careful planning. Given the news as it currently was, altering the schedule would be an overreaction.

And even if the betrothal was genuine, engagements usually lasted for many months and sometimes even years.

He looked again at the announcements and wondered. Although he'd assumed he would have a year and more to carefully maneuver, Carsely wasn't that young, and although he wasn't sure if he was remembering the right chit, if Miss Melissa North was who he thought she was, she wasn't any debutante, either.

Regardless, he would wait and see; with stakes such as those he was aiming for, playing safe was key.

Meanwhile, however, he would think about advancing his plans, developing them further, firming his options and getting his troops into place—just in case the unexpected happened and the newly affianced couple thought to marry this year.

If that proved to be so, then the period available to prosecute and win his campaign would be foreshortened. Nevertheless, he really couldn't see, Carsely being who he was, that the lead-up to any wedding would be reduced to a prohibitive degree.

The Gazette lying open on his lap, he sat and weighed and debated.

Eventually, he folded the paper and laid it aside, then rose and crossed to the desk between the windows.

It wouldn't hurt to write a few more letters.

CHAPTER 4

$\mathcal{B}$y Sunday morning, Melissa was growing exceedingly weary of being the cynosure of ton attention. Even in church—even during the sermon—she was conscious of the unrelenting scrutiny of those in the nave behind them. As they'd claimed a place toward the front of the church, those staring included most of the congregation.

Flanked by Julian and her mother, she tried to keep her mind on the minister's words.

The three soirées she and Julian had attended the previous evening had been every bit as trying as she'd feared. The announcement of their betrothal was so new, many had only learned of it that day and were all but lying in wait to ambush them and, under the guise of congratulating them, extract further details, such as when their engagement ball might be held and when the "happy event" of their wedding might occur.

Sadly, she couldn't reply that she really had no idea on either count.

She was relieved when the minister reached his benediction. Minutes later, she took Julian's proffered arm, and with appropriate smiles on their faces, they followed her transparently proud mama toward the door. They'd hung back slightly so that most of the congregation was ahead of them, but once they'd exchanged the customary greetings with the minister, who had heard the news and tendered his smiling congratulations as well, they emerged onto the porch, which was teeming with other worshipers.

Noting the horde poised to descend on them, she gripped Julian's sleeve and, smile brightening, determinedly steered him directly to Lady Halliwell, one of her mother's oldest friends.

She was gratified to find Julian quick to respond; he moved so smoothly, without hesitation, that it appeared that he as well as she had always intended to speak first with the Halliwells.

Lady Halliwell was delighted to be thus singled out. Melissa spent several minutes introducing Julian to her ladyship and her two daughters, accepting their congratulations, and deflecting the expected questions, which gave her time to take stock of those transparently awaiting their turn, and with input from her mother, who elected to remain with the Halliwells, select which group to acknowledge next.

The strategy left her in charge of who they spoke with and for how long; there were always others hovering, eager to have their say.

While she knew the majority of those present, at least by name, Julian's acquaintance was more limited; she duly introduced him and, when she sensed he was entirely at sea, added a comment or two to nudge him to make the correct connections.

She was pleased that he proved adept at picking up the hints she cast his way. As they circulated among the groups thronging the porch, she felt reassured by how well they coped, increasingly smoothly working as a team in acknowledging the felicitations while deflecting the overly curious.

They were nearing one end of the porch when an older lady stepped into their path. Perhaps a trifle younger than Melissa's mother, the lady had curly blond hair, pretty but sadly faded features, and bright blue eyes. She smiled delightedly at Julian and rather more shyly at Melissa. "Julian, dear." She held out her hand. "I vow your news took me utterly by surprise."

With his customary grace, Julian took her hand and half bowed. "Cousin Helen." He glanced Melissa's way and, in a reversal of their recent roles, introduced her. "My grandfather's niece-by-marriage, Mrs. Helen Delamere, allow me to present my fiancée, Miss North."

"Oh, do please call me Helen." Mrs. Delamere smiled delightedly and held out her hand. "I'm very pleased to meet you, Miss North."

Smiling, Melissa lightly clasped her fingers. "Just Melissa to family." Mrs. Delamere's open expression suggested she was intrigued as to the circumstances of their unexpected betrothal, but also genuinely happy for them.

"Oh!" Mrs. Delamere turned to include a gentleman who had just left

another group and now ambled up to join them. "Do allow me to introduce my lodger and dear friend, Captain Findlay-Wright. George, you're
just in time to meet Miss North, Julian's fiancée."

The captain was a tall man, almost Julian's height but leaner, with
sun-bleached gingery hair and the pale freckled complexion that often
went with that. His features were even, pleasant without being in any way
remarkable.

Smiling easily, Melissa extended her hand, and the captain took it and
very correctly bowed over it. "A pleasure, Miss North." Releasing her
hand, he straightened and nodded with ready bonhomie to Julian.
"Carsely. Don't often see you here."

His expression serene, Julian caught Melissa's eye and lightly
shrugged. "Needs must, you might say."

"Oh, but have you heard from your aunts?" Mrs. Delamere's face lit.
"They'll be so *thrilled*. And I daresay your sisters will be as well.
Well"—she laid a hand on Melissa's sleeve—"they'll be relieved that
Julian will have a countess, which presumably means he'll settle down
and be responsible with the estate. Not, of course, that he was irrespon-
sible before, but well, we really don't know what he did in Ireland, so one
can't be certain."

Barely pausing for breath, Mrs. Delamere rattled on, her monologue
effortlessly skittering from a comment about Julian's mother living at
Carsington Castle and therefore not being present to rejoice in their news,
to an inquiry as to Melissa's parents, to a comment about her son Gordon
—at which point, Melissa realized the connection—before veering into a
paean of Julian's virtues as a young child.

Stunned, Melissa tried to keep up and take appropriate note of all the
useful tidbits Mrs. Delamere let fall.

Suddenly, Mrs. Delamere gripped her hand tightly and squeezed. "I
can't tell you how pleased I am that dear George drew my attention to the
notice in *The Gazette*. I hadn't yet got to it, you see, but I wouldn't have
missed offering my felicitations for the world. I mean, family must rally
around at such moments and lend their voice to the happy chorus. Why, I
recall when Julian's father married his mother." And on she went without
pause.

Increasingly taken aback, not just by the unending stream of words
but even more by the potentially embarrassing revelations, minor though
they were, contained within the gushing deluge, Melissa slid a look at

Julian and saw that, contrary to the impression given by the easy smile on his face, he wasn't all that happy, either.

She was about to somewhat unceremoniously put an end to the torrent when the captain caught one of Mrs. Delamere's waving hands. "Helen, my dear, time is getting on, and I fear I have a luncheon appointment and will need the carriage." With a hint of apology in his eyes, the captain smiled at Melissa and Julian. "I'm sure Miss North and Carsely will excuse us. Likely they need to get on as well."

"What? Oh! Yes, of course. I quite forgot the time." Still smiling, Mrs. Delamere turned to Melissa and Julian. "Well, at least I've tendered my felicitations in person, and I can see you two have others still waiting to do so, so we'll take our leave."

Hugely relieved, Julian murmured an appropriate farewell, and Melissa did the same, and the captain drew Helen away, and finally, Julian could hear himself think.

"Phew!" Melissa glanced at him sidelong as she turned to greet the last group of well-wishers still dallying on the porch. "So that's Gordon's mother."

"Indeed." His socially adept smile in place, Julian acknowledged the greetings of Lord and Lady Holden while his mind ranged over all Helen had let fall.

The Holdens were the last couple waiting to offer their congratulations, and they did so with commendable brevity.

After parting from them and confirming that Lady North had already quit the scene, Julian led Melissa down the church steps and into Hanover Square, where the North carriage was waiting.

Her arm linked with his, Melissa asked, "Is Mrs. Delamere always so…chatty? Her tongue seemed to run on wheels—I've never met anyone who fitted that description so well."

"Indeed, and I believe the word you were searching for is 'indiscreet.' And the long and short of it is that I honestly don't know. I'll have to ask Mama. She keeps in touch with Helen, although I suspect that's mostly by letter."

"Your mother spends most of her time in the country, doesn't she?"

"She does, and so do my sisters. My aunts are in and out of town, but Mama will know whom to ask to check if Helen rattles on like that to everyone or only to members of the family."

Melissa nodded. "It might be an outcome of nerves—she talks like that with family, but with others, she's shy and reserved."

"One can only hope."

They reached the North carriage, and the footman opened the door. Julian handed Melissa up and followed.

~

On Monday evening, at half an hour to midnight, Julian escorted Melissa and Lady North into Lady Mollison's ballroom.

All but instantly, Lady Mollison materialized from the crowd to welcome them. "Henrietta!" She caught and squeezed Lady North's hands. "I am utterly delighted to see you and thrilled that you could persuade these young people to join us." Her ladyship's eyes gleamed with triumph as they rested on Julian and Melissa. "I'm sure they're much in demand."

Calmly smiling, Melissa greeted Lady Mollison and said all the right things. For his part, Julian smiled charmingly and bowed over her ladyship's hand, which earned him an openly approving look. He then stood by as the ladies exchanged the usual social chitchat before Lady Mollison consented to allow him to steer Lady North and Melissa on.

They were immediately surrounded by guests eager to congratulate and speak with them, but he'd resigned himself to that. This was their third and, thankfully, last event of the evening; the earlier two had been smaller affairs, and they hadn't dallied overlong at either. In contrast, Lady Mollison currently ranked as one of the foremost hostesses in the ton, and her ballroom was packed with society's elite. The colorful, babbling melee was the very epitome of an unholy crush.

Lady North settled with several other older matrons gathered on a pair of sofas halfway down the room. After being introduced to the bevy of avidly intrigued ladies and withstanding their interrogation, Melissa and Julian were allowed to stroll on.

As they did, he murmured, "I am beyond glad that this is the last event of the evening. Over the past few days, it's been borne in on me that, until now, socially speaking, I've led a remarkably sheltered life."

Melissa huffed. "I cut my social eyeteeth at gatherings such as this, and I can assure you it never gets any easier. The instant you let down your guard, you'll trip and land in goodness only knows what mire."

He glanced sidelong at her. "Do I detect a certain weariness with the ton's never-ending demands?"

"Why do you think I was planning on insisting that this would be my last Season?" She paused, then added, "I can appreciate that, by any and all standards, courtesy of my family's status and connections, I've gained a degree of experience and understanding of the ton and those who comprise it that few young ladies, or even not-so-young ladies, could aspire to. I anticipate that knowledge will be useful in whatever future I pursue."

"I see. In that case, can you enlighten me as to why that gentleman to our left has chosen such a color for his waistcoat? Is it a statement of some sort or an insignia?"

She glanced at the gentleman in question, who was sporting a waistcoat in a particularly virulent shade of mustard yellow, and made a disparaging sound. "That's Hildebrand Clayton. He fancies himself a connoisseur of art and has, I understand, declared that color the ultimate in fashion."

"Has anyone else taken it up?"

"Good Lord, no! His last year's selection was an eye-watering puce. No one thought that a good idea, either."

They continued strolling, and in between pausing to chat and receive the apparently unending congratulations and fend off the inevitable inquisitive queries, they exchanged comments and observations.

At one point, Julian murmured, "Carmichael over there looks surprisingly intent."

The rakish lord was hanging on every word uttered by the lady beside him.

Melissa chuckled. "I wish him luck with Lady Jeffers. She's a widow just out of mourning and is intent on enjoying life, and everyone knows Carmichael's pockets are to let."

"Ah. I see." Julian smiled, and they continued to wend their way through the gilded throng, entertaining themselves as they went.

Then a group of musicians tucked away in an alcove set bow to string, and the guests obligingly drifted toward the walls, yielding the floor to those who wished to dance.

"Shall we?" There hadn't been dancing at the previous events they'd attended, at least not while they'd been there, and something in Julian leapt at the chance. He looked at Melissa and saw a similar explorative eagerness in her eyes.

She slid her hand from his arm and offered it to him. "Indeed, my lord. I believe we should."

He took her hand, and they moved onto the floor. She turned into his arms as he reached for her. Their hands settled, his at her back, hers on his shoulder, and their free hands clasped, then he stepped out, into the slow swirl of couples.

The music swelled, and the dance took hold, and they stepped out with increasing confidence.

Their complementary heights, their suppleness, and the ease with which she matched his steps all contributed to a sensation that was just this side of floating. They whirled down the room with effortless, faultless grace.

He smiled into her eyes. "I always knew waltzing with you would be perfect."

She all but rolled her eyes, yet the smile that curved her lips stated she felt as he did, that this was yet another indication of their marital compatibility.

Melissa's senses had come alive, and she was acutely aware of how easily he moved her around the floor. She couldn't recall any similar experience; none of the other hundreds of gentlemen with whom she'd waltzed had ever made the moment this…magical.

This pleasurable.

She enjoyed dancing, waltzing especially, but had never come across any partner as accomplished as he. She met his eyes. "I recall hearing that Wellington always insisted his officers knew how to waltz and waltz well. I've never thought to ask if the Home Office and Foreign Office have the same rule."

He smiled. "After a fashion, they do. It's not written anywhere, but it's understood that your chances of advancement are significantly greater if you can waltz to a certain standard."

"You are clearly a high achiever."

He chuckled. "I have to confess my skills hail from skating. I always loved it as a child and continue to enjoy it whenever I can. Hence—" He stepped farther and whirled her into an effortless glide, then gracefully swept on without missing a beat.

She laughed. "Yes, I can sense that now." She smiled up at him. "I remember skating on the village lake at Little Moseley."

He smiled into her eyes, and for an instant, it seemed as if they were both looking back at the younger people they had been.

Then the music slowed, and they did the same. The dance ended, and he released her, stepped back, and bowed. She curtsied, then he raised her.

Looking around, she felt as if she was seeing those about them for the first time since she'd stepped into the dance with him.

He twined her arm with his and, when she glanced his way, nodded toward a nearby archway. "It seems that supper is upon us."

They ventured into the supper room and joined the queue for the buffet table. They nodded and chatted to others as they progressed, but once they'd helped themselves to a selection of the delicacies on offer, Julian spotted a small table tucked in a corner—a table large enough for only two.

Melissa subsided onto the chair he held with something akin to relief. She smiled as he sat across from her. They settled to consume the tidbits, freely sharing likes and dislikes as they did. As the minutes sped past, she grew increasingly aware that, even in this setting, she was far more relaxed with him than she'd ever been with any other gentleman. Perhaps it was her habit of holding herself aloof, always at a slight distance, untouchable in a way, that shone such a clear contrasting light on her very different feelings when sharing time with him.

He had such a dry sense of humor—one that meshed well with hers—and a ready appreciation of the absurd; they spent their later minutes in the supper room in an irreverent exchange revolving about matrons' evening caps.

When, finally, they reluctantly rose to return to the ongoing crush in the ballroom, she took his arm and tipped her head closer to his. "As a recently affianced couple, we can stay together, and if we keep moving, we should be able to hold the vultures at bay."

"Vultures as in those determined to pick our secrets from our brains?" He nodded. "I'm all for that."

They managed reasonably well. During the next hour, Julian allowed Melissa to steer them through the chattering horde while he kept a weather eye out for the sharp-eyed ladies and gentlemen who made it their business to always know the latest sensational story and whose welcome at ton events largely rested on their ability to satisfy others by recounting the juicy details.

The entire ton, or so it seemed, wanted to know *exactly* how their unexpected engagement had come about.

Of course, he had to check with Melissa that he was correctly attributing motives to those hovering, but his instincts proved sound; in all but one instance, after glancing at the person he indicated, she took evasive action.

The previous afternoon, he'd found time to look up Gordon and ensure he understood that sharing any details of the circumstances preceding Julian and Melissa's shock announcement would result in Gordon's allowance from the earldom's coffers being cut off. Gordon had fallen over himself to assure Julian he hadn't breathed a word and wouldn't dream of doing so. He'd been convincing, and Julian felt confident that source of sensational titillation had been blocked.

As they tacked through the crowd, via the introductions Melissa made, it eventually dawned on him that the people she deemed worthy of their time were socially useful, politically useful, or both. Thereafter, he paid greater attention to the people and their affiliations, and as his realization firmed to fact, he glanced at her, but could read nothing in her serenely assured expression.

The next time they moved on, before they joined anyone else, he dipped his head close to hers and murmured, "Are you deliberately choosing to introduce me to people it will help me to know?"

She looked at him as if surprised he had to ask. "Of course." She shrugged. "If we have to be here—and there's really no help for that— then we might as well put our time to good use." She arched a brow at him. "Don't you agree?"

"I do, indeed. And thank you. After my years away, I'm seriously rusty when it comes to who's who in the ton."

She huffed. "I'd noticed."

He smiled and allowed her to lead him on. He'd never appreciated crowds of this magnitude, where shoulders and elbows constantly brushed, yet he was entirely content to remain by her side.

Shortly after, when they were once again in transit between groups, he softly said, "We seem to be attracting a number of supplicants who, apparently, are keen to remind you of their existence."

"Now that I'm in line to be your countess?" Melissa dryly added. "Indeed."

In truth, she wasn't all that surprised. If she became his countess, she would be a sure conduit to his attention, and there were many in the ton who saw value in such indirect routes to influence.

The observation made her realize she'd been operating under an assumption. "I should have asked earlier. Do you harbor political aspirations, and if so, what are they?"

"Having only just taken up the mantle of the earldom, at least in a political sense, I'm currently very much feeling my way. I do share

Rufus's concerns regarding the corn prices and similar issues, but while in Ireland, I became more aware of the inadvisability of consistently ignoring the well-being of our people, those who have a right to expect our protection in a general sense." He frowned. "While forming any political agenda will necessarily have to take second place to the estate and my pending change of circumstances"—he briefly caught her eye, one dark eyebrow lifting—"I suspect my ultimate political direction will be a synthesis of what I learned while away and the realities of managing the earldom."

She steered him away from the group she'd intended to join; by keeping moving, she could continue this discussion. "What you learned while you were away—does that include your impulse to rescue Kieran?"

He inclined his head. "In part. He's an orphan with a valuable skill, and I was there and could offer him a way to make a living from it." He paused, then added, "If I can do that for others nearer to home... I'd like to explore that."

She filed the information away; she was a trifle stunned to realize how closely his interests in such matters aligned with hers.

"After my time in the Home Office," he went on, "I accept that effecting meaningful change is often best done from within the halls of power, and regardless, it's a long-term process."

"Indeed." She met his gaze. "As a daughter of the Foreign Office, so to speak, I couldn't agree more."

That was another insight they shared, one others without such exposure would not possess.

While she'd scoffed at the label of a perfect match, theirs seemed to become more perfect with every hour they spent learning about each other.

The musicians started playing again, and Julian cocked a brow at her. "Shall we escape onto the dance floor again?"

She smiled and held out her hand. "Indeed, my lord. That's an excellent idea."

◊

Early the following evening, Julian was seated in the library, wrapping up a long session with the estate accounts, when sounds of an arrival came rolling from the front hall.

He raised his head, listened, then muttered, "She must have left at sunrise on Sunday." As soon as possible after his missive regarding his betrothal to Melissa had reached the castle.

Resigned, he shut the ledger he'd been working on, stacked it with its fellows on the desk, then rose and walked out to the front hall.

On hearing his footsteps, his mother, Veronica, Countess of Carsely, looked his way and beamed. "Darling! Such news! Of course, I came straightaway." With her blond hair expertly coiffed and barely streaked with gray, blue eyed and still vivaciously beautiful, his mother held out her arms, her face alight with exuberance despite her having traveled for almost two days.

Julian went forward and bent to kiss her cheek and allow her to gather him into a scented embrace. "Mama. You must have had poor Henry set out before dawn."

"Oh, faugh!" His mother released him and waved dismissively. "Everyone at the castle is utterly agog, including Henry. Of course, I had to come racing down."

Smiling delightedly at him, she looped her arm in his and turned toward the drawing room. "While they take up my things and prepare my room—although of course, Mrs. Crosby has already done so, having known I would arrive—you must tell me all about it. You don't need me to state that congratulations are in order—I'm quite sure half the ton will have lined up to say so by now."

Acquiescing, he nodded. "Indeed, they have."

"Naturally. Persuading Melissa North to accept your offer is quite the coup."

Hiding a smile, he ushered her into the drawing room and firmly shut the door. "You know," he said, following her to the grouping of chairs before the fireplace, "many might have thought the shoe on the other foot —that Melissa was lucky to have hooked me."

His mother sat and, still smiling, looked up at him. "Indeed, as I've already heard from several correspondents—and yes, three sent missives that arrived with yours—the general consensus is that this match is beyond perfect." Her blue eyes studied his face, and her gaze grew shrewd. "So why don't you tell me how it came about? Because until now, I had no idea you were even acquainted with Miss North."

He sighed, sat, and explained the whole—from their years-ago meetings in Little Moseley under her grandmother's aegis, through their mutually-agreed-upon parting, to his return to the capital with the intention of finding the right bride—

"Really, darling! You might have warned me *that* was why you were heading down."

He met her gaze. "Mama, warning you would have been entirely counterproductive. I wanted to look over the field without anyone trying to direct my gaze to this chit or that."

She humphed and waved at him to continue.

After regathering his thoughts, he explained about seeing Melissa with Gordon and following them out to the gazebo. Glossing over the kiss took finesse, but he'd learned a great deal in his time in Ireland, enough at least to have his mother focusing instead on the three ladies who had walked in on them.

"Those three are Helen's friends!"

"So Melissa realized. As you had warned me might happen, we believe that Gordon had set his sights on Melissa's dowry and had engineered a situation he intended to use to force a betrothal with her."

His mother shuddered dramatically. "That poor girl—what a lucky escape!"

"She said that as well."

"Hmm." His mother regarded him with a knowing eye. Many made the mistake of thinking the Countess of Carsely a beautiful lady with no more wit than the average ton female, and in that, they were very wrong. "So what happened next?"

She listened carefully as he explained, then he outlined the agreement he and Melissa had reached to avail themselves of the opportunity created by circumstance to assess if, after all, they might, indeed, suit.

"The Norths have agreed with our tack and have been entirely supportive."

His mother nodded. "Indeed. I can't see why they wouldn't be— neither are fools." She studied him for a moment, then leaned closer and asked, "Tell me, is Melissa as shrewd, intelligent, and"—she gestured expansively—"as they say?"

"As immersed in the ton, chapter and verse, and unwilling to suffer fools gladly?" He smiled. "She is, indeed."

If anything, his mother looked reassured. "Well, she is the daughter of Henrietta, who is Osbaldestone to the core, and North, after all. At the very least, she should have a sound grounding in the ways of the higher civil service and much of politics as well as the wider workings of the ton."

He nodded. "She does." He hesitated, then admitted, "She's already been of considerable help in smoothing my way back into wider society. I hadn't truly appreciated how much had altered while I've been away—even the list of major hostesses has changed."

His mother nodded. From her expression, he gathered she was quietly pleased that Melissa was assisting him. Given that, had he not had Melissa to rely on, he would have turned to his mother for help, he hadn't been entirely sure how she would react to being effectively usurped. He was relieved that she showed no signs of having expected him to revert to holding her apron strings in the social sphere.

The clock on the mantelpiece whirred and chimed for six o'clock. He glanced at it. "I need to go up and change. I'm dining here, but I'm due to escort Melissa and Lady North to several events this evening."

"Yes, of course!" His mother rose. "That's entirely how things should be."

He got to his feet and trailed her to the door.

"I'll join you in the dining room shortly." On reaching the door, she threw a still-delighted smile his way. "As it's just family, we don't need to foregather in the drawing room."

He nodded agreement, opened the door for her, and followed her into the front hall.

Mrs. Crosby, the housekeeper, was waiting to greet her mistress. Julian watched as the pair climbed the stairs, heads together, already conferring; he suspected he knew what about.

Crosby, the butler, was hovering.

Julian asked, "Are either of my brothers dining in?"

"No, my lord. Both said they would be out for dinner."

Julian stifled a sigh and nodded. "Just me and the countess, then." He started up the stairs. At least he and she would be at either end of the table, not that that would restrain his mother in any way.

As he'd foreseen, over the dinner table, his mother blithely informed him of her plans to call on the Norths.

"Do remember me to her ladyship when you see her tonight and assure her I will call on her and Lord North at my earliest convenience." She barely waited for his nod before rolling on, "I'll have to hold a family dinner, of course, and the sooner the better."

Startled, he looked up. "Is that really necessary"—he remembered and quickly tacked on—"at this point in time?"

His mother looked at him as if he'd missed something obvious. "Everyone will expect me to hold such an event to introduce Melissa to the family, and that has to happen as soon as possible, well before any engagement ball."

He lowered his knife and fork and fixed his mother with a direct look. "Mama, the situation being what it is—namely that Melissa and I haven't yet decided to go through with our engagement—then we have no firm notion of when or even if any engagement ball might take place."

"Indeed, and trust me when I say that's all the more reason to get the family event scheduled, done, and out of the way."

"Can't we wait until we're certain we'll be going forward with the engagement and ultimately the wedding?"

"Good gracious, Julian! Of course not!" In the tone of someone patiently explaining a point to one deficient in understanding, she went on, "If you and Melissa wish to be given the time to come to your own decision, then everything must proceed as expected, or you'll have people wondering and whispering, and you certainly won't want that!"

He thought, swallowed, then as mildly as he could manage, said, "I see," and went back to eating his beef.

His mother viewed him for a moment and, detecting no further signs of rebellion, declared, "Don't worry. Lady North and I will sort everything out."

He bit his tongue against the impulse to confess that was exactly what he feared. But from experience, he knew there was no sense even attempting to argue, and he'd run out of time, regardless. He set down his cutlery, laid his napkin aside, and pushed back from the table. "I fear, Mama, that I need to leave you. I have to hie around to North House."

His mother beamed beatifically at him. "Of course, darling boy." She dimpled up at him as she waved a dismissal. "Do enjoy yourself."

He managed a smile in return, then quit the room and the house before she told him any more disturbing news.

~

After weathering Tuesday evening, with the arrival of his mother capped by three crowded ton events, Julian was desperate for escape—to have just a few hours of surcease, of peace away from the hothouse of the ton.

Inspired and determined, at the unfashionable hour of ten o'clock, he drove his curricle to Mount Street. As he'd hoped, he found Melissa up and ready for the day and persuaded her to join him on a jaunt to Richmond. He didn't have to press; she leapt at the chance, as eager as he to get away from the incessant attention.

She paused only to don her bonnet and pelisse and grab a travel rug, then she gave him her hand, allowed him to lead her down the steps and hand her up, then he joined her, and they were away.

As he set his horses trotting down the Knightsbridge Road, she tipped back her head and laughed. "I feel like we're running away."

He grinned. "We are." He flicked the reins and sent his horses quickly past a lumbering coach. Once the beasts were trotting steadily again, he said, "I thought we could stop at the Star and Garter for lunch, then wander down by the river and just watch it flow along."

"After the past week, that sounds heavenly."

A week before, they hadn't been engaged, hadn't known the other was in London or that they would meet. Neither had imagined they would be thrust into the spotlight as they had been.

At that hour, traffic heading out of the capital was light. As the horses trotted on toward Hammersmith, Melissa said, "You mentioned your mother was intent on hosting a dinner?"

He nodded. "To introduce you to the family. She says if it's not held soon, people will start to speculate as to why not, so..."

"Hmm. She's right about that. Did she give you any idea of a date?"

He admitted his mother hadn't, and Melissa quizzed him on the extent of his family and the members likely to attend.

That nudged him to ask for a verbal sketch of her family, most of whom, it seemed, were resident in London.

"The Osbaldestones and Norths have long held office in the civil service, so while some of the family have had country properties at various times, their duties fix them in the capital so they rarely got to use them." Melissa shrugged. "It's difficult to entertain in the way high office demands from a country house, even one in Kent, Surrey, or Essex. The family have largely become London-based."

"I imagine your parents' household must be accustomed to constant entertaining."

"Perpetual and unceasing." She paused, then added, "It sounds tiring, but once everyone is used to what has to be done, how things need to be done, it becomes easier and easier to the point where it's virtually a way of life." She glanced at him. "I suppose that's what I meant by saying we're London-based—our family is truly immersed in that lifestyle."

He nodded in understanding. "In contrast, my parents came to London only when they had to—for instance, to marry off my sisters. My father preferred country life—he rarely occupied his seat in the Lords, preferring, instead, his seat on his hunter. Consequently, Mama had little entertaining of a political nature to do. She entertains socially while in London, and rather more when at the castle. You could say her social base is there rather than here."

Melissa tipped her head, studying what she could see of his face. "If your parents were distanced from the political scene, how did you come to go into the Home Office? I always understood your family was behind that."

He smiled fondly. "That was my uncle Claude's doing. He was in the Home Office for years and loved it. He died in harness, so to speak, about seven years ago. From when I was relatively young, he used to tell me of his work, and I found it fascinating—it was so different from anything I saw my father do, all of which revolved about managing the estate. As I grew older, my conversations with Claude evolved into long discussions on matters of current social and political import. I suppose you could say he lit the spark of interest that eventually led to me joining the Home Office. Somewhat strangely, my father was keen on the idea as well. Looking back, I suspect that, despite his own inclinations, he felt that me having a wider experience socially and politically would be better for the earldom in the long run."

Bluntly, she asked, "Did you get on well with your father?"

He nodded readily. "We rubbed along well—despite our divergent interests, in other spheres, our concerns overlapped. He loved to ride and so do I, and it was the same with loving the castle and being devoted to seeing the earldom as a whole function smoothly and well. We always had those things in common, and he was, in fact, a very shrewd man."

From his tone, she surmised that he and his father had been close.

He checked his horses and turned them south, over Kew Bridge. As the hooves clopped loudly and the wheels rattled, she glanced at the river running east, wide and unstoppable on its journey to the sea.

She would meet his mother and brothers soon enough and could observe and form her own opinions regarding his relationships with them. What else did she need to know? This seemed the perfect time to further her knowledge of him and his life. Given she was seriously considering linking her life to his, it behooved her to use the opportunity he'd handed her.

Before she could decide on her next interrogatory tack, they reached the Star and Garter. He turned in under the archway to the inn's stable yard, and ostlers came running, their eyes lighting with appreciation as they took in the magnificence of the pair of bays and the elegant curricle.

After surrendering the reins, Julian gave her his hand and assisted her down to the cobbles. As they approached the side entrance, she read the sign above the door and smiled. "I've never been here, but I've always wanted to visit."

He pushed open the door and ushered her inside. "After we lunch, then stroll the river banks and relax, perhaps we can return and sample their high tea before heading back to town?"

She smiled. "That sounds wonderful. It's the high tea I've heard tales of."

The owner bustled up, took one look at them, and beaming, bowed them to a prime table before a window. They were promptly served, and while they ate, they looked out over the river, noting the occasional boat that glided past and commenting on those strolling the towpath. A few might be locals taking the air, but many were, like them, refugees from London down for the day.

Over the table, their conversation remained light with a humorous bent. Once they were replete, they rose, and after Julian had paid their shot, he had the rug fetched from the curricle and, hand in hand, they headed for the riverbank.

In companionable silence, they walked a little way along the towpath and found a suitable spot between two trees in which to spread the rug and sit in the dappled sunshine.

Side by side, they looked out over the quietly rippling river, then Julian heaved a long sigh and flopped back. He stretched out full length beside her, linked his hands behind his head, and closed his eyes. "This is peaceful."

While it was hardly silent, the sounds that reached them—birds twittering in the trees, water lapping at the bank, the occasional *plunk* of an oar—were, indeed, soothing.

Melissa looked down at him and smiled at the sight. She debated joining him but, for the moment, remained sitting. Lifting her face, she closed her eyes and reveled in the cool caress of the light breeze on her cheeks.

Proving that, despite his closed eyes, he wasn't somnolent, he said, "You've asked about my political interests. Do you have any of your own? Causes you feel drawn to?"

Eyes still closed, she arched her brows lightly. "I mentioned at the outset that I'd intended this Season to be my last—my admittedly vague notion of what to do with myself subsequently was to investigate how I could best assist those devoted to bettering the lives of the far too many orphaned children in London and elsewhere in England." She paused, then, without waiting for him to prompt, went on, "I realize that, in having the sort of upbringing I've had, I've been one of the lucky ones in life. Given that, it seems only right that I do what I can for those who, through no fault of their own, have not been so lucky."

He made an approving sound. After a moment, he said, "You should talk to Kieran. It takes a while to get him to open up, but once he does... it's instructive."

She could imagine. "I will sometime." Assuming they married.

"Apropos of our earlier discussion about living in London and living in the country, it's always seemed to me that to make any sort of difference on any major issue, one has to be prepared to live in London and contend with the social-cum-political scene. There's no getting away from the fact the two spheres are inextricably linked."

"Indeed." She thought of the prospect he was alluding to—where they would live if they married. After a moment, she glanced at him, then lowered herself to lie alongside him.

A good few inches separated them, but then he drew one hand from beneath his head, reached and found her hand, and twined his fingers with hers.

While innocent enough, in the circumstances, the gesture felt strangely intimate.

Without letting herself think too hard, she lightly gripped his fingers back.

She stared up at the shards of blue sky framed by the greening branches overhead. After a second of sorting through her thoughts, she said, "I have to confess that I view London society purely as an arena in which useful contacts and connections are made. It's the value of those contacts and connections in facilitating one's ability to accomplish things —as you said, to make a difference—that makes the fuss and bother of the ton worthwhile." After reviewing her words, she wondered, "Is it terribly cold-blooded to view social events in that light?"

He huffed cynically. "Not at all. In fact, I guarantee that a large percentage of those with any power at all hold much the same view. Having to endure ton events—the crushes, the often-inane conversations, the furious matchmaking, and so on—isn't attractive to most of us and certainly isn't what keeps us coming back."

"Hmm. Well, in that case, I confess I've never been fond of crowded entertainments, but I've learned to tolerate them in pursuit of a meaningful goal, which is to say that I accept the ton and its events as a necessary evil."

He laughed, raised her hand, and brushed a light kiss to her knuckles. "I've never heard it put so well."

She tamped down her reaction to the light caress and steadfastly ignored the warmth spreading through her.

"So," he went on, "given all that, how would you feel about spending most of the year in the country—in Derbyshire, to be precise? Would you be—could you be—happy if we came down to London only for the height of the Season and a few weeks in autumn?"

That gave her the perfect opening to command, "Carsington Castle and that estate—tell me about it, in detail this time."

He did. They spent nearly an hour with her questioning—interrogating—and him freely answering.

When she ran out of questions, she felt confident in stating, "In light of all that, I'm sure I'll be able to find duties, endeavors, and interests sufficient to keep me occupied." She already had ideas for several improvements she would like to explore. She turned her head and met his eyes. "That's really all I need to be happy—things to accomplish."

His smile was swift. He came up on one elbow and, leaning over her, with his free hand brushed back a strand of hair that had fallen across her forehead.

The look in his gray eyes...stole her breath.

For long moments, she stared at him, at what he allowed her to see, fascinated, mesmerized...wanting to know yet more.

But while they seemed to be enclosed in their own private space, in reality, they were in public, and the towpath ran only yards away.

Yet she couldn't bring herself to shatter the moment. She raised a hand and lightly stroked the side of his face.

He turned his head and pressed a heated kiss to her palm, and what little breath she'd managed to catch fled all over again.

His lids, which had fallen, rose lazily. He looked down at her, then his lips quirked into a gentle smile. "Perhaps, all things considered, it might be time for our high tea."

She laughed and nodded. He shifted back, then rose and held out a hand to help her to her feet.

Julian closed his fingers about hers. He felt heartened, reassured, not just by her responses but by the tenor of their exchanges. The latter testified to the closeness that was steadily building between them; he was quite sure neither would speak to anyone else in such an unrestrained, uncensored way.

As he waited for her to flick out her skirts, he felt quietly content. All was progressing as it should; he had absolutely no qualms in going forward with their engagement and was increasingly confident she was coming to feel the same way.

With luck, he would be able to ask her for her decision soon. As he tensed to haul her up, he scanned her face, but balked at pushing the point that afternoon; he was not quite ready to risk all yet.

With a grin, he hauled her upright, briefly steadying her with an arm around her waist.

She laughed, but then her gaze went past him, and the smile fell from her face.

Instantly, he released her and turned. "What?"

She pointed to the left, where the towpath meandered around a stand of trees. "Isn't that the man from the theater? Peeking out from behind that tree?"

He spotted the dark-haired man.

The fellow stepped out, onto the path. He stood there, apparently debating whether or not to approach.

Julian inwardly swore and strode forward.

As if interpreting that as encouragement, the man started toward him.

Five young men, jostling each other and horsing around, came ambling along the path from Julian's right; their noisy if lighthearted argument had him glancing their way.

Immediately, he looked back at the dark-haired man, only to discover he'd vanished.

Julian pulled up, swallowed a curse, then swung on his heel and retraced the few steps he'd taken.

As he reached Melissa, he met her eyes, grimaced, and shook his head.

She'd gathered up the rug. Clutching it to her chest, she stared after the man. "Why did he run?"

"Because of those idiots coming along."

She frowned and transferred her gaze to him. "Why should that bother him?"

"That, indeed, is the question." Gently, he took the rug from her, tucked it under his arm, then offered her his other arm.

She slipped her hand into the crook of his elbow. "Do you have any idea who he is?"

He cast one last glance at where the man had been. "I've never met him before."

The sharp glance she threw him stated very clearly that she was aware he hadn't actually answered her question. Briefly meeting her eyes, he admitted, "At this point, I honestly don't know what to think."

That, she accepted. With a nod, she matched her stride to his, and they made their way back to the inn.

There, they indulged in a scrumptious high tea. With the servers about, their conversation reverted to a light banter.

Afterward, Melissa waited with Julian in the inn's stable yard while the smiling ostlers brought out his curricle and horses. The lads were transparently proud of the care they'd lavished on both. While bestowing suitable largesse on the pair, Julian added several words of praise, leaving the lads glowing.

She gave him her hand, and he helped her to the seat. She bided her time until they were out of Richmond proper and had crossed the bridge and were once more rolling steadily toward London before asking, "What was it that you actually did while in Ireland?"

She kept her gaze forward, but felt the glance—as sharp as any of hers—that he threw her. Then he, too, fixed his gaze ahead. She didn't prompt, just waited.

Eventually, he replied, "I mentioned that I was a negotiator." Without her having to press, he explained what that entailed, ending with, "Because the Irish hierarchy were willing to treat with me, I ended up being the one sent to discuss every little thing with them. Sometimes, I was merely a messenger, but most often, my role was to present our side of an issue and try to gauge their response."

She frowned. "Even I know that must have been dangerous."

He lifted one shoulder. "Potentially, yes. But as I said, for whatever reason, the Irishmen decided they could trust me, at least to the extent of using me as a conduit to get their point across to Dublin Castle."

She knew that all parties involved referred to the British administration in Ireland as "Dublin Castle."

He added, "That was why Gregory moved heaven and earth to keep me there for as long as he could. Initially, my appointment was only supposed to last two years."

She spent several minutes wondering what might have happened had he not been so good at his job, so valuable to the administration in Ireland, but instead, had returned to London when he'd originally expected to... Then she set the past aside and refocused on the present. "So you were a trusted contact of the Irishmen. Did you acquire any enemies from that time?"

She was pleased that he considered the notion before slowly shaking his head.

"I'm not aware of any, and I know of no reason any Irishman would want me dead."

"That man—he had curly black hair and a faintly swarthy complexion. He could be Irish."

He nodded. "He might be."

They were clattering along Kensington High Street when she put into words what she felt sure they were both thinking. "So the Irish, at least those in Ireland, trust you as a conduit to the government. Could that man be wanting to use you to pass a message along?"

He didn't say anything for some time, but whether that meant he was thinking or having to concentrate too intently on the increasing traffic to formulate an answer, she couldn't have said. But when they turned up Park Lane into the quieter streets of Mayfair, he glanced at her. "I thought that might be it, but the way he keeps vanishing whenever anyone else hoves in sight... That's the part I don't understand, and that bothers me."

By mutual consent, they let the topic lie. In truth, she was rather grateful to the unknown, possibly Irish man; if it hadn't been for his repeatedly popping up, she might never have thought to ask the questions she had—might never have learned about that aspect of Julian's life.

Thinking back to what she'd seen in him all those years ago confirmed that this more serious side of him, one encompassing a devotion to country and to duty of several kinds, was one she'd sensed, even then, was there. Even while he'd been acting the fool, as young gentlemen were wont to do, there'd been an awareness of others and of ever-present duty to his name and station running beneath his glib and highly polished exterior.

Being the daughter of Lord North and, even more pertinently, a scion on the Osbaldestone family tree, she knew what value to place on such fundamental convictions. They formed the bedrock of men's souls.

Julian drew up outside North House and came around to help her down.

As he hadn't brought his tiger with him and there was no helpful urchin in sight, they parted on the pavement.

Smiling, she gave him her hand. "Thank you for a lovely day free of the madding crowd."

He smiled easily, took her hand, raised it to his lips, and kissed her knuckles. "It truly was my pleasure." His gray gaze held her with almost mesmerizing power, drawing her in, tempting her, luring her nearer.

For an instant, she teetered on the precipice of stepping closer and brazenly demanding a proper kiss. Her lips throbbed hungrily.

She hauled in a breath and, with a warning look, retrieved her fingers.

He smiled faintly and released her. "Until tonight."

"Indeed. Lady Hetherington expects us in good time for her dinner."

He sighed dramatically. "No rest for the wicked." With a last commiserating smile, he saluted her, and she turned and went up the steps.

Curtin, her parents' butler, opened the door and bowed her in. On the threshold, she turned and saw Julian, once again on the curricle's seat but waiting to see her safely inside. She smiled and raised a hand.

In reply, he flourished his whip, then gave his horses the office and drove off.

She watched him go, then still smiling, went inside, entirely happy with the outcome of her day.

CHAPTER 5

a full week after finding themselves unexpectedly engaged, Julian sat beside Melissa in the front row of the Carsely box at the Royal Opera House and wondered, yet again, when the ton would lose interest in them.

Too many people still found the sight of them fascinating, as if waiting for him or Melissa or both to do something sensational. He had no idea why; it wasn't as if either of them was given to behaving in outrageous or scandalous ways.

He liked opera as well as any of his peers, which was to say that while the soprano caterwauled on stage, he was thinking of other things. His mother had been busily organizing, which was why he and Melissa, attended by their mothers and three of their aunts, were there that evening, once again on display for the entertainment and—beneath that—edification of the elite of London's society.

Having no need to think further on that, he let his mind drift over the past week. While he'd spent what he considered far too many hours at social events, other than on the days they'd gone to Surrey and Richmond, he'd been able to devote some of his waking hours to dealing with estate business. Given the size of the earldom's holdings, managing them properly was a constant, never-ending endeavor.

"What did you get up to today?"

Melissa's whisper floated across his senses. Without shifting his gaze from the stage—not that he was watching the drama enacted upon it—

under his breath, he replied, "I had to go through the projections for this year's harvest and sign off on the planting plans."

"I daresay that was more exciting—and certainly more rewarding—than attending three at-homes."

"Very likely." He stifled a grin. "I also learned that we put up over three hundred pound jars of honey."

"You have beehives?"

"Dozens. They're scattered through the orchards on all the properties."

"Hmm, I do like honey. What sort of orchards?"

They continued their sotto voce exchange, with her questioning and him describing a range of minor details about the castle and the earldom's other properties.

Despite staring at the stage, Melissa saw nothing of the action upon it; she didn't even truly hear the music and singing, so engrossed was she in expanding her knowledge of Carsington Castle and the household there. While she'd found Julian's mother, Veronica, charming, she couldn't imagine asking her the sort of questions she freely, without the slightest hesitation, put to Julian. Such as whether the butler and house-keeper were young enough to remain in their posts for a good long while.

He answered without reservation, and she was reassured to learn that the Phelpses were unlikely to retire soon. The idea of having to take on such a large household only to soon lose her principal lieutenants wasn't a prospect she wished to face.

They'd reached that point in their discussions when it dawned on her just how far she'd traveled down the mental path of converting their faux engagement into a genuine one. She glanced sidelong at Julian's chiseled features, but could detect nothing more than his usual relaxed confidence. Inwardly humphing, she shifted her gaze forward. No wonder he was so happy to answer all her queries.

Still... Fractionally, she tipped up her chin. If she was to make an informed decision as to whether to become his countess, then it was only wise to learn all she could from the most well-informed source.

After a moment, she murmured, "Did you say there were dovecotes?"

"Yes. There are three."

"Just so you know—I hate dovecotes."

There was a hint of laughter in his voice when he replied, "I'll bear that in mind."

Julian was, in fact, entirely happy to satisfy her near-endless queries; that she was asking about such domestic details was patently a good sign.

He'd sensed the instant she'd realized what her litany of questions revealed, the moment marked by the sudden break in the steady flow, the suspension of her breathing, the slight widening of her eyes as realization had struck.

She'd paused, thought, then she'd continued.

He'd almost blown out a breath of relief, then he'd inwardly grinned and calmly continued answering her questions—questions that were only pertinent were she actively considering marrying him.

He held fast to his conviction that, ultimately, she would accept his suit.

Finally, the music and massed voices swelled in a great crescendo, then cut off, and the performance was at an end. With relief, he rose, clapping with the rest of the audience in what was a standing ovation; apparently, the opera had been exceptional.

He couldn't remember any of it.

He glanced sidelong at Melissa and caught her glancing at him. Their gazes met and held, then they both burst out laughing.

They were still chuckling as he drew out her chair, allowing her to move deeper into the box. Before following her, he swept a comprehensive glance around the pit, but saw no familiar head of black curls.

He turned to assist the other ladies. Melissa helped them untangle their wraps while he held their cloaks.

When everyone was ready, they quit the box; allowing their elders to precede them, he and Melissa brought up the rear.

He noticed his mother and hers had their heads together, avidly arranging, no doubt. He caught Melissa's eye and, with a tip of his head, directed her gaze to the disconcerting sight.

She looked, then sent him a resigned glance and patted his sleeve. "There's nothing we can do, I fear."

He swallowed a disaffected huff; he was an earl, yet apparently, escaping whatever their mothers were planning was beyond him.

While they slowly descended the stairs to the ground floor, he kept an eye peeled for their mystery man, but he didn't appear.

Then they were outside the theater, and while their party waited for the Carsely and North carriages to arrive, he bent his head and murmured by Melissa's ear, "I haven't seen our mystery man anywhere." When she glanced at him, he asked, "Have you?"

She shook her head, a slight frown in her eyes. "Did you think he would be here?"

"I thought he might show. It's not that difficult to engineer a meeting in a crowd."

"Yes, but..." She glanced back at the packed foyer. "Maybe he couldn't afford a ticket? Or the attire? And don't forget, this performance has been sold out for weeks."

"Has it?" He hadn't known; his mother had the box for the Season. "Perhaps that—or the clothes—was his problem." He frowned. "I wonder what that tells us about him."

The man clearly wanted to avoid being noticed by anyone other than Julian and Melissa, and if he hadn't known about this performance, even to turn up in the street, it seemed likely he hadn't been in London that long.

~

The following afternoon, Melissa sat on the sofa in the drawing room of Winslow House and smiled benevolently as she accepted a cup of tea from an all but bouncing Lottie.

Now fifteen, Lottie had come to town with their grandmother, Lady Osbaldestone, who had been sojourning at Lottie's home in Northamptonshire when the news of Melissa and Julian's unexpected engagement had reached that branch of the family.

Unsurprisingly, the instant her grandmother had arrived in the capital, Melissa and Julian had been summoned to attend this entirely private afternoon tea.

"Well!" Over the rim of her teacup, Lady Osbaldestone, archgrande dame and arbiter of ton sentiment, eyed Melissa and Julian, who was seated beside her, with open approval. "I don't know how this came about, and frankly, I don't care." She raised her cup in a toast. "I am simply delighted that you have finally embarked on this journey. It's one I long feared you'd never take."

Melissa sipped and, from the corner of her eye, caught Julian's equally relieved gaze. Although in years past, her grandmother had been well disposed toward Julian, they hadn't known what to expect from her now. Luckily, it appeared that in announcing their engagement, they'd satisfied some long-held expectation of hers—never a bad achievement.

After delivering a teacup to Julian, Lottie retreated with her own cup to sit in a chair alongside their grandmother's. "Incidentally," Lottie said, "Jamie and George send their regards. Both hope to come down at some point and deliver their congratulations in person." Lottie's blue eyes twinkled. "Like Grandmama, the three of us feel a certain vindication over your engagement."

Julian lowered his cup. "Melissa mentioned that Jamie and George are at Oxford and Eton, respectively. Do they have any particular futures in mind?"

"Jamie's eighteen," Lottie replied, "and is reading history and hoping to attach himself to the school of archeology. George is in his final year at school and has been bitten by the antiquities bug. He forever has his nose in a book, reading about some artifact or other. If you put him and Jamie in the same room and allow them to lead the conversation"—Lottie rolled her eyes—"all you'll hear is ancient news."

Lady Osbaldestone humphed. "You're no better, my girl, with your talk of digs and excavations."

"But I don't want to dig myself, Grandmama—I just want to be there and watch." Lottie paused, then added, "And catalog what they find." To Melissa and Julian, she explained, "I can't see the point in getting excited over bits and pieces in a museum. Finding them, however, is a different story—so much more exciting to my way of thinking."

Melissa grinned. "I remember the day we found the Roman hoard behind Grandmama's house. The three of you were in the thick of it."

Julian nodded. "And you, Miss Charlotte, jumped into the pit as soon as you could and were grubbing about in the dirt just as furiously as your brothers were."

Lottie tried to suppress a grin and lifted one shoulder in a disconcertingly adult gesture. "That was then. I've grown past such behavior."

Julian chuckled, and Melissa smiled. In truth, they were all older and more mature than they had been then.

As if to underscore that, her grandmother stated, "I remember those Christmases well. Quite a time we had. Tell me, Carsely, are you still in touch with Sir Henry and the others?"

Julian nodded. "We never lost touch, although these days, we only see each other perhaps once a year. As you know, we continued our Christmas get-togethers in Little Moseley even after I went to Ireland, as that was one of the times of the year when I was allowed some weeks' leave."

"I well remember the year we caught that French spy," Lady Osbaldestone said, her black gaze steady on Julian's face. Then she switched that always terrifying gaze to Melissa. "That was the year after you last visited, my dear. You and Mandy missed the most exciting imbroglio, what with your uncle Christopher meeting his Marion and us all chasing after…what was his name?"

"De Mille," Julian supplied. "One of Napoleon's favorite agents." Smiling, he glanced at Melissa. "That was quite the coup, capturing him. It made your uncle's career and didn't do mine any harm, either."

Melissa hadn't known Julian had gone back to Little Moseley after they'd agreed to part. Yet apparently, he had, year after year. That, she was aware, was what her grandmother wished her to know, although quite what she was supposed to deduce from the knowledge, she wasn't sure.

Regardless, as their conversation continued, memories of years past mingling with observations of the present and expectations for the future, despite what her grandmother termed their "unconventional approach," her view of their marriage as a connection that was fated to be shone through.

Her grandmother wasn't one to form such a view without sound reasons.

Increasingly, Melissa felt that Julian—and indeed, Mandy—had been correct in suggesting that their past association, steeped in mutual youth though it had been, was nevertheless a valid indicator of the potential for an adult relationship.

Julian kept a wary eye on Lady Osbaldestone while the bulk of his senses remained focused on Melissa as he tracked how she was reacting to the subtle yet unrelenting pressure her grandmother was bringing to bear—on multiple fronts. She really was a grande dame extraordinaire, yet he was in two minds over her championship. After the past week, he was even more certain that his best strategy for winning Melissa to wife was to allow her to convince herself of what he already saw clearly—namely, that they were, in fact, the perfect match the ton had labeled them.

Finally, their reminiscing ran down, and with the tea drunk and the cakes consumed, Melissa and he rose to take their leave.

After Melissa had kissed Lady Osbaldestone's cheek, he took the old lady's hand and bowed over it. Her fingers clutched as tight as any claws, and she caught his gaze and whispered, "Don't let her slip through your fingers."

He met her obsidian gaze. "I won't."

She smiled, reached up, and patted his cheek. "Dear boy. See that you don't."

With that nebulous warning ringing in his ears, he farewelled Lottie, then followed Melissa from the room.

He didn't breathe easily until they were going down the front steps and the door of Winslow House closed with a thud of finality behind them.

Abruptly, Melissa halted, looking along the street to their left. "There's our mystery man."

Julian looked and saw the man—dressed in a heavy black overcoat and, today, sporting a cap—standing on the opposite pavement a little way along.

As he watched, the man started walking their way, but then a carriage rumbled down the street, two gentlemen came out of another house and started walking toward them, and a messenger came hurrying along, in his haste unceremoniously brushing past the man.

The man halted, then the carriage came between them, blocking Julian's view.

When the carriage passed, he looked again and wasn't entirely surprised to see that the man had, once again, disappeared.

Melissa stared. "What on earth...?"

"Come." Looping his arm with hers, Julian drew her around and set off for Mount Street. He tipped his head toward hers and, lowering his voice, explained, "I think he's been warned not to approach me while there are others about who might spot him."

She frowned. "Why?"

He quirked a brow. "I imagine because whatever message he's carrying is sensitive, and there are fears others might be watching me, ready to ensure, one way or another, that I never receive it."

Her gaze fixed on his face, sharp and openly concerned. "So you are in danger!"

Anxiety swam in her blue eyes, and he couldn't stop his heart from leaping just a little; clearly, she cared for him. He would willingly accept that as his advance for the day.

He smiled gently, reassuringly, and shook his head. "No. It's not me who's in danger. It's him."

~

The days fled past in a haze of balls, soirées, and formal dinners. A week after their successful outing to Richmond, Julian and Melissa stole away to spend the day at Greenwich.

He'd arranged for them to take a water taxi from the stairs by Westminster Bridge. After stepping into the boat and setting down the loaded picnic basket provided by the Carsely House cook, he turned to where Melissa waited on the stone step. Smiling, he reached up, closed his hands about her waist, and lifted her down. The shift in weight made the boat rock. They held still until it steadied, then he handed her to the plush, chair-like seat in the bow. He waited until she settled her skirts, then sat beside her and nodded to the two watermen sitting at the stern, patiently waiting to get under way.

With indulgent grins, the watermen dipped their oars in the dark water, and in seconds, the boat drew smoothly away from the bottom of the granite stairs.

As the buildings of Whitehall slipped away on their right, Julian and Melissa relaxed on the surprisingly comfortable padded bench with its raised back. He'd told the watermen that they were in no especial hurry, but the river was running strongly, enough that the men had to work to weave the lighter boat past the ferries, barges, and other watercraft likewise busily navigating the space.

Regardless, out on the expanse of murky water, the noises of town were muted, and although the shouts of watermen, the occasional horn, shrill steam whistles, and the raucous cries of jostling gulls were far from silent, they belonged to another world. All awareness of London faded as the experience of the river engulfed them.

They passed under Waterloo Bridge, then Blackfriars Bridge and Southwark Bridge and, eventually, slid beneath the span of London Bridge and left the city behind.

After a time, Julian broke their companionable silence to observe, "Although we're children of the haut ton, it seems we share a liking for savoring moments without words in the open air."

Smiling, she tipped her head back, closing her eyes as the weak sunshine bathed her face. "You're right—that's another thing we have in common. Neither of us feel we have to be conversing all the time." She raised her lids enough to glance at him from beneath her lashes. She studied his face and, when he arched a questioning brow, said, "You do realize that the coming weeks—those leading to the height of the Season —are going to be even worse than those we've weathered thus far?"

He blinked. "Are they? I thought Sunday bad enough. Whatever happened to the notion of a day of rest?"

She smothered a snort. "This is the ton, and at the height of the Season, there is no rest afforded to anyone, wicked or otherwise."

"So it appears." He thought of the crowd that had thronged the porch of St. George's Church, followed by the luncheon, the party, and two evening events that had forced them to adopt their social façades virtually throughout the entire day.

Monday and Tuesday had been only marginally better, at least for him. Melissa, he suspected, had had luncheons and at-homes to contend with while he had taken refuge in his study with the excuse of having to attend to estate business. True enough, but also a major relief.

"I don't understand," he said, "why the fascination with us has yet to wane. If anything, people seem to be watching us even more closely."

She sighed. "It's the 'perfect match' stigma. They're all watching to see how matters play out and if we'll stumble."

They can watch, but that, they won't see. Stumbling wasn't an option. He was determined on that.

The boatmen had their work cut out for them in avoiding all the ships crowding the Pool of London, but eventually, Rotherhithe fell far behind, and they passed through Limehouse Reach and continued toward Deptford.

The farther they traveled down the river, the more the sense of leaving behind the mad carousel of ton events grew, until finally, they fetched up at the appropriately named Garden Pier that gave access to the royal park. They stepped out of the boat and, after Julian paid off the watermen, walked the few short blocks up Church Street, past the church itself and onto the tree-lined paths of the park. Melissa looped her arm in his and, with a smile on her face, looked about her. He carried the picnic basket in his other hand, idly swinging it as they strolled.

While not quite bucolic, the atmosphere was a far cry from that which prevailed in London. Here, children romped and laughed as they raced across the lawns, sometimes with maids or footmen chasing after them, laughing in turn. No one stood on ceremony or dignity; this was a place for enjoying a day free from censorious eyes.

Inevitably, there were members of the ton indulging as they were, but although several others recognized them, no one ventured more than a polite nod in passing.

"Bliss," Julian murmured after the third such encounter. Melissa simply smiled, and they strolled on.

They found a grassy spot shaded by an old oak and spread the picnic blanket and sat. After staring out and up and commenting on the kites that, despite the feeble breeze, several children had managed to get aloft, they turned to the basket and unpacked the repast Julian's cook had—clearly—taken great pride in assembling. There were small game pies, with light flaky pastry and a succulent filling, golden cheese balls, roast chicken, hard-boiled quail eggs, several other delicacies, fresh crusty bread, cheddar cheese, dried apples and pears, and a bottle of sweet wine and several bottles of cider with which to wash everything down.

"Hmm." Melissa closed her eyes and savored the tastes bursting on her tongue. She swallowed, then opened her eyes and studied the small pie. "These are scrumptious. You must convey my compliments to your cook."

Propped on one elbow and demolishing his own pie, Julian nodded. "I convey mine regularly. Usually daily. She's a gem."

"I have to say, I'm always torn by the arguments over which is better, French—or at least French-trained—chefs, usually male, or English cooks, usually female. While I appreciate and approve of some of the French-inspired dishes, I've generally found, especially when in the country, that local cooks do better, especially those willing to incorporate some of the continental ideas into their own recipes."

Julian held up another of the delicious delights—a quail breast stuffed with prunes and nuts—in illustration. "My thoughts exactly."

Many of the children had been taken home for their luncheons or had been called to attend family groups picnicking under the trees. The March sun had decided to rule the day and was beaming down, warm enough to make the temperature pleasant.

She continued to nibble on the pie, then dusted off her fingers and reached for the next morsel. "When you were young, did you come here with your brothers?"

He nodded. "A few times during each of the years that we came down with our parents. Of course, we were more interested in viewing the navy ships that are docked just a little farther along."

She softly huffed. "We only came here twice—I think because the second time, Christopher fell into the river. Before we'd had our picnic."

Julian chuckled. "With three boys to keep occupied, I think our nurse-maids and later our tutors were always glad to bring us here—plenty of space to run off excess energy, and then there were the ships and, when we were somewhat older, the observatory to visit." He turned to look at her. "So if you didn't come here, where did you go? Or rather, get taken?"

"The Royal Menagerie, countless times. Christopher was fascinated with the lions. Mandy and I always found the rooks frightening, but as Christopher was completely oblivious to their threat, as older sisters, we had to keep our upper lips stiff."

He laughed. They returned their gazes to the lawns before them just as two young boys ran out from the trees, bowling a hoop along.

Julian pointed. "I remember doing that and not just here. All around Hyde Park as well. Once, Felix and I lost control of our hoop, and it bowled across the avenue and caused a team to rear and set the ladies in the carriage screeching—literally sent them into hysterics. No real calamity, but we grabbed the hoop and raced home, utterly breathless from laughing." Grinning, he met her eyes. "Boys will be boys, and the footmen with us couldn't stop laughing, either."

They continued exchanging memories and anecdotes as they ate and drank.

Once the food was reduced to mere crumbs, Julian reclined on one elbow and sipped the last of the wine, while Melissa sat upright, her legs stretched before her and her ankles crossed, and cradled a pottery mug of the cider.

With post-prandial peace washing over him, he looked across the neat lawns toward the river and the taller buildings of the city, visible in the distance.

He sipped, then, keeping his gaze on the view, said, "All this talk of us being the perfect match—what do you think people mean by that?"

From the corner of his eye, he saw her lightly shrug.

"I suspect," she said, "that the phrase means different things to different people."

"Such as?"

She thought, then offered, "Mutual respect. A working partnership based on each other's strengths. A relationship that works for both parties. A solid foundation both can rely on. That, and always having the other's support."

Without shifting his gaze, he quietly said, "And love?"

He sensed her swift glance, then she inclined her head. "For many, that, too."

"And for you?" He turned his head and met her eyes. "What does a perfect match mean to you?"

For a long moment, she held his gaze, then said, "I haven't used that term to describe us."

He dipped his head in acknowledgment. "Nevertheless."

She sighed softly and looked out, over the lawns. "I seriously doubt anyone or anything that's human-based is ever truly perfect. That's simply asking too much."

"You'll get no argument from me on that score, yet...whatever's between us, perfect match or not, I suspect it's time we started defining what, in that mutual connection, however one wishes to describe it, is important to us. To each of us. In what lies between us, what does each of us value?"

He waited until, faint puzzlement in her eyes, she again met his gaze, then he stated, "They haven't yet started to actively press us, but soon, they will."

Melissa knew he was right. Despite their private agreement to explore and consider, they would be allowed only so long before their families—currently holding back—would expect to hear some definite decisions. When he waited, patient as ever, she faintly grimaced. "I realize we have limited time, that we can't put matters off forever, yet..." Where to start?

When she didn't immediately go on, he sat up and shifted to face her. His gray gaze steady on her face, he said, "If you were asked to design your ideal relationship, how would you describe it? What elements would you include?"

She drew in a breath and, before she could overthink things, gave voice to the words that leapt to her tongue. "I'd want someone to share life's ups and downs with. Someone who sees and responds to things in the same way I do."

"Someone with the same or at least similar views and attitudes?"

She waggled her head. "They wouldn't necessarily need to think exactly as I do. Perhaps I should say they would need to share the same overarching values I hold."

He smiled. "Because it never hurts to hear different perspectives?"

"Exactly!" Of course, he understood. She went on, "Discussing and even arguing points clarifies one's views, so I should also stipulate someone to whom I can speak freely and engage with without reserve."

He nodded. "We're making progress, and I wholeheartedly agree with your points." He hesitated, then offered, "While my view of my perfect match doesn't notably differ from yours thus far, I would add that my someone would be committed to the same ideals and, in terms of those, be prepared to work to advance them and to hold a line if challenged..." He trailed off, then amended, "The crux of that is they should share my commitment to making things better for others and to building something that lasts."

Regarding him, she said, "That sounds entirely laudable." She tipped her head. "Are you speaking of the earldom specifically?"

"The earldom, yes, but not only that." Julian paused, ordering his thoughts, then went on, "I can see both a broader and also a narrower focus. For instance, more narrowly, the family at the center of the earldom, while on a wider stage, the situation of all who live in the county or even the country."

"Do you feel the same sense of purpose should extend to those other arenas?"

He smiled. "This illustrates what you said earlier, about being able to talk freely and the benefits of the same. But to answer your question, I suspect my prioritizing would move outward, like concentric rings, from my immediate family, to those dependent on the earldom, to those in the surrounding communities, to all in the county, and ultimately, to all in England."

"Concentric circles." She nodded. "That's an illuminating way of thinking of it."

"And if you think of commitment as a defined amount of paint spread over the increasingly larger areas, then the analogy works in that respect, too, with the intensity of the color indicating the degree of effort applying to each ring."

"Each ring of ambition and influence. Yes, I see. The farther out from the center, the more diluted one's force will be."

They fell silent, both thinking, then he smiled ruefully and met her eyes. "We've become rather philosophical and strayed from our original focus."

She arched her brows in question, and he replied, "Us."

When she looked at him challengingly, he sat straighter, then captured and held her gaze. "You haven't married because no gentleman offered sufficient incentive to entice you to favor him with your hand. Is that an accurate statement?"

His years of negotiating were coming to the fore, but if that was what it took...he was willing to use all the skills he possessed to achieve his goal—namely, her as his wife.

She tipped her head, then conceded, "That's a fair assessment, but I'm not sure where it gets us."

"I'm trying to learn what it will take to persuade you to put your hand in mine and front an altar."

She almost smiled at his dry tone, but she straightened her twitching lips and said, "You want to make our engagement real."

That wasn't a question, but he nodded and confirmed, "I do."

When she continued to regard him with what he was coming to think of as her assessing look, he baldly asked, "What about you?"

Such a short, simple question. Melissa returned his regard as the magnitude of all that hung on her answer weighed on her mind. But they were here, and he was right; they had to address this issue and, at least between them, decide what they wanted.

It's time.

"I had all but turned my back on marriage," she admitted, "precisely because of what you said—because no gentleman offered me reason enough to consider marrying him."

He spread his hands to either side. "You know what I have. You know what I can and will offer you as my wife."

She couldn't stop a faintly cynical smile. "I know the tangibles—the title, the estate, the houses, the wealth and position—but it's the *in*tangibles that make all the tangibles worthwhile, that give them real value. It's not being your countess that matters, it's what I can achieve and create through being your countess that carries weight with me." She took a moment to canvass her thoughts, then sensing that she finally had a grip on them, went on, "To my mind, it's the intangibles that make a marriage work, certainly over time."

He cocked his head. "By intangibles...you mean respect, honor, caring, affection?"

She nodded and, greatly daring, added, "And love."

He didn't look away. He held her gaze for several long moments, then asked, "Owning to love as well?"

She swallowed and nodded. "Yes. For what worth is love if it's hidden away?" She tipped up her chin. "So yes, love acknowledged, not love concealed or denied." She paused, searching his eyes, then as bold as he had previously been, asked, "Will you—are you prepared to—offer me even that?"

She could barely believe they'd pared away all the usual obfuscation and got down to the essential, fundamental question.

He continued to hold her gaze, his own open and steady as a rock. "I'm not one hundred percent certain I know what love is, but if love is what we feel for each other"—he waved a hand between them—"if that's what's grown and is still growing between us, then yes." His voice deepening, he vowed, "I'm ready and willing to offer you—and to own to and acknowledge—all that I feel for you." His lips quirked. "I'm not sure it's possible for me to do anything else. This"—again, he waved between them—"whatever it is, is too powerful a feeling to suppress or even hide. That much, I already know and readily admit."

The look in his eyes—steady, sure, and true—ensured that she couldn't keep her response from her lips. "I don't know that it's love I feel for you, either. I haven't experienced this sort of feeling for another before."

He was watching her with the same all-consuming intensity with which she was regarding him. "So can we agree," he said, "that if this is love, we'll own to it? That we'll go forward with our marriage and, in doing so, acknowledge our love, claim it, and make it an integral part of our shared life?"

She felt compelled to point out, "We can't see the future—we can't know if any enticing picture you and I conjure today will weather even the next few months, let alone through the years."

"True." He didn't even attempt to argue, to tell her she was wrong. "But one thing I learned during my time in Ireland, dealing with so many others with their own agendas, is that you can never truly know another's heart and soul. Ultimately, in every relationship, there comes a point where each party has to offer trust—to trust in the other."

His gaze didn't waver as he went on, "The reality is that we can each make declarations and promises, but neither of us can know with absolute certainty that the other will remain true to our initial shared vision, our initial shared goal. Short of there being some sort of test or demonstration, each of us can only trust that the other will prove steadfast."

He paused, then, his voice low yet certain, concluded, "If we want to go forward, all we can do is place our faith in each other and take that chance."

Held captive by the power in his gaze, she drew in a slow breath, then slowly exhaled. "In marriage and in loving, there are no guarantees."

"No. There are only promises and hope. But if we don't take the chance—if we don't pursue love but instead decide to protect our hearts and turn aside—we'll leave all potential benefits behind, unrealized."

She dipped her head in agreement.

After a second of searching her face, he went on, "For us, today, here and now, what we do next hinges on one question—with respect to our putative marriage, are the potential benefits enough to tempt you to take a chance, accept the unavoidable inherent risk, and trust me when I swear that, if you place your hand in mine and make our faux engagement real and subsequently marry me, I will continue to feel as I do about you, and because of that, I will put your welfare and your wishes ahead of my own for the rest of our lives?"

She felt as if she should deliberate long and hard. Instead, she let the single word her mind supplied fall from her lips. "Yes."

He blinked, then searched her eyes. "Just that? Yes?"

She let her smile grow, then laughed at the faintly stunned look on his face. She reached out and gripped his hand and shook it. "Yes, I trust you. I always have, even in those long-ago days in Little Moseley. And since then, you've only grown more obviously honorable and trustworthy." She knew to her bones that was so; his true colors were so obvious, so evident, that he'd become the Home Office's ace negotiator because people on both sides trusted him and had faith in his honor, in how he would behave. "I know," she said with absolute conviction, "that any promise you make, you will move heaven and earth to keep."

Despite her "yes" being precisely what Julian had wanted to hear, she'd just proved his point that one could never entirely be sure of another's heart. He hadn't even fully understood the depths of his own feelings, and he certainly hadn't foreseen her conviction and clarity regarding her own.

She just agreed to marry me.

He'd never craved anything more intensely.

Lost in her eyes, he reminded himself to breathe, then felt compelled to confirm, "So from here, from now, we go forward." He turned his hand, captured hers, and raised her fingers to his lips and kissed them. "And make our supposedly perfect match into the union we want it to be."

She tightened her fingers on his. "Yes, just that. We make our marriage into what *we* want it to be, a union that encompasses all that's important to us." She held his gaze. "Including love."

That sounded like a challenge, one he was perfectly willing to accept. "If love is ours," he stated, "we'll embrace and claim it."

They stared at each other as those words sank in, then using his hold on her hand, he drew her to him and bent his head, and as she lifted her lips, he covered them with his.

The exchange started off poignant and sweet. She kissed him back, and moving slowly, he closed his arms about her, drawing her deeper into his embrace, before angling his head and extending the caress, sinking progressively deeper into the kiss.

Her lips parted on a sigh, and he took immediate advantage. The engagement spun out and on, into realms of evocative and increasingly provocative sensation, until passion rose, steady and sure, thrumming beneath their escalating hunger and infusing the desire that had ignited and started to simmer, gradually building to a slow, steady, compulsive thud in their veins.

Sensation swirled and beckoned, luring them on.

The tightening grip of her palm at his nape and the scoring of her nails as her fingers raked through his hair were just novel enough to register—and remind him of where they were.

Mentally, he came to a dead halt, then after a fraught moment of lecturing himself regarding their reality and his wider purpose, inexorably, he drew on their reins.

She realized and, reluctantly, came about, and inch by inch, step by step, together, they retreated from the all-consuming kiss.

When he finally managed to raise his head, they were both breathless and hungry for more. Their gazes met and held; for a long moment, they stared into each other's eyes, reading the truth blazoned there, then slowly, rather smugly, they smiled and eased apart.

Hands clasped, fingers twined, they remained staring at each other, each, he knew, feeling the beat of passion still thudding in their veins.

Eventually, he cleared his throat and said, "We'll make our families very happy when we announce—or should I say confirm—our direction."

Her smile deepened. "I'm just glad I won't have to explain crying off to Grandmama."

He shuddered, then rocked back onto his feet, rose, and held out his hand to help her up. "Is it wrong to keep track of the horrors continuing on our path will allow us to avoid? Purely in terms of congratulating ourselves on our wisdom?"

Regaining her feet, she laughed. "I'm reasonably certain that acknowledging avoided horrors counts as permitted encouragement."

Lighthearted and happy, he grinned at her, then together, they repacked the basket. She folded the blanket and tucked it over the top, then he picked up the basket and offered her his arm. She took it, and they started back toward the pier.

With smiles on their faces that would have instantly revealed their news to anyone who knew them, they strolled along. Unable to quell the impulse, he scanned the lawns and the trees bordering the paths.

She noticed. "Are you looking for our mystery man?" She started searching as well.

"I wondered if he might seize this opportunity to approach me. I'm fairly certain he's Irish and wants to speak with me alone, with no one else close enough to overhear and, if possible, no one to witness our meeting, either, except perhaps you."

They kept walking. When the pier came into sight, she sighed. "It appears he hasn't followed us here."

"Indeed." To be truthful, he was just as glad the man, whoever he was, hadn't appeared to distract them from what had proved to be an afternoon of momentous importance.

They reached the pier, and he waved in a water taxi. When it arrived, the wooden side grating against the stone steps, he handed Melissa into the gently rocking boat and followed. As he settled on the cushioned seat beside her, this time facing the bow, and the boatmen pushed off, he took in the hazy outline of the roofs of London and felt elation rise.

He'd achieved his immediate objective, and his campaign in pursuit of his perfect wife, namely the lady leaning her shoulder against his, with her hand tucked snugly in his, was proceeding exactly as he'd hoped.

CHAPTER 6

*F*our evenings later, Melissa sat beside Julian at the middle of one long side of the immense dining table in the formal dining room of Carsely House and fought to keep her entirely false smile firmly fixed on her face.

They were a little over halfway through Julian's mother's "family dinner" to formally introduce Melissa to his family and Julian to hers. During the earlier hour in the drawing room, on Julian's arm, she'd formally met all those of his family who were present and had introduced him to those members of her family he hadn't previously met.

The dining room was large, with twin chandeliers bathing the long board in bright white light that glinted off the crystal and silverware and set sparks flashing in the jewels gracing many of the ladies' throats. Melissa herself was wearing a necklace of aquamarines set in rosettes of diamonds, with single rosettes dangling from each ear. The hue of the aquamarines matched the vivid shade of her silk gown, one of her favorite colors for evening wear as it made the most of her pale skin, dark-blue eyes, and dark-brown hair.

About her, various members of Julian's family, most of them Delameres, were intermixed with Norths and Osbaldestones. Julian's brother Felix sat on her left, while his younger brother, Damian, sat a few seats down on the opposite side of the table.

She'd been pleased to discover that Gordon had been seated farther up the board, on the same side as her and Julian and effectively out of their sight. She wasn't sure whether she was still annoyed with Gordon or, perversely, whether, given the outcome of his interference in her life, she should thank him. However, when she and Julian had come upon Gordon in the drawing room, she'd detected a certain constraint between the pair, and Julian had cut short the exchange, and she'd smiled and moved on with him.

Clearly, Gordon had not yet been forgiven by the head of his house.

"My dear Melissa." One of Julian's connections, a matron in her forties, who was seated a little way along the board, leaned forward to say, "You must be looking forward to seeing Carsington Castle." She widened her eyes and looked from Melissa to Julian. "I daresay you plan to spend the summer there?"

Melissa quashed an urge to roll her eyes. They'd been fending off such leading questions all evening. Maintaining a serene expression, she looked at Julian. His connection; he could deal with this.

After briefly meeting her eyes, he looked up the table. "As to that, I really can't say. We haven't yet decided."

Increasingly through the evening, that was the reply to which they'd steadfastly clung.

Yet still the questions kept coming. She turned to deal with one from her aunt Catherine regarding which modistes she was considering consulting. The words "for your wedding gown" weren't uttered but were clearly implied.

She pretended to be oblivious.

Sadly, as all her family knew her far too well to believe she didn't understand the inquiries they were attempting to make, that tactic failed dismally in halting the sometimes subtle but often not so subtle inquisition.

She'd expected some degree of curiosity, but the barrage of questions was more than she'd anticipated. She told herself that, given the majority of those present were not aware of their back-to-front wooing, she shouldn't be so surprised.

On the journey home from Greenwich, she and Julian had discussed how best to move forward. They'd decided to keep their decision to proceed with the engagement and wedding to themselves for the moment in the hope of gaining time to explore the possibilities and further define exactly what they wanted—for instance, with the marriage settlements and details of the wedding—without having to endure a higher level of helpful interference than that to which they were already subject.

Inciting heightened interest was the last thing they wished to do.

And indeed, the past three days spent crafting a satisfying joint life and examining and discussing the aspects they might include within that framework had been fascinating and illuminating. They'd skipped as many daytime events as they possibly could and, instead, had spent time talking with each other, exchanging ideas and putting flesh on the bones of their emerging vision of their future life.

As part of that, they'd attended a meeting of one of the charities favored by ton ladies, one devoted to the care and education of orphans in London. Both she and Julian had been warmly welcomed, and he'd found several other gentlemen present and, like her, had ended the excursion wanting to further their ideas in that sphere. After subsequent discussion, they'd agreed to first examine what the situation was like around Carsington Castle and Derbyshire in general before making a firm decision as to exactly which project to support and where to direct their energies.

She'd been especially pleased over how he and she had come together over that.

Their evenings hadn't been as rewarding. Throughout the impossible-to-avoid events, the ton's scrutiny hadn't wavered and, if anything, had grown more intense—that sense of people watching and waiting for something to happen. That expectation had grown to be a palpable thing, an almost-smothering weight.

Increasingly, it was putting both their backs up; neither were the sort to appreciate being pushed, and that was what it felt like—being pushed to satisfy society's expectations.

And now, this.

After Julian had deflected yet another thinly veiled inquiry attempting to define when their engagement ball would be, she smiled, determinedly serene, and murmured so only he would hear, "How much longer do you think we can keep this up without one or other of us snapping and saying something we really shouldn't?"

His expression relaxed and easygoing, but with temper clouding his gray eyes, he replied, "This has been far worse than I expected. I can see it was naive of us to imagine we might be allowed a week or two to ponder our future before declaring ourselves." He lightly arched one dark brow. "They're not going to let us have that, are they?"

Smile widening as if at some shared joke, she shook her head. "Definitely not." After a momentary pause, she added, "I suspect their patience is nearly exhausted. Any day now, someone is going to confront us and demand to be told when our engagement ball will be held and what date we've settled on for our wedding."

Inwardly, Julian grimaced. It seemed their hopes of being left in peace to define their own way forward were doomed. Although naming dates for their engagement ball and subsequent wedding might seem minor issues, the instant they capitulated and did so, they would be swept along on an irresistible tide that wouldn't release them until after they were wed. Melissa had explained that, and his recollections of his sisters' engagements and weddings bore out her prediction. Once they committed to their engagement ball, they would be helpless to influence much at all, not until after they were wed.

Neither he nor she liked feeling helpless, liked surrendering the reins to anyone, let alone giving in to the demands of the nameless, faceless ton. But...

His mother tapped her water glass, then rose, beaming, to declare that it was time for her to lead the ladies back to the drawing room, leaving the gentlemen to pass the port and brandy.

He rose and drew out Melissa's chair for her, using the moment to murmur, "Each to our own ordeal."

She threw him a speaking glance, but wore a delighted smile as she moved past him and, after joining the other ladies, indeed, being engulfed by them, followed his mother from the room.

Tightening his hold on his temper, he resumed his seat as the other men moved to take the chairs around him, forming a large knot at the center of the table.

As he'd expected, as the decanters did the rounds, the questions came thick and fast. Some were straightforward, such as a query from one of his maternal cousins as to how much involvement he still had with the Home Office, and Melissa's father's question as to whether he missed the work, both of which he handled with ease; indeed, he extended his answers to take up as much time as possible, hoping to stifle the more intrusive queries, such as the brazen question from one of his maternal uncles as to whether he could confirm the date for their engagement ball.

His smile a trifle tight, he replied, "No."

His uncle merely nodded. "Thought as much, but I had to ask, you know?"

Everyone chuckled, understanding that to mean he'd been ordered by his wife to do so.

That broke the tension, and the same uncle further helped by asking where he'd got his matched bays. "Noticed them in the park the other day. Lovely steppers."

That led the conversation into less-fraught waters, and Julian started to relax.

After their digestive tipples of choice had been consumed, at his suggestion—his mother being quite capable of sending a footman to summon them if they dallied too long—the company rose and started back to the drawing room.

He found himself strolling with Felix on one side and Captain Findlay-Wright on the other. The captain was often included in family gatherings as Helen's escort; the family had accepted that, in assisting her to bring the body of her husband, Colonel Maurice Delamere, home from India, Findlay-Wright had done the family a significant service, and as he continued to lodge with Helen, squire her about, and rein in her frequently wild notions, they'd fallen into the habit of inviting him to attend with her.

"Well," Findlay-Wright said, "all this talk of engagement balls and weddings aside, given your interest in your acres, I imagine you'll be back at the castle as soon as you can manage it." The look he cast Julian was commiserating. "I can't imagine you're enjoying this. You must be keen to seek refuge in Derbyshire."

Julian smiled easily. "I won't say you're wrong, but as I came to London intending to find a suitable bride, I can hardly complain about the outcome."

Findlay-Wright faintly frowned. "I hadn't realized you'd reached the point of looking about you for a wife."

Julian lightly shrugged. "I decided to be proactive rather than having some lady foisted on me."

"Ah." Findlay-Wright nodded. "That, I can understand."

They'd reached the drawing room; the door had been left wide, and the three of them continued into the spacious chamber.

Instantly, Julian looked for and located Melissa. She was seated on a sofa, flanked by two of his great-aunts and Helen, and her expression as she stared at him looked distinctly brittle.

Vaguely aware that the captain and Felix had ambled on to join some others, Julian went directly to Melissa.

As he approached, he saw that while she fought to keep that definitely fragile smile in place, her eyes were bright with temper. Then he realized that his great-aunt Hortense was droning on about weddings she'd attended.

Hortense broke off as he fetched up before the sofa. She raised her quizzing glass and peered at him. "Ah, Carsely. There you are."

She drew breath to say more, but reaching for Melissa's hand, he cut in with, "I'm afraid I've come to"—*rescue*—"steal Melissa away. There's an issue on which I require her opinion."

"Oh?" His great-aunts and Helen looked intrigued.

Melissa gripped his hand and popped to her feet. "Of course, my lord. I'm happy to help." She waved toward the doorway. "Shall we?"

The pointed look she cast him stated they needed to leave the room before she did something regrettable.

He tucked her hand in the crook of his elbow, inclined his head to the three older ladies, and with Melissa, walked smoothly but quickly from the room.

"I take it," he murmured as they stepped into the front hall, "that your ordeal was worse than mine."

"Horrendous," she confirmed through clenched teeth. "I need to be away from them all for a while."

He glanced at her now-set face. "Do we need to talk privately?"

She hesitated, then nodded. "That might be a good idea."

The tension in her voice was alarming. He led her down a minor corridor and around to the garden parlor, a small but pleasant room that overlooked the side garden.

He opened the parlor door and looked in. As he'd expected, there was no one else there, but as the room was a reception room and on the ground floor, a lamp had been left burning, turned low, on the end table beside the sofa facing the windows.

Melissa looked past him, sighed feelingly, drew her hand from his sleeve, and walked in. She made for the sofa and slumped down upon it in a susurration of silks. "The past half hour has been my worst experience in the ton bar none."

He winced, closed the door, and went to turn up the lamp. "That bad?"

"I literally know of no words sufficient to do it justice."

He debated sitting beside her, but then he wouldn't be able to see her face. He stepped around the sofa, pulled up an armchair, and sat more or less facing her. He reached out and took one of her hands. "Words aside, what happened?"

Puzzled, Melissa looked at him, then waved toward the drawing room. "Didn't you see?"

"Just then?" He shook his head. "I looked at you, not anyone else—well, except my great-aunts and Helen, and even then, I wasn't paying attention to them."

She stared at him, then humphed. "Well, that's nice in its way, but if you had looked, you would have seen that every single eye in that room—literally every female eye—was trained on me. From the moment we regained the drawing room, no matter what they were doing—chatting to each other or simply standing and waiting—every single one of them angled themselves so they could keep an eye on me! It was"—she waved her free hand wildly—"unnerving!"

He grimaced.

Lowering her hand, she paused, recalling the moments. "It was as if they were *willing* me to break—to give up and tell them what they want to know. Even my mother and my aunts were doing it."

To her relief, he didn't suggest she was overreacting. Instead, he regarded her steadily. "They're waiting for a declaration, and they're not going to back down."

She huffed. "I strongly suspect this evening is a sign of things to come."

His gaze on her face, he blew out a steady breath, then asked, "Have you in any way changed your mind about our deliberations of Wednesday?"

She shook her head; of that, she was sure. "It feels...right."

He nodded. "Yes, it does. Simply put, everything about us seems to fit."

"Exactly."

"In light of that"—his eyes sought and held hers—"and given that, no matter how much we would prefer to move more slowly, at our own pace, not even the pair of us together can withstand the social might of the ton, we're going to have to step up to the challenge of taking our next step now and making our declaration—our ultimate commitment—or they'll badger us until we do."

She studied his face. "Your negotiator side is showing. It's not stepping up to a challenge but bending to their will. However"—she held up her hand in a staying gesture—"now that I can think more clearly, I can see the necessity. Gritting our teeth and clinging to our preferred timetable isn't going to work."

His lips twisted wryly. "And ultimately, the end result will be the same."

She hesitated, then said, "Once we take the next step and speak of dates for our engagement ball and our wedding, there'll be no going back."

He looked at her, then rose, drawing on her hand to bring her to her feet. From a distance of mere inches, his eyes held hers. "I don't want to go back."

This close, she could feel the attraction thrumming between them. She licked suddenly dry lips and, trapped in his gray gaze, murmured, "Nor do I."

The ends of his lips lifted. "Well, then."

He bent his head, and instantly, she lifted her lips to his.

To her delight, this kiss was different again—firmer, more passionate, immediately more fiery—as if their decision had freed something inside him and inside her as well.

The hunger that had, it seemed, grown since Wednesday reared up and demanded, and they supped and sipped and sought to appease it, only to have it grow greater still.

His arm tightened about her, and she willingly pressed closer. Nearer. The heat of him, reaching through the silk of her gown, was intoxicating. He was all lean muscle, supple and so warm; her senses rioted, reaching, wanting.

Yearning for more.

Julian sensed her need clearly; it was there in the blatant offering of her lips, in the evocative teasing of her tongue stroking his. In the pressure of her breasts against his chest, in the tensing of her fingers on his shoulders.

He had to fight to keep hold of the reins—his as well as hers. She was new to this, but so avidly eager, she steadily eroded his control.

Given where they were—no matter the whispering devils in his brain —they couldn't further indulge.

Increasingly desperate, he thought of those waiting in the drawing room—including Lady Osbaldestone.

A mental picture of that grande dame provided the necessary impetus for him to ease back, reluctant step by step, from the whirlpool of sensation that was Melissa's kiss.

Finally, he brought the caress to an end and raised his head. He looked down into her starry midnight eyes and, his voice gravelly and low, murmured, "Let's take that kiss as sealing our troth."

Her lips lazily lifted in a cat-considering-a-bowl-of-cream smile. Before she could tempt him to resume, he took half a step back and angled his head toward the door. "Now, we need to tell the others."

She considered that, then inclined her head in acquiescence. "They'll be in alt."

"Indeed." He took her hand and towed her to the door, opened it, and with a flourish, bowed her through. "Lead on, my lady." *My countess.*

Almost as if she heard the words he didn't say, she studied him for an instant, then wound her arm in his, and together, they walked back to the drawing room.

Naturally, the instant they appeared in the doorway, every conversation ceased, and every pair of eyes locked on them. As far as he could tell, everyone was in much the same place they had been when he and Melissa had left; judging by the almost apprehensive expressions on many faces, he could imagine the consternation they'd left behind.

Melissa had halted just over the threshold and drawn her arm from his. Placing a reassuring hand at the back of her waist, he adopted an affable smile and announced, "Melissa and I believe that it's time we set our wedding date."

The ensuing eruption of delight was unfeigned; the ladies were understandably thrilled, while the gentlemen, for all that they were more restrained, were also notably pleased and, possibly, relieved.

Their mothers, in particular, could barely contain their joy-cum-relief.

He and Melissa exchanged glances, then together, moved farther into the room, only to be engulfed by a cacophony of exclamations, giddy observations, and expressions of delight.

It was left to Lady Osbaldestone, smiling approvingly though she was, to call the company to order. She rapped her cane on the floor several times, much like a judge's gavel, and into the ensuing silence, said, "Well, then, you two, when's the date to be? And once we have that settled, your engagement ball needs to be fixed as well." She pinned them with a black and rather beady gaze. "I assume you're not about to tell us that you've decided to elope?"

Julian cut a glance at Melissa, and she caught his eye.

Why hadn't they thought of that?

Of course, by then, it was far too late. Plastering on bright smiles, with perfect sincerity, they assured everyone that the thought hadn't crossed their minds.

Focused by Lady Osbaldestone's decree, the mothers, aunts, and assorted female relatives took over. Melissa was instructed to sit in an armchair that placed her as the focal point for all the other ladies.

As she settled, the look she sent Julian had him sinking onto the arm of the chair; they would weather the storm together.

The suggestions flew, and even the gentlemen gathered around. Ultimately, after weighing reasons that stretched from the likely weather to the royal calendar, it was decreed that May 26 would be the most propitious for their wedding, which, by general agreement, would be celebrated in the chapel at Carsington Castle.

When, having declared that to be the best of all selections, the company looked to Julian and Melissa for approval, they shared a glance, then Melissa regally inclined her head. "That will suit."

Reassured, the ladies immediately turned their minds to the date of their engagement ball. That necessitated much consulting of memorized diaries of upcoming events, but finally, the date of April 7 was nominated and put forward for approval.

Again, Julian glanced at Melissa. Resigned, she arched a brow at him.

He looked back at the waiting throng. "That seems perfect."

Only he was close enough to hear Melissa's half-suppressed snort of derisive laughter.

With the dates agreed, Melissa found herself drawn into the preparations for their engagement ball, which, after all, was only two weeks away.

"That said," her mother declared, "given the entire ton have been waiting to learn the date, as long as we get the invitations out by Monday, I expect everyone we invite will be able to attend."

Her grandmother snorted. "You won't be able to keep them away."

As Melissa had suspected, the entire ton had been hanging out for the news.

While the arguments about this and that raged, Julian remained beside her; she found comfort in his amusement over how deeply invested so many others were in their nuptials. Given he and she were not expected to contribute ideas but only to give their opinions when solicited, they fell into their habit of trading sotto voce observations and comments that, more than once, had her battling highly inappropriate laughter.

At one point, he observed, "Have you noticed? Your wily grandmama is using this exercise as a means of merging the families. More than anyone else, she's in charge."

Melissa smiled fondly. "She always is."

Ultimately, with the tea brought in and duly drunk, and tea toasts raised to the mothers of the bride and the groom and, more generally, to the outcome of the evening, the company deemed it a night well lived and rose and said their farewells.

Melissa walked out to the front hall with her grandmother and a thoroughly excited Lottie. As this had been a strictly family dinner, Lottie had been allowed to attend.

"It was so exciting!" She all but bounced on her toes. "I'm so glad you chose this evening to finalize your dates."

"Indeed." As always, her grandmother's black eyes seemed to see into Melissa's brain. "I'm glad you've both agreed to move more decisively forward."

She smiled and let the comment lie. "I just wish Mandy could have been here and been a part of it all." Reference to her impending first great-grandchild could usually be counted on to distract even her grandmother.

"A pity, yes, given you and she are so close," her grandmother replied, "but I'm relieved that Rufus has put his foot down. Your sister is too close to her time to endure the jolting journey to town."

Smiling at the success of her deflection, Melissa merely inclined her head.

Only to have her grandmother lightly rap her arm with her furled lorgnette. "I predict this marriage will be the making of you both." Uncompromisingly meeting her gaze, her grandmother informed her, "From the moment you two first met, this was meant to be."

Grinning, Lottie nodded. "It truly was. We all knew it."

Refraining from shaking her head, Melissa hugged them both, then watched them walk out of the front door, solicitously attended by two Carsely footmen.

Several gentlemen had been waiting to approach her and make their farewells, including Gordon, who bowed over her hand and insouciantly remarked, "Well, that didn't turn out too badly after all."

Melissa narrowed her eyes at him, then Julian appeared at her elbow, and Gordon promptly bid his cousin a reserved farewell and sloped off.

Julian humphed. "He might have unwittingly assisted, but he's still a cad."

Then his uncle tapped him on the shoulder, and he turned away, leaving Melissa facing Captain Findlay-Wright. She smiled and gave him her hand. "Thank you for coming, Captain, and for escorting Mrs. Delamere. I'm sure she's glad of your support."

"I do my poor best, my dear." The captain bowed over her hand, then, straightening, with a twinkle in his eyes, remarked, "I have to say that I was quite surprised that any young lady could so rapidly catch and fix Carsely's attention."

She recognized that the captain was fishing for information and was relieved by the evidence that Gordon had kept his mouth shut regarding the role he'd played in bringing her and Julian together. Still smiling, she simply replied, "Indeed," and shifted her gaze to Helen Delamere, who, trailing after the captain, had come to take her leave.

Julian had always wondered why farewells took so much longer than introductions. It seemed a good hour before there was only Melissa and her parents left in the front hall. Her mother and his still had their heads together; as a group, they walked out onto the front porch.

Only then did Lady North say, "We'll talk tomorrow," to which his mother replied, "Call whenever you're free."

Lord North met Julian's eyes, resignation in his, then after a final round of farewells, led his wife down the steps to their waiting carriage.

Julian followed with Melissa on his arm. "I believe," he murmured, "that all in all, we weathered that well." He caught her gaze. "Nothing we can't live with was decreed."

She smiled. "You're right. In the end, it worked out. And at least all the avid watching should now cease."

"We can but hope." They paused before the carriage, and he raised her hand to his lips and kissed her fingers. His gaze holding hers, he murmured, "Sleep well, my dear countess-to-be. I'll call around later tomorrow morning."

Her smile deepened, and she inclined her head. He handed her into the carriage and stood back while the North footman closed the door, then swung up to his perch. The coachman flicked the reins, and the horses started plodding.

Julian remained on the pavement, watching the carriage roll southward along North Audley Street.

He was about to turn inside when movement across the street caught his eye. He halted, and their mystery man stepped out of a pool of shadow.

The man glanced swiftly around.

Julian's mother and the footmen had retreated inside, and there was no one else on the street.

Julian took a slow step toward the man to show he was willing to meet.

The man saw, nodded, and started across the road.

The door behind Julian opened, and light flooded down the steps. "Julian?"

Julian mentally swore. He turned and brusquely waved Felix back. Although his brother halted, he didn't go inside but stood watching.

Julian glanced back at the man, hoping to reassure him.

Only to discover an empty street.

He sighed. He hung his head for a moment, then turned and walked back to his house. He went up the steps, waving Felix inside, then followed his brother through the door.

Crosby shut the door and threw the bolts.

In the hall, Felix turned and frowned at Julian. "What were you doing out there?"

Realizing he hadn't mentioned the Irishman to Felix, Julian waved toward the study. "Come, and I'll explain. After all that, I could do with a nightcap."

Felix followed him into the study. They found Damian already there, sprawled in an armchair and savoring Julian's brandy.

Damian grinned. "I thought you'd end up here. What a night! I wouldn't be in your shoes for anything."

Julian humphed and poured two glasses of brandy. He handed one to Felix.

Accepting the glass, Felix said, "All things considered, I thought you and Melissa managed rather well."

"Although disappearing like that in the middle of things rather threw the cat among the pigeons," Damian said. "Just as well you returned with the news they were all hanging out to hear. That pleased everyone."

Felix sank into one of the armchairs. "But what were you doing outside just now?"

"Heh?" Damian looked between his older brothers. "What did I miss?"

Julian sank into his favorite armchair, took a sip of brandy and savored it, then swallowed and told them about the mystery man he'd now seen three times. "I'm increasingly certain he's Irish and has been sent here with some message for me that he's been ordered to deliver in secret, including letting no one see him speak with me. That's why he keeps vanishing whenever anyone else—well, anyone other than Melissa —appears."

Felix frowned. "But you're no longer at the Irish desk—not even at the Home Office anymore. Surely they—whoever they are—realize you're in the Lords now?"

Julian nodded. "I'm sure any political group over there would know that, which is why I think there has to be some particular and sensitive reason this man has been sent expressly to speak secretly with me." He drained his glass, then lowered it and observed, "While the Home Office know I've left, the Irish might yet be inclined to see me as someone they can use to pass on information. Whether I'm in the Lords or not, they know I have access to the right ears."

Damian huffed. "Well, if we see this blighter lurking about, we'll make a point of hauling him in."

"Please don't." Julian shook his head at his little brother. "While I admit I'm now curious to speak with the fellow, the last thing I need is for you to act overexuberantly and land me in the middle of some political crisis."

Damian looked unconvinced. "Really?"

Julian leveled a stern look at him. "Yes. Really."

Four mornings later, Melissa did something she hadn't had a chance to do for years.

She drew up from their first gallop down the tan of Rotten Row and flashed Julian a beaming smile. "I'd forgotten how much I enjoy being on a horse. These days, I only get to ride when we visit Winslow Abbey." She met his eyes. "Thank you for suggesting this."

Beside her, mounted on a black gelding, Julian returned her smile with a lazily satisfied smile of his own. "I'm glad I thought of it. We'll have to look into getting you a mount of your own here in London."

He'd explained that he and his brothers rode on most days, even when in the capital, but as there was no suitable horse for her in his London stable, he'd arranged to hire a neat bay mare for the occasion.

By unvoiced consent, they headed back to the beginning of the riding track so they could indulge in another gallop. As they guided their horses along the grassy verge bordered by a remnant of woodland, she asked, "What sort of riding is there around the castle?"

"The bridle paths are extensive, and of course, there's the local hunt as well."

She listened attentively as he described the general layout of the bridle paths relative to the castle; an image of the place was forming in her mind, and she added in those details. She was conscious of rising excitement over their impending marriage, although her interest was focused more on what would follow than on the occasion itself.

As they trotted slowly into the more inhabited areas of the park, he observed, "At least people aren't staring as much as they were, although whether that's due to the hour and the particular people about or the announcement of our engagement ball and wedding, who's to say?"

"I suspect the latter has more to do with it. Our news was all over the ton by the very next morning!"

"Given their reaction at church, the ladies must have had the story delivered with their morning cocoa."

She chuckled. "Very likely. But as you say, at least people are no longer hovering in anticipation with their attentions glued to us."

"True. The details of the ball and the fear of not receiving an invitation have eclipsed us as the most pertinent point of interest."

"Thank heaven for that."

"Mind you," Julian continued as they turned their horses and joined the short queue of riders waiting to gallop down the tan, "I foresee the quest to secure an invitation growing fraught in coming days. Lord Hillcrest bailed me up at White's on Monday. I haven't spoken to him since our days at Oxford. Then Lady Ferrars pounced on me in Piccadilly, apparently to remind me that her younger son had been at Eton with me."

Melissa laughed. "I'm getting many of the same approaches. Wherever possible, I refer them to Mama."

He arched his brows. "There's a thought."

They'd reached the head of the queue, and the open track beckoned. He glanced at Melissa and found her grinning, waiting to catch his eye.

He grinned back and tipped his head. "After you."

With a laugh, she tapped her heel to the horse's side and shot off.

He held his horse back for a second, then loosened the reins and set the powerful gelding thundering in her wake. Although the groomed, well-pounded tan was tame compared to a woodland bridle path, the exercise gave him an opportunity to assure himself of Melissa's abilities.

When she'd told him she hadn't ridden in years, he'd been concerned that she might not possess the skills and confidence to ride about the estate. That anxiety had been laid to rest; she had an excellent seat and steady hands, and even though the hired horse was new to her, she managed the animal without a second thought, and the horse responded without hesitation.

Relieved, reassured, he raced close behind as she flew down the track.

They reached the end and wheeled, exhilaration singing in their veins and lighting their eyes and expressions. They slowed the horses to a walk as they started back along the swath of clipped grass between the track and the woods.

The next group of riders—a trio this time—pounded down the track.

A shot rang out, the sound almost buried beneath the thunder of hooves.

Several yards ahead, a divot appeared as a ball plowed into the ground between his and Melissa's horses.

Both animals shied.

Shocked, Julian instinctively tightened the reins and looked back.

Because of a slight bend in the track, a stand of trees lay directly behind them. The shot had come from there.

Melissa's horse was dancing, but she remained in control.

Grim-faced, he met her eyes, wide and startled in a suddenly pale face, and nodded forward. "Go!"

Her lips clamped tight, and she swung her horse toward the top of the track, then gave the mare her head.

He followed close behind.

Several people threw them curious looks as they rode full tilt into the more populated areas of the park, and they slowed their headlong dash to a less eye-catching trot, then to an unremarkable walk.

Julian looked at Melissa.

She met his eyes, disbelief and sheer flabbergastedness writ large in her expression.

He grimaced and nodded in sympathy. "I..." He shook his head. "Did that just happen?"

"I think so." She drew in a breath, then admitted, "I don't know what to say."

"Nor do I." He glanced around, then nodded ahead. "Let's ride back to Mount Street."

They crossed the track, skirted the end of the main body of the Serpentine, and started trotting up the path to the Grosvenor Gate.

The sound of hoofbeats coming up behind them had them glancing around.

Julian relaxed and slowed to a walk as Felix came riding up. He'd known his brother had intended to go riding sometime that morning.

Felix greeted Melissa, then with a faint frown in his eyes, looked at Julian. "What's going on? I saw the pair of you racing back beside the track as I was going down."

Julian met Melissa's gaze, then looked at Felix. "Not here. We were heading to Mount Street, but on reflection, it might be better to go to Carsely House." To Melissa, he added, "Mama won't be down yet, and for what we want to talk about, assured privacy might be preferable."

"Indeed." She nodded decisively and shook her reins, setting the mare trotting again.

Trying to conceal how grim he felt, Julian signaled to Felix to ride on Melissa's other side and urged his horse alongside hers as the three of them made for the Grosvenor Gate.

Fifteen minutes later, Julian ushered Melissa into the study at Carsely House and steered her to the group of armchairs angled before the hearth.

Despite the sun, the breeze had been chilly, and Melissa paused to warm her hands at the fire before sinking into one of the wing chairs.

Julian claimed the chair across the hearth, his usual seat, while Felix, after following them in and closing the door, took the armchair to Julian's right.

Julian exchanged a glance with Melissa, then looked at Felix. "The reason we were racing is because someone shot at us."

"What?" Felix's eyes flew wide. "Did you see who it was?"

Julian shook his head. "They shot from somewhere behind us. We were on our way back, just past the bend. I think he was in the woods, on that wooded hillock that, at that point, was more or less directly behind us."

Felix nodded his understanding, but his gaze was flicking back and forth between Melissa and Julian. "I assume he missed?"

"The ball passed between us." Julian knew that had to be the case. He gazed at Melissa. "The ball plowed into the dirt some yards in front of the horses."

Felix's frown deepened. "So who was he shooting at? You?" He looked at Julian, then shifted his gaze to Melissa. "Or you?"

Julian shrugged. "I don't know that we can say."

Melissa made a disparaging sound. "I assure you I have no unexpected enemies lurking. No rejected suitors or anything of that ilk." She stared hard at Julian, then her eyes narrowed. "Tell me"—she switched her gaze to Felix—"in firing a pistol over any distance, don't you have to allow for the breeze?"

Felix nodded. "You do. And this morning in the park, it was coming from the southeast." He looked at Julian. "So who was riding on the right?"

Julian grimaced; that had been him. "Regardless, I don't think we can make any assumptions about which of us was the intended target. Don't forget, the news of our engagement ball has reignited talk about our marriage. While you may not be aware of a disgruntled former suitor, he might yet exist."

Anxiety had crept into Melissa's dark-blue eyes. Lips thin, she shook her head. "I can't imagine anyone wanting me dead." Her gaze remained leveled at him. "That said, who would want you dead?"

Some perverse part of him felt pleased that she was agitated on his behalf, while the rest of him felt compelled to ease her mind. "Like you, I can't think of anyone who might want to kill me."

Felix scoffed. "Yes, you can. You know what you were doing in Ireland. Plenty of possibilities there, and what about this Irishman who's been secretly trying to make contact?"

Melissa looked from Felix to Julian. "Have you seen him again?"

He explained about glimpsing the man in the street after their family dinner. "There was no one else about, and he was heading my way when Felix came out to see what I was doing." He grimaced. "When I looked back, the man was gone. Regardless, he's no threat to me. Almost certainly, he's been sent to deliver a message that some group in Ireland wants me to pass on, and I can't do that if I'm dead."

"Indeed!" Felix was growing animated. "And that's my point! If this blighter is trying so hard to deliver his message secretively, then presumably you receiving the message and passing it on is something others won't want to happen. And even if those others are in Ireland, obviously, they have agents here. Otherwise, the blighter wouldn't be so skittish."

Worry in his face, Felix met Julian's gaze. "And now, with our mystery Irishman having been in town for weeks, perhaps that other group, having just learned of his mission and not knowing whether he's succeeded or not, has decided that the easiest way to ensure you don't pass on his message is to eliminate you."

Under the pointed gazes of his transparently exercised brother and his fiancée, Julian clung to impassivity. He didn't want to admit that scenario was possible, but unfortunately, it was. When both waited, clearly not intending to let him off their hook, he calmly said, "As I have yet to learn what the Irishman's message is, I can't judge if it's critical enough to warrant someone trying to kill me to prevent it getting through."

He saw Melissa's eyes widen and her stare intensify and inwardly swore. He'd just confirmed that the work he'd done in Ireland had, indeed, been of the sort that could have got him killed.

Seeking to distract her—and Felix—he focused on her and stated, "Be that as it may, I don't think it's wise to blinker ourselves to the possibility that the shooter might have been aiming at you." Despite the evidence suggesting otherwise, he was genuinely concerned that might have been the case.

Her eyes narrowed to deep-sapphire shards. "The only thing that's recently changed in my life is that I've accepted your offer and the dates for our engagement ball and wedding have been fixed and promulgated throughout the ton. I really cannot see even the most avid husband hunter resorting to murder as a means of stopping me from stepping into your countess's shoes."

He almost winced at her acerbic tone and grudgingly admitted, "I agree the notion is far-fetched."

"It's ludicrous to imagine that anyone is intent on killing me." Her gaze remained locked on his face. "So who is after you?"

Felix nodded seriously. "Because someone is, and we need to learn who."

Julian inwardly sighed and resigned himself to a lengthy discussion.

As he could have predicted, listing and describing all of the many factions in Ireland, both Irish and English, left them no further forward and, if anything, even more confused.

CHAPTER 7

"*This*"—on Julian's arm, Melissa gestured, indicating the scene in the Carsely House ballroom—"is far more glittering, in every sense of the word, than I'd anticipated."

The massive chandeliers illuminated a throng that included the most beautiful and also the most powerful among the ton. The colors of the ladies' silks and satins created a scintillatingly brilliant palette, while the level of noise would have given Babel a run for its money.

"It's certainly a night to remain on our toes." Julian kept his genial, easygoing social smile in place as, leading Melissa through the crowd, he acknowledged the beaming nods of several ladies and gentlemen.

About them, their engagement ball was in full swing. They'd spent the opening hour of the event on the receiving line, smiling and welcoming what had, at the time, seemed a never-ending stream of the elite of the ton, socially and politically. Everyone who was anyone was there, and the joint hostesses—their mothers—were in alt. It was the height of the Season, and there were at least two other major balls being held that evening, but by now, everyone who had been invited to celebrate the engagement of Julian, Earl of Carsely, and Miss Melissa North was standing in the Carsely House ballroom.

After being released from the receiving line, they'd shared the first waltz—a magical interlude in which they'd been able to focus solely on each other—but that had ended far too quickly, and they'd had to don their social faces and cling to their social graces and respond to all who had come to wish them well and be seen doing so.

While the wishes tendered were, in the main, sincere and receiving them was a pleasant enough occupation, constant repetition of the same words and phrases, listening and responding to the same exclamations, and deflecting the same probing questions gradually eroded their patience.

The only reason they were presently unencumbered by guests was that they were strolling in a fixed direction as if on a mission; it was one they had invented, namely, to check on Melissa's grandmother. As that august lady continued to terrify a good portion of the ton, they'd reasoned that as they were currently in her good books, by taking refuge in her orbit, they would be able to catch their breaths.

Since the first guests had arrived, they'd been greeting, chatting, and accepting congratulations nonstop; the activity had started to grow wearying after the first thirty minutes. Two hours on, and Julian had admitted he was approaching his limit of being unfailingly polite. As Melissa had been in much the same case, she'd joined him in casting about for a means of gaining some respite; visiting her grandmother had been her idea.

As they approached the chaise on which the old lady sat in state, presiding over a circle of older matrons who were busy watching their descendants with varying intents, with a last wary glance at the rest of the room, Julian admitted, "I'm not overly surprised by who is here. After all, attending events such as this is part and parcel of being in the upper echelon. What does surprise me is the unremitting delight everyone is exuding."

They halted by Lady Osbaldestone's side, and she proved that, despite her age, her hearing was excellent. She fixed them with a gimlet gaze. "Naturally, everyone here is thrilled by your engagement. For the ton at large, it's a positive sign, a good omen for the future." She searched their faces for signs of understanding, then detecting none in their bemused expressions, humphed and explained, "Everyone has great hopes of you both. It's transparently obvious to everyone that, with any luck at all, this marriage will be the making of you both and the foundation of something remarkable." She waved. "No doubt your mothers will have been hearing that from every possible source."

Julian and Melissa shared sidelong glances, then Melissa asked if her grandmama was comfortable and required anything, and after being assured she wanted for nothing, rather than dally close and catch their breaths—and invite further disturbing insights—they moved on as fast as they dared.

They clung to the wall, and leaning close on Julian's arm, Melissa grumbled, "Now we've reassured the ton regarding our engagement and eventual wedding, apparently, they've shifted their expectations to what we're going to do next!"

His social smile once more in place, Julian nodded at several guests and, biting the bullet, steered Melissa in their direction; at least there was no one likely to gush at them in that group. In contrast to his easy expression, his tone was grim as he replied, "If I'm reading this correctly, the elite are now watching us with great interest in anticipation of seeing us evolve into some sort of ideal socio-political couple."

"Exactly!" She sounded disgusted. "I just wish they'd stop *expecting* things—it's as if they're writing rules for us to live by."

He couldn't deny that. Now that Lady Osbaldestone had opened his eyes, several comments he'd previously thought somewhat strange made greater, albeit unwelcome sense. "At least," he murmured, in the seconds before they came within hearing of the group, "being inside Carsely House means we don't have to constantly look over our shoulders in search of errant assassins. That does make a pleasant change."

"There is that." Melissa increased the brightness of her smile as they joined the group, most of whom were married couples of similar age to them.

While they chatted, endeavoring to allow none of their weariness with the social round to show, she reflected that being safely inside Carsely House and also the center of all attention was, indeed, a good thing and something of a relief. Ever since the incident in the park, at all times that they'd been out of their respective homes, she'd been on high alert, and so had Julian. He'd even insisted on accompanying her to her appointments with her modiste, causing considerable consternation as everyone else present was adamant that he could not see any of her new gowns and especially not her wedding gown.

He'd merely smiled at the fussing, unmoved and unmoving, and left Madame Henriette to reorganize her showroom and fitting rooms.

While Melissa understood that his intention was to ensure she came to no harm—even though it was obvious it had to be him who was the assassin's target—she reasoned that in keeping his guard high, he would also end up protecting himself.

Of course, she'd kept watch as well, just as religiously, but neither they nor Felix, who had taken to accompanying them on their rides, had seen hide nor hair of the Irishman or of any would-be assassin.

The constant tension and the escalating anxiety had added to the already trying situation and further eroded their holds on their tempers. Even more frustratingly, they couldn't directly confront the targets of their ire, meaning the assassin and the wider ton.

Although they both had tempers, presumably because of his service in Ireland, he was more adept at managing his than she was hers.

When, still smiling brightly, they moved on toward the next group of guests eager to speak with them, she murmured, "I had hoped to make this my last Season, and now that I'm so delighting the ton by marrying you, I can only hope that once we're wed, we'll be less..." She gestured.

"In the ton's eye?"

She nodded. "Exactly."

He smiled, bent his head, and whispered, "In that case, you'll be delighted to discover how far Carsington Castle is from anywhere the ton gathers."

Her smile more genuine, she met his eyes. "I'm already looking forward to escaping there."

Their gazes held for a second, then as one, they faced forward and engaged the next knot of guests.

Later in the evening, after waltzing with several of her ex-would-be suitors, all of whom had claimed to be devastated to have lost their chance with her—not that even one of them had had a chance with her in the first place—Melissa finally found herself once more in her intended's arms, whirling slowly around the ballroom.

She sighed. "This is pleasant." It was heavenly to be able to relax, place her trust in her partner, and let go and allow her senses to revel in the sensation of his arm banding her back, his hand splayed across her spine, the contact searing through the fine silk of her new celestial-blue gown. He moved with accomplished grace, and all she had to do was let her feet follow his lead.

From beneath her lashes, she studied the aristocratic planes of his face and smiled. "If we could only spend the rest of the evening here, slowly waltzing, I would be content."

He huffed softly. "You and me both." He drew her closer as they went around the turn, and the silk of her bodice brushed against the fabric of his coat, and a frisson of heat bloomed and sank deep.

Once they were on the straight again, he murmured, "I don't know if it's because I've been away from London for so long, but I can't recall there being quite so many predatory ladies haunting the ton." His lips quirked as he confessed, "I've been subtly propositioned three times."

She laughed. "I should have warned you. Those ladies do like to hunt, and they're very much of our circle, but for their purposes, a gentleman isn't fair game until at least officially engaged." She tipped her head consideringly. "And truth be told, they're usually careful to ensure that the wedding is definitely on." She returned her gaze to his face and arched an amused brow. "Apparently, we've been convincing, and no one any longer doubts that."

He grunted and gathered her closer, a possessive reaction she didn't miss but to which—oddly for her—she didn't feel compelled to take umbrage. "Luckily," he continued, "our wedding *is* going to take place in seven weeks at a place very far from here."

Her inner smile was much more smug than the one curving her lips.

As the music slowed, then ceased, she looked at him assessingly. He released her and bowed, and she curtsied. When he raised her, she gripped his hand and met his eyes. "It's grown rather stuffy in here. I believe the doors to the terrace are open. Shall we take a stroll out there?"

He glanced toward the terrace.

Through the uncurtained windows, they could see several couples ambling in the cooler air.

"I'm all for escaping this hothouse for a while." He returned his gaze to her face. "But I know of a place where we can savor the fresh air without having to interact with others." With a teasing light in his gray eyes, he quirked an eyebrow. "Of course, it's not a spot of which our mothers would approve. Are you game?"

She laughed. "You've piqued my interest, my lord." She waved toward the garden. "By all means, lead on."

It wasn't a simple matter for them to slip away without being noticed. By degrees, stopping and chatting along the way, they made for the far corner of the ballroom on the opposite side of the room from the terrace.

Intrigued, Melissa followed Julian's lead, including in engaging with the others they were using as cover for their escape. In due course, they fetched up with their backs to the room's corner and a group of guests in a circle before them, screening them from the rest of the room.

Then the musicians started playing the introduction for the next dance.

As everyone in their circle looked toward the dance floor, Julian caught Melissa's eye and turned the other way, reached out and touched the paneling, and a concealed service door popped open. He whisked her through, followed, and drew the door shut. It clicked almost silently into place.

As far as Melissa had seen, none of the group they'd been conversing with had noticed their departure. "That was slick," she murmured.

In the gloom, with the only light coming from a distant wall sconce, she saw Julian's teeth flash in a grin. "I've always wanted to do that."

He grasped her hand and moved past her. "Come on."

Of course, he knew where he was going. They stepped out of another door into a side corridor, and he swiftly drew her on. The sound of the ball faded as he turned down another hallway. "We're in the other wing that gives onto the rear lawn." He stopped by a door, opened it, and confidently led her through.

While he paused to shut the door, she looked around at what was clearly a summer parlor. On the opposite side of the room, double French doors gave access to a small balcony-cum-terrace.

Without needing more light than what seeped through the uncurtained windows, Julian moved past her, catching her hand and, avoiding the shadowy furniture, towing her across to the French doors.

They were locked and bolted, but the key was in the lock, and it was the work of a moment to set both doors wide, then he bowed and waved her forward. "Our own private terrace."

She walked out onto a narrow balcony draped in shadows and silvery moonlight.

A few feet above ground level, the balcony overlooked one shorter side of the rectangular rear lawn while the ballroom terrace lined the longer side to their left. The two areas were separated by a section of the building and garden beds, and trees and leafy bushes shielded the balcony from the larger terrace and the ballroom beyond and muted the music and chatter emanating through the open ballroom doors.

The balcony was more open in the other direction. Looking that way, Melissa saw deeply shadowed garden beds backed by large trees and, above those, a section of the night sky, black as ink with a bright crescent moon riding high and stars twinkling through the darkness.

With the cool night air caressing her arms and shoulders, she placed her hands on the top of the stone balustrade and tipped her face up to the moon and stars. After the crush of the ballroom, with its noise and pressure, the peace on the small balcony held a magical appeal.

Julian joined her, and instinctively, she turned to him.

The moonlight etched his smile as he drew her to him, then he bent his head, and she slid her hands over his shoulders and let her lids fall as his lips found hers.

The kiss held confidence and certainty. They savored, sipped, supped, then he licked the seam of her lips, and she parted them, and his tongue found hers and stroked and lured.

Their slide into passion was gradual, yet inexorable. The compulsive power built and swelled until it became an aching tide. At some point, he'd drawn her fully into his arms; now, they tightened, and he crushed her to him. She sent her splayed fingers to tangle in his hair; they clenched and gripped as a whirlpool of desire, of heat and yearning, rose and swept her—swept them—away.

Hunger surged, steady and sure and unrelenting. Like a drumbeat in their blood, it pounded and drove them on.

His hands shifted, sliding over her silk-clad curves, tracing, sculpting, then one rose to close about her breast, and her breath hitched, then she tightened her grip on his hair and, through the kiss, urged him on.

He kneaded, slowly, possessively, then his artful fingers went roaming. His fingertips circled her aching nipple, then closed and delicately nipped, then more firmly squeezed.

She gasped, then brazenly pressed closer, boldly demanding, and he responded with experienced understanding, the play of his fingers sending her senses leaping, then reeling, until she felt battered by their insistent, persistent *need*.

She ached to seize the moment, but...

On a gasp, she broke the kiss and, eyes closed, tipped back her head. "Oh Lord! We can't."

His chuckle was dark. "No, my darling. Sadly, we most definitely can't. We'd never live it down."

His hand continued to stroke and caress her breast, pandering to her senses at least that much.

She gave a throaty purr of appreciation. With the tip of her tongue, she traced her swollen lips. "Now I understand why Mandy wrote so firmly, warning me to ensure I had only the least-crushable silks for my gowns and to make sure the bodices were fitted and smooth." The words tumbled from her, a realization she didn't hesitate to share.

He chuckled again. "I always knew your sister would be a good influence on you."

She softly huffed and raised her head, and he swooped and reclaimed her lips. The kiss surged anew, heat and passion and desire erupting, threatening to consume them whole, but then reluctantly, he eased back, and she followed suit as, metaphorical inch by inch, they drew back from the precipice over which they would have preferred to fall.

Eventually, Julian raised his head. He looked down at Melissa's Madonna-like face, illuminated by starlight. Her lashes fluttered, then rose to reveal eyes the color of the midnight sky—a blue so dark it was almost black—in which embers of desire and passion still smoldered.

Despite that, she heaved a huge sigh and said, "I suppose we'd better get back."

Resigned to ending the interlude and with the promise of the exchange a beacon for the future, he smiled and, leaving his arms loosely about her, shifted to lounge against the balustrade. He glanced fleetingly at the ballroom. "I'd much rather stay here, at least for a while longer."

She drew back and regarded him through narrowing eyes. "How much longer?"

"I was thinking along the lines of an hour or so."

She huffed "As I thought. You're bamming." She caught one of his hands, backed toward the doors, and tugged. "Come on! You know as well as I do that we can disappear for only so long before the whispers start."

"I'm not sure I care—"

"Yes, you do. And no matter how I kick at the traces, I care, too. So..." Determined, she tugged harder.

Laughing, he allowed her to haul him away from the balustrade.

Crash!

Something large smashed onto the balustrade immediately behind him.

Instinct propelled him forward, shielding Melissa from flying shards and thrusting her back through the French doors. He followed. The instant they were safely inside, they whirled to stare out.

The shattered remnants of one of the stone urns that adorned the parapet of the house lay strewn about the balcony, centered on where he'd been standing seconds before.

An icy chill clamped about his nape.

Before he could stop her, Melissa popped out again, swung around, and stared up at the roof.

Cursing, he joined her and looked as well.

She pointed. "There was someone up there—a man—leaning over and looking down, but he drew back when he saw me look up."

There was no sign of anyone there now.

He shook the shards and dust from his coat and felt his features set like granite. He seized her hand. "Come on!"

A glance at the ballroom terrace showed it was empty. He realized it must be time for supper. There'd been no one on the terrace who might have seen what had happened.

After pausing to shut and lock the French doors, he joined Melissa at the parlor door. Grasping her hand, he led her out and on via a different series of corridors. Over his shoulder, he explained, "This is the quickest route to the front hall."

They stepped into the rear of the front hall, at that moment deserted except for two footmen flanking the front door, ready to assist departing guests. Julian murmured, "You should return to the ballroom. You'll be safer there."

"No." The word was uncompromising. Briefly, she met his eyes, her own dark with temper. "I just saved you from being killed. I'm not leaving your side."

There was something in her features that warned him not to push his luck. He looked ahead and continued walking along beside the stairs, making for the foyer. "There are only two ways to reach the roof—via the main stairs or by the staff's back stairs."

Melissa nodded. She kept a tight hold on his hand and fought to subdue the tumult of emotions raging through her as they walked toward the hall proper, to where they would be able to see up the main stairs and along the wide corridor leading to the ballroom.

This was their engagement ball, held inside his house, an earl's mansion in Mayfair, currently hosting the larger part of the haut ton, and yet whoever it was had tried to kill him there!

How dare they!

She felt very much as she imagined her grandmother did when confronted with the insensitivity of the uncouth.

Fury and fear comingled in a potent brew, but she thrust the surging emotions deep; she—and he—needed to keep their wits about them.

They rounded the newel post of the grand staircase and looked up.

Felix was leisurely descending, settling his coat as he came. He saw them and smiled. "Is it winding down yet? Or like me, are you trying to sneak away?"

Julian ignored that and demanded, "Did you see anyone up there?"

Realizing something was wrong, Felix halted and frowned. "No. But until a few minutes ago, I was hiding in my room. Now you're off the matchmakers' lists, they've realized I exist and are hunting me." His frown deepened, and he glanced up at the gallery. "Why would anyone other than family be up there?"

Succinctly, Julian told him about the falling urn and the man Melissa had spied on the roof. From the corner of his eye, he saw that Melissa was watching Felix closely, eyes faintly narrowed, but his brother's shock was evident.

"Good Lord!" Felix stared up the stairs. "But they won't still be up there." He turned to Julian. "I didn't see anyone going up or down. Chances are they used the back stairs."

Curtly, Julian nodded, then grimaced. "They'll be long gone by now."

Felix continued down the stairs and joined them, then quietly said, "Assuming that, whoever they are, they're not a guest."

Julian glanced at Melissa; from her expression, that thought had occurred to her as well. He dipped his head. "Assuming that."

"I'm no longer so certain we can assume that," she said.

A door opened down another corridor, and voices could be heard heading their way from the rear of the house.

Felix exchanged a look with Julian. He nodded fractionally; one of the group was Damian.

Julian summoned a genial smile and plastered it on. He squeezed Melissa's hand in warning and saw her expression lighten, then Damian strolled into the hall, surrounded by a pack of six gentlemen guests.

The gentlemen were all smiling and ambling, plainly in good spirits. A few looked not quite steady on their feet, but all professed delight at encountering Julian, Melissa, and Felix.

Julian took note of who was in the group. All were known to him— three friends of Damian's, all his age, plus two older very distant cousins and Findlay-Wright.

Julian smiled and replied to their various quips while doing his best to encourage the group to return to the ballroom. Melissa realized his intention and assisted, using her more polished social skills to steer the group on.

Meanwhile, Julian signaled Damian to remain.

Curious, Damian dutifully hung back, and they watched the others go. Once the group vanished beneath the archway leading to the ballroom, Damian turned to Julian. "Is something wrong?"

"First," Julian said, his tone hardening, "did you see anyone unexpected back there—anywhere near the back stairs?"

Damian frowned. "No." He tipped his head toward the ballroom archway. "That lot needed the water closets and weren't in any state to remember directions. I didn't want them wandering about aimlessly, so I acted as a guide."

"So all those gentlemen were with you from the time you left the ballroom?" Melissa asked.

Puzzlement deepening, Damian shook his head. "I took four of them —my friends and Roddy, one of our cousins. And Brian, our other cousin, and Findlay-Wright joined us while we were there. All of us came back in a group."

"Was there anyone still there?" Felix asked.

Damian shook his head. "No." He looked at Julian. "And I didn't see anyone about the back stairs, either. Why?"

Once again, Julian recounted what had occurred on the parlor balcony.

"Good Lord!" Damian's expression reflected every emotion Julian was sure they all felt. In his little brother's case, incredulity won out. *"Here?"* Damian demanded.

"Yes." Julian glanced toward the ballroom and exhaled through his teeth. "Unfortunately, we can't simply vanish from our engagement ball. We all need to go in there and pretend nothing whatever's amiss."

Melissa linked her arm in his. "We should also all go in together, as if we've been chatting about some family matter."

He nodded and settled her arm in his. "Good idea." He started for the corridor leading to the ballroom.

"But"—Felix fell in beside him, his tone suggesting he wasn't going to be gainsaid—"tomorrow morning, instead of going to church, we need to sit down and seriously discuss who is trying to kill you."

"Indeed." Julian felt the weight of the look Melissa bent on him.

"I'll be there, too," she declared. "What time?" She looked past him at Felix, then glanced at Damian, beside her. "Eleven?"

His brothers growled agreement, and when they all looked at him, Julian nodded. "Eleven. In the study here." He met Melissa's eyes. "I'll come and fetch you. And now…bright smiles, everyone."

They all knew how to play ton games; apparently relaxed, with easy-going, patently happy smiles on their faces, they strolled back into the fray.

~

The following morning, Julian walked the short distance to Mount Street, with a footman and his groom, both not in livery, unobtrusively trailing ten or so yards behind.

He was not of a mind to allow Melissa to venture forth without suitable protection, not even over the short distance between their homes. He also accepted that he was likely the attacker's target and couldn't help wondering if the sight of him, idly strolling along the pavement, might draw the villain out.

That said, he doubted the ruse would work; the more he thought of what had occurred the previous night—or rather very early that morning —the more it seemed clear it had been a spontaneous, opportunistic attempt.

On reaching North House, he set aside his cogitations, went up the steps, and rapped on the door. He'd arranged with Melissa to be there at a quarter to eleven, and it was close to that time.

The door swung open, and she walked out, garbed in her pelisse and with her bonnet and gloves already on. Her gaze immediately raked him as if checking for damage.

Apparently reassured, she stepped forward and took his arm, looking around as she did.

When the door shut behind her, she stated, "I'm not at all sure parading before a potential assassin is a good idea."

Inwardly buoyed by her open concern for him, he steadied her down the steps to the pavement. "If they haven't already made an appearance, I seriously doubt anything will happen on our way back."

His mild reply did not, apparently, reassure her; she humphed in response, and as they strolled—quite swiftly—back to Carsely House, she kept a tight hold on his arm and constantly scanned their surroundings.

As he'd predicted, they reached Carsely House without incident, without even sighting anyone suspicious.

After helping Melissa remove her coat and handing it and her bonnet to Crosby, Julian ushered her into the study, where they found his brothers already waiting.

Both immediately came to their feet.

Melissa smiled and waved at them to sit. "Standing on ceremony is going to become tedious—let's dispense with it between us."

Felix and Damian grinned and murmured ready agreement. They waited until she sank into the chair to one side of the fireplace, then as Julian claimed his usual chair opposite, Felix and Damian relaxed into the other two chairs grouped before the hearth.

Damian looked from Melissa to Julian. "So, where should we start? From what Felix has told me, I gather this latest effort wasn't the first attempt on your life."

Julian caught Melissa's eye and smothered the instinctive urge to make light of what had occurred. "It seems not," he admitted.

"And," Melissa said, tugging off her gloves, "there have been other strange happenings as well, like the mystery Irishman." She fixed Julian with a level look. "Why not start by listing all the incidents? Perhaps there's a pattern."

He held her gaze, then cast a swift glance at Felix. "Actually, the first attempt to at least injure me occurred before I came down to London."

"What?" Both Melissa and Damian stared at him. Melissa added, "You haven't mentioned that before."

"I didn't know what to make of it at the time, and I still don't." Briefly, he described the thorn that had been found wedged into his saddle. "Luckily, because Argus, my mount, went slightly lame and I took out Regis, my father's hunter, who needed the run, I had to use a different saddle, and in putting my saddle away, the groom found the thorn."

Resting his forearms on his knees, Felix leaned forward. "You've never had any such attacks before? While you were in Ireland?"

He shook his head. "I've received threats, and frankly, there'd be few of us in my section in Ireland who haven't had some, but actual attempts? No. Nothing."

Melissa nodded. "All right. So let's assume the thorn in the saddle was the first attempt." Her gaze remained fixed on his face. "What was the next incident?"

Reluctant but resigned, he cataloged the happenings and was taken aback to realize there'd been seven in total, four of which involved the Irishman. "But there was no hint of danger during any of those four incidents." He frowned. "I really can't imagine how an Irishman haunting my steps, presumably wanting to speak with me secretly, connects with attempts on my life."

"Not unless, as I suggested," Felix said, "it's the other side of the Irish equation trying to stop you from acting on the message. If you're dead, there'll be no danger of that."

Melissa watched Julian shake his head.

"Trust me," he said. "The Irish groups fight each other constantly, often murderously, but they are not usually so Machiavellian in their planning, especially not on this side of the Irish Sea."

He paused, then went on, "And then there's opportunity. While our mystery Irishman or his Irish opposition could have shot at us in the park, I can't see how either party could have lodged that thorn in my saddle at the castle and, yesterday, somehow got through the house, onto the roof, happened to see me standing on the terrace below, pushed an urn over, then got out of the house without anyone seeing him."

Damian wrinkled his nose. "Put like that, the Irishman does sound more like an incidental distraction."

Julian nodded. "My thoughts exactly."

"But," Felix said, "that still leaves us with the thorn, the shot in the park, and the falling urn to explain."

My thoughts exactly. Melissa saw Julian hesitate, as if inwardly debating some point.

Eventually, he admitted, "Except for Melissa seeing the man on the roof, any of those three incidents, had they succeeded, might have been explained away as an unfortunate accident. However, taken together, especially with the man on the roof, they're too much to swallow as mere coincidence."

"No, indeed." She felt somewhat reassured that he was taking the threat seriously. She looked at Felix and Damian and saw the concern she felt reflected in their features.

She expected one of them to say *"So what's our next step?"* but instead, the gong for luncheon resonated through the house.

All three men looked up, then got to their feet. Julian reached for her hand and, when she surrendered it, drew her up. "I forgot to mention— Mama and Uncle Frederick hoped you would join us for luncheon. If you're free?"

"Yes, of course." She hadn't actually thought of luncheon, but her mother knew where she was. "I'll be delighted to join you." In truth, she was curious about this household, for which she would soon be responsible.

She walked with Julian to the family dining room, which proved to be a pleasant parlor giving onto the side lawn. She was relieved to see that the small terrace was out of sight around a corner of the building; she wondered whether Julian had thought to have the staff clear the damage and also to suggest that his mother did not need to be informed of an urn falling from the roof. Given that, before strolling into the room, the three brothers all adopted expressions of relaxed unconcern, she felt reasonably confident one of them would have thought to give the necessary orders. She followed their lead, smiling easily as she greeted Veronica, who had insisted she call her by her first name, and Frederick, a dapper and kindly gentleman.

They all sat about the round table, and the butler, Crosby, assisted by two footmen, ferried out the platters.

The countess was patently delighted to have Melissa there, and the conversation progressed in bright, breezy, and engaging fashion and was never allowed to lag. In ensuring the latter, the countess was aided and abetted by her sons, who strove to keep the atmosphere lighthearted and far removed from anything serious. Melissa got the distinct impression that none of the countess's sons wished her to become alarmed.

For his part, Frederick was keen to encourage Melissa to view herself as one of the family. She found him a gentle soul and quite a dear.

Knowing that Mandy's relationship with Rufus's mother was still rather starchy and strained, Melissa hadn't expected so quickly to feel relaxed in Veronica's and Frederick's company, yet there was no denying she did. Both exerted themselves to that end, and she readily responded in kind.

By the end of the meal, they were, indeed, dealing with each other much as family members would, cutting across each other's comments and amending others, transparently having set aside all constraint.

As everyone pushed back from the table, Julian rose and came to draw out her chair. "Come. I'll walk you home."

Veronica and Frederick came to see her off.

In the front hall, Veronica took Melissa's hand, drew her close, and kissed her cheek. "My dear," the countess whispered, "you've no idea how pleased Frederick and I are that Julian chose you."

Melissa smiled back. "Thank you."

After she took her leave of Frederick, Julian gave her his arm and led her to the front door that Crosby promptly opened. She inclined her head to Crosby as she passed, and he bowed; she glimpsed the tiny smile that lifted his lips as he did, and that made her smile as well.

They went down the steps and started along the pavement, and she shifted her smiling gaze to Julian.

He studied her expression, then arched a brow in question.

She chuckled and lightly squeezed his arm. "I'm pleased that I'm finding it so easy to become one of your family. I truly didn't expect it to be such smooth sailing."

His smile bloomed as well, and he looked down. After a moment, he said, "I'm glad that's so, but I feel I should confess that Mama is in alt over the prospect of having another lady at the castle."

When she, in turn, looked at him questioningly, he went on, "She's been the only female at the castle—well, female of the family—since my younger sister married, and that was more than five years ago. I know Mama misses female company and having another female to discuss things with."

"I can understand that." Melissa thought of her own family, which was well supplied with female members. "I still miss having Mandy beside me, to share secrets with."

Julian threw her a resigned look. "I believe I can predict that you and Mama will end thick as thieves, united against us poor hapless males."

She laughed, but then her smile faded, and her expression grew serious and sober.

He felt an urge to make her smile again, but with the most recent attack still fresh in his mind, he was as troubled as she.

As they neared the corner of Grosvenor Square, she raised her head, drew in a deeper breath, then looked at him and, when he met her eyes, asked, "Could Felix be behind the attacks?"

He blinked. "What?" Astonished, he halted and stared at her. "No. Of course not."

When she didn't look convinced, he asked, "What made you think that?"

She looked at him in mild frustration and opened her mouth to reply, then noticed other pedestrians walking past and thought better of it.

He agreed. Privacy was required for such a discussion, and in this area, both of them stood a good chance of being recognized.

They'd halted at the corner of Grosvenor Square. He scanned the square's central park and spotted an unoccupied bench along one of the paths. He nodded that way. "Come on. Let's sit and discuss this."

They crossed the cobbled street and walked into the park. After claiming the wrought-iron seat, shaded by the branches of a cherry tree, currently in full bloom, Melissa shifted so she could more easily see his face and said, "When you were shot at in the park, Felix was there, remember? And last night, when the urn fell, he's the only one we know for certain had been upstairs. There's no evidence anyone else was, and I assume you've checked with the staff this morning and no one saw anyone by the back stairs?"

He was forced to concede the point. "No one saw anyone unexpected near the stairs, much less going up or down them."

She nodded. "Well, then, was Felix at the castle when the incident with the thorn occurred?"

He met her gaze. After a moment of inner debate, he admitted, "Felix met me as I left the stable, just after I'd learned about the thorn." When she stared—all but glared—at him, he took her hand and gently squeezed. "While I admit Felix is one of the few who might have put the thorn in place, and he couldn't have known that I wouldn't use that saddle that morning, you're going to have to think again, because I know it's not him."

Frowning, she studied his eyes. Eventually, she asked, "Why are you so certain he isn't the culprit?"

He closed his hand more firmly about hers. "Because Felix and I are close. It's not simply a matter of being brothers of similar age who've grown up together, although that's part of it. Once, when he was ten and I was eleven, I saved his life. He nearly drowned, and while I was the stronger swimmer, he panicked, and I had to fight him to get him to shore. He and I know that, at one point when we went over a low weir, it would have been much safer for me to let him go, but I wouldn't. He's never forgotten that. I've never tried to make him feel he owed me—I don't think of the incident in that way—but that's the way he sees it. He's been my champion and would-be defender ever since, even if I don't need defending, and over the years, that's become an ingrained part of who he is. He would be as likely to cut off his own arm as try to harm me."

Her frown lightened, but she was clearly still uncertain.

Struck by inspiration, he asked, "Would you ever believe Mandy would deliberately set out to murder you?"

She sighed. "No, of course not." After a moment, she shook her head. "That could simply never happen. So yes, I understand. And you and Felix do seem similarly close."

Julian nodded. "We're not twins, but as near as makes no odds." After a moment, he asked, "Aside from his proximity—in all three instances, I admit—was there any other reason you focused on him?"

Once again, she looked at him as if he was being obtuse. "He's your heir, isn't he?"

He blinked. "Well, yes. He is." Then he shook his head. "But as we've now established, it isn't him."

"Hmm." After a moment of frowning cogitation, she met his eyes. "Is it common knowledge how close you and Felix are?"

He thought about it, then admitted, "I doubt it. We've never lived in each other's pockets, certainly not while in London."

Her eyes narrowed, and her gaze fixed unseeing across the park. Eventually, she murmured, as if trying out the thought, "Could it be that, assuming you and Felix are no closer than some brothers—and let's face it, not all brothers are close when there's a wealthy earldom at stake— someone has thought to cast him as their scapegoat?" She met his eyes. "Might we be supposed to leap to the conclusion that Felix is behind the attacks? Him being near on three separate occasions is surely more than coincidence."

He frowned. "I'd like to say you're wrong, yet three times does stretch belief. But I can't see why anyone would want to make it appear that Felix is at fault."

She almost hissed in exasperation. "Because if you're murdered and Felix is convicted of the crime, he can't inherit."

"But that just passes the title and estate to Damian, and before you ask, it's not him, either. Just thinking of something this convoluted and complicated, let alone organizing it, is far, *far* out of character for my little brother." He caught her gaze. "Damian is very much as he appears— cheery, devil-may-care, easygoing, and essentially harmless."

Her eyes narrowed. "But is he in debt? Perhaps someone suggested the scheme as a means of accessing the Delamere wealth?"

He was already shaking his head. "No." He paused, then admitted, "I keep a very close eye on Damian. His personality being what it is, he was always going to attract those looking for an easy mark. He did get into debt the first year he came up to town—and I let him. It was all entirely predictable and somewhat understandable, but I wanted him to have the stomach-churning experience of being entirely out of his depth. And I wanted to see what he would do." He held her gaze. "He came to me and made a full confession. I paid off his debts, and in return, he swore never to go that road again." His lips twisted. "I admit I still watch and check, but thus far, he's kept that promise."

Frowning, she tipped her head. "You're sure?" she asked.

But it was purely to hear him say, "I'm certain. I don't take chances with those I care about."

Melissa studied his eyes, then nodded in acceptance and faced forward. "So it's neither of your brothers, and we can trust them to help with this. However…it still seems to me that it's possible someone, for whatever reason, is taking aim not just at you but at Felix as well, by casting him as the prime suspect."

Julian tipped his head her way. "I can't say that's impossible."

She waited, then prompted, "So what now? Do we slow things down and see what happens?"

Swiftly, he glanced at her. "We can't postpone the wedding." His tone suggested he'd already considered it. "That would cause a furor."

"Of immense proportions, but I would rather a furor and a delayed wedding than to find myself with no groom."

He squeezed the hand he still held. "That's not going to happen. I don't think me marrying you has anything to do with the attacks. The incident of the thorn in my saddle—which could not have happened without someone deliberately putting it there—occurred before I even made up my mind to come to London. And given the subsequent attacks, we have to accept that it's me—not you or the prospect of our marriage— that's the true target here."

She stared at him, then said, "That's not reassuring."

He smiled in what he doubtless hoped was a reassuring fashion. "We'll get to the bottom of it, but just so we're clear"—he raised her hand to his lips and brushed a kiss to the backs of her gloved fingers—"no putting off the wedding."

She blew out a breath and nodded. Aside from all else, the lead-up to the wedding would necessitate them spending a great deal of their waking hours together, which would allow her to watch his back, especially when he forgot to. And she would be there to help catch whoever was behind the attacks; on that, she was determined.

As if attuned to her thoughts, his voice hardening, he said, "Aside from all else, I'm not inclined to allow some nameless, faceless villain to disrupt our lives."

Bravo! "Not now that we've finally come together, found our right path, and are moving ahead in a manner of which even the grandes dames approve."

He smiled and straightened on the seat. "You and I are on our right path, and we'll follow it come what may."

"Indeed." She squeezed his hand back. "And if necessary, we'll fight for what we want—a peaceful, satisfying life together."

Julian felt his smile spontaneously deepen. She sounded so fierce. In a way, he felt humbled by her determination to champion him. He possessed clear and fond memories of the girl she'd been, but the woman she was now, strong, confident, and in her own way, growing into her inherent power, was so much more.

He had to admit he loved this staunchly protective side of her, one he hadn't until recently dreamt she possessed.

Despite the current uncertainties, he felt solidly confident as he declared, "So we go forward and keep our wits about us, and we ensure that whoever is behind these attacks doesn't succeed."

She met his eyes, her dark-blue gaze determined. "More, we're going to figure out who that person is, then we'll deal with them appropriately."

To his ears, she sounded positively vengeful. Was it wrong to feel faintly thrilled?

Regardless, still smiling, he rose and drew her to her feet. "Your mama will be wondering what's become of you. I'd best get you home."

She dismissed the concern with a wave, but linked her arm with his once more and allowed him to steer her out of the park and on along the pavement toward Mount Street.

As they left Grosvenor Square behind, her words about identifying who was responsible for the attacks echoed in his mind. He was fairly sure they would have to do just that, because it seemed highly unlikely that whoever was behind the attacks would stop.

It was Sunday evening before the man behind the attacks attained the right frame of mind to review what had come to pass at Carsely House.

With as much detachment as he could muster, he made himself go over his actions step by step and, ultimately, forced himself to admit that it had been a worryingly close call.

But Carsely *and* his bride-to-be standing alone on a small balcony, away from all the other guests and even out of sight of the staff, had simply been an opportunity too perfect to pass up.

He'd been right to seize it; he couldn't regret doing so, even now. Yes, it had come to naught, but… "By Jupiter! I so nearly succeeded!"

He dwelled on the moment, savoring again the burst of excitement he'd felt in the instant when he'd thought he'd triumphed, then the memories of Miss North's white face looking up and the stomach-churning fear that had gripped him for the rest of the night rose to haunt him.

Determinedly, he consigned the incident to the past and turned his mind to what he should have been following—his carefully thought-out master plan. He needed to be patient. Despite knowing full well how rarely spontaneous attacks worked, he'd acted impulsively on two occasions, and while neither action had brought him the result he craved, they had, instead, put Carsely on alert.

That had not been a part of his plan.

He brooded on the situation as the minutes ticked by. Eventually, he accepted that he would have to make amends of a sort. He would have to back away, hold off for a time.

"Let Carsely think all danger has passed. I need to give him a chance to forget and grow dismissive and careless of his safety."

Even with the wedding looming, there was plenty of time, and there was no denying that arranging the right sort of accident was very much easier in the country.

He paused, thinking of the latest pawn he'd moved into position.

It was tempting—undeniably so—to see what might be achieved by putting that agent to work.

CHAPTER 8

*S*ome two weeks later, a faintly exasperated Julian summoned Felix and Damian to his study.

When the pair arrived, he held out the list of wedding invitees. "I need you to tell me if anyone's missing who should be there, and then we have to go through and note those we think should stay at the castle."

The list was four pages long. Felix took the sheets and handed two to Damian, and the pair lounged in the chairs before the desk and started to read.

Julian watched them peruse the pages. The past weeks had grown increasingly hectic; he'd had no idea preparing for a wedding involved so many decisions, so much fussing over this and that, much less that he would be called on to have an opinion on matters such as the decorations for the castle ballroom in which the wedding breakfast would be held. That he didn't have an opinion hadn't been an acceptable answer, although it had made Melissa fight to hide a smile.

In between too many meetings with his mother, his future mother-in-law, and his bride, he'd had to deal with estate business as well as the inevitable meetings with his solicitors and Lord North over the marriage settlements. And wedged between all that, he'd tried to get some inkling of what the Irishman might wish to tell him; he'd ambled through the corridors of the Home Office several times, but had been loath to make his inquiry official. Given he had no idea what the issue at hand was, he felt a need to tread warily. That said, all the information he'd been able to glean suggested that there was nothing of a major nature going on.

In light of that, he'd wondered if the Irishman had given up. Regardless, unless the matter was truly urgent, once Julian headed for Derbyshire, he doubted the Irishman would follow.

As for his attacker, whoever the blighter was, at least he appeared to have drawn back.

Julian wasn't naive enough to imagine he'd given up.

Felix stirred, then asked after a distant cousin.

Julian frowned. "You're right. His name should be there."

Felix and Damian hunted through the lists and confirmed the cousin's name wasn't on them.

Julian handed Felix a pencil. "Add it."

Clearly reluctantly, Damian recalled a crotchety old lady, a relict of some ancient connection, and was transparently relieved when Julian assured him she was no longer alive. When his brothers looked at him strangely, Damian explained, "She always used to pinch my cheeks. Hard."

They moved on to discussing the accommodations.

"Mama says she needs to know by the end of the day," Julian said. "The castle might be large, but I'd rather not overburden the staff— they'll have the wedding and wedding breakfast to manage as it is."

Felix shrugged. "Wirksworth is close enough, and there's Matlock and Ashbourne for those coming from those directions."

"And Belper and Derby for those heading back to town." Damian looked at Julian. "I assume you and Melissa will be remaining at the castle?"

Julian nodded. "We've decided to spend the summer there. Melissa wants to get to know the place."

Damian grinned. "Lord knows, it's big enough."

Felix tapped the list. "Getting back to this, why not just put up the close family, hers as well as ours? If you limit it to that, no one's going to argue."

"True." Damian tossed onto the desk the sheets he'd been holding. "And regardless of the castle being huge, that's still not a small number of guests to be housing under its many roofs." He stretched, then made to rise. "So that's done."

"Not quite." Julian lifted another list from the pile on the desk. "These are the staff from here who'll be going up to assist at the castle. Mama said the Crosbys need to know to organize transport and also to organize those remaining here to man this house, and the Phelpses have asked for the numbers to be accommodated at the castle. Check it before I hand it on to Mama."

Felix took the list, scanned it, and grunted. "Looks right to me." He passed the list to Damian.

Damian's gaze raked the names, then paused. "Aha!" He held out his hand. "Give me that pencil. You have my groom, but not my new man."

Felix turned wide eyes on Damian. "You have a man? Since when?"

For reasons known only to himself, for years, Damian had resisted getting someone to oversee his wardrobe.

Damian pulled a face at Felix. "I'm twenty-four. I decided it was time." He handed the amended list to Julian.

Julian took the list and glanced at it. "And his name is…?"

"Manning." Damian pointed at the list. "I stuck his name near the other valets' names."

"Is he the man I saw in the corridor this morning?" Felix asked. "Middling height, early thirties perhaps, close-cropped dark hair, roundish face, and just starting a paunch."

Damian nodded. "That's him."

Felix frowned slightly. "I have to say he appeared a little…well, not exactly rough but less polished than the usual gentleman's gentleman."

Julian snorted. "That's probably why he suits Damian."

When Damian merely grinned, Felix rolled his eyes.

"Where did you find him?" Julian half expected Damian to say at some boxing match.

"I'd mentioned to Gordon about needing a man, and he recommended Manning, who's apparently a relation of some other gentleman's gentleman Gordon knows."

Julian tended to forget that Damian and Gordon, being cousins of much the same age, were friends.

"Well," Felix said, "one can only hope the fellow will keep your coats in better state."

"Not to mention your boots," Julian added. Ignoring Damian's reply, he initialed all the lists, then signaled to Damian to ring for a footman. "I'm sure Mama will be happy to receive these ahead of her deadline. As I'm relying on her to organize the logistics, I need to keep her sweet."

After tugging the bellpull, Damian asked. "Are you finished with us?"

Julian shook his head. "Wait a moment."

The footman arrived, and Julian handed over the lists to be ferried to his mother. Once the door had shut behind the footman, he returned his gaze to his now-attentive brothers.

Both read his expression and immediately grew serious.

"We have to consider," he said, "the possibility that whoever has tried to attack me several times might well have been at the engagement ball as a guest. Consequently—"

"Whoever the blighter is, he might also be at the wedding." Felix blew out a breath. "I hadn't thought of that."

Damian raised a hand and waved it. "I did." He met Julian's eyes. "You'll need guards of sorts. I was going to suggest that we ask all the staff and everyone we trust to be on guard for any strange happenings, and if they see anything even minor that's odd, they should tell Felix or me immediately."

Felix was nodding. "You won't be in any position to react quickly if anything untoward occurs."

Julian grimaced. "Sadly, you're right. I'm liable to be dancing or surrounded by guests."

"Who will most likely be the very last guests you'll want to know of any potential emergency," Felix added,

"As much as I'd like to argue, I can't." Julian looked from Felix to Damian. "So in addition to the staff, who are we thinking of?"

They tossed around names, discussed, and decided.

"Keep it simple," Julian stated. "Just say there might be someone—a guest, or staff, or anyone at all—who might try to cause trouble, and we'd rather not have any incidents disrupting the day."

Felix nodded. "The staff will accept that, and our friends will, too. No need to be specific."

"Not that we can be specific," Damian pointed out.

Julian grunted. After a moment, he admitted, "One of my main concerns is that, as we don't know the attacker's motive, we can't rule out the possibility that, on finding himself blocked from striking at me, he'll turn his sights on Melissa."

That made his brothers grow as grave as he felt.

Frowning, Felix suggested, "You could alert the staff to be particularly vigilant where their new mistress is concerned. You can make it vague, and they'll put it down to husbandly protectiveness, which they'll probably think very appropriate, and because they all love you, they'll make sure they keep a close eye on Melissa."

Damian nodded. "I second that. You know the castle staff are yours to command. They always have been."

"And of course," Felix added, "we'll help. At least during the wedding itself, you'll be by her side, and when, during the breakfast, you get drawn into other duties, we'll step in and at least stay close enough to make sure nothing happens to her."

Julian took in his brothers' committed expressions and, after a moment, inclined his head. "Thank you. I suspect that's the best we can do. That, and hope that whoever it is, they continue to lie low."

A week later, Melissa steered Julian through the crowd assembled on Lady Jersey's rear lawn at Osterly Park. The occasion was one of her ladyship's famous alfresco luncheons, and the cream of the ton had gathered to enjoy the bright May day.

While she and Julian smiled and chatted and steadily circulated among the crowd—constantly moving being the best defense against being surrounded and metaphorically taken hostage—in a moment between groups, he tipped his head down to hers and murmured, "Why do I get the impression that we're one of the principal attractions?"

Her polite smile in place, she met his eyes. "Because we are."

She faced forward as a lady swept up. "Lady Trelawny. How delightful to see you again. And your daughter as well. Imogen, isn't it?"

After the necessary introductions and obligatory chatting, as they moved on again, Julian murmured, "And we're here because...?"

Still smiling, she patted his arm. "Lady Jersey has always been kind to me. Strange to say, she was one of the few major hostesses who didn't try to pressure me into marrying—meaning marrying someone else."

"Ah." After a moment, he added, "In that case, I'm happy to be able to lend our presence to her event."

Melissa chuckled and led him on.

As was now the norm when they appeared at such venues, the insatiably curious descended, chatting eagerly in the hopes of learning more about their wedding. In this rather exclusive setting, the numbers of the curious were further bolstered by their own connections.

Mrs. Helen Delamere was one such who popped up in their path. "So delightful to see you both!"

Melissa wasn't surprised when, after exchanging the barest minimum by way of greetings, Mrs. Delamere, her eyes bright with curiosity, leaned close, set a hand on Melissa's wrist, and whispered, "I can't wait to witness your wedding! It's been years since there was a wedding at the castle. Both Constance and Eleanor married in St. George's, which I always thought such a shame." Her expression turned sorrowful, then brightened again. "But *finally*, I'll get to see a wedding in the chapel at Carsington Castle." Eyes alight, she laid her hands across her bosom. "It will be ravishingly romantic, I'm sure." She turned her pale-blue gaze on Julian. "Don't you think so, Carsely?"

His face an impassive mask, he replied, "No doubt."

Melissa smothered an urge to kick him.

Mrs. Delamere returned her attention to Melissa. "But tell me, my dear, you must be looking forward to your wedding trip. I daresay you're going to some fabulously wonderful place. I hear Italy and the south of France are lovely at this time of year." She looked at Melissa hopefully.

Melissa smiled and replied, "I'm sorry to disappoint, but I plan to spend the summer at the castle, learning the ropes of how to run the place from Veronica."

"Oh." Mrs. Delamere blinked. "I see." She released Melissa. "Somehow, I'd got it in my head that you were off on a jaunt about the Continent." She sounded and looked confused.

Julian relented. "We are considering such a trip later in the year, but of course, being free to leave the country depends on the estate, business concerns, and to some extent, the political situation as well."

Mrs. Delamere looked relieved. "Ah." She nodded. "That's what I must have heard." Her bright smile returned, and she beamed at them both. "I'm so glad I wasn't entirely wrong." She glanced about. "And now I must allow all these other lovely people to have their time with you. Farewell, and I'll see you at the castle!"

On that note, she swanned away, apparently quite happy.

As the next group approached, Melissa glanced at Julian. "Did you understand that? Why she's so glad she wasn't entirely wrong?"

Lips thinning, his gaze on Mrs. Delamere's departing back, Julian shook his head. "Helen doesn't always make sense, at least not in the way others think of it."

Already smiling, Melissa held out her hand to the next matron wishing to speak with them. "Lady Huntwell. I hadn't realized you were up from Devon."

Julian plastered on his practiced smile and nodded and exchanged the usual glib phrases. In that, his years with the Home Office stood him in good stead; he'd long ago lost count of the balls, parties, and other social events he'd had to attend while in Dublin.

Gradually, the reality of being on such hallowed ground as Osterly Park sank in and eased the tension that had become second nature whenever he and Melissa were in public. Having no idea of the attacker's motives, or of how the villain might think, had left him prey to an unyielding protectiveness he understood, but had underestimated. However, no attacker, no matter how well-connected, was going to attempt anything while surrounded on all sides by the elite of the ton. Being able to relax his vigilance, at least for a few hours, was a welcome relief.

At Lady Jersey's direction, with the other guests, he and Melissa started along the wending path toward the bluebell dell where the picnic was to be held. On noting that they were temporarily out of ready earshot of others, he murmured, "Did I tell you that the order to provide me, Felix, and Damian with attire for the wedding has turned my tailor into a nervous wreck?"

She laughed. "No. How?"

He told her of his last fitting and how the normally mild and even-tempered man had nearly broken down. "Not over me, although he wasn't happy about the material I chose for our waistcoats—he wanted something flashier—but Damian had him literally pulling out what little hair he still has. Apparently, my little brother's shoulders have somehow grown a full inch since his previous fitting. For a while there, Felix and I thought Saxby would have an apoplexy. Luckily, we managed to soothe his ruffled feathers, and he ended promising to have the coat and waistcoat remade and ready in time."

She glanced suspiciously his way. "I'm surprised that a twenty-four-year-old would have such a growth spurt over such a short time."

He snorted. "More like Damian, who hates standing still, wriggled while being measured." They strolled on, and he glanced at her. "So, what's your most excruciating experience in this circus of wedding preparations?"

"Ah—that would undoubtedly be when Mandy came up for the fitting for her matron-of-honor gown on Monday."

Three weeks previously, Mandy had been brought to bed of a healthy baby girl. By all accounts, mother and daughter were faring well, and Rufus was utterly besotted with his offspring.

Briefly, Melissa glanced at Julian. "You know how determined Mandy has been to be my matron of honor. She persuaded—or possibly badgered and verbally bludgeoned—Rufus into bringing her and little Charlene up to town, just for the fitting. Mama, of course, was delighted to have a chance to hold her first grandchild, so she remained at North House with Charlene and Rufus while Mandy and I went to see the modiste.

"Well, Madame Henriette had assured us she could work with the measurements for Mandy that she already had—she's been our modiste for years. She was adamant that she knew exactly how to adjust the measurements to accommodate a lady only just out of her confinement."

She paused, and he prompted, "I sense a 'but'..."

Lips setting a touch grimly, she nodded. "The gown was a disaster. I had Mandy wailing, and Madame in tears, and the poor assistants didn't know what to do. They cowered in the workshop and wouldn't come out. In the end, I had to lightly slap Mandy to get her to stop wailing and pay attention, and I had to speak very sternly to Madame."

She shook her head. "Both were so fixated on the gown and expecting it to be perfect, they'd entirely forgotten that there were a full three weeks before the wedding—before the gown absolutely has to be done." Exasperated, she waved. "And Mandy was right there! I had to stand over the lot of them and get Madame and her assistants to do a completely new set of measurements. And I got Mandy to promise to come up to town again in a week or so for a final fitting."

She glanced up at him from beneath her lashes. "In order to get everyone to behave, I might have threatened to elope."

He laughed aloud. "I must remember that. In our current circumstances, it's the perfect threat."

She grinned and nodded. "I certainly found it effective."

Still chuckling, he caught her hand and lightly squeezed.

After a moment, he raised the hand and pressed a kiss to her fingers. Lowering his arm, he stated, "It appears that, thus far, we've weathered all the ton, in its many and varied guises, has thrown at us."

She nodded. "We have, and we've just over three weeks to go."

He mock groaned, then dipped his head close to whisper, "About that threat of yours...?"

It was her turn to laugh.

Smiling, relaxed and happy, he swung her hand as they continued down the path.

Lady Jersey's notion of a picnic was to have her guests lounge in groups on rugs spread on the grassy area that overlooked the park's famous bluebell dell and sip champagne while consuming delicacies displayed on silver platters and served by a small army of footmen.

The champagne was cool, the various comestibles beyond delicious, and once everyone was seated, the company Julian and Melissa found themselves in proved surprisingly comfortable. The two other couples Lady Jersey directed their way were acquaintances of similar station and, like them, engaged to be wed. After establishing their respective wedding dates—Julian and Melissa's wedding would be the first to occur—the six of them agreed to avoid all talk of weddings, engagement balls, and such and, instead, entertained themselves with more lighthearted banter, much as they would have had they not been engaged.

That was another sort of relief.

Like any good hostess, Lady Jersey wandered between the rugs, checking that her guests had everything they needed. When she passed nearby, Julian caught her eye and raised his glass to her in appreciation. Her ladyship smiled, nodded, and glided on.

Far more relaxed than he'd expected to be, he snagged a bunch of grapes from the platter of a passing footman. He popped one in his mouth, then noticed Melissa eyeing the bunch. He pulled another grape from the stalk and held it out, offering it to her.

She caught his eye, then instead of reaching for it with her fingers, she leaned nearer and plucked the grape from his fingers with her lips.

His breath seized; his libido came alive. Desperate for immediate distraction, he plucked another grape, tossed it up, and caught it in his mouth.

She laughed, and he plucked another and arched a brow at her.

When she nodded, he lobbed it—and she dipped and successfully snaffled it.

They laughed, and eating the rest of the bunch became a contest, which, after distracting him, she won, much to their shared delight.

He hadn't recently seen this side of her—the more lighthearted girl he'd caught glimpses of long ago—and he was delighted to find her again.

For her part, she, too, seemed to soften, to allow her feelings for him to show in her features, in the way she leaned her shoulder against his.

Being with the other couples—by then, likewise focused on each other—afforded them greater license, and they both took advantage.

Eventually, it was time to rise and return to the house.

Leaving Melissa chatting with the other couples, Julian took their glasses to a nearby table for collection.

After setting the glasses down, he turned and found Lady Jersey standing beside him. Her haughty gaze had been resting on Melissa, but she transferred it to him and nodded regally. "I'm very pleased to see Melissa smiling so much more frequently than she used to. She's much more beautiful when she smiles, don't you think?"

Subjected to an arched eyebrow and a penetrating look, he was pleased to be able to answer truthfully. "I do."

"Indeed. I heartily approve. Keep it up!" With that firm admonition, Lady Jersey swanned off.

He blinked, shook his head, then, a smile slowly forming, returned to Melissa's side.

She looked after Lady Jersey. "What was that about?" Suspicion rang in her tone.

"Nothing bad." He offered his arm, and she wound hers with his. They started back with the others, making their way to the beginning of the path. "Apparently, she approves of us."

"She does?" Melissa stared at him. "She actually said those words?"

Puzzled, he met her gaze. "Yes. Specifically, she said 'I heartily approve.'"

"Well!" She faced forward. "That's one for the books."

"It is?"

She nodded. "She very, *very* rarely indicates unequivocal approval." She smiled, gave a happy little skip, and caught his eye. "We obviously pass muster. I must remember to tell Mama."

He smiled, then raised a hand and tucked an errant strand of her hair behind one of her ears.

All she could see in his gray eyes was contented happiness; the sight moved her to vow that she would work to keep that particular expression permanently infusing his gaze.

They reached the lawns and joined the company in making their farewells and waiting for their carriages to roll up. Before Julian's curricle arrived, a short, rather dumpy, dark-haired lady accosted them.

"Carsely, Miss North." Lady Esterhazy exchanged nods. "I'm

delighted to see you both. I wished to say how pleased I was to learn of your betrothal."

Melissa shot Julian a swift glance, then her smile unabated, gave her attention to the second major ton hostess—indeed, the second of Almack's powerful patronesses—seeking to bestow her imprimatur on their union.

~

Three weeks later, in preparing to quit London for Derbyshire, Julian and Felix sat in the study of Carsely House, going through the estate records, of which Julian insisted Felix keep abreast.

They paused for Julian to shut one ledger and open the next.

Seated on the opposite side of the desk, Felix sighed and stretched, then critically surveyed Julian. "I don't know how you've survived the past weeks and retained your sanity—some semblance of it, at least. The earlier weeks were bad enough, but the last two have been horrendous! And if it's been bad for Damian and me, keeping up appearances while worrying that an attack might occur at any moment, I can't imagine what it's been like for you."

Julian grunted. He almost quipped that he'd grown used to it, only he hadn't. The barrage of invitations had been relentless, with many events being ones they couldn't avoid attending. Meanwhile, the unremitting tension of being constantly on guard, prey to an unforgiving compulsion to watch over Melissa like a hawk, had steadily eroded his social façade until, at times, he'd felt like snarling.

The only saving grace had been that Melissa had been there, by his side, sharing the ordeal. Their sotto voce exchanges of cynical comments and shrewd observations had helped anchor him and keep him sane.

The knowledge that had slowly seeped into his awareness—that she was watching over him as much as he was watching over her—had also grounded him in a way he couldn't entirely explain.

Felix was still regarding him anxiously.

With a wry quirk of his lips, he admitted, "It has been wearying, but"—he shrugged—"Melissa's been there with me, which has made the moments bearable." He paused, then darkly added, "Just."

Felix studied him for a moment more, then sighed. "The pair of you... you really are the perfect match the ton has labeled you."

He winced. "Don't let Melissa hear you say that. She's still not recon-
ciled to that description."

"Oh?"

"She says it places unrealistic expectations on us, and she doesn't like
being told she has to live up to anyone else's ideals."

"Ah." Felix nodded sagely. "I can see how that might be. She's
rather...strong. Stronger than she appears."

Julian smiled. He'd known that from the first, when they'd met in
Little Moseley. "We are who we are. I'm just grateful she was still unmarried when I came back." He opened the next ledger.

"Speaking of Ireland..." Felix caught his eye. "Have you or anyone
else sighted that damned Irishman?"

He shook his head. "He seems to have gone to ground. He might even
have gone back to Ireland. If what he wanted to tell me is truly important
enough, he'll reappear." He tapped his finger on the ledger. "Now stop
trying to distract me and pay attention to this."

Felix groaned, sat forward, and dutifully stared at the accounts while
Julian ran through the current issues.

After he'd succeeded to the title, as Felix was his heir, Julian had
insisted on these meetings. While he'd had a basic understanding of the
estate from his late teens, after his father's unexpected death, he'd had to
find and pick up all the reins without any recent knowledge of the far-
flung holdings. That had been a challenge, one he'd sworn that whoever
succeeded to the earldom after him would never have to face.

Hence, Felix's introduction to all matters affecting the Delamere
holdings.

One such matter was the various deeds that would be altered courtesy
of the marriage settlements. After finishing with the accounts and closing
the last ledger, Julian moved on to explaining the settlements' impacts in
detail.

When he finished, he sat back and eyed Felix's frowning face. "Any
questions?"

"As a matter of fact, yes." Felix met his gaze. "What about the Scottish holdings? Are there any stipulations in those deeds pertaining to your
marital status?"

Julian blinked. "Good point." He thought, then admitted, "I don't
believe my marriage will affect them, but I haven't checked."

He rose and crossed to the large bookcase that stood against the wall
to the right of the desk. He scanned the titles of the volumes, found the

one he sought in the center of the middle shelf, gripped the spine, and drew it out.

At least, he tried to, but the book stuck an inch out from its fellows.

He frowned and wiggled the tome, trying to free it of whatever it was catching on. He pulled evenly, but that didn't help. Grimacing, he gripped the spine more firmly and sharply tugged.

The book jerked out and came free in his hand.

The bookcase started to tilt, then fall.

Stunned, he looked up.

"Watch out!"

Felix crashed into him.

They fell, sprawling on the floor, Julian trapped half under Felix.

The bookcase crashed down, the upper section slamming onto the edge of the large desk. Heavy leather-bound books rained down on Julian and onto Felix's back.

"Ow!" Felix shifted, dislodging several tomes. "Damn it!" He turned his head enough to see the bookcase propped at an angle over them, supported by the edge of the massive and immovable desk. "What the devil...?"

Felix turned back and stared dumbfounded at Julian.

Grimly, Julian nodded. "My sentiments exactly." He urged Felix upward. "I can't move until you do. Crawl out."

Felix rolled off Julian, then wriggled and, pushing fallen books out of the way, crawled out from beneath the angled bookcase. He stopped when he was clear, turned, and sat, still staring, stunned, at the wreckage.

Free of Felix's weight, Julian rolled onto his stomach, crawled out, and joined his brother.

They sat and stared while their hearts slowed. From the floor, what might have happened was plain to see.

"I think we're even," Julian said. "If you hadn't launched yourself over the desk and knocked me down, I would have been crushed between the bookcase and the desk."

And he would, almost certainly, have died.

After a moment, Felix said, "I saw all those ledgers passing before my eyes and knew I'd regret letting you die."

They both managed a shaky laugh.

Felix glanced toward the door. "No one's come."

"Crosby told me all the staff have been cooped to polish the silver before packing it to be sent to the castle."

The wedding was three days away, and the atmosphere in the house was approaching frenzied.

Julian hauled in a deep breath and exhaled. Then he drew in another breath, pushed to his feet, and extended a hand to Felix. "You all right?"

Felix gripped the proffered hand and allowed Julian to haul him upright. "I think so. Well, other than several bruises from the books." Looking at the fallen bookcase, Felix frowned. "There are wires. Why are there wires?"

Julian looked and saw the fine wires looping over the back of the bookcase in a pattern that was plainly deliberate. The wires twisted together, and one end ran upward to some sort of contraption that had sat on the bookcase's top, from which steel rods now protruded; the rods had pushed the top of the case away from the wall. The wires' other ends passed through the back of the case, threaded through tiny holes all along each shelf. Julian crouched and looked at the books that had fallen out, then grunted and rose. "All the books have wires looped through the spines."

He stepped to the wall and examined the remnants of the bolts that had once anchored the bookcase to the wall.

Felix came to peer as well. "They've been cut!"

Grim-faced, Julian nodded. "Someone knew how to make the case tippable and how to rig it so that when a book was pulled out, the entire case would fall."

"That's...ingenious."

It truly was. Someone understood mechanics. Julian shook his head. "I can't imagine who might have done this." He put a hand to the bookcase and tested the weight. "This isn't something you and I can clear up— I'll have to tell Crosby and get him to deal with it."

Felix looked at him. "This is serious. A lethal trap laid inside Carsely House—in your study, for heaven's sake!"

Grimly, he nodded. "The point hasn't escaped me. The house should have been safe, but either someone broke in, or the attacker, or someone working for him, is on the staff."

His gaze resting on the fallen bookcase, Felix blew out a breath. "At least we're leaving for the castle tomorrow."

"And most of those in this house are going with us."

Felix's face fell. He looked at Julian. When, face set, Julian simply stared back, Felix asked, "What are we going to do?" Then he swallowed and amended, "What can we do?"

"Exactly." Lips thinning, Julian looked at the bookcase, then, exasperated, raked a hand through his hair. "At this moment, with the wedding so close, we can't do anything constructive." He thought, then added, "As far as I can see, our only way forward is to work out who did this, lay our hands on them, then assuming they aren't the principal perpetrator, follow the trail from them to whoever is." He imagined that, then exhaled. "And the truth is that all of that will be very much easier at the castle, given I'm lord and master there."

CHAPTER 9

their wedding day dawned bright and clear—a perfect summer day for the perfect wedding of the ton's perfect couple.

The point wasn't lost on Melissa, but she was almost taken aback by the intensity of the surging joy that swept her up and buoyed her on, into the events of their most momentous of days.

Over the past weeks, she and Julian had spent at least a portion of every day together. Over that time, she'd constantly questioned her decision—to go forward with him and embrace love, if it came, within their marriage—but at no time had she detected even a quiver in her inner certainty or in his steadfast commitment to what had formed in her mind as their ideal.

Their definition of their perfect match.

Everything had fallen into place, exactly as if Lottie's view that their marriage was fated was, in fact, the case. The kisses and increasingly blatant caresses they'd shared had only added to that conviction.

So now she was there, and their wedding day had dawned, and soon they would be man and wife. She'd expected to feel some degree of hesitation, of uncertainty. Instead, all she felt was eagerness and an impatience to have the day done.

She was definitely looking forward to the night that would follow.

She, her parents, and the rest of the bridal party had arrived two days ago, just as the westering sun was painting the castle's stone walls in warm tones of rose-tinged gold. The castle itself, with its gatehouse, battlements, and towers, had proved to be a far more romantic, fairy-tale setting than she'd imagined it would be; on being shown around the chapel and the other reception rooms, she'd realized that Helen Delamere's excitement over witnessing a wedding there was entirely understandable.

Now, with the morning well advanced, in the large chamber allotted to her, she sat on the stool before the dressing table while her maid, Jolene, assisted by Lottie, put the finishing touches to her hair, and felt somewhat like the eye of a storm with winds of excitement and eager anticipation swirling all around her.

Eventually, with oohs and aahs and escalating anticipation in the air, Lottie and Jolene lifted the fine lace veil and draped it over the creation of curls and braids they'd confected from Melissa's long dark hair, then carefully anchored the veil in place with the pearl-encrusted combs her grandmother had loaned her.

Mandy stood on Melissa's right, critically surveying the outcome. Melissa glanced at her sister and smiled. Even faintly frowning, Mandy looked elegant in the turquoise-blue satin gown Madame Henriette had— to everyone's relief—finally fitted to perfection. Currently, Mandy was shifting from foot to foot with ill-concealed excitement.

Jolene and Lottie were fussing with the veil, determined to get the fall of the delicate fabric just so. Melissa looked into the mirror to check their progress.

Lottie was also gowned in the turquoise satin and, with her blond curls twisted into a topknot, looked significantly older than her fifteen years. She'd been delegated to act as chief flower girl in charge of the two junior flower girls and pageboy, who were Melissa's uncle Christopher's three children, the youngest trio in the wider Osbaldestone family. Under the eyes of Lottie and Melissa's brother, the trio were supposed to walk up the aisle ahead of the other bridesmaids, liberally distributing rose petals along the short nave of the chapel.

Melissa shifted her gaze and, in the mirror, studied her mother's transparently delighted expression. Her mother stood farther back in the room, but was watching the activity about the dressing table keenly. For her, this moment presaged a singular achievement. By the end of the day, she would have successfully married off both her daughters to highly desirable partis, an accomplishment few of her peers could claim. One daughter, yes, but two settled so well was rare, and her mother was as

eager and as impatient as Melissa to have the knot tied and the deed
done.

Beside her mother, Melissa's grandmother stood regally erect, her
cane anchored upright before her. Melissa scanned her grandmother's
face and saw a softness in the haughty features that wasn't often there.
Even more than Lottie, her grandmother had believed this marriage was
one of those that "should be" and was commensurately pleased and, it
seemed to Melissa, a touch triumphant, given she and Julian had first met
under her grandmother's aegis.

Melissa's second bridesmaid, her cousin Genevieve North, also clad
in a turquoise satin gown, was presently straightening the neckcloth of
Melissa's brother, Christopher. At twenty-two, Christopher had been
assigned to accompany Lottie down the aisle and assist in keeping the
younger trio in line. Given the children's natural exuberance, that would
be no idle task.

In the mirror, Melissa could just see the trio in question as they lurked
in one corner of the room. Someone had wisely set the three baskets filled
with fresh rose petals, harvested that morning by the castle gardeners
from the extensive rose garden, on top of a tall chest of drawers, out of
reach of the children. Even from the other side of the room, Melissa could
smell the luscious scent rising from the petals.

But the three children were standing, silent and still, staring down at
the floor in the far corner of the room, and Melissa found herself blessing
the farsightedness of one of her grandmother's oldest and closest friends,
Helena, Dowager Duchess of St. Ives. Helena was another of the ton's
grandes dames, and Melissa had known her socially for all her adult life.
Consequently, she hadn't been surprised when, on arriving at the castle,
her grandmother had informed her that Helena, unable to attend due to a
previous family engagement, had sent a bridal gift and delivered a large
box into Melissa's hands.

She and Julian had been stunned to discover the box contained a
squirming bundle of golden fur, a puppy who had promptly attached
himself to her.

When she'd appealed to her grandmother for an explanation of the
unusual gift, her grandmother had met her gaze and informed her that
Helena believed Melissa and Julian would have need of the puppy, and in
matters of perspicaciousness, her grandmother had learned long ago that
it never paid to argue with Helena.

Although Helena was nearly as old as Melissa's grandmother, no more than that august dame was Helena mentally failing. Melissa and Julian had accepted the gift with suitable if wary grace.

Subsequently, being of a decidedly adventuresome bent, the puppy had been dubbed Ulysses and allowed to spend time in Melissa's room; if they tried to shut him out, he would sit in the corridor outside the door and howl until admitted. Thus far, he'd behaved himself and hadn't chewed anything vital, although on more than one occasion, Jolene had had to rescue the ballroom slippers Melissa was wearing, the ones that matched her wedding gown, from the playful pup.

At that moment, Ulysses was asleep on a folded blanket in the corner of the room, actively contributing to the general peace by keeping the youngsters mesmerized. Melissa sent a mental thank-you winging Helena's way.

"There!" Lottie raised her hands and stepped back to view the results of her and Jolene's efforts. She caught Melissa's eye in the mirror and beamed. "You're simply perfect!"

There was that word again; if she'd been at all superstitious, Melissa might have been concerned.

Instead, as she slowly rose and felt the ivory silk of her gown, with its fitted bodice and draped skirt overlaid with gauzy lace studded with tiny pearls, its high waist marked by a twisted rope of larger pearls, settle around her, a sense of serene calmness descended and embraced her.

Just as well, given the flurry of excitement that gripped everyone else in the room—all except her father, who, throughout, had stood stoically watching from beside the door.

Mandy's eyes were shining. She reached out and squeezed Melissa's hand. "You look *ravishing*. Carsely is going to swallow his tongue."

Melissa laughed and turned to see her mother raise a lace-edged handkerchief to her eye. "You do look superb, my dear," she managed with a trembling smile. She waved aside her happy tears. "Don't mind me."

"Really, Henrietta." Melissa's grandmother shook her head at her eldest daughter. "Now is not the time for tears."

Yet as her redoubtable grandmother turned her way, Melissa noticed her black eyes were suspiciously shiny as well. Her grandmother looked her up and down, then nodded. "You look lovely, my dear. I believe Mandy has it right."

As Melissa stepped forward, twitching the trains of gown and veil to trail behind her, her grandmother stepped nearer, leaned close, and brushed her cheek to Melissa's. "Just remember, my dear," her grandmother murmured, "to keep that handsome husband of yours in line—at least, for the rest of the *day*."

The emphasis her grandmother placed on that last word and the knowing look in her black eyes nearly made Melissa blush.

Her grandmother stepped back and rapped her cane on the floor. "Come along now—it's time for our toast."

Melissa's father had already opened the bottle of champagne, and he poured small amounts into the crystal flutes waiting on the dresser. He handed around the glasses, then held his up and proposed, "To my darling Melissa—a happy marriage to you, my dear, and a happy life."

"Hear, hear!" came from many throats as the other adults raised their glasses.

"And don't forget the grandchildren," her mother added.

Everyone laughed and drank while the youngest trio looked on wide-eyed.

Noticing that the noise and movement had brought Ulysses out to investigate, Melissa held out her barely sipped glass to Jolene and said to the maid, "Thank you for all your help, and please don't forget to take Ulysses down to the kitchens and lock him in."

Beaming, Jolene took the glass. "Don't you worry about that scrap of fur. I won't let him wander. And I'll be there later, at the back of the chapel, to see you wed, miss—my lady." Jolene's grin widened. "I'm going to have to get used to calling you that now, aren't I?"

Melissa smiled, then Mandy clapped and called, "Form up, everyone. It's time we went down!"

Under Mandy's and her grandmother's direction, the bridal party scurried into line. Genevieve hurriedly brought Melissa her bouquet of white roses with cornflowers mixed in, then handed smaller bouquets to Mandy and Lottie and took one up herself.

Amid all the flutter, Melissa's mother and grandmother went ahead, then the procession started off, with Lottie and Christopher herding the three younger ones as the advance guard.

"No, Barton!" Lottie caught the little boy's hand. "Not yet, remember? You have to wait until we get to the churchy place—*then* you can start throwing petals on the ground."

Mandy gently lifted the front of the veil over Melissa's head and drew it down so that it screened her face. "There!" Mandy sighed. "Lottie was right—you truly are the perfect bride for this time and place."

Melissa smiled back, then Genevieve called, "Here I go!" and set off behind Lottie and Christopher.

Mandy squeezed Melissa's hand and, with a last smile, stepped out in Genevieve's wake.

Jolene had already slipped out, carrying a whining Ulysses toward the servants' stairs.

That left Melissa and her father.

He smiled, walked to her side, and offered his arm. "Well, my girl, it's finally just us. And can I say how happy I am that the others have gone ahead? So much flutter and fuss all morning isn't good for the digestion."

She laughed and, resting her hand on his sleeve, allowed him to lead her out of her chamber and along the corridor behind Mandy.

Lottie and Christopher performed a minor miracle and managed to slow the children so that the bridal party progressed in suitably stately fashion down the corridor to the gallery around the head of the main stairs. From there onward, Melissa was touched to see that their way was lined with staff, all smiling in delight at the sight of her.

She and her father paused at the top of the stairs, then once Mandy was halfway down, started down themselves. Melissa found she was smiling with genuine happiness as, with stately tread, their procession reached the front hall, then veered around into the corridor that ultimately ended in the chapel.

There were quite a few male guests lining the walls outside the chapel doors. Plainly, the chapel was packed to its limit, and the gentlemen intended to close about the doorway once the bridal party had passed and view the ceremony from there.

Everyone was smiling; there wasn't a serious or even impassive expression to be seen.

As the advance guard—the three children and Lottie and Christopher —filled the chapel's entrance, the organ swelled, and a march rang out.

The children—freed at last to fling petals willy-nilly—managed not to go too fast. All the guests turned or craned their heads to watch them with universal expressions of amused delight.

As soon as the group reached the end of the aisle, Genevieve raised her head and stepped out in a measured walk, and when she was halfway down the short aisle, Mandy fell in behind her.

Melissa drew in a slow, deep breath and finally allowed herself to look past her sister and focus on the gentleman standing straight and tall at the end of the aisle, waiting for her to join him.

He looked...exactly as she'd imagined he would in her youthful dreams. In form, in attire, he was elegance personified. His near-black hair was burnished by the light streaming through the rose window above the altar, while his gaze, steady and sure, rested unwaveringly on her.

She realized she'd forgotten to breathe again and quickly rectified the fault.

Her father patted her hand. "Well, my girl, now it's your turn. Are you ready?"

Without taking her eyes from Julian, she whispered, "Yes."

And started walking.

Julian couldn't look away as, in time with the stately music, Melissa walked down the aisle of his family's chapel and to his side.

This was a moment of triumph and of promise. And of immense relief.

As she neared, he felt blessed—amazingly, astoundingly blessed.

She was all and everything he wanted and needed; he felt faintly giddy as she covered the last few feet. When she halted a mere foot away, he drew in a much-needed breath. He couldn't drag his eyes from her face, from the glint of dark eyes he could see through the screen of her delicate veil.

She was a picture; she was a fantasy. His fantasy. And soon to be his forever more.

He held out his hand, and her father transferred her hand from his sleeve to Julian's clasp. He fought not to clench his fingers around hers and only lightly grasp.

Then he and she, together, side by side, turned to face Reverend Fairweather, who held the living of St. Mary's Church in Wirksworth and was beyond thrilled to be officiating that day.

The ceremony passed in a blur; the familiar phrases and Julian's straightforward responses required so little thought they didn't distract his senses from their fixation on his bride.

Felix and Damian stood alongside him in silent support, and when the time came, Felix produced the simple gold band, and Julian took it and slid it carefully onto Melissa's delicate finger.

And then the reverend, beaming, pronounced them man and wife.

Julian's heart leapt. He turned to Melissa and saw the same riotous mix of joy, hope, eagerness, and impatience that surged through him shining in her deep-blue eyes.

He drew her to him as she moved to close the distance. Without conscious direction, his arms encircled her and drew her closer still as he bent his head, and they kissed.

Their first kiss as husband and wife, as a couple committed to forging a shared life.

This, then, was their beginning, and he felt it in his bones.

Her lips moved beneath his, and the promise that welled in the simple caress made his head spin.

Stunned, grateful, and uplifted all at once, he raised his head, and they drew back from the kiss.

For one shining moment, there was only him and her, standing in the shaft of light that shone through the chapel's rose window in celestial benediction. Lost in the other's eyes, they savored the moment, then as the rustling of the congregation intruded, he and she shared a private smile and, as one, turned to face their world.

For the first time as Julian's countess, Melissa faced his family and hers with a mix of giddy delight, unalloyed happiness, and a deeply rooted confidence in him and herself—in their ability to make their marriage into all they wished it to be.

That confidence lived so powerfully within her, it armored her in strength and serenity as Julian wound her arm in his, and they stepped down into the nave, where their eager well-wishers waited to mob them.

In seconds, they were surrounded and being congratulated and lauded on all sides. People pressed close to kiss her cheek or her free hand, while others pressed or pumped Julian's hand or slapped him on the back.

The noise was Babel-like; it was difficult to know who said what, much less remember each encounter.

Eventually, Julian's mother—now the dowager countess—clapped her hands, and into the momentary silence, in a stentorian voice, Julian's uncle Frederick directed everyone to repair to the ballroom, "Where our celebrations will continue!"

Everyone happily fell in, and at the encouragement of all there, Julian guided Melissa to the head of the crowd, and unable to stop smiling, they led the guests out of the chapel, along the corridor into the castle's central section and—accompanied by cheers and applause from the assembled staff—on into the grand ballroom that took up the rear of that wing.

The wedding breakfast that followed proved to be a time of untrammeled joy, much to the very real relief of Julian, Melissa, Felix, and Damian, all of whom, regardless of their duties and nonstop demands on their time, beneath their genuinely delighted façades, remained alert, on guard, and ready to react.

Since Melissa's arrival at the castle, she and Julian had managed only a very short interlude together. He'd offered to show her the rose garden, an excursion their elders had thought sufficiently romantic to allow them to venture forth on alone, albeit within sight of the house. While he and she had strolled amid the rioting blooms, he'd told her about the incident in his study. She'd been horrified, but on returning to the house, the pandemonium of last-minute preparations had swept her up, and she hadn't had time to even think of the incident.

Now, as they circled the ballroom floor in the wedding waltz, she waited until they'd completed their first solo circuit and other couples had joined them so they were less on show, then with her expression still one of delighted joy, she smiled at her husband and asked, "Nothing more's happened, has it?"

Involuntarily, her hand tightened on his shoulder; she was so very grateful he'd survived the latest attack. Attack by bookcase; it was hard to credit, let alone accept.

His expression a mask of all the emotions their guests expected to see, he replied, "No. No reports of any unusual activity from anyone."

In the rose garden, he'd told her that Felix and Damian would act as his lieutenants in liaising with the small army of staff and also selected friends who had been asked to be on the lookout for what they'd vaguely described as suspicious behavior. During the reception thus far, she'd noticed that the castle butler, Phelps, as well as the butler she'd met in London, Crosby, were somewhat on edge.

She said as much and added, "Crosby, especially, seems to be trying to look everywhere at once."

"I had to leave cleaning up the detritus in the study to him and the footmen. Consequently, all the staff who came up from London to help today understand the threat is real." Julian drew her closer as they went through the turn. Once they were revolving smoothly again, his lips quirked, and he added, "Crosby seems to have taken the incident as a personal affront."

"Hmm. I can see that. Luckily, if any guests notice anything, they'll put it down to the stress of the day."

"Speaking of which, I'm starting to wonder if leaving London will have thwarted our attacker. The business in the study could have been the work of someone sneaking into the house. It's quite a different matter to sneak into the castle."

She started to frown, then remembered and banished the expression, reinstating her delighted smile. "I thought you suspected it was the work of someone on the staff."

He dipped his head in acknowledgment. "That's one possibility, but on reflection, it's just as possible someone broke in and rigged it one night."

The frown continued to threaten. "Did Crosby find any signs of a break-in?"

He shook his head. "But it's a huge old house with lots of external doors and windows with lots of different locks. It's possible someone broke in and Crosby hasn't found the evidence yet, or there wasn't enough evidence to notice."

The last notes of the waltz floated over the heads now crowding the dance floor.

Moving with easy grace, they halted, stepped apart, and Julian bowed as Melissa curtsied.

Still smiling, he raised her. As he wound her arm in his, she tipped her head close and murmured, "Perhaps now we're finally wed, the attacks will cease."

Julian met her gaze. "As we've no idea of the motivation behind them...then yes, perhaps they will."

As, with their expressions suitably relaxed and happy, they turned to meet the guests waiting to waylay them, she murmured, "You don't believe that."

"You don't, either."

She sighed. "Regardless, I've a feeling they're not going to attempt anything today—not with so many people, so much of the haut ton, in attendance. In light of that"—she threw him an openly challenging look —"might I suggest we truly relax and give ourselves over to enjoying our wedding day?"

The smile that overtook his face was entirely genuine. "Your wish is my command, my lady." With an elegant flourish, he waved. "Lead on."

She laughed and promptly did.

Her uncle Christopher and his wife, Marion, both of whom Julian had met long ago in Little Moseley, were waiting to have a word with them. With a wide grin on his face, Christopher, who was rather senior in the Foreign

Office, shook Julian's hand. "It was a surprise to learn you two knew each other from Christmases spent in Little Moseley"—releasing Julian, Christopher glanced fondly at his wife—"given that was where we met, too."

Marion smiled benevolently, then looked at Melissa. "You weren't there that year, when I chased your uncle into Hampshire."

"No." Melissa's smile deepened. She exchanged a glance with Julian. "I was busy elsewhere that year."

According to Mandy, Melissa had deliberately avoided the place in order to ensure she didn't run into him. He arched a brow at her, but she only laughed, then Christopher and Marion tendered their farewells, as they had arranged to travel on to visit Marion's brother and his family, who lived near Chesterfield.

"Going on a journey with children," Christopher informed them, "is an entirely different experience to any other form of travel."

Marion poked him in the ribs. "You're the one who plays games with them until they're so exhausted they fall asleep."

"And why," Christopher said, laughing, "do I do that?"

Marion shook her head at him. To Julian and Melissa, she said, "You'll understand when you have your own."

After exchanging handclasps and kisses, Marion swept off in search of her children, towing a smiling Christopher behind her.

The next guests to accost them were Melissa's cousins Jamie and George, along with Sir Henry Fitzgibbon, Thomas Kilburn, Roger Carnaby, and George Wiley, now Viscount Worth.

Julian and Melissa had been thrilled when they'd learned all six would be there.

Henry enthusiastically kissed Melissa's hand. "Everyone at Fulsom Hall was delighted to hear of your news. Aunt Ermintrude claims she always knew you two would wed, and Eugenia and Christian send their best."

Thomas Kilburn grinned unabashedly at Julian and Melissa. "When you two met in Little Moseley all those years ago, the rest of us always thought you'd tie the knot someday—and here we are, on that day, celebrating with you. It's like we're the wise men, and our prediction came true."

The others all nodded.

"It was fated," George, her cousin, declared. "Jamie, Lottie, and I were certain of that, even all those years ago, and apparently, Grandmama was, too, and you know she's almost always right." George grinned, then said, "Remember the Roman hoard?"

Yes," Roger Carnaby said. "Whatever happened to that?"

They spent a comfortable twenty minutes catching up with who had done what. It was evident that Jamie and George truly had been bitten by the archeological bug, and George planned to join Jamie at university with the intention of specializing in the study of antiquities.

"I hope to specialize in archeology," Jamie said. "So George's studies will complement mine." He exchanged a glance with his brother. "Who knows? Eventually, we might go on digs together."

Judging from George's expression, that was a shared dream.

The other gentlemen had visited the castle often during their school and university days and, on leaving, would head toward London, stopping in nearby Derby for the night.

In releasing Julian and Melissa to the others waiting to speak with them, Thomas companionably bumped Julian's shoulder. "You're the first of us to fall, but once you met Melissa, we expected that. Mind you"—he exchanged a suddenly sober look with the others, which they all returned —"that's not to say that any of us are lining up to follow your lead."

Julian laughed. "Good luck with that and with any plans you might harbor regarding managing your future lives. If there's one thing I've learned through our experience, it's that when it comes to love and marriage, Fate goes her own way."

George Wiley, now Lord Worth, grimaced. "I was afraid you'd say something like that."

Julian and the others clapped him on the back and teased him over being the other titled one and, therefore, higher on the matchmakers' lists than the others.

Mock frowning, George wagged a finger at Henry, Thomas, and Roger. "Titles are one thing, but you're all wealthy enough and well-connected enough to be targets. Best keep your eyes open, gentlemen!"

On that note, with laughs and grins, the group broke up.

With Melissa, Julian turned and found two of his female cousins and their husbands waiting to pay their respects.

Although both cousins were younger than he was, they were in their later twenties and already the mothers of burgeoning broods. He introduced Melissa to the two couples and was pleased to note the honest welcome the others gave his new countess.

My new countess.

The thought put a faintly silly smile on his face. His cousins' husbands noticed, but thankfully, all they did was smile understandingly. Julian decided he owed them the better brandy next time they visited.

After parting from the four, he and Melissa weathered a platoon of his relatives and connections. All were universally charming, and Melissa effortlessly charmed them back. She even engaged with Helen Delamere —and given Helen's peripatetic attention, that was no mean feat—by returning to Helen's comment when they'd met on the porch of St. George's, regarding the romantic nature of a wedding at the castle.

"Once I reached here and saw the castle and the chapel and even this ballroom"—Melissa gestured to the high, painted ceiling and the many windows giving out onto the terrace and parterre beyond—"I completely understood what you meant."

That set Helen off recounting all the specific moments of their wedding day that had struck her as particularly romantic, in the main forgetting that they had, in fact, experienced those moments themselves.

But while she might be frustrating and sometimes irritating, there was no harm in Helen, and Melissa seemed to have taken her measure.

As usual, Captain Findlay-Wright hovered at Helen's elbow. Some in the ton viewed him as a hanger-on, but Julian exchanged polite nods with him and traded inconsequential comments about the latest news from the capital. When Helen, well away describing something, flung out her arms, while Findlay-Wright looked faintly pained, Julian gave the man credit for not rolling his eyes. Regardless of any other aspect of his character, in dealing with Helen and watching over her, the man was something of a saint.

Subsequently, Julian and Melissa were bailed up by his widowed aunts, Sophie and Gertrude. Through the ensuing conversation, he realized Melissa had put in the time to learn the details of the various branches of his family tree, saving him from having to tax his memory; she knew which offspring belonged to each aunt and what those offspring —all daughters—were currently doing.

When they finally moved on and, at last, had a moment to call their own, he teased her over having done her homework. She looked at him in a haughty manner that forcibly reminded him of her grandmother. "Of course, I asked about your family. I would be a ninny if I turned up to an event such as this without the slightest clue."

He grinned and debated whether to inform her that he found her mock haughtiness arousing, but refrained; he'd sternly lectured his libido that it had to behave until they managed to escape and gain the earl's apartments.

Then his new wife dipped her head closer and admitted, "However, there was one family issue I didn't like to ask anyone else about."

He guessed. "Findlay-Wright?"

"Yes." She met his eyes. "He seems to be universally tolerated as Helen's...well, cicisbeo if nothing else, yet I understand he lives under the same roof. On the face of it, that should be deemed scandalous, yet no one seems to react in that way."

Smiling politely, he steered her clear of some distant connections they'd already spent time with and onto a route that led along the windows of the long room, angling his shoulders so it appeared he was directing her attention to sights within the gardens and park beyond. "In a nutshell, the story is this. Helen married my great-uncle Horace's only son, Maurice Delamere. He was a colonel, and about ten years after Gordon—their only child—was born, Maurice was posted to India with our troops in support of the East India Company. A few years later, Maurice was shot and killed in the field, and Helen, who was in India at the time, fell apart. On the other side of the world, where none of us could reach her or easily arrange for help.

"Findlay-Wright had been a captain under Maurice's command and, by all accounts, had become close friends with Maurice and Helen. He comes from a completely unremarkable family, a younger son of a lower gentry family sent into the army. As it happened, he was ready to sell out, and through various contacts, the family requested and Findlay-Wright agreed to accompany Helen and Maurice's body on the journey back to England."

"And by the time the pair reached London," Melissa said, "Helen and the captain were inseparable."

Still pacing slowly with their gazes trained unseeing outside, Julian inclined his head. "My uncle and aunts tell me that Helen was always a clingy, dependent female, and no one was really surprised that she turned to Findlay-Wright for support. It was she, not Findlay-Wright, who insisted he take rooms in the house Gordon has inherited, but that Helen has the use of for the rest of her life. She views it as the least she can do in gratitude for Findlay-Wright's help through her most difficult time." He paused, then added, "Having met Helen, you can imagine that coping with Maurice's death would have prostrated her, and dealing with the inevitable tasks involved in organizing for Maurice's return and all the rest would have been far beyond her."

"So Findlay-Wright stepped in," Melissa said, also looking out at the gardens.

"Indeed. And rest assured, Papa checked, but there was no hint of any sort that in doing so, Findlay-Wright had lined his own pockets. If anything, the opposite seemed true—he'd assisted Helen when she couldn't readily access funds over there."

After a moment, he went on, "So to answer your question about why no one views Findlay-Wright and his association with Helen in any scandalous light, the truth is, the family was and to this day continues to be grateful, both for what he did in India and in getting Helen home and for what he does these days, when he squires Helen about and manages to rein in her…"

Melissa supplied, "Flights of fancy?"

He nodded. "Close enough. He seems able to manage her as no one else can. In many ways, he's relieved us all of having to worry about Helen."

After a moment, Melissa nodded. "Thank you for explaining. That now makes sense. I simply couldn't see them as lovers."

Julian huffed. "Unsurprisingly, no one else can, either, which has rather stymied the gossips."

They reached the end of the long line of windows. Melissa tightened her hold on his arm and turned to survey the guests. "Now that we've done our duty by family and close friends"—she cast an arch look at him —"are you ready to face the powers that be?"

He knew to whom she referred. By anyone's standards, this wedding, linking her family with his, was a major haut ton event, and the powerful, both in society and in politics, were very much in attendance.

He sighed and, resuming his relaxed and charming façade, bowed. "Lead on, my lady." He doubted he'd ever get tired of saying that.

Arm in arm, they did the rounds, stopping to chat with the major hostesses and their spouses, then moving on to exchange comments and observations on the issues of the day with the senior men in the Home Office and also the Foreign Office, who had come to witness a marriage that merged two families, each of which had served one or other office for many years.

Ultimately, Julian and Melissa found themselves in the rarefied company of a highly elite group that included the two most powerful viscounts in the land—Castlereagh and Sidmouth, respectively the Secretary of State for Foreign Affairs and the Home Secretary.

Despite the company, they held their own with commendable ease. Julian discovered that his new wife was entirely comfortable in Castlereagh's presence, and if she could manage the often-difficult statesman with such ready aplomb, he needn't fear she would require his protection at any political gatherings.

The presence of the Earl of Liverpool, Prime Minister and Leader of the House of Lords, who had earlier waylaid them to deliver a few quiet words encouraging Julian to become rather more engaged with political affairs than his late father had been, made it certain that attending further political gatherings was, indeed, in their cards.

When they'd paid their respects to all who had traveled to Derbyshire to see them wed and, arm in arm, strolled on, Julian dipped his head to Melissa's and murmured, "It's as if by marrying, in their minds, you and I have stepped onto their stage."

She whispered, "I know what you mean. I might have expected their attitude to gradually change as we, as a couple, become better known among their set, but it seems they've already made up their minds about us—about what they expect of us socially and politically."

He nodded. "They've already decided that we're on their level and that we're a couple to watch."

"I agree—we appear to have been accorded a status that should have taken years to achieve."

He met her eyes. "I seriously doubt either of us could have claimed that status on our own, meaning if we'd married some other person." He glanced around. "The breadth and depth of our consolidated background in both social and political spheres derives from both of us, and apparently, that's catapulted us to a prominence few just-married couples could command."

Felix ambled up. They paused as he joined them and, with an easy smile, said, "Absolutely nothing untoward has happened. No hint of anything even vaguely disturbing."

Damian arrived from the opposite direction in time to hear Felix's report. Damian nodded. "Not a whiff of anything remotely nefarious. Either the villain's lying low, or he isn't here."

Julian inclined his head. "Thank you for playing captains of the guard."

Felix smiled, and Damian flashed Julian and Melissa a grin. "Actually, it quite made my day."

The sound of clapping drew their attention to the musicians' dais at the far end of the room. His mother stood there; it was she who had clapped. As everyone paused in their conversations and looked her way, she announced, "Our musicians have done us proud." She turned toward the quartet and applauded, and the assembled company joined her. "But now," she went on, "they must leave us, so this will be the last dance of our wonderful afternoon."

Looking over the crowd, she spotted Julian and Melissa and extended her hand in invitation. "Won't you lead the way, my dears?"

As the musicians put bow to string and the opening chords of a waltz wafted through the ballroom, smiling easily, Julian swung Melissa around, bowed elegantly, then raised her from her curtsy and drew her into his arms, and in perfect accord, they stepped out and revolved across the floor.

Other couples followed. After several moments, Melissa looked into Julian's face and, still smiling, said, "I heard several of the grandes dames declare that this has been the perfect wedding for us, their perfect couple."

He let his smile deepen. "Sadly, I can't see us losing that label any time soon."

She shook her head in resignation, yet she was smiling as he whirled them on.

A sense of gladness, of almost magical assurance that all was well—indeed, *perfect*—on this, their special day, took hold. The feeling was so complete, so certain, it escalated his protectiveness—the compulsion to protect what they had at all costs—and had him surreptitiously scanning the room for any potential threat. Even though not a ripple of danger had reached them, the need to protect what they'd already fostered and grown lingered.

At last, as the music faded and they halted, bowed and curtsied, then, once more, turned to the company, their mothers advanced on them, declaring it was time for them to retire.

Sweeter words, he'd never heard.

First, however, Melissa had to ceremonially toss her bouquet to a hopeful crowd comprised of all the unmarried young ladies.

Her mother handed her the bouquet, while the dowager said, "It will work best on the main stairs."

She waved Julian and Melissa toward the front hall and, as they left, hand in hand and grinning as they hurried off, the other guests noticed, heard his mother's announcement, and rushed to follow.

Even those already married—indeed, the bulk of the remaining guests —joined in, eager to watch the fun. The exodus from the ballroom only added to the escalating excitement.

Julian led Melissa halfway up the first flight of the grand staircase. "From here," he said as he halted and turned her.

Smiling widely, Melissa swung to view the crowd of eager ladies rapidly forming at the base of the stairs.

Standing beside her, Julian murmured, "Best wait until they're all here, then close your eyes and lob it their way."

Melissa dutifully waited until the gathering at the bottom of the stairs was no longer growing, then scanned the upturned faces and arched a brow. "Ready?"

"Yes!" came from many throats, while others nodded.

She closed her eyes, paused, then using both hands, tossed the bouquet high above the assembled heads.

Squeals rang out, and she opened her eyes and watched the bouquet descend—into the hands of a frankly startled Genevieve.

Melissa laughed delightedly and flung a kiss Genevieve's way.

Julian caught and squeezed her hand, and she glanced at him. Smiling, he met her eyes. "Time to take our leave."

She looked down at the wider crowd; virtually all the guests were there.

Julian raised his free hand, and everyone quieted and waited expectantly.

"Thank you all for coming and being a part of our day."

Inspired, Melissa raised her voice and added, "Your company—each and every one of you—helped make this day complete."

"But now, it's time for us to bid you adieu." He raised their linked hands. "We hope you enjoy the rest of your day. We certainly intend to enjoy the rest of ours."

Melissa swallowed a gasp. *Really?* But she was already turning.

Julian released her only to allow her to turn, then seized her hand, and they hurried up the stairs, followed by laughter, cheers, catcalls, and the inevitable shouted recommendations. The noise faded as they rushed down the long corridor deep into the central wing.

Relief struck, and suddenly feeling gay and carefree, she tipped back her head and laughed, and smiling more unrestrainedly, more genuinely than he had until then, he laughed with her.

The day had been glorious, and now, at last, the public part of it was over and done, and they could set aside their polished, sophisticated masks and simply be themselves. Now, at last, they would have the peace, the silence, the privacy to turn their full focus on themselves. On each other. On being together.

To explore and appreciate what the day had wrought.

They were in the family wing, an area of the castle into which she hadn't previously ventured.

Julian pointed to doors nearer the gallery as belonging to Felix's and Damian's rooms, but he led her on, all the way to the double doors at the corridor's end.

His hand on the doorknob, he caught her eye. "The earl's apartments." He set the door swinging and gestured her inside. "Now yours as well."

She walked into a small foyer with an archway on the right and a closed door to the left. She passed through the archway and found herself in a comfortable sitting room, well-lit by large windows that caught a sliver of golden light cast by the westering sun. The furniture was oak, the upholstery green leather, with the curtains and tasseled cushions in a darker shade of green. A large fireplace with a sculpted overmantel provided a focus for the grouping of armchairs and sofa, although no fire presently burned in the grate.

Melissa crossed to the nearer window and looked out, orienting herself. The room filled one corner at the end of the wing, and that window, on the room's longer side, looked out on a section of the formal parterre, bordered by trees beyond which green fields stretched away to end in distant woodland. She moved to the window at the wing's end, through which the sunshine presently lanced, and discovered a view of lush lawns that extended to a line of large, established trees edging denser woods.

She glanced around. It was a restful room, serene yet with signs of being lived in; there were books left on the occasional tables, and a well-stocked tantalus sat against one wall.

The fireplace was the dominant feature in the long interior wall, and to either side of the mantel stood doors that, presumably, led to the rooms that occupied the other half of that end of the wing.

She glanced at Julian.

Smiling, he waved her to the door closer to the windows. "The countess's bedchamber is through there." He pointed at the other door. "That leads to the earl's bedroom." He met her gaze. "But I don't plan on using it much."

She tried to smother her smile, but failed.

He waved between the doors. "We each have bathing chambers and dressing rooms between."

She couldn't control her curiosity any longer. She walked to the door to her new bedchamber and pushed it wide. She halted on the threshold and let her eyes feast.

She felt him approach, then he halted behind her, wrapped his arms about her waist, and holding her against him, lowered his chin to her shoulder. "Your mother told me those were your favorite colors, but of course, you can make whatever changes you wish."

She drank in the buttery tones of golden oak that formed the perfect complement for curtains and upholstery in a fabulous pattern featuring her favorite dark blue and turquoise, with accents of grass green, swirled together in a stylized pattern. The base on which the intricately sweeping colors had been laid was a very pale sky blue. She'd never seen anything like it.

As if reading her mind, he murmured, "I had them create the pattern just for you. There isn't another even similar."

Her heart swelled as her gaze roved over the large, four-poster bed, hung with curtains of heavy silk printed in her pattern. Two wing chairs were angled before the fireplace, and a love seat sat facing the window at the end of the room, which also looked out on the lawns, trees, and woods.

Two large windows flanked the bed. The curtains, which matched those on the bed, had been left open, and she glimpsed a view of rising wooded hills in the distance; given the orientation, she suspected the nearer view would include the castle's rose garden.

She drew in a long, slow breath, then she turned in Julian's arms. Resting her hands on his shoulders, she looked into his gray eyes, took in their watchful, waiting expression, then let her lips curve in her most glorious smile. "Thank you." She hoped he could hear that the words came from her heart. "This is…just *wonderful*."

His lips quirked, and he arched a brow. "Perfect?"

She laughed and conceded, "Yes, husband mine—this is, indeed, perfect."

"Good." Without waiting for more—he'd waited long enough—Julian bent his head and kissed her. Not as he'd kissed her before the altar but passionately, letting all he felt for her—all he desired—well and pour through him and infuse the exchange.

Unleashed, ardor raged, and with lips and tongue, she met him, her hands rising to frame his face and hold him to the kiss—not that he was going anywhere.

He waltzed her step by step into the room, pausing only to blindly reach behind him and send the door swinging shut. Then he caught her to him, flagrantly molded her hips to his, and felt the flames of passion burn.

She was as eager as he, as committed and determined to claim this, to take the next inevitable step on the road they'd started down so long ago.

Heat built, and desire grew and compelled them. Burgeoning hunger drove them on. Caresses grew more intent, more explicit, more laden with hunger and need, pushing them past the inevitable fumbling as, with neither willing to break from the kiss, he reached round her and undid the tiny pearl buttons that ran down her spine.

Finally, the last slid free. She didn't wait for him to brush the puffed sleeves from her shoulders but freed her arms, then pushed the gown down to pool about her ankles.

Through the haze of lust fogging his brain, he recalled just how delicate the fabric of her wedding gown was and seized the excuse to wrap his arms around her and lift her, freeing her feet of the puddle of silk, lace, and pearls, then he carried her to the bed.

He halted by the bed's side, eased his hold, and let her slide, sensuous and wanton, down his body. He was already rock-hard and aching, and the sensations the contact sent surging through him made him suck in a breath.

On her feet, she broke from the kiss to fall on his clothes in a near-ravenous frenzy. Not that he attempted to dissuade her. Quite the opposite. He shrugged out of his coat and flung it aside, then rapidly sent his waistcoat the same way.

She'd managed to unknot his cravat. She slid the long band from about his neck, tossed it away, and fell on his shirt. The instant she drew the tails free of his waistband, he brushed her hands aside and stripped the linen off over his head.

As the garment slid from his fingers to the floor, he realized his mistake.

Her eyes gleamed, midnight dark, as she set her palms to his heated skin.

He closed his eyes and bit back a groan as she spread her fingers and sculpted, then played.

For one long moment, eyes still closed, he wrestled with his demons, but he'd held them at bay for far too long, and really, where was the need?

There was no real reason to slow down, to try to manage her—to manage this.

Then she pressed close, reached up, framed his face and drew it down, and kissed him—with longing and yearning and urgent entreaty—and all prospect of control vanished.

With her lips and tongue, she spoke to him—all of him—and lured. She moved against him in innocent seduction, her tightly peaked breasts pressing into his chest, with only a thin layer of silk gauze separating skin from skin.

He responded and reached for her, angled his head, and took the lead in the kiss, in the raging, out-of-control incitement to plunder.

He took her mouth and sent his hands to claim her body. Savoring each curve, exploring every hollow.

Soon, her chemise, garters, and stockings were gone, and her skin felt like silk beneath his palms.

Ridding himself of his trousers, shoes, and socks was the work of seconds, then together, they fell on the bed.

They both had long legs, which tangled and slid against each other's as they rolled and explored, and hunger rose and demanded its due.

By unvoiced agreement, they did their best to stave off the inevitable long enough to satisfy their mutual craving to know and be known. To trace and lick and savor all that gave delight, every tactile pleasure.

But the flames were unstoppable, the pressure to race to completion undeniable, and when, gasping, she tugged him over her, he surrendered to the relentless drive.

He sheathed himself in her, and she caught her breath, clamping hard about him, but almost immediately, her instinctive reaction faded. From beneath heavy lids, she caught his gaze, then deliberately, with a challenge he couldn't mistake, she moved suggestively beneath him.

It was his turn to have his lungs seize, then the whirlpool of sensations—of her luscious body clasping his erection, of her soft silken flesh sliding against his harder frame—crashed through him, and he responded to her invitation, withdrew and thrust in again, and rode her.

The age-old dance caught them up and swept them away, and although she was a novice, the moves came easily, naturally—*perfectly*.

Melissa clung to sanity, awash on a sea of sensation. Her body rocked beneath his in a rhythm it seemed to instinctively know, while the tactile sensations welled and swelled and all but overloaded her mind.

Glorious.

She now understood the whispers, the eagerness of ladies who had indulged, like Mandy and her married friends.

She'd known the theory, of course, but the practice was so much more. So much more alluring, appealing, and altogether consuming.

She gave herself up to it—drank in every moment, every sensation—and luxuriated in a feeling that in this, through this, she'd somehow attained a freedom she hadn't known was there to be claimed.

The passion, the heat, the hunger all built, driven even more relentlessly by their joining.

The compulsion to cling, to hold tight and fly, to reach and strive drove her on, and he was with her every step of the way. A tension she'd never known before coiled deep in her belly, ratcheting tighter with every powerful thrust, every flex of his long body over hers.

Then something sparked deep inside, and sensation intensified, spread and grew, then gripped hard and abruptly released—and she felt as if she flew.

Her senses broke apart, disintegrated, and she lost touch with the world.

He gave a low groan, and she sensed him joining her as his body went rigid in her arms.

They hung there, in that altered state of being, and whether for seconds or minutes, she couldn't tell.

But they were together, fused and joined in a way that seemed to reach to their souls.

That forged them into the perfect match so many were sure they were.

Her lips lightly curved at the thought.

The flames faded, and all tension gone, he slumped upon her, and she held him in her arms, glorying in the sense of closeness.

Of intimacy as it was meant to be.

She closed her eyes and savored.

～

Some time later, Julian managed to summon sufficient wit and strength to relieve Melissa of his weight. He grunted softly, disengaged, and lifted from her.

They disentangled themselves, then reoriented themselves on the bed, and he lifted the covers over them, and they settled.

Sleepily, she rolled on her side toward him, raised a hand, and traced her fingers down his cheek. She let her hand slide away and sighed, the sound redolent with contented satiation. "That was...amazing."

He felt the same. He laughed softly, caught her hand, raised her fingers to his lips, and pressed a gentle kiss to the tips. "Amazing and..."

When he didn't finish the sentence, she murmured, "Amazing and what?"

He stared up at the canopy and, eventually, said, "Amazing and glorious."

"Hmm." She was falling asleep.

He angled his head and brushed a kiss to her forehead. "It was perfect," he whispered and meant it.

She softly humphed, but she was already sliding into slumber.

He studied her face, lit by the glow of sunset falling through the uncurtained windows.

He watched sleep claim her and, with his eyes, traced every feature.

Beloved.

That was what she was to him. He'd known that in the instant he'd first seen her all those years ago.

And now she was here, sharing her bed with him, and everything he'd thought he'd known of intimacy had changed.

He hadn't lived the life of a hermit. Quite the opposite. He'd had more women than he could count, all of whom had been far more experienced than she, yet in terms of intensity, this encounter put every past interlude to shame.

He'd been going to say "Amazing and eye-opening," but then she would have asked what had surprised him.

The difference love made—that being in love made—was what had accomplished that, but the understanding was new to him, and he wanted to dwell on it. To define and appreciate it—and to embrace it.

He was very aware that the togetherness he and she already shared and would share going forward was something few of their peers ever had the chance to claim.

That instinctive togetherness was what had already set them apart in the eyes of the more experienced in society.

The most important, most immediately relevant element in his newfound understanding was that their togetherness—their marriage and the love that was its foundation—was precious.

Precious and worthy of being protected at any and all cost.

CHAPTER 10

*T*wo evenings later, having returned from Derbyshire with his plans solidly in place, the man with designs on the Earl of Carsely's life settled in his favorite armchair before his sitting room's empty grate and calmly took stock.

"A pity, perhaps, that no suitable moment arose while I was there." He considered that, then resignedly grimaced. There'd been far too many people on watch—the staff, even some of the guests. Within minutes of arriving, he'd noted the heightened tension. He'd been far too wise to fall into such a trap.

"That said, now they're wed, the clock is definitely ticking."

He pondered that, weighing the possibilities against all he already had in place, and concluded that, regardless, there was still plenty of time for his plan to roll forward and, indeed, no reason to act precipitously and risk exposure.

Indeed, it would serve him better to allow the happy couple a few days to relax, to get comfortable and forget about the previous incidents and imagine, consciously or unconsciously, that the threat had passed. That they were safe and could lower their guard.

"Yes," he murmured, eyes glinting in the lamplight. "That is clearly the course of wisdom."

He had his pawns in place. They would obey his orders; he didn't need to fear they would hesitate, regardless of any reluctance they might feel.

He smiled coldly. He had them all well and truly harnessed, and the reins were in his hands.

That had been the one task he had been able to accomplish while at the castle. He'd met with each of his carefully selected agents and given them their orders. Each knew what he expected of them, and he'd made sure that each had also understood the price of not acting as he wished.

As ever, his planning was thorough. He had multiple routes forward, multiple chances to achieve success. As per his directions, his people—his pawns—would progressively work through each gambit, and eventually, ultimately, one would work, and he would win through.

He smiled, the gesture chilling. "Patience." Soon, his path ahead would be clear, and he could concentrate on pulling the strings that, ultimately, would give him access to the earldom's coffers.

And that would be so very satisfying.

It would be the pinnacle of his life's achievements.

He considered the prospect, then nodded to himself. "Playing a long game always works."

~

Five days after the wedding—after four days of blissful married life—Melissa rode beside Julian as they returned to the stable at the end of their morning ride.

They clattered into the yard and drew rein. She waited, watching appreciatively as Julian, who had ridden Argus, his fabulous black Arab, lithely swung down from the saddle. After handing Argus's reins to Mitchell, the middle-aged groom who'd come out to attend them, Julian walked to the side of Melissa's neat bay mare. She freed her boots from her side-saddle's stirrup. He caught her gaze as he reached up, closed his hands about the midnight-blue velvet encasing her waist, and lifted her down.

As he set her on her feet, she beamed at him. "Every time we go riding, I'm grateful all over again for your gift." Rosa, the bay mare, had been one of his wedding gifts to her.

A slow smile broke over his handsome face. He raised a hand and plucked a piece of bark from her hair. "I know. Just as I know that, at some point in the day, I'll find myself exceedingly grateful for your gratitude."

She humphed and hoped she wasn't blushing.

"Come back here, you wretched beast!"

They both turned to see Ulysses scampering toward her as fast as his stubby legs would carry him with Hockey and two stable lads in hot pursuit.

They'd left the puppy confined in a stall after he'd twice tried to track her after she'd ridden out, causing consternation among the staff, who had had to catch and carry him back.

Ulysses reached her and reared up to place his paws on her skirt.

Melissa crouched and patted him. "It's all right." She smiled up at Hockey as he came to a puffing halt. "He's found me."

His hands on his hips as he caught his breath, Hockey apologized. "He heard Rosa's hoofbeats, and I swear he knew it was you coming in. Squirmed between two boards and got out of the stall, and then nothing would do for it but that he had to come racing out to you."

Melissa smiled at the puppy, who was trying to crawl into her lap, and stroked his silky head. "You're a clever one."

Hockey huffed. "Don't encourage him." He fished in his pocket and hauled out a length of rein. "Here." He held it out. "I fashioned a ring clip on the end to go around his neck—I can let it out as he grows—and there's a loop for you to hold at the other end. That way, you can take him for walks in the garden without him scenting a rabbit and getting away from you again. I made it long enough to allow him to run a bit, but if he gets in trouble, you'll be able to haul him back."

"Thank you." Smiling gratefully, Melissa took the leading rein, swiftly examined it, then crouched and fastened the makeshift collar around Ulysses's neck, avoiding the puppy's attempts to catch and chew the leather. Once the collar was secure, she rose and let the lead play out. Ulysses sat for a moment as if catching his breath, possibly contemplating what the strange thing around his neck was, then he streaked off to fling himself on Julian's boots.

Julian laughed, bent, and patted the golden bundle, then straightened and waved Melissa toward the house. "Let's see how he behaves on the rein."

With a last smile for Hockey, Melissa swept up the train of her velvet riding skirt into the crook of one arm, then let the rein play out and walked beside Julian along the path that led to the castle's side terrace.

They strolled, allowing Ulysses to scamper about. He quickly learned the limits of the rein, and by the time they reached the terrace steps, he was more or less keeping pace with Melissa, stopping to sniff and snuffle, but responding to the lightest tug, entirely happy to remain within her orbit.

Melissa halted before the steps and looked assessingly at Ulysses. "I was going to go up and change, but I suspect he's been napping while we were out. It might be best to take him for his walk now."

Julian nodded. "That might also assist in fixing the notion of being on a lead into his doggy brain."

Melissa laughed, then cocked her head and looked at him questioningly. "Are you going to join us?"

He hesitated, clearly torn, then sighed. "Hagerson sent up some contracts I need to review and sign and get back to him as soon as possible. I'd better get started on them before lunch, or I won't get through them today, and I really should."

"Never mind. Ulysses will keep me safe." She saw concern infuse the clear gray of Julian's eyes and smiled reassuringly. "Don't worry. We'll stick to the gardens and be back within the half hour." She looked at Ulysses. "His little legs probably won't last even that long."

Julian nodded. "All right. Stay safe." He bent his head, and she lifted hers, and they exchanged a swift, sweet kiss.

Then she smiled, waved, and stepped out along the path around the terrace to the lawn beyond.

She felt Julian's gaze resting on her, then heard the sound of his boots go quickly up the steps. A second later, the terrace door clicked shut.

Ulysses had scampered ahead, but now came gamboling back.

"Well"—she shook the rein—"apparently, it's just us, so where should we go today?"

Ulysses wasn't the only one still exploring their new home. Intent on furthering her knowledge of the extensive gardens, she'd taken to walking a different section each day. She looked around. She'd already been through the rose garden and had walked the lawn leading down to the river on the castle's other side. Although walking trails through the home woods beckoned, she wasn't game to take Ulysses that far yet, and she had said she would stay within the gardens. "The shrubbery, then."

She headed for the high green hedges that screened the stables from the house. Ulysses gamboled hither and yon, venturing out, then returning.

As she strolled across the well-kept lawn, she reviewed the past few days. From her first morning as Julian's countess, everything had rolled on remarkably smoothly. Step by step, she was settling into the role, in no small part thanks to Veronica and also Frederick, who still lived at the castle, which, indeed, had always been his home.

Frederick and "Veronica's boys," as she termed her sons, got along well. There was no friction between the members of the family living at the castle, which was something of a relief. Indeed, Melissa had yet to detect friction of any sort between anyone at all. All the senior staff had been in their positions for decades, and most had been born and raised on the estate. It was that sort of household, deeply rooted in the local community, and she knew enough to be grateful for that, too. No friction made life for everyone that much more relaxing.

With Veronica's help and active encouragement, Melissa had been steadily taking up the reins of the castle household and learning a little of the London household along the way. She was also pleased that Jolene, the only staff Melissa had brought with her, had been welcomed into the castle staff with no bother at all.

That didn't always happen, any more than a new mistress easily settling into a home with an already established household.

As she and Ulysses reached the entrance to the shrubbery, she smiled and informed him, "I've been blessed."

She certainly felt that way as she strolled down the path delineated by the dense green walls. She reached a grassy rectangular clearing hosting a stone-edged lily pond with a stone bench placed at one end, perfect for quiet reflection. But with a puppy on a leash, reflection would have to wait.

Four archways, one at each corner of the rectangle, framed paths leading away from the clearing. She'd walked in along one, but had no idea where the others went. After resettling her heavy train more firmly in her bent arm, she allowed Ulysses, nose to the ground, apparently tracking some animal, to tug her through the nearest archway and along another green-walled avenue.

The path turned right, then left, then twenty feet farther on, turned left again.

Straining at the makeshift leash, snuffling nonstop, Ulysses swung around the corner. She followed—only to almost trip over the puppy, who had halted in the center of the path, legs splayed, a whiny growl issuing from his throat.

She frowned. "What's the matter?" She looked along the grassy path as the tone of Ulysses's growl deepened. The path ran straight on, ending in another grassy enclosure. "There's nothing there."

Ulysses thought differently; his growl rose to a whiny yelp, and he turned tail and dashed back the way they'd come.

"Wait!" She swung around, dropping her train to grab the leash with both hands.

Clap!

The sudden sound so close behind her had her whirling back—to discover the train of her riding skirt clamped in the steel jaws of a trap.

The leash jerked taut, but she held on as she stared at the torn and crumpled fabric mangled between the metal teeth.

A chill brushed her nape.

She drew in a steadying breath, then another, then she leaned to the side, far enough to look up the path they'd followed from the pond.

Ulysses was sitting facing her with a determined look on his furry face. She gently tugged, but he refused to budge.

"That's all right. Stay there." It was probably better that he remained at a distance rather than bouncing around her feet. She studied the trap. Why it was there was a question she thrust aside. More important was how to get free. There had to be some way of releasing the jaws.

She crouched and tugged at her train. It was ripped and ruined, yet even yanking hard, she couldn't drag it free of the trap's teeth. Gingerly, she tried to ease the jaws apart, but the force holding them shut was simply too powerful.

If it hadn't been for Ulysses's superior senses and his instincts, and him trusting them and acting as he had, he and very likely she would have been seriously hurt. Small as he was, he would likely have died, and she could easily have lost part of her foot or even her leg.

Given the distance the shrubbery was from the house, she might even have bled to death.

She swallowed and, closing her eyes, breathed in and slowly out, pushing down the fear that tried to choke her.

Thanks to Ulysses, he and she hadn't walked into the trap.

Clinging to the fact that they were both unharmed, she opened her eyes, drew in one last steadying breath, then rose and, avoiding looking at the trap, leaned across to look along the grassy avenue to where Ulysses still stubbornly sat. Grimly, she studied him. "Now what?"

As if he understood her, the puppy tipped back his head and let out a long howl.

Given his size, the sound was surprisingly loud and clearly the canine equivalent of "Help!"

He paused only to fill his lungs, then repeated the call.

She started to hope. The gardeners would be somewhere about, and the shrubbery wasn't all that far from the stable.

The next time Ulysses paused, during the momentary silence, she raised her own voice. "Help!"

Ulysses seemed to think that meant they were in competition and threw himself into howling even louder and longer.

She continued to add her voice to his chorus, and within minutes, she heard voices in the distance. Even though she couldn't make out the words, she could sense the consternation. The voices drew nearer, and she yelled, "I'm here—in the shrubbery!"

Ulysses let out a series of high-pitched yips and stood and turned to face the other way.

"Where?" Julian called from somewhere close.

She felt faint with relief. "Down the path leading from the northeast corner of the lily pond court!"

Ulysses was yipping and bouncing, adding to her directions.

Then a bevy of people came rushing down the avenue, Julian in the lead, with Felix close behind, and Hockey and the head groundsman and several grooms and undergardeners following.

As they neared, Melissa held up her hands in warning. "Don't step around the corner. There's a trap. It caught my train, and I'm stuck."

The looks of concern on everyone's faces grew even starker.

Julian reached her and swept her into his arms, crushing her to him. Feeling the tug on the back of her gown, he looked around her and down. "What the devil…?" A second later, his stunned incredulity was swamped by a thunderous expression. "Edgerton. Hockey. What the devil is a mantrap doing in the shrubbery?"

"What?" Edgerton was the head groundsman. Frowning, he pushed past Felix—who had reached Melissa and Julian and was also goggling at the trap—and stared down at the metal jaws. "Good God!" After a moment, he glanced at Hockey. "We haven't had any mantraps on the estate for…how long?"

"At least a decade." Hockey leaned to peer past Felix, then his face set in grim lines, and he looked at Julian. "Your father got rid of them all years ago."

"That's what I thought." Julian forced himself to haul in a deep breath, rein in his reactions, and focus on the fact that Melissa was unharmed and in his arms, alive and well; he told himself to cling to that.

Edgerton had crouched and was examining the trap. "This wasn't here when we went through with the scythes day before yesterday. Couldn't've been—we tramped all over this path."

When Edgerton looked at Julian, clearly waiting for direction, he managed a nod. "We'll worry about where it came from later. The first thing we need to do is to free the countess."

Ulysses had followed Julian to Melissa and now plonked his rear on Julian's boot.

He glanced at the pup. "Lucky he didn't come around the corner first."

"He did." Melissa looked at Ulysses. "If it wasn't for him, I would most likely have walked into it." She explained how the puppy had reacted, how he'd fled and forced her to turn, releasing her train.

Edgerton reached out and patted the pup on the head. "*Good* dog." Then he looked up and said, "Seems like the trigger's been set too light, which in this case, ended well, because the weight of her ladyship's train was enough to spring the trap."

"Be that as it may, now that it's sprung, how do we release it?" Julian's question had Edgerton and Hockey conferring, then both sent grooms and undergardeners running for various tools.

The exodus allowed Julian to see his mother, who had followed him and Felix from the house, but had hung back some way along the path. Despite the distance, he could see she was white-faced and, judging from the way her hands were tightly gripped, deeply rattled and upset.

Luckily, Frederick had followed as well; although also shocked, he'd remained by Veronica's side. Julian caught Frederick's gaze, glanced at his mother, then looked back.

Frederick nodded. Gently, he touched Veronica's arm. "My dear, Julian and the others have this well in hand, and Melissa, it seems, is unharmed."

Realizing what was happening, Melissa, who'd been watching Edgerton and Hockey work their way around the trap, freeing it from the turf that had been laid over it to conceal it, looked at Veronica and Frederick, smiled, and called, "I truly am unhurt, Veronica. Quite unharmed."

Julian saw his mother drag in a breath.

"That's a relief to hear, dear," Veronica replied.

"Perhaps," Frederick suggested, "we might return to the house and order some tea. I'm sure Melissa will want some once she's free."

"I will, indeed," Melissa confirmed. She glanced at Julian, then at

Felix, who had crouched and was helping Hockey and Edgerton. "Once we have this sorted out, I daresay we'll all want some tea. And perhaps some cake as well?"

Veronica nodded with something of her customary decisiveness. "I'll see to it. Join us in the parlor as soon as you can."

Julian watched Frederick offer Veronica his arm and was relieved when she took it and allowed Frederick to lead her toward the castle.

Julian returned his gaze to the mantrap Edgerton, Hockey, and Felix had unearthed. It didn't require any great effort to imagine what might have been.

The vision chilled him to the core.

Although he'd eased his compulsive grip, he kept his arms loosely around Melissa as two undergardeners and a groom rushed up, carrying crowbars, picks, shovels, and several screwdrivers.

Edgerton took charge, and at his direction, the men heaved and strained and prized the jaws half open. Edgerton poked a screwdriver into the mechanism, then grunted, "Got it," and the jaws relaxed and settled apart.

Melissa reached down and, with Felix's help, lifted her wrecked train from the steel teeth.

Edgerton, who had continued to work on the mechanism, sat back and nodded. "That's fixed it. I've unscrewed the spring. It can't be made to snap shut again." He waved to his men. "You can lift it now—it's safe."

Although the two groundsmen took him at his word, they nevertheless avoided the sharp metal teeth. But Edgerton was an old hand and knew what he was about; when the pair hoisted the contraption free of the ground, the heavy spring rolled out, and the jaws remained wide and inert.

Everyone breathed silent sighs of relief.

As Edgerton levered to his feet, Julian caught his eye. "Can you and Hockey examine the thing—see if you can get some idea of where it came from?"

Both men nodded. "We'll take a good long look, my lord," Edgerton assured him, "but I doubt there'll be anything useful."

Julian accepted that with a nod. "Let me know if you find anything or have any other ideas. Once you've finished examining it, take it apart. I don't want it to be useable again."

"Aye, we'll do that," Hockey said. "Terrible things, mantraps."

The undergardeners carrying the trap, along with the groom with most of the tools, had already trudged back up the path. With nods to Julian, Melissa, and Felix, Hockey and Edgerton followed, heads together as they discussed mantraps.

Julian turned to find Melissa examining her train. "It's ruined," he said.

Melissa gathered the ripped and marked velvet into the crook of her elbow. "I'll get Jolene to cut the damaged bits off and rehem it. That will do for now. I'll send to Madame Henriette to have another riding skirt made and sent up."

He nodded, then looked down at Ulysses. In the wake of too much excitement, the pup had curled up and fallen asleep at Julian's feet.

He sighed, bent, and scooped up the bundle of golden fur. As he settled the puppy in one arm, Ulysses woke, but only to sleepily register who was carrying him. Then he yawned widely, tucked his head down again, snuffled, sighed mightily, and fell silent.

Julian took Melissa's hand, and without another word, he, she, and Felix headed back along the path.

By the time they reached the lily pond, Ulysses had decided that he didn't like being carried by someone who was walking. He wriggled and squirmed until Julian set him down.

Still on the leading rein but heading in the right direction, the pup started to quest about. When they walked out of the shrubbery and started across the lawn toward the rear terrace, he was nosing several yards ahead of them, at the limit of the leash.

Abruptly, Ulysses's head came up. He halted, alert, standing and staring at the line of trees that bordered the woods. His body quivered, as if unsure whether to dart back to Melissa and safety or stand his ground. Then he started barking, clearly in warning, darting a few steps, then retreating, but with his attention fixed on the woods.

Julian, Melissa, and Felix halted and rapidly scanned the shadows.

"There!" Melissa pointed to a figure flitting deeper into the woods. Eyes narrowed, she squinted. "Isn't that our mystery man?"

Julian and Felix looked.

Then Felix shook his head. "I didn't see him."

Julian grunted. "I did, but not well enough to identify him." He looked at Melissa.

She sighed. "He's vanished. Again."

"Are you sure it was him?' Julian asked.

She hesitated, then nodded. "He was the man we saw outside the theater and at Richmond."

Felix looked at Julian. "It must have been him who set the trap."

His expression grimly frustrated, Julian shook his head. "No. If he's here for the reason I suspect, then I seriously doubt he set the trap. If he or whoever he represents wants my help with something—and I'm increasingly certain that's why he's stalking me—then he would hardly wish to harm me."

Felix frowned. "But—"

Julian held up a staying hand. "However, I've had more than enough of playing hide-and-seek. He won't get far on foot, and the chances are good that he's putting up somewhere within easy reach." After one last glance at the woods—now empty—he waved toward the castle. "Come on." He started walking again.

Melissa kept pace as they walked briskly toward the terrace. "What do you plan to do?" By now, she knew him well enough to know that he'd come to a decision.

He threw her a swift, sidelong glance, then looked toward the castle. "I'm the local magistrate. After discovering a mantrap set in my shrubbery, no one will be surprised if I conduct a sweep of the immediate area and haul in any man unknown to the locals for questioning. The assumption will be that it's about the trap, and that will serve as the perfect cover to have the Irishman brought in so he and I can talk."

Later that day, Melissa sat in an armchair, placed to one side of Julian's desk in the castle library, and watched as Phelps ushered out the first of the three men Julian's sweep, conducted by the local constable assisted by various castle staff, had snared.

As expected, none of the castle staff had known anything about the mantrap, and neither had the faintly bewildered Scotsman, a traveling salesman engaged in the wool trade, whom Phelps was showing out.

Essentially, interviewing the first two men brought in was all for show. The man Julian—and she and Felix—wanted to speak with was the third man, the Irishman, who had been found at a small local inn.

The door closed behind Phelps, and Melissa looked down at Ulysses, who was curled at her feet and fast asleep. Although he'd opened one eye when the Scotsman had entered the room, he'd otherwise shown no interest in the visitor and had settled to sleep again.

That was quietly reassuring; Melissa was learning to trust Ulysses's instincts. She'd spent the hours since coming in from the shrubbery assuring the entire household that her nerves were completely intact and she wasn't in any danger of fainting—indeed, that she was no more fragile than she had been earlier that morning. As for Ulysses, news of his deeds had made the puppy the toast of the castle and the recipient of probably far too many tasty treats. Melissa had had to stop Veronica from rewarding him with a slice of seed cake.

Julian and Felix were talking about the mantrap. As Edgerton had predicted, he and Hockey hadn't found any clue as to where the trap had come from. What they were adamantly certain about was that it hadn't been something that had been left lying discarded in some castle store; it had been too new for that.

Julian and Felix broke off their discussion as a rap on the door heralded Phelps with the second of the three non-local men.

The middle-aged man, another man traveling on business if his neat but well-worn clothes were any guide, was understandably wary. When Julian waved him to the straight-backed chair before the desk, he sat and, on being invited to tell them who he was and what he was doing in the area, admitted that he was a clerk for a foundry, on his way to deliver a contract to a customer in Coventry.

The poor man was patently taken aback when Julian asked if his company manufactured mantraps. "No, my lord. We specialize in nails and rods."

"Not springs?" Felix asked.

The man shook his head. "Straight and small. That's all we do. We're not one of the majors, you see."

After establishing that the man hadn't seen anything that might have been a mantrap during his time in the neighborhood and that, until brought to the castle, he hadn't set foot on castle grounds, Julian released him to Phelps to see out.

"Right." Julian sat back. "That's our cover story in place. Now for the real point of this exercise."

Phelps returned, ushering the Irishman into the room.

He was of medium height, tending stocky, with curly black hair, a pale complexion, and bright-blue eyes. Melissa judged him to be about thirty years old, but he carried the air of one who had seen hard times. He wore nondescript clothes—coat, breeches, and boots that would be unremarkable in town or country. If it wasn't for his black curls, he wouldn't stand out in anyone's memory.

As it was, after Julian waved the man to the chair before the desk and nodded a dismissal to Phelps, when Julian briefly glanced Melissa's way, she nodded decisively. The Irishman was the man she'd seen outside the theater, at Richmond Park, and under the trees earlier that day.

Julian clasped his hands on the desk and studied the Irishman, who, rather boldly, stared back.

After a second, Julian's lips curved in a faint yet intent and satisfied smile. "As you know, I'm Carsely." He arched his brows. "I don't suppose you know anything about a mantrap set in a path of the shrubbery here?"

The Irishman blinked.

"Or," Julian continued, "anything about the other recent attempts to kill me?"

"What?" The Irishman's eyes widened. Then he shook his head. "I don't want to kill you. I've been trying to catch you to tell you something."

Julian nodded. "Indeed. So what is it you wish to tell me?"

The Irishman hesitated, then looked pointedly at Melissa and Felix.

Julian waved. "My wife and my brother. You can speak freely before them."

The man weighed that, then straightened and said, "My name's Dally Watkins. The Ribbonmen leadership sent me to tell you that Davy O'Donnell's been thrown in Ulster nick on the say-so of the Orangemen."

Julian shut his eyes and groaned. "Why on earth…?"

Melissa suspected he'd intended the question to be rhetorical, but Watkins answered, "No real reason, but that new bloke, Goulburn, is one of theirs, so he decided to stick Davy inside to shut him up."

Julian opened his eyes. "Surely someone's told Gregory by now?"

Watkins shrugged. "They might have tried, but we don't know because Gregory's been over here. But he needs to get himself back over there and sort things out, or they're saying there'll be hell to pay."

Julian muttered, "I can imagine." His gaze on Watkins, Julian tapped his finger on his blotter, then stopped. "You and your leaders do know that I'm no longer with the Home Office?"

Watkins nodded. "Aye. We knew you'd left." His gaze slid to Melissa, then returned to Julian. "But the bods on the Irish desk will listen to you, as will those in Dublin Castle. You were their top negotiator, and even Goulburn will listen to what you have to say—and the Lord Lieutenant certainly will. He's one as likes to keep things calm, so he'll back Gregory in sorting this out."

In Julian's view, that assessment was accurate in all respects. He thought, then sighed. "All right." On leaving the service, he'd vowed to himself that he wouldn't get sucked back into Home Office affairs, but he couldn't just leave this to slide and land God knew where. He hadn't spent ten years of his life working to keep things calm in Ireland to have some idiot act belligerently and pitch the whole applecart into turmoil for no reason. Lips thinning, he nodded. "I'll write to Gregory as well as to a few others in Dublin Castle, pointing out the inadvisability of jailing one of the few men able to and likely to help them keep a lid on things."

Watkins looked pleased. He grinned as if a weight had sloughed from his shoulders. "Thank you. That's all we ask."

Julian eyed him. "Were you followed?"

"They had people tracking me in London, but when I reported back that I was having trouble getting you alone, those at home suggested I head up here and wait for you to come north, so I left and made for Liverpool as if I'd given up and was going home, but instead, I came across here. I think they lost me—I don't think they followed me when I left London."

Julian nodded. "Regardless, I suggest we put you up for the night. I'll dispatch letters tomorrow, and you can take the one for your masters and start on your way back to Ireland then."

Watkins bobbed his head. "If I could just nip back and fetch my things from the inn?"

"You were at the Pig and Whistle, I believe?"

When Watkins nodded, Julian said, "I'll send a groom to fetch your belongings and drop a word in the owner's ear that you're a guest at the castle, and we'd be obliged if he would keep that to himself, and if anyone inquires after you, he should steer them to Chesterfield, farther north."

Watkins looked impressed. "Aye, that'll help."

Julian nodded to Felix, who rose and rang for Phelps.

Watkins got to his feet and rather awkwardly bowed. "Thank you, my lord. I—we—know you don't have to help, and we're grateful."

Julian inclined his head. "Please tell your masters that they need to establish a connection with someone in Dublin Castle—Hillworth comes to mind. I'll write as much in my letter and that, as you've discovered, hunting me down over here won't necessarily be straightforward."

Watkins nodded. "Aye. I'll make sure they understand that."

Phelps arrived, and Julian gave his orders, then handed Watkins into Phelps's care. Plainly rather curious, presumably about how things were done in an earl's house, Watkins went off with Phelps quite happily.

As the door shut behind the pair, Felix returned to the armchair angled before the desk and fixed his gaze on Julian. "Well, that's one mystery solved, but it leaves us with the question of who's behind the lethal accidents that keep happening to you." Felix looked at Melissa. "Both of you."

Julian glanced at Melissa as well. "Indeed. And sadly, whoever is behind those incidents has followed us here."

"Well," Melissa said, "on the bright side, as all the London staff have returned to Carsely House and, according to Edgerton, the mantrap must have been laid in the past day, the person responsible isn't one of our London people."

Julian nodded. "And equally, none of the staff here were in London when the bookcase fell—I don't think anyone here has been down there in living memory."

"True." Felix looked happier. "So if it's none of the staff, then presumably, in London, someone broke in and set up the bookcase, but was careful to leave no trace. And here"—he shrugged—"while there might be staff around during the main part of the day, either very early in the morning or even more so after six in the evening, when everyone's inside, anyone slipping into the grounds would have had ample time to set that trap."

Julian grimaced. "The trap was well camouflaged—they spent time doing that—but even from the castle roof, you can't see into that part of the shrubbery. They would have had plenty of time yesterday evening or even the evening before, and as you say, at this time of year, the light lasts for hours, long after the staff down tools and come in or go home."

Felix nodded. "Easy enough to keep watch and seize their opportunity."

"Although we've verified that the trap itself had to have been brought onto the estate," Julian said, "I can't see any viable way of tracing who brought it here. Even if one of our workers or someone on the neighboring farms had noticed a wagon passing, what are the chances of them having taken note of the people driving the wagon?"

Felix snorted. "Let's just accept that there's no way forward there."

Silence fell as they pondered that.

Eventually, Julian said, "As far as I can see, we have no way of identifying who set the trap, just as we have no way of identifying who put the thorn in my saddle, or shot at us in the park, or pushed the urn off the roof of Carsely House, or tampered with the bookcase." He met Melissa's darkened gaze. "It seems the one thing we can be sure about is that, whoever he is, he's not going to stop."

The statement hung in the air.

Unsurprisingly, no one argued.

The clock on the mantelpiece whirred. They all looked at it as it chimed for six o'clock.

Julian pushed away from the desk. "We'd better get changed for dinner or Mama will get the wind up even more than she already has."

"God, yes." Felix got to his feet. "That's something we don't need."

Melissa rose as well, awakening Ulysses.

As they walked toward the door, Julian took her hand and twined his fingers with hers. He literally felt better for the contact, and the way her fingers curled about his suggested she craved it, too.

With Ulysses gamboling about their feet, they left the library, paused in the front hall to hand the puppy over to an impassive Phelps, and with Felix trailing at their heels, started up the main stairs.

Julian glanced at Melissa's face. Her expression stated she was deep in thought.

He shifted his gaze forward. Regardless of anything and everything else, he'd be keeping a much closer eye on her from now on. Indeed, through every minute of every day until they apprehended the villain and removed all threat—even indirect—to her.

CHAPTER 11

*T*hree quietly tense but uneventful days later, Melissa sat in an armchair before the desk in the library and watched Julian, seated opposite, peruse the list of neighboring gentry Veronica had compiled at Melissa's request.

The room's long windows looked out over a narrow flagstone terrace to the side garden, an area of green lawns and shady trees basking in the afternoon sunshine. After years in London, she was finding the peace of the castle grounds relaxing, and the weather today had been especially pleasant.

That said, there was a snake lurking somewhere in their Eden. Ever since the incident with the mantrap, the entire household had been metaphorically holding their breaths, waiting to see what would happen next, poised to defend against any threat in whatever way was required, yet not having the slightest clue from which direction that threat would come.

The tension was very real, yet everyone tried to pretend it wasn't there, primarily to avoid escalating Veronica's and Frederick's anxieties. Both tended to become consumed by worry, which was bad enough, but they would try to help, and that was…even less helpful.

After much discussion, Melissa, Julian, and Felix had agreed that, at present, their only viable way forward was to wait for the snake to launch his next attack and hope that, this time, quite aside from them success-fully evading said attack, they would gain enough clues to identify him.

Julian reached the end of the list and humphed. "I take it Mama mentioned the Midsummer Ball?"

Melissa refocused on her handsome husband. "She did. She's been unreservedly helpful, and I thank my lucky stars every day that she's been so amenable to handing over the household reins. It's not every newly-wed wife who can say that. And your uncle's been extraordinarily kind and helpful, too."

Julian set down the list. "Even more than Mama, Uncle Frederick knows how the castle runs. He would be an excellent source for any of the details Mama might not know—like what's stored in the attics."

Lips twitching, Melissa arched her brows. "If I wanted to know what's in the attics, I would have thought to ask you or one of your brothers first."

Julian paused, then dipped his head. "Good point. Anyway, if Mama is unavailable, Uncle Frederick will be delighted to assist." He met her eyes. "They're both very happy to have you here, you know."

She smiled. "I did get that impression. But to return to the Midsummer Ball, I gather that's the next event the castle regularly hosts"—she pointed at the list—"and all those people usually attend."

He nodded. "You'll meet all our neighbors at the ball. After that, the next event is the Harvest Fair, which is held in the grounds, and everyone from around about attends. Mama can tell you more, but of the three annual castle events, I imagine that's the most difficult to organize. The other is the Hunt Ball, which is straightforward enough."

"Does the local hunt ride from here?"

"No, but the Wirksworth Ride—the mock hunt before midsummer—leaves from the forecourt here."

Ulysses, who'd been napping at Melissa's feet, leapt up and, whining, tail wagging but not furiously, hurried down the room to the open French doors. He halted on the threshold, looked out, and yelped.

Julian and Melissa rose.

Before they could move, Felix, white-faced, disheveled, and with his right hand clamped to his left shoulder, came staggering into view on the terrace.

Ulysses yelped encouragingly, and Felix stumbled to the open doors and all but fell through.

Already striding down the room, Julian leapt to catch his brother and steady him. "What the devil happened?"

As he steered Felix to the nearest armchair, through gritted teeth, Felix gasped, "Get me a drink—something strong." He fell into the chair.

Julian straightened, took in Felix's white face, and his own expression turning grim, headed for the tantalus.

Melissa bent over Felix and reached for his right hand. "Let me see." Felix allowed her to lift his hand enough to peek beneath, then she set his hand back and gently pressed it down. "The ball's ripped a long furrow through your coat, but luckily, the wound is shallow. That said, it's bleeding rather profusely, so keep your hand there for the moment." She glanced at his coat. "Are you carrying a handkerchief?"

"Right breeches pocket."

Julian returned. "Here, drink this." As Felix grasped the glass in his left hand, Julian passed a clean handkerchief to Melissa. "Use this. I'll get his."

He retrieved Felix's handkerchief and handed it to her as well.

Melissa folded both into a thick pad, then lifted Felix's hand, positioned the pad over the wound, then set his hand back in place. "Hold that there for now. You'll need to get out of your coat and shirt soon."

Felix swallowed a second mouthful of brandy. "I liked this coat, and now, the bastard's ruined it."

Deducing from that plaint that his brother was regaining his composure, Julian drew up an armchair for Melissa and another for himself. As he sat, he repeated, "So, what happened?"

Felix's color was returning. He lowered the glass and sighed. "I was on my way to the old fish pond. After we talked about it this morning, I thought to go and check what state it's in. If we're going to restock it, we'll want to be sure it's still in sound condition. I took the usual path off the lake—well, there really is only one direct path to the pond, I suppose, which probably explains why our attacker had thought to set up a spring gun along the way."

"A spring gun?" Julian stared.

Melissa looked back and forth. "What's a spring gun?"

His face setting, Julian replied, "It's another, rather more deadly form of mantrap."

Felix waved his glass. "Blows your head off instead of cutting off your leg."

"Good Lord!" Melissa turned wide eyes on Felix. "Thank God it only winged you."

"Yes, well, that wasn't through any mistake on our would-be murderer's part. I saw an odd mushroom and turned back to look at it just as the gun went off. The trip wire was hidden beneath fallen fern fronds, and I'd stepped right on it."

Melissa paled. "You"—she looked from Felix to Julian—"or you were supposed to have been killed."

"Exactly." Felix took another sip of his brandy. "Not much doubt of that, not with a spring gun." He looked at Julian.

Julian was accustomed to maintaining an impassive expression, but now his features felt set in stone. "I believe we can take it as read that someone wants me"—he met Felix's gaze—"and possibly you as well, dead, and they're not fussy over how they achieve that."

Melissa was frowning. She met his eyes. "But if I understood what you and Felix said this morning at breakfast, neither of you had been down to the fish pond for years."

Felix nodded. "That's why I went to take a look."

Julian caught the point she was making. "But given we don't usually visit the fish pond, why put a spring gun on the path that leads to the fish pond and nowhere else?"

Melissa nodded. "Exactly. The only reason to do that—"

"Is if," Felix grimly stated, "the blighter heard us discussing the fish pond this morning and knew that, eventually, one or other of us would go down to check on it."

"Not necessarily heard," Melissa cautioned, "but heard of. Any of the staff who passed in and out of the breakfast room while we were talking of it—and there were at least four because Veronica and Frederick had just come in and Phelps was replenishing the sideboard—could have heard and innocently mentioned it in passing to others."

"Or even not so innocently." Julian thought, then grimaced. "But I take your point. We can't leap to any conclusions and, sadly, once again, we can't even produce a limited list of suspects. Nor can we haul the staff in and attempt to find whoever set up the spring gun. Just as with the mantrap"—he waved, indicating the land around the castle—"it could easily have been someone from outside the estate."

Melissa was nodding. "It's too easy to imagine a scenario of Phelps going into the kitchen to pick up a dish and mentioning to Mrs. Phelps or even Edgerton that you're discussing restocking the fish pond, just as Cook is dealing with the butcher boy at the other end of the table, and then the butcher boy mentions it to his friend, who's the fishmonger's son…" Grimacing, she shrugged. "Even I know that's how news spreads in the country."

Julian and Felix grimaced as well. "You're not wrong," Felix said and drained the rest of his brandy.

Over the next half hour, they discussed what they should do. Regarding how to deal with the spring gun, they agreed it would be best to take Phelps, Edgerton, and Hockey into their confidence, tell them of the spring gun, and note that despite any assumptions that it might be tempting to draw, there was no firm evidence linking any member of the staff to the attack.

"I'll ask Edgerton and Hockey to take care of the damned thing themselves," Julian said. "They'll understand the need to keep quiet about it, but they'll also be put on guard." He winced. "More on guard."

They remained concerned over further escalating Veronica's and Frederick's anxieties, understandable though those were, and decided not to mention the incident to them or, indeed, anyone else beyond the Phelpses, Hockey, and Edgerton.

"And my man," Felix said. He'd lowered his hand from the handkerchiefs, which showed only a small bloodstain. "I'll have to get Hicks to bind this up and dispose of the evidence, but he's as loyal as old boots. He'll do it and keep mum."

Julian nodded. "It might be wise to include Keogh, my man"—he looked at Melissa—"and your maid as well."

Melissa nodded. "I'll tell Jolene."

"And I'll write to Damian as well," Julian said, "just so he's abreast of the situation."

"Removing the spring gun," Felix said, "and keeping quiet about the incident might at least confuse the blighter."

Julian grunted and rose. "At present, it seems there's precious little else we can do. I'll go and speak with Edgerton first, then find Hockey."

Melissa pushed out of the armchair. "I'll come with you. I've been meaning to speak with Edgerton about the borders for autumn." She linked her arm with Julian's. "We can use that as our excuse for seeking him out."

Felix grunted and got to his feet as well. "I'll slip upstairs and get Hicks to fix me up." He looked at Julian and Melissa. "I'd take the back stairs, but the servants gossip far worse than anyone else. Can you clear the way to the main stairs?"

They grinned and did, walking ahead and ensuring that no one was about to see Felix trailing behind them.

They reached the front hall without encountering anyone, and Felix slipped past and up the stairs.

Julian watched Felix go. His brother was still alive but...

Jaw firming, with Melissa on his arm, he made for the front door.

Three days later, having completed their morning's ride, which today had taken in the lands all the way to the estate's western boundary, Melissa and Julian cantered home along the well-maintained bridle path through the thick woods that covered the rise to the west of the castle.

In the lead, Melissa turned her head and called back, "I can see why this is your favorite route back to the castle. The glimpses of the walls and roofs are intriguing."

Julian replied, "As I child, I loved those teasing vignettes—I still do."

Smiling, Melissa faced forward—and her hat was swept from her head. "What?"

She hauled on the reins. Rosa obediently responded, and Melissa half wheeled to a halt. Settling in the saddle, she stared back along the track and saw that Julian had reined Argus in hard and had stopped level with her fallen hat.

He seemed to be staring at something directly in front of him, something she couldn't see.

She frowned. She'd expected to see an errant branch or some such thing—whatever had hit her hat with sufficient force to rip it from its anchoring pins.

Julian stared at the taut wire that stretched across the path. In something close to disbelief, he raised a hand and, with one gloved finger, tested the tension.

It was as tight as a piano wire, half as thick, and infinitely more deadly.

And at the perfect height to hit him across the throat when he leant over Argus's neck.

Puzzled, Melissa came trotting back.

"Careful," he warned.

If he'd been in the lead or riding alone, as had generally been the case before their wedding...

He blew out a breath, then forced his lungs to work and draw in another. Beneath him, Argus twitched and shifted.

Melissa had finally come close enough to see the wire. Like him, she instantly understood the implications. She looked at him and paled. "Good Lord. It's another attack." She halted on the other side of the wire and stared at it. "What would have happened if you'd ridden full tilt into that?" She raised her gaze to his face. "I'd wager that, knowing the path so well, normally, you would have been galloping."

He was about to nod when the *crack* of a snapping branch reached them, followed by the unmistakable thud of boots running away. The sound quickly faded.

Julian quelled an instinctive urge to give chase. He couldn't ride through the woods themselves—the trees grew too thickly—and even if he rode hard and circled around...

He looked at Melissa. She didn't know the ground and would fall behind. He didn't want to leave her undefended or, potentially worse, lead her into danger. Who was to say there wasn't more than one murderous thug lurking?

He glanced around, but the woods seemed silent, wrapped in their usual pervasive peace.

Trusting his senses, he swung down from Argus's back. "That there was someone waiting answers the question of what would have happened had I been riding alone. At the very least, I would have fallen from the saddle." At worst, he would have opened his throat from ear to ear. "I suspect the intention was to topple me from the saddle, and then whoever was waiting would have finished me off."

Incredulous, Melissa stared at him, then shook her head. "I can barely believe this."

Leading Argus, he walked under the wire and halted level with her. He held up the reins. "Hold him while I get the wire down."

She took the reins and watched—and kept watch, scanning the woods around them—while he followed the wire back to the trees around which it was tied.

When he rounded the first, he discovered small horizontal marks cut into the trunk, each a foot higher than the one before. He crouched and confirmed that the first mark was level with the ground along the track. Straightening, he found that the wire had been held in place by a buckle-like contraption tacked into the trunk. He used his pocketknife to pry out the tack. "They've measured this. They've gone to significant lengths to get the height of the wire just right."

Melissa's head came around, and she stared anew.

He didn't need to look at her to know she would follow the same deductive trail his mind had leapt along. He knew she'd reached the same conclusion when she turned her head to look at Argus.

"Argus isn't as tall as some of the other horses." She looked back at Julian. "That suggests someone knew how tall you sit when on his back."

He walked out from behind the tree and wound the wire into a ball as he crossed the path to the tree used as an anchor on the other side. "That points to someone in the stable."

She tipped her head consideringly. "Or someone who spends time within sight of the stable yard, enough to have seen you ride out often."

He reached the other tree and studied the bole. "There are the same measuring marks on this one." He detached the wire and pocketed the ball, then returned to the bridle path, bent, and picked up her hat. While walking to where she waited on Rosa, he dusted off the blue velvet, then tweaked the dyed ostrich feather until it stood tall once more.

On reaching Rosa's side, he held up the hat. Melissa took it and handed him Argus's reins. He remounted while she fiddled, reanchoring the hat. Lowering her hands, she shook her head, testing, then satisfied, picked up her reins and fixed him with a frowning look. "I suppose we'd better get on."

He nodded, waited until she'd wheeled her mare, then followed as she rode on along the bridle path, not as quickly as they had been and with both of them openly scanning the woods to either side.

They left the cover of the woods and reached the spot where he often paused to look down at the castle. Melissa didn't stop but slowed Rosa to a walk and, over her shoulder, declared, "I don't like this."

He brought Argus up to amble beside Rosa. "I don't, either. We're getting far too accustomed to incidents like this. They happen, we survive unscathed, look to see if we can identify the culprit, and when we can't readily do so and something else demands our attention, we let the matter slide and, more or less, wait for the next attempt."

"That's too passive to suit either of us." Her expression darkened. "It's frustrating not to be able to deal with it—to sort out what's happening and put a stop to it."

He mulled over her observation for several paces. She was correct in that their essential helplessness was grating on their tempers. Not reacting in some definite fashion was growing more untenable with every attempt. "There has to be something we can do." When she glanced at him hopefully, he caught her eye. "Let's start by analyzing what today's incident tells us."

She arched her brows and looked forward. "Well, presumably whoever set up the wire—so carefully calculated to incapacitate you—didn't know that I planned to go riding with you."

"True. And that means whoever it was didn't, in this case, have any insight into our discussion over the breakfast table this morning."

She wrinkled her nose. "I'm fairly certain only Phelps was there at the time, and we really don't suspect him."

Julian grunted in agreement. "That there was someone waiting in the woods, presumably to finish me off, also suggests they thought I would be riding alone."

"Yes, but"—Melissa looked toward the stable—"if they'd been watching the stable yard this morning, they would have seen you ride out by yourself." She glanced at him. "You rode out ahead of me and went to the dovecotes, remember?"

Before they'd left the house, when they'd been walking along the corridor, heading for the side terrace and the stable beyond, Mrs. Phelps had come hurrying after them, wanting an urgent word with Melissa about the menus for the coming week. As Julian had intended to check on the dovecotes and she'd always found that many birds all gathered together unnerving, they'd agreed he would go on alone, and once she'd finished with Mrs. Phelps, she would ride out and meet him at the orchard before they rode on together to explore the western reaches of the Carsington estate, eventually returning via the woods.

Julian nodded. "Clearly, whoever organized that wire must have seen me ride out, but not been there to see you do the same later." He arched a brow at her. "How long was it between me riding out and you reaching the stable yard? Do you have any idea?"

Frowning, she thought back. "I was with Mrs. Phelps for at least ten minutes—we had to rearrange the entire week's worth of menus. Assuming you rode out within two minutes of reaching the stable—" She caught his eye. "Did Hockey have Argus saddled and waiting?" When Julian nodded, she went on, "Then assuming that you and I took close to the same time to reach the stable from the house, you must have ridden out at least eight minutes before I walked into the stable yard."

"That's enough time for someone inside the stable or watching the

yard to decide I'd ridden out alone and leave to go and set up the wire."
He paused, then went on, "Given they so carefully measured the height of
the wire, I think we can safely assume I was their target, and they
couldn't have set up the wire earlier because others use that path as well.
Some of those who work in the house and gardens but live in cottages
about the estate walk along that path every morning and evening."

"So we can be certain the wire was set up some time after those
people passed this morning."

"And they wouldn't have wanted it up if there wasn't a good chance
of catching me riding back, and everyone knows I always take that path
home." His jaw firming, Julian nodded. "They would have waited to
confirm that I was riding out and that I was alone."

They walked the horses on, then Melissa observed, "It can't be
anyone who works in the stable." She glanced at him. "You'd asked for
Rosa to be saddled as well as Argus, and she was ready when I got to the
stable yard."

He grimaced. "You're right. Rosa was ready and waiting when I
mounted Argus, so yes, everyone in the stable ought to have known you
would be riding out as well."

"So we come back to someone watching the stable yard long enough
to see you ride out alone, then leaving before I walked out."

Lips compressed, Julian said, "We need to sit down and work out
what each incident tells us of the person responsible. Given the number of
incidents we've weathered, we should be able to produce a list of possible
suspects or at least define who the culprit can't be."

Melissa's face set, and she nodded briskly. "Enough of this. Like you,
I'm heartily sick of our apparent impotence. Let's get back, put our heads
together, and see if we can find some way forward. Some way to get to
the bottom of this."

She shook Rosa's reins and urged the mare into a trot, and Julian
brought Argus alongside.

~

After leaving the horses in the stable, they retreated to their apartments to
change their clothes, then as the maids were in their sitting room,
descended to the library.

Julian ushered Melissa through the door. He followed and closed it
behind them as Melissa exclaimed, "Damian! You're back."

She went forward, hands outstretched, as along with Felix, his little brother rose from one of the armchairs in the group before the fireplace.

Julian arched a resigned brow and followed more slowly. Unnerved by the attacks in London, after the wedding, Felix and Damian had both wanted to remain at the castle, but as Julian had pointed out, that would have raised eyebrows all around. In the end, he'd agreed that Felix could stay, his presence excused by unspecified estate business, and rather grumpily, Damian had returned to town with his friends.

After the more recent incidents, Julian had written to Damian purely to keep him apprised of developments, but of course, Damian had come haring back.

As Julian's sometimes rapscallion little brother, Damian had quickly become a favorite of Melissa's. When she finally released him, and Damian turned, rather more warily, to Julian, resigned, he held out a hand.

Damian grinned, gripped, and shook, then as they moved to claim seats, sank into the armchair he'd earlier occupied and, in more sober vein, said, "Felix has told me about the latest attacks. Good Lord! It's—" Lips compressing, he shook his head. "I mean, this is England. We don't go about bumping off aristocrats."

Despite the situation, Julian almost smiled. "I seriously doubt it's any of my tenants trying to 'bump me off.'"

"Yes, well," Felix said, "these attacks are getting too serious to simply brush aside. We need to find who's responsible and string them up by their thumbs."

Julian inclined his head. "That's more or less the reasoning that's brought us here." He exchanged a glance with Melissa, then looked at his brothers. "Because speaking of attacks, we've just weathered another."

"What?" Felix demanded.

Damian looked incredulous. "When?"

Between them, Julian and Melissa described the latest incident, including their staggered departure from the stable yard.

Both Damian and Felix listened intently.

Leaning forward, his forearms braced on his thighs, Damian said, "So whoever it was thought you would be riding alone, as you used to do all the time, and returning—as you always do—along that particular path."

"That they were so particular about the height of the wire..." Felix shook his head. "I really don't like that."

"But," Melissa said, "it suggests that whoever put up that wire knew how tall Julian sits on Argus and that whoever it was left soon after he rode out."

Frowning, Damian looked at Julian. "Can we...I don't know." He gestured. "Call in all the outdoor staff and work through who was where, when?"

"Whoever left to put up the wire wouldn't have been about to be seen by others for at least twenty minutes, more like half an hour." Felix looked at Julian. "And we can't forget someone was in the woods, ready to do you in after you fell."

Melissa grimaced. "But that person could have been anyone—even someone from outside the estate."

"And there," Julian grimly said, "lies the rub. Even the setting up of the wire could have been done by someone from outside the estate. All they would have needed was the right information, albeit fed to them by someone on staff."

He paused, staring unseeing into space as he imagined the outcomes of the various tacks they could take. After several moments, he refocused on Melissa, then looked at his brothers. "If I call in all the staff—for it could just as well be a junior footman or even a maid who'd kept watch from the house and signaled someone—we'll achieve two things immediately. We'll put the perpetrator on notice that we're actively after them, but of even greater concern, we'll signal to all our staff that we do not have faith in them, in their honesty, their integrity. That is no small thing."

He waited to allow those words to sink in, then said, "As far as I can see, the person who gathered the critical information—how high to put the wire, on which bridle path, and when—could have been anyone on staff." He immediately qualified, "At least theoretically. In practice, we know our senior staff are loyal and solidly behind us, and that goes for the staff who hail from local families." To Melissa, he added, "We have and have had no disagreements or even vaguely difficult situations with the local estate families, and the majority of our staff are drawn from their ranks."

Melissa, Felix, and Damian all frowned, but none of them argued.

That gave Julian the chance to say, "Incidentally, Damian, we're saying as little as possible to Mama and Uncle Frederick about any of this, and at this point, they know nothing of this morning's incident."

"Good God, no." Damian looked aghast. "You know what they're like. Worrywarts, the pair of them. They'd fuss and hover and try to smother us all." He licked his index finger and crossed his heart. "I won't breathe a word."

Julian couldn't suppress a smile. There were times when Damian was still ten years old.

Felix stirred. "While I don't like not being able to react, I agree that we can't simply call in all the staff and start interrogating them." Felix looked at Damian, then Melissa, and finally at Julian. "But there has to be some way forward."

Julian had been juggling possibilities like the pieces of a jigsaw. "Potentially, there are several people involved, and we need to identify and capture them all. Putting aside the three attempts in London, not because I think they're unconnected but because they're well-nigh impossible to follow up"—he held up a single finger—"we have the person who got the information—for instance, that the groundsmen had scythed the path in the shrubbery and wouldn't return for at least two weeks, or how tall I sit on Argus, and when I rode out from the stables alone. Let's call that person our informant."

The others were following; they nodded.

"The next person who must exist is the one who actively puts the traps in place—who strung the wire or set the mantrap in the shrubbery lawn and the spring gun along the path to the fishpond. Let's label him the perpetrator."

"And," Felix put in, "it's certain our perpetrator is a man. No woman could have put that trap in place."

Julian nodded. "Indeed. And continuing with our list of people we need to identify, the third and last is whoever is behind the push to kill me, because as far as I can see, no maid, footman, gardener, or even an ordinary person from outside the estate who would know to set up a spring gun or mantrap has any motive or reason to murder me. Not on their own behalves."

His eyes on Julian's face, Damian observed, "Very few people would gain anything from seeing you dead."

"Exactly. It makes no sense that someone has, for no real reason, decided to attack the head of the House of Delamere. Yet there've been seven attempts thus far—three in London and four here, including the thorn stuck in my saddle." Julian paused, then added, "More than anyone else, we need to identify who's behind this, because they'll be the one actively driving each and every attempt, and ultimately, they are the one we have to stop. Catching and removing their agents won't stop the attacks."

"A person with a real motive to kill you." Melissa's dark-blue gaze met his. "Do you have any idea who that might be?"

"I've wracked my brains, and I can't think of anyone—or even any reason that might suffice." After a moment, he went on, "But to return to our list of people—or in actuality, roles—we have an informant, a perpetrator, and a motivator."

Felix's eyes were narrowed in thought. "As far as I can see, in all the attacks so far, the roles of informant and perpetrator could have been filled by the same person."

Julian nodded. "But the motivator has to be someone else. Someone unlikely to be at the castle or even anywhere close."

"Someone lurking in the shadows," Melissa said.

"That's certainly how it looks and feels." Julian contemplated that scenario.

Melissa stirred, and when Julian glanced her way, she caught his eye. "The informant"—she glanced at Felix—"who may or may not be the perpetrator. I know none of you want to think it, but the informant, at least, must be one of the castle staff."

The three brothers stared at her, reluctance in their expressions. She ignored that and went on, "Our only real way forward is to try to identify that person." She glanced at Julian. "We didn't tell anyone else about the wire today. Who did we tell about the spring gun?"

"Only Phelps, Edgerton, and Hockey," Julian supplied.

She nodded. "Those three, and Mrs. Phelps, we all agree we can trust. And if you think about it, the informant must by now be getting nervous. Two attacks have now passed without anything happening. You're walking about, plainly unhurt, unharmed, and very much alive, and what must be even more confusing, you're not reacting and demanding someone's head."

"*That*," Julian said, "is a very valid point." He paused, plainly furiously thinking, then went on, "I've been wondering why anyone would stage such a succession of strange attempts. Except for the incident in Hyde Park and the bookcase falling, they've all been of the sort that might at a stretch be deemed an accident. Even the Hyde Park incident could have been someone shooting at something else, something relatively innocuous, and the bookcase could have been a politically motivated warning from the Irish, not an actual attempt to kill me."

Damian frowned. "I'm not following." He looked at Melissa, then Julian. "How does confusing the informant explain the strange nature of the attempts?"

"Not confusing the informant," Julian replied, "but the assumption that I would react and how others would expect me to react. What if the thinking behind the attacks is that if they succeed, well and good, but even if they don't, they'll result in me thundering about and accusing the staff and ending alienating the entire staff? If I did that, and subsequently, I was killed anywhere on the estate, the likely suspect list would be—"

"Very large, indeed." Felix looked grim. He met Julian's gaze. "Thankfully, you haven't yet done anything to sow seeds of discontent among the staff."

"No. Nor do I intend to."

"*But*," Melissa insisted, "holding back entirely won't get us any further forward, and I believe we're agreed that we can't continue to let matters slide?"

She looked pointedly and questioningly at Felix, Damian, and finally Julian.

Damian also looked at Julian. "Whoever our madman motivator is, he isn't going to—indeed, as far as I can see, he has no reason to—stop."

"And eventually," Felix added, "there'll come a day when Melissa isn't riding ahead of you to scupper his plans, and our fiend will succeed in his aim."

Julian grimaced, but nodded. "You're right. Clearly, our motivator isn't going to stop. He has some reason, some goal, and this is obviously a long-range plan. But given all the above, what's our best way forward?"

"I agree we can't investigate the staff as a whole," Melissa said, "and I accept that it's likely true that none of those who've worked here for decades or who belong to estate families will be the one we're looking for." She smiled faintly. "Indeed, that's something I've noted as I've been going around learning the household ropes and meeting all the staff—the vast majority have worked here for years and are part of the local community. There are, however, a handful who are more recent additions."

She looked from one brother to the next, until she met Julian's eyes. "This household has recently changed from what was essentially a widow-and-bachelor sons' establishment to that of a socially and politically active married couple. While I only brought with me my maid—who we can also trust—there have, of necessity, been several recent hires. Why don't we start with them? Not speaking to them directly, not interrogating anyone, but first, purely learning who those potential informants are?"

Julian's eyes narrowed, then he nodded. "I'll get Phelps to make up a list of the staff." He arched a brow at Melissa. "I'll say that you and I want to go over it to gain a better understanding of our staffing situation both here and in town."

She nodded. "That's entirely believable and won't alert anyone. I'll mention it to Mrs. Phelps as well."

Julian continued, "While we trust the Phelpses and the other senior staff, there's no sense adding further stress at this point by telling them of our suspicions, not until we get some idea of who our informant might be."

"You can ask for the list to include how long each staff member has worked here," Felix suggested.

Damian agreed. "That'll make the newcomers easy to identify, and don't forget, that thorn in your saddle means you need to go back before the wedding."

"Before I even went down to London." Grimly, Julian nodded. "But I agree—concentrating on those hired in the past year or so holds out the best hope for identifying who on the staff is working against us."

CHAPTER 12

*T*wo days later, Melissa sat beside Julian in the castle's gig, and while they bowled along the track leading to one of the estate's farther-flung farms, she scanned the list the Phelpses, with the help of Hockey and Edgerton, had prepared.

Every now and then, the rocking of the simple carriage as they rounded a bend forced her to look up. As they rattled around another curve, her gaze took in a vista of neat fields, slumbering in gentle midmorning sunshine and bordered by hedgerows, with thick copses dotting the green and golden expanses. There were fallow deer in the area; they'd passed two small herds along the way. The sky was mostly clear, and the mild June sunshine was pleasant, while the breeze was almost nonexistent, barely ruffling the leaves.

As the well-beaten track, bordered by ditches and running between two fields, straightened once more, Melissa returned her attention to the list. "There's eleven, all told, employed within the past two years. Actually"—she rapidly calculated—"within the past twenty months. Beyond the twenty-month mark, the next most recent hire is over six years ago."

Julian nodded. "It's hard to imagine why someone who's been on staff for more than six years should suddenly turn on the family. So who are the eleven we need to focus on?"

"In order of hiring, the one from twenty months ago is Mitchell, the groom. Then comes Biggins, an undergroom, and Walter, a junior stable-man, followed by Richards, a footman, and Cantrell, who's a junior footman, then Benton, a senior housemaid, Polly Fisher and Enid Wise, both junior maids, Billy Botham, the scullery boy, Joe Carter, a groundsman, and last and most recent, Damian's valet, Manning." Melissa glanced at Julian. "Any ideas how to winnow that crowd?"

Julian steered the horse, an older bay gelding, along the track by rote; he knew every inch of these lands and didn't need to concentrate on the road. "Given the mantrap and the spring gun, it's tempting to point at Carter, the groundsman, but as we've already established that both the mantrap and the spring gun assembly had to have been brought in from outside the estate, then in reality, it could be any of the men. I can't see any woman, or the scullery boy for that matter, managing to lay and set the mantrap."

"Hmm. And Carter could have been the one who, on seeing you ride out from the stable, rigged the wire on the bridle path, but so, too, could Mitchell, Biggins, Walter, and even Richards, Cantrell, or Manning."

"Mitchell, Biggins, and Walter—if our attacker is one of them, then unless he left the stable before Hockey called for our mounts to be saddled, he should have known you would be out with me…" He paused, then went on, "Actually, I'm not sure anyone in the stable *would* have known you intended to join me rather than go riding somewhere on your own." He glanced at Melissa. "Did you say you'd be joining me?"

She was silent for a moment, clearly thinking back, then said, "I only mentioned it to Hockey as I rode out. He and I were out by the mounting block. No one else was near enough to hear."

The track swung left to follow the base of a shallow valley, with rising pasture on the left, studded here and there with mature coppices, while on their right, the fields were replaced by a stand of woodland angling up the valley's side. The track grew more rutted, furrowed by runoff from the woods, which came right to the edge of the track.

Julian kept the bay trotting onward at a steady pace. "I told Hockey that you'd been detained, but would be along shortly, and others probably overheard that. I didn't tell anyone you would be joining me."

"Hmm. Richards helps Phelps in the breakfast parlor most mornings, so he might have heard that we would be riding together, which suggests he isn't involved, but who else of the indoor staff might have heard of our intentions…" She frowned. "This is getting complicated. I need another sheet of paper—"

A snapping *crack* rang out directly beneath them—from under the gig's seat.

Melissa yelped and clutched the gig's side.

Julian swore and hauled on the reins as both wheels tipped outward, then in a succession of smaller snapping cracks, splintered and fell apart, and the baseboard beneath the thankfully well-padded seat thumped onto the hard track.

They bumped along for several yards before the experienced yet nevertheless spooked horse consented to respond to the reins and slowed to a walk, then halted.

The horse blew out a noisy breath and shook his head.

Julian and Melissa did much the same.

Stunned, they looked at each other. "Are you all right?" he asked.

She nodded. "You?"

"Unhurt, but..." Still holding the reins and seated as if driving along, he turned and surveyed the wreckage strewn along the track behind them. "I'm not sure I believe this."

He rose and stepped out of the gig, the baseboard of which now sat on the track. He watched as Melissa carefully stood and stepped free of the gig on the other side. While she looked around in stunned amazement, he walked to the horse's head. He murmured to the gelding, soothing the uncertain beast, then stepped across the narrow verge and tied the reins to the nearest tree.

When he turned, Melissa had walked back along the track.

He joined her as she stood frowning at the two largest pieces of the wrecked wheels—the hubs from which most of the spokes and rim had snapped off. The hubs lay more or less flat on opposite sides of the track, having fallen that way when the axle—an old wooden one—had snapped.

Still frowning, Melissa glanced at him. "Is it normal for wheels to fall off like this?"

He shook his head and crouched to examine the ruined wheel closer to him. "Axles don't normally snap like that, meaning without cause." He examined the end of the obviously roughly snapped axle that still protruded from the hub, then looked at the piece that remained in the other wheel hub at her feet. "There's a good section of the axle missing."

He rose and walked along the track, scanning the litter of shattered spokes and rims.

Melissa followed, surveying the detritus on the track's other side. "Here's a piece!" She bent and picked up a section of axle that had fallen in the longer grass of the verge.

"And here's the rest." He bent and picked up another section. He studied the ends, then frowning more definitely, walked to where Melissa waited, holding her find. He took it and brought the two pieces together. "Let's see…"

Set end to end, the pieces fitted snugly—and it was evident that the axle had been sawn through for more than half its thickness.

Melissa sucked in a slow breath, then looked back along the track. "When we hit those ruts…"

"Exactly. Whoever did this left enough strength in the axle so no one would immediately guess that anything was wrong and we would drive away from the castle, but once we hit the rougher tracks, it would only be a matter of time before the axle snapped."

She met his eyes, confusion in hers. "But why?" She gestured to the gig's seat, resting on the track. "While the experience was a shock, it was hardly life-threatening."

He looked at the pieces of axle in his hands, then assessingly at the carriage. Eyes narrowing, he replied, "Wheels do sometimes fall off carriages, usually because of some weakness where the wheel connects with the axle. In such a case, only one wheel gives way, and usually, that's at high speed and the occupants are thrown. Sometimes, they die. Carriage accidents of that sort aren't infrequent. But"—he looked at the pieces of axle he held—"in this case, someone made the mistake of weakening the axle in the center of its span, so when it snapped, with similar weight on either side of the carriage and on a straight stretch of track, both wheels fell off at more or less the same time."

Melissa had turned to survey the gig's body. "So while we were dumped down and ended riding along the road, we weren't tipped sideways and flung out of the carriage."

After tossing the pieces of axle to the ground, he waved at the gig. "That's what happened."

She looked at him. "Your mother and Frederick used the gig yesterday afternoon to go into Wirksworth. When did you ask for it to be made ready for us?"

He grimaced. "I mentioned it to Phelps last night, before we retired. He would have sent the message straight on to the stable."

"So someone had to have got to the gig sometime between late last night and this morning—very early this morning, because they couldn't have risked being caught sawing at an axle."

Voice hardening, he said, "Hockey has been locking the stable and carriage barn at night, but one of the grooms or stablemen could have hidden and remained inside." He paused, then added, "I can't imagine anyone else being able to—the Phelpses would have noticed if any of the indoor staff weren't in their rooms when they locked up for the night."

Melissa hauled out the list she'd stuffed into her pocket and consulted it. "That means our prime suspects are Mitchell, Biggins, and Walter."

Grimly, he nodded. "All the rest of the stable staff have been with us for years if not decades." He turned and looked back along the track.

She noticed. "What?"

"I was just thinking about what you said earlier, about this not being a life-threatening accident. Even if they'd sabotaged the axle more effectively, chances are good that at least one of us would have survived, possibly both of us, although we would have been almost certainly injured and incapacitated. So"—he blew out a breath—"if their aim is to kill me...I assume someone will be along shortly."

She swung to look in the same direction. "They'll have followed us out, intending to finish us off?"

"I can't see how this attempt was otherwise supposed to work." He studied the woods, then looked the other way, and almost smiled in satisfaction. "However, I believe we shouldn't wait openly in the lane."

He grasped Melissa's hand and nodded to the coppice in the field twenty yards back from the track. "Let's take cover there—the undergrowth is nicely thick—and keep watch to see who arrives." He wasn't interested in getting into any altercation with someone who would almost certainly come armed. More, his most urgent impulse was to ensure that she wasn't exposed to any danger.

She readily followed him to the stile, but paused to look at their horse. "What about old Ned?"

"He's secure and can graze on the verge. I can't see any reason anyone would harm him."

Accepting that, she turned to the stile, and he helped her over it, then followed. After dropping to the ground, he took her hand again, and they quickly climbed the slope to the coppice.

They rounded it and slipped between the thick regrowth until, still well within the trees, they could crouch and, sure of being concealed, peer out at the track and the forlorn-looking remains of the gig.

Melissa scanned the track, then fixed her gaze on the spot where the lane entered the small valley. "They'll be coming from the castle, won't they?"

"I imagine so," Julian murmured.

They waited. The minutes ticked past, but then the sound of a horse trotting reached her ears. She glanced at Julian and saw his gaze sharpen on the farthest point of the track visible from where they were.

With the same eager tension—at last, they would learn unequivocally who the attacker was—she stared at the same spot.

A rider came into view, trotting quite quickly along.

Julian bent his head close and whispered, "That's Mitchell."

She watched the groom as he neared the start of the wreckage. He was a well-built man of above-average height and, judging by the way he sat the horse, a strong rider. He had dark hair cut fairly short, and his clothes were practical and nondescript, exactly what one would expect a groom to wear. She studied his face as, slowing, he looked farther along the track, then frowned at the sight of the gig's seat sitting squarely on the ground. She turned her head slightly to whisper to Julian, "The other day, when I went to get Rosa, I didn't see him in the stable."

His gaze trained on Mitchell, Julian nodded. "He would have been in the woods, rigging the wire, but we can check with Hockey as to whether he knew Mitchell was gone or whether the others saw him slope off."

Mitchell halted his horse and surveyed the scene. Far from showing any innocent surprise, much less concern, he scanned the surrounding area thoroughly, then his face setting, he pulled out a pistol from the holster in his saddle. He checked the gun, then his left hand strayed to the hunting knife on his hip, loosening it in its scabbard, then pistol in hand, he started his horse walking slowly toward the gig's stranded seat.

When he reached the point where he could see there was no one in the seat or lying on the ground in front of it or anywhere close, he swore.

Even Melissa heard his "Damn it!"

Mitchell halted his horse, seemed to dither, then he replaced the pistol in its holster and dismounted.

They watched as he walked back along the lane, plainly searching through the debris. Eventually, he paused, then bent and picked up the two main sections of the axle.

"The bits that prove it was sawn almost through," Julian murmured.

They watched Mitchell, apparently satisfied, walk back to his horse. He stuffed the sawn pieces into a saddlebag, then mounted again, shook his reins, and set his horse trotting on.

Julian straightened.

Melissa looked at him and saw he was almost smiling, but there was no warmth in his expression—quite the opposite. "What now?" she asked.

Julian glanced at her, then looked at where Mitchell was disappearing along the track as it wended along the valley. "I assume he thinks we've walked on toward the farm. It's closer than the castle."

He hadn't liked the look of that pistol or the knife. As far as he was concerned, simply by turning up, even without Mitchell's actions once he had, the groom had marked himself as a condemned man.

Mitchell passed out of sight. Julian reached for Melissa's hand and drew her upright. "Let's go down and fetch Ned and ride him back to the castle." The old hunter would easily carry them both."

Melissa followed him out of the coppice. "What if Mitchell comes back and sees Ned has gone?"

"The farm is some way on, so it'll be a while before he returns, and I imagine he'll think he's missed us and we've come back and taken Ned—as, in fact, is the case—or that someone else has found the wreck and taken Ned back to the castle." They started down the sloping field. "Either way, I think he—Mitchell—will return to the castle, if nothing else to learn what's happened."

"Until he sees us or hears that we've returned hale and whole, he won't know if we're alive or"—she gestured—"whether we tried to walk for help but collapsed in the woods, too injured to go on."

"Exactly." He climbed over the stile, then helped her over it, and they hurried back to Ned.

Within minutes, he'd freed Ned from the gig's shafts, refashioned the reins, and they were perched on Ned's broad back, Melissa sitting sideways before him, as the old hunter readily cantered for home.

Melissa, it transpired, was thinking along much the same lines as Julian was. "What do we do once we reach the stable?" she asked.

"I want to be there when Mitchell rides in, but I don't want him to see either of us until he's off his horse."

"And," she concluded, "he has no chance of escape." She nodded. "I approve of that plan, but don't think I'm going to retreat to the house until we have him in chains."

He heard the determination in her voice—the ruthless focus—and smiled and didn't try to argue.

∼

When Mitchell was spotted riding in, Julian and Melissa hid behind a stall wall, out of sight of anyone in the stable yard, but near enough to hear whatever words were exchanged.

Hockey and the other stablemen had been livid when they'd heard the tale of what had happened that morning. Apparently, Mitchell was one of the grooms delegated to exercise the various hunters the four male Delameres housed at the castle. Consequently, when Mitchell approached Hockey that morning, saying one of the horses he tended needed a run, Hockey hadn't hesitated to send Mitchell out on the horse.

When Mitchell rode in, Hockey, outwardly his usual relaxed self, was waiting close to the main stable doors.

Six of the other stablemen were engaged with routine chores nearby, two inside the stable and four not far from where Hockey stood.

As Mitchell reined in and walked the horse forward, Hockey reached out and caught the horse's bridle. "Has he settled, then?"

Mitchell smiled and dismounted. "I rode out his skittishness. He's right as rain now."

Hockey took the reins and handed them off to the stable lad who ran up—Walter, as it happened. "Anything else to report?" Hockey asked. As Walter led the horse away, not into the stable but to the side, Hockey turned an innocently inquiring look on Mitchell.

Mitchell appeared nonplussed by the question. He arched his brows, pretended to think, then shook his head. "No. Nothing untoward."

Hockey smashed a fist into Mitchell's face—so fast Mitchell had no time to counter the punch. The blow was so ferocious, the impact flung Mitchell back to sprawl on the cobbles of the yard.

Instantly, the other stablemen—who happened to be carrying pitchforks and shovels—closed around him.

One hand cradling his jaw, Mitchell blinked groggily, saw the circle of angry faces, and with a blank expression, focused on Hockey. "What was that for?" His flat tone made it clear he'd already guessed.

His meaty fists on his hips, Hockey almost spat, "For being a lying traitor, that's what."

"Come on." Julian grasped Melissa's hand and, with her, walked out of the stable and into the yard.

Mitchell didn't try to get up. Propped on one elbow, with a mix of wary apprehension and defeated resignation in his eyes, he watched Julian and Melissa approach.

Julian halted beside Hockey. He studied Mitchell, then in an even tone, said, "The countess and I saw you ride up to the wreckage of the gig. We saw you pause, check your pistol and also your hunting knife before approaching the wreck. When you realized there were no dead or injured bodies to be found, you swore, then—and this is the most telling part—you dismounted, walked back along the track, hunting through the debris for the pieces of the axle that showed where you had sawn the axle almost through. You found the two pieces and put them into your saddlebag."

Without shifting his gaze from Mitchell, Julian pointed at the horse Walter still held in full view of all in the stable yard. "That saddlebag."

He'd ordered the horse to be kept in full view, hoping that in searching for him and Melissa, Mitchell would forget about the pieces of the axle and ride back to the castle carrying the damning evidence, and indeed, the saddlebag in question was still bulging as it had after Mitchell had thrust the wooden sections into it.

Mitchell glanced at the horse and paled.

Julian caught Hockey's eye and tipped his head toward the saddlebag. "Why don't we see what's in there?"

Hockey grunted and walked to the horse, and Mitchell hung his head and deflated.

The sight of the pieces of axle that Hockey drew forth and showed to everyone, displaying the clean, sawed cut that went two-thirds of the way across the shaft, had the other men muttering, shifting restlessly, and glowering darkly at Mitchell.

He didn't look up again, and after waiting for a moment, Julian went on, "Hockey and the other stablemen have confirmed that no one saw you in the stablemen's quarters after Hockey locked the stable and barn last night. You were first seen this morning by Hockey and Walter after Hockey unlocked the barn. Everyone else is accounted for from the time the stable and barn were locked to the time they were opened again. The evidence against you is conclusive—you were the person who engineered today's accident. We're left to infer that you are also responsible for the spate of accidents that have recently occurred."

Mitchell had kept his head down, staring at Julian's boots, but Julian thought he frowned at that.

When no further reaction eventuated, Julian coldly went on, "For all we know, you might be responsible for the death of my father and also the death of Campbell, his groom."

At that, Mitchell looked up, a protest obviously on his lips, but at the last second, he froze. Then he bit the words back and dropped his gaze once more.

Puzzled, Julian stared at the man. Around him, deep-seated anger and transparent thoughts of vigilante justice swelled in the air, an almost palpable force. A quick glance at the expressions of the men gathered around confirmed that if Julian wanted Mitchell dead, all he had to do was say the word, and the deed would be done, the body disposed of, and no one else the wiser.

But these were modern times, and justice wasn't supposed to be meted out like that.

Even more importantly, Mitchell had information Julian wanted.

Into the almost vibrating silence, he said, "Clearly, you've been acting on someone's orders. Whose?"

Mitchell's head came up, a vestige of hope sliding through his eyes, but again, the hope faded, and he drew back, although his lips tightened into a thin line as if he fought to stop himself from answering the question.

When Julian finally succeeded in catching Mitchell's gaze, the man stared at him for a second, then fractionally shook his head and looked down again.

During his years in Ireland, Julian had witnessed the same sort of behavior when people were acting under orders and were too frightened of the reactions of those who gave those orders to identify them.

He'd learned there was value in being patient, even when it was the last thing he wanted to be.

"Very well." He bit out the words. "I assume you're aware that I'm the local magistrate and able to bind you over to the next assizes without further trial."

Mitchell didn't react to that at all. If anything, his posture seemed to indicate he'd expected as much.

Julian glanced at the other men, then looked at Hockey, whose color was still high and whose hands remained tightly fisted. "Let's see how he feels after spending a day or two in the dungeon." That was another benefit of being the local magistrate. There was a proper cell for holding prisoners in the castle dungeon, which had long ago been converted into a simple cellar, but in this instance, "dungeon" sounded more appropriate.

Hockey slapped a fist into his palm. "Leave it to us—the boys and I'll see he's put into the cell."

Julian murmured under his breath, "Undamaged, please. I want him to cooperate, and I won't be able to trust anything he says if he makes statements under duress." He'd learned that lesson in Ireland, too.

Hockey looked disgusted, but nodded. "Aye. We'll deposit him in the dungeon without harming a hair on his head."

Looking back at Mitchell, who had looked up to try to listen to what Julian and Hockey were saying, Julian caught the man's eye. "While on your own in the cell, you might want to ponder whether you wish to go to the gallows for attempting to murder an earl, a countess, an earl's son, and anyone else who might have got caught in those traps you laid, or if you'd rather tell me all you know and sail off to Botany Bay. Your choice. I would counsel you to exercise wisdom in making it."

With that, Julian offered Melissa his arm and, when she took it, entirely ignoring Mitchell, walked with her out of the stable yard.

As they started up the path to the side terrace, Melissa let out a long sigh.

When he looked her way, she met his eyes and smiled. "There is one definite bright side to this morning."

He arched his brows, inviting her to tell him.

"With our perpetrator caught, we won't have any further accidents."

He smiled in turn and inclined his head. "There is that. We might not have discovered who's behind the attacks yet, but we've reached that point at least."

With Mitchell in the dungeon, life in the castle calmed and returned to something approaching normality.

Julian, usually with Melissa in attendance, spoke with Mitchell on several occasions over the following two days, but the man remained stubbornly silent. While he didn't attempt to deny responsibility for any of the attacks, neither did he confirm his involvement, and most crucially, he refused to open his lips and name whomever it was who had given him his orders and, presumably, was also behind the attacks that had occurred in London.

On Sunday, Julian decided to leave the man to his own thoughts. "Perhaps uninterrupted solitude in which to contemplate his future will soften his stance and loosen his tongue."

"We can but hope," Melissa replied. There was definitely something holding Mitchell back, some compulsion forcing him literally to bite his tongue regarding whoever had sent him to murder Julian. Yet as both she and Julian had noted, Mitchell hadn't denied that such a person existed or that he'd been acting at someone else's behest.

Setting aside their frustration, they went down to breakfast late, then Melissa ambled about the rose garden with Ulysses while Julian retreated with Felix and Damian to the library to read the London papers. After a relaxed family luncheon, Julian reminded her of his suggestion of the previous evening, namely that he and she take the castle punt and drift along the stream and out onto the castle's lake.

The day was warm, the air almost balmy, and she readily agreed.

Located at the bottom of the sloping south lawn, the boathouse was built on the banks of the stream that wended down through the wooded heights to the west of the castle to flow eastward along the southern edge of the grounds and spill into the lake, which lay southeast of the castle.

Frederick had mentioned that the stream continued eastward and eventually joined other minor tributaries and turned south, ultimately merging with the river Derwent a little way north of Derby.

Inside the boathouse, Melissa helped Julian launch the single punt, then scrambled in as he took up the pole and pushed them out onto the lazily meandering stream.

With a sigh, she lay back in the prow and, past the rim of her straw hat, looked up at the cerulean-blue sky. A few puffy white clouds sailed majestically across the expanse, while the sun beamed steadily down; it was truly the most perfect early-summer day.

She filled her lungs with fresh air carrying the evocative tang of freshly cut grass and the scent of flowing water. Birds sang from the branches of the trees overhanging the stream and flitted in the rushes. A dragonfly appeared and hovered before her face, as if staring into her eyes, then darted off, skimming over the water's gleaming surface.

Under Julian's direction, the punt glided slowly eastward, then the lazy current slowed even more, and they floated out onto the so-called lake, formed by a widening of the stream in the southeast corner of the castle grounds. The lake was perhaps two hundred feet at its widest and twice that in length. The stream entered at the western end and flowed out at the easternmost point.

Peace, bucolic and pervasive, wrapped about her.

She lowered her gaze and drank in the sight of her handsome husband, standing on the platform at the punt's stern. He'd left his coat and waistcoat in the boathouse and had rolled up the sleeves of his shirt to his elbows. Lean muscles bunched and released as he wielded the long pole with practiced ease.

Only now that the danger had passed could she appreciate the tension that had previously afflicted them, since well before their wedding; its sudden absence made its previous existence starkly obvious. For both of them, that heightened awareness had become such a persistent habit that being able to relax and let it go, allow it to fade, felt rather like setting down a physical burden—a tangible relief.

The punt angled, and she raised her hand to shade her eyes as she continued to allow them to feast on Julian. His gray gaze idly scanned the water as he poled them slowly along. She smiled. "Are there fish in this lake?"

He looked at her, and his lips curved in appreciation and simple happiness. "Most definitely. Felix and I often fish here and in the stream. There are roach and tench, and we get the occasional pike as well, so don't trail your fingers in the water." He grinned. "Pike bite."

After glancing up and checking their progress, he returned his gaze to her. "Did you ever go fishing when you were a girl?"

"No. There never was anywhere to try it, but I wouldn't mind learning. It seems a very soothing activity."

His smile deepened. "It is. And it certainly teaches one patience."

That was one virtue that came to neither of them naturally; any patience they exhibited was a learned skill.

The sleepy silence rolled over them again, and they let it.

Melissa's thoughts rambled, touching on how much more at ease the whole household had become after Mitchell had been locked in the dungeon. Veronica and Frederick were patently relieved and, yesterday, had organized a family outing to the monthly market in nearby Wirksworth. Along with Felix, Damian, Veronica, and Frederick, Melissa and Julian had spent a very pleasant morning strolling among the market stalls, admiring the local craftwork, and Julian and Felix had spent some time chatting with the local farmers who had brought livestock to sell.

Later, the family had lunched in a private parlor at the Wirksworth Arms, then as a group, had diverted to admire the fabulous designs created out of flowers by the village women in dressing the local well head—an early June tradition in Derbyshire. After that, she, Veronica, and Frederick had climbed into the landau and been driven back to the castle, while Julian, Felix, and Damian cantered in their wake.

Smiling, she refocused on Julian. "It's so peaceful around here. Even in Wirksworth, everyone was at ease, genial and happy. For someone who's lived most of their life in London, it's quite eye-opening."

He arched his brows. "Wirksworth might be larger than a village, but its roots lie in all the surrounding families and their rural endeavors. You'll find Derby more like London. I'm sure Mama will suggest she take you to Derby soon, if only to introduce you to the local shopping."

His resigned grimace made her laugh. "I have to admit I've never stopped in Derby long enough to gain any real sense of the place."

He studied her face. "Do you miss town—the bustle and undeniable amenities of London?"

She thought, then shook her head. "To be perfectly truthful, I've been utterly content wandering the gardens and going out with you, exploring the estate, getting to know the various tenants and farms, and seeing the land, the valleys and hills." She smiled up at him. "It's home to you, but it's new to me, and in a way, that newness—the novelty in all I see—feeds my eagerness to work out a future that embraces it all!"

She spread her arms on the last words, smiling up at him, and he smiled back. "I'm glad. I'm looking forward to our joint future, too." He leaned on the pole and pushed them onward.

Still smiling, she drew in her arms and resettled, shifting her feet. Her heels made a small splash.

What? She frowned and sat up. The sudden shift in her weight made the punt dip and wallow.

Julian bit back a curse and swayed, but managed to keep his balance.

After confirming he had, Melissa returned her gaze to her sandals—and the inch of water sloshing about in the bottom of the punt. "Is there meant to be water inside the boat?"

Julian frowned. "What?" He drew up the pole, set it down along the length of the punt, then stepped down from the raised platform at the stern. Immediately he did, the punt wallowed again, and a second later, the water covering the base rose, wetting the bottom inch of his boots. He crouched and stared, then grimly stated, "No. There shouldn't be any water at all." He dipped his head and felt around under the middle bench. "There must be a hole…"

They searched and found a neat round hole about an inch in diameter underneath the platform on which Melissa had been lounging.

He swore. "They plugged it with wadding so it would take a little time for the water to soak through, but now the wadding's saturated, the water's pouring in."

"So we're sinking?"

He nodded and swiveled to survey the nearest shore, which happened to be the edge of the south lawn. He bent, snatched up the pole, and stepped back onto the raised stern. "The lake's not that deep, at least not between us and the south lawn. Let's see how close I can get us."

He turned the punt, but with the water in the boat rising, his initial push only moved them a yard closer to shore. He tried again, getting a little farther as the punt sank lower.

"We've taken on too much water." He stood upright, balanced the long pole in one hand, and flung it like a javelin toward the bank. It landed in the water a few yards short of the shore. "We can fish it out later."

He looked at her. "I'm a strong swimmer. Can you swim at all?"

She'd stripped off the sash that had secured her hat to her head and used it to bind the hat and her sandals into a bundle. She humphed as she tied the other end of the sash to her wrist. "Despite my having little experience of country ways, swimming is the one outdoor activity I can do, mostly due to trips to the seaside. That and having a little brother who was always issuing challenges." With a determined light in her eye, she fixed her gaze on the bank. "I don't swim well, and I'm certainly not fast, but I won't sink."

Julian exhaled in relief. Few of their peers, indeed few of their countrymen, could swim at all. "Right, then." The punt was sinking deeper and deeper. "I'm going in. I'll wait for you, and we can swim in slowly together."

She nodded, and he stepped off the stern and plunged into the water. At least it was summer, and although cold, the water wasn't icy.

He resurfaced, slicked back his hair, and opened his eyes to see her sitting on the sinking prow with her legs in the lake, then she pushed off, sliding into the water.

She floundered somewhat, and when she finally struck out, her style was ungainly, but as she'd promised, she didn't sink.

He swam across behind her and, with one hand, caught the ring at the front of the punt. Dragging the boat through the water behind him wasn't easy, but it wouldn't be for long, and he wanted the evidence.

Half on his back with his left hand gripping the punt's ring, with a few strong kicks, he swam up alongside Melissa. He kept a few feet away, avoiding her paddling arms and hands. With his free hand, he fished and caught the bundle of her hat and sandals so that the weight of it no longer dragged on her wrist. With sure, steady kicks, he swam parallel to her. "That's it. It's not much farther before we'll be able to stand and walk out."

A few minutes later, he tested the depth and found he was just tall enough to reach the bottom. He kicked on a few more feet, then stood. The water came to his upper chest. Changing hands, using his right to tow the boat behind him, he waited until Melissa had swum a few more feet, then gripped her elbow. "You can stand, I think."

She blew out a breath, then tried and discovered he was right. With a sigh of relief, she stood, retrieved her sodden hat and sandals, and waded beside him as they covered the last ten feet to the bank.

"There's a bit of a step to get out." He held one hand as, with the other, she hauled her drenched skirts up above her knees, then with his help, she clambered onto the bank.

She paused, catching her breath, then bent and gathered her wet skirts and wrung them out. After releasing the wet fabric, she took three dragging steps up the lawn, swung around, sank down to sit on the thick grass, then slumped back full length, flinging her arms wide.

Not a bad idea. The sun was streaming down, and although the water had been cool, with no wind to further chill them, they'd be warm again soon enough.

He pulled the punt close, then stepped onto the bank and heaved the boat onto the grass. He released it and stared at it for a moment, then looked at his ruined boots. It was tempting to take them off, but he would struggle to do it, and the thought of expending that much energy then and there had him turning to where Melissa lay. He walked to her side, sat, and stretched out beside her.

The caress of the sun on his face felt like a blessing.

He closed his eyes, and they lay there for several minutes, soaking in the warmth.

Eventually, without opening his eyes, he murmured, "Clearly, we have more than one perpetrator on the premises."

The sound she made signified how deeply unimpressed with that state of affairs she was. After a moment, she asked, "Could Mitchell have done it? Drilled the hole some time ago and left it as another little trap for you?"

"There's only one punt, and Mama and Frederick took it out yesterday, after we came home. That's what gave me the idea for an excursion of our own."

"Ah. I see." A minute later, she sighed and asked, "So what should we do?"

He considered various options, then said, "We can leave the punt where it is for the moment. Let's see if we can creep inside and get changed into dry clothes, then meet in our sitting room and figure out our next move."

"All right." Melissa sat up, and he followed suit.

She waited while he rose, then took the hand he offered and wobbled to her feet. She gathered up her hat and sandals—she had no idea if Jolene could resurrect the hat—and hand in hand with Julian, crept toward the house by a roundabout route that gave them cover almost all the way to a side door.

They slipped inside and reached the bottom of one of the numerous secondary stairs without meeting anyone. They had to pause at the top and take refuge in an alcove to avoid a pair of maids, but once the chattering girls had passed, they hurried to the family wing and their apartments at the end.

As she led the way into the foyer, she murmured, "I'm surprised you haven't worked out a better route to clandestinely go back and forth. Like a passage in the walls or something of that ilk."

He flung her a laughing glance. "These weren't my rooms while I was growing up."

"Ah. Of course." She headed for her bedroom and the bathing chamber beyond. "Are there passages in the walls?"

"Of course."

She didn't look back, but from his tone, she could tell he was smiling.

They both made short work of stripping off their damp clothes, drying off, and getting dressed in suitable attire. She found and donned a lightweight summer gown, then combed out her damp hair before twisting it up into a knot and anchoring it. She looked in the mirror, decided that was good enough, and went out to join Julian in the sitting room.

He was standing by the window, looking out.

She walked up and halted beside him. "Now what? How can we learn who scuppered the punt?"

"Do you have that list of the staff?"

She crossed to her escritoire, opened the panel, and extracted the list from the drawer into which she'd put it. After closing the desk, she returned to his side and held out the list.

He took it and scanned the names. "I think we can leave the women out of our calculations. Drilling a hole through such seasoned wood wouldn't have been easy, and they would have needed to find and fetch the right tool and in such a way that no one saw or suspected them, all of which seems unlikely. For the same reasons, I think we can excuse the scullery boy as well. With Mitchell definitely out of contention, we have six possible suspects—Biggins or Walter from the stable, Carter the groundsman, Richards or Cantrell, the footmen, or Manning, Damian's valet."

She folded her arms and narrowed her eyes on the horizon. "Did your mother and Frederick definitely take the punt out late yesterday afternoon?"

From the corner of her eye, she saw him nod.

"I met them coming in," he said. "They were exclaiming over a king-fisher they'd seen as they punted back to the boathouse."

"So the punt was watertight at that time. Yesterday at about...?"

"Six o'clock," he supplied. "We were all on our way upstairs to dress for dinner." He paused, then went on, "No one mentioned punting during dinner, but after dinner, you and I spoke about taking the punt out while we were on our way to the drawing room. I can't recall who might have been around to hear us. Can you?"

She shook her head. "That's the trouble with being constantly surrounded by staff. They fade into the paneling."

He snorted. "Regardless, I think we can be certain someone heard us, and that would have been about nine o'clock yesterday evening."

"So the deed must have been done between then and when? Two o'clock this afternoon?" She glanced at him and saw his eyes narrow in thought.

"No. I don't think so." He looked at the list of staff again. "Yes, it's Sunday, but they all still have various duties. Finding time during the day to fetch a drill—and all such tools are kept in a cupboard in a room off the carriage barn—going down to the boathouse, and spending at least half an hour down there, all without anyone seeing them, would have been diffi-cult. The chances of being noticed would have been ridiculously high—indeed, almost a certainty. I can't believe any would-be murderer would have risked that."

He glanced at her. "Yesterday evening, when we spoke of going out in the punt, did we say 'tomorrow' or 'tomorrow afternoon'?"

She reviewed the moment in her memory. "Just 'tomorrow.' We didn't specify."

"That's my memory of it, too. And if whoever it was didn't know when we would go out—morning or afternoon—he would have done the deed between nine o'clock last night and, at the latest, ten o'clock this morning." After a moment, he added, "And ten o'clock is stretching it."

She tried to imagine what it must have been like for the perpetrator. "It's not really something that could easily be done in the dead of night, is it? Not without a decent source of light. Even getting down to the boathouse at night wouldn't be easy without a lantern."

He huffed. "The boathouse is open to the water. A lighted lantern down there shines on the river and reflects up into the trees." He caught her eye and faintly smiled. "I know because we tried it once—Felix and I. The light show is rather significant. Felix's, Damian's, and Uncle Frederick's rooms face that way, and in this weather, Felix and Damian sleep with their windows open—one or other would likely have noticed."

She frowned. "If our perpetrator didn't do the deed at night, when did he manage it?"

"First thing in the morning." He paused, then increasingly certain, went on, "I've just remembered—Hockey's been locking the carriage barn overnight. That means from about nine in the evening until dawn, which currently occurs before six o'clock. So unless as soon as he heard or learned of our plans, our perpetrator rushed straight down to the barn to fetch a drill…" Lips setting, he shook his head. "That's unlikely as well. That leaves us with the early morning hours. Hockey opens up the stable and barn at dawn, then most if not all of the grooms and usually Hockey himself are busy taking the horses out to the paddocks before mucking out the stalls. There's a window of time when getting into and out of the barn undetected would be possible, and of course, our perpetrator didn't have to return the drill—he could simply have hidden it."

"Anywhere at all." She nodded. "From his point of view, that would have been the least risky plan."

"And given that, to date, our attackers have been very careful, that's most likely the plan he followed." He glanced at the list. "That means we're looking at which of these six men could have gone down to the barn and the boathouse between dawn and ten o'clock this morning."

"That's a relatively short window." She cocked her head and looked at him. "So how do we go about learning where Biggins, Walter, Carter, Richards, Cantrell, and Manning were during that period?"

"It's not Biggins or Walter, because over those hours, Hockey would have them running hither and yon. We can ask, but it won't be them. For much the same reason, I doubt it will be Carter. Edgerton and his men come in early, but we can ask." Julian looked at Melissa, then strode to the bellpull, tugged it, and turned back to face her. "I'm going to have the Phelpses, Hockey, and Edgerton come up here. They already know about the attacks, and I'm sure they'll have been keeping an eagle eye on all the staff."

He dispatched the footman who responded to the bell to find and send up the senior staff.

While they waited, Melissa sank into the armchair she favored angled before the hearth, but Julian couldn't settle enough to sit. A restless energy crawled beneath his skin. He paced, trying to make the action seem absentminded rather than agitated.

The tension that had vanished after they'd caught Mitchell had returned in full force, indeed, ratcheting tighter, more demanding than before. Having been free of it for three days made its return all the more noticeable and compelling. More disturbing.

When a knock fell on the door, he forced himself to halt before the fireplace and, clasping his hands behind his back, in an even tone, called, "Come."

Melissa glanced at him; he doubted she was fooled.

Phelps looked in, then stepped past the door. "You wished to see us, my lord?"

"I did." He waved the four into the room. "Please, come in, all of you."

The Phelpses were more confident than Hockey and Edgerton, who hung back, clearly uneasy as they stepped onto the polished boards and glanced around at the luxurious furnishings.

Melissa smiled reassuringly. "We just have a few queries regarding members of the staff."

Julian caught the questioning look she flashed him. How open did he want to be?

He considered the four lining up at an angle so they faced both him and Melissa and decided secrecy would be counterproductive. "The countess and I had another close call an hour ago." Briefly, he explained how the punt had sunk and why.

That all four were deeply shocked—that, like him, they'd believed Mitchell to be the only rotten apple in their barrel—was written plainly in their faces.

Melissa leaned forward. "Mrs. Phelps, please do sit down."

The housekeeper had grown distinctly pale. She dithered—her instinct over what was proper intervening—but then she dipped her head and murmured, "Thank you, my lady. I do think I had better." She sank down to perch rigidly upright on the edge of the armchair opposite Melissa's.

Julian looked at Phelps, Hockey, and Edgerton. "Consequently, we're trying to determine who might have holed the punt." He explained their reasoning regarding the period of time in which they thought the deed must have been done, and why they were focusing on the six recently hired men other than Mitchell. "So the question we have for you is whether you noticed where Biggins, Walter, Carter, Richards, Cantrell, and Manning were during the hours between dawn and ten o'clock this morning."

Edgerton was quick to say, "It can't have been Carter. He lodges with the Brinks family on the estate, and he and Fred Brinks walk into work together every morning. This morning, they were in as usual, about seven, and that means they would have set out around sunrise—you know how far the Brinkses' cottage is from here. And once they'd arrived, I had them working together all morning, alongside several other lads, clearing up the west border. I saw them all there, on and off, and none of them, Fred or the others, said anything about Carter sloping off."

Julian nodded. "So Carter is vouched for." He looked at Hockey, who had been frowning.

Hockey met his eye. "I've been trying to think if I saw anyone about the barn who shouldn't have been there." He grimaced. "But I was out with the horses for much of that time. It was my morning for checking hooves. But as for Biggins and Walter, they turned up as usual with the others for orders at sunrise. Both had chores, and I saw them in the fields where they should have been on and off over those hours, and neither of them missed completing their tasks. Given what I'd set them to do, if either had gone down to the boathouse, I doubt they'd have managed to it all get done."

Julian dipped his head, accepting that. "So Biggins and Walter are accounted for." He turned his gaze to the Phelpses.

Mrs. Phelps cleared her throat. "I remember seeing Richards at his usual time. They're all in the kitchen by seven, and Richards looked to be his usual sleepy self. It takes a good strong cup of tea to wake him up most days. But he was there, as usual, joking with Cook, and then, as far as I know, doing his regular chores." She seemed to puff up a little and sat even straighter. "As for Bobby Cantrell, he came in from his parents' farm as usual at six, on the dot. Never a minute late, that boy." It was obvious Cantrell was a favorite with her and a local to boot.

She looked questioningly at her husband, but Phelps was faintly frowning and staring absently at the rug.

Mrs. Phelps reached out and tugged his coat. "Hugh?"

When he blinked and looked at her, she asked, "Were Richards and Bobby Cantrell there for their usual duties this morning?"

"Heh?" Then Phelps shook himself and glanced sheepishly at Julian and Melissa. "Sorry." He glanced at his wife. "Yes. Richards and Bobby were both busy with their usual tasks, and Manning was about as well." He frowned and looked at Julian. "But Master Damian doesn't rise until late, so for the early part of the morning, Manning is left to his own devices." Phelps straightened, raised his head, and more formally reported, "This morning, I happened to be in the west wing, fetching one of the lamps there to refill it, when I encountered Manning coming in through the side door at the end—the one the family use when going to the boathouse."

Julian appreciated the distinction; if the staff went to the boathouse, they would leave via the kitchen door and walk around. Phelps didn't approve of Manning using an entrance the staff would not normally use, and that meant that the incident had stuck firmly in Phelps's memory. "When was this?" Julian asked.

"Just on seven, my lord. As you might expect, I asked Manning what he'd been doing. He smiled and said he'd just been out to take the air— that it was a wonderful morning and it had seemed a shame not to enjoy it." Phelps snorted. "You may be sure I explained to him that, wonderful morning or not, staff were to come and go via the kitchen door." Phelps all but sniffed in disparagement, then his frown deepened, and he added, "That door is half glass, so I saw him as he came toward it." Phelps met Julian's gaze. "I didn't think anything of it at the time, but he was brushing some sort of dust from his sleeves as he walked up the path."

Julian held back a sharp-edged, predatory smile. "Thank you, Phelps. That's most helpful." He nodded to the other three. "And our thanks to you as well. You've helped us winnow the guilty from the innocent. It seems it's Manning we need to speak with, but please, leave him to us."

Mrs. Phelps rose, and at Julian's nod of dismissal, the four bowed and filed from the room.

"Well." Julian blew out a breath and looked at Melissa, only to see her frowning. "What?"

She raised her dark-blue gaze to his face. "Damian mentioned to me that Manning had been recommended to him by Gordon."

Julian's smile grew grim. "Indeed." He paused, then tipped his head toward the door. "Let's find Damian first, then we'll hunt down Manning and see what he has to say for himself."

They found Damian and Felix relaxing in the library. One look at Julian's and Melissa's set faces and Julian's brothers came alert.

"What?" Felix demanded, his gaze searching Julian's face.

"Don't tell me Mitchell's escaped from the dungeon." Damian was equally concerned, but cloaked his worry in flippancy. "Well, he can't have—no one's ever managed that."

Ignoring that, Julian saw Melissa to her usual armchair, then sat and, between them, they told Felix and Damian the story of the sinking punt.

Predictably, both were horrified.

"Thank God you weren't that far out and can swim," Felix said.

Damian was frowning. "Mama and Frederick took the punt out yesterday, so whoever it was had to have drilled the hole during the night." His frown deepened. "But how on earth did they know you two intended to take the punt out this afternoon in time to put a hole in it first?"

Julian and Melissa explained what they believed must have happened and their deductions and investigations leading to Phelps's revelation. "So," Julian finally concluded, his gaze fixing on Damian, "it looks like it's Manning we need to interrogate."

Damian's expression had grown dark and grim. He shook his head in transparent self-disgust. "I should have known something was wrong." He looked at each of them. "I've been wondering over the last few days if Manning is even a real valet. He mixed up my hairbrush and my coat brush, and his ironing..." Damian gestured. "Suffice it to say that *I* could do a better job."

Looking like a thundercloud, he pushed to his feet. "Let's hunt him down and see what he has to say for himself. I haven't seen him since about eleven, when I left my room."

Julian held up a staying hand. "There's no need to chase the man." He waved at the bellpull. "Ring for Phelps and have him send Manning in."

Damian hesitated, but then tugged the bellpull, returned to the chair, and grumbled beneath his breath, "I'm going to have words with dear Gordon when next I see him."

Julian suspected his little brother would have to wait in line for that honor, but chose not to further provoke his clearly exercised sibling.

Phelps duly answered the summons and, once apprised of Julian's wishes, after confirming that Manning had lunched with the staff, assured them he would send the man in straightaway.

After Phelps left, Julian caught Felix's, then Damian's eyes. "Any wagers on whether Manning will be found?"

Melissa caught Julian's gaze and shook her head, but as it transpired, he'd hit the mark.

Three minutes later, Phelps returned and reported, "Manning isn't downstairs, my lord. I've sent Richards and Thornley to find him and tell him that Master Damian requires his assistance."

"Thank you, Phelps," Julian replied.

The thud of rapidly approaching footsteps heralded the arrival of Thornley, somewhat out of breath.

The senior footman appeared in the open doorway, and when Julian waved him in, he stepped over the threshold and halted. He bobbed his head to Julian and Melissa and, when Phelps gestured for him to speak, stated, "We looked through the upstairs rooms, my lord, but couldn't find Manning anywhere, so we tried the staff quarters. He's not up there, and all his belongings are still in his room. But when we were on our way down, we passed Harriet on the stairs, and she asked what we were about, and we told her we were after Manning, and she said she'd seen him hurrying down to the stable as fast as his legs would carry him. She thought he must be chasing after Mr. Damian for some reason."

Julian smiled. "Thank you, Thornley." He nodded to the butler. "And to you, Phelps."

"And," Melissa added, "do pass on our thanks to our sharp-eyed Harriet as well."

"Indeed." Julian rose. "We'll handle things from here."

Phelps and Thornley bowed and retreated.

Julian collected his brothers with a look, then glanced at Melissa as she rose.

"Don't think I'm staying here," she warned him and led the way out of the room.

Five minutes later, with Melissa's hand in his and Felix and Damian striding on either side, Julian walked into the stable yard. The sounds of an altercation rolled out through the open stable door.

"No." Hockey sounded belligerently adamant. "You cannot have a horse to ride to Wirksworth nor anywhere else. Not unless his lordship says so, and that's my last word on that."

Julian smiled and strolled into the stable.

Hockey, his huge arms crossed over his chest, legs planted like oaks, stood blocking the aisle that led to the stalls.

Facing him, Manning had plainly been pleading his case, but at the sound of their footsteps, he whirled.

For one instant, guilt and horror warred in his expression, then a flash of animal cunning had him glancing around, searching for escape.

But all around stood various stablemen, drawn by the argument and looking increasingly suspicious of the Londoner in their midst.

As Manning recognized the futility of attempting to break free, his shoulders slumped, and his expression grew strangely blank.

The valet, who was almost certainly not a valet, made no attempt to defend himself as Damian strode up, grabbed him by the collar, all but shook him, and barked, "What have you been up to, you conniving mountebank?"

Julian released Melissa, walked forward, and dropped a hand on Damian's shoulder. "Take him up to the house. I have questions for which I would like answers."

Damian drew in a deep breath and visibly shackled his temper. After a second, he shook Manning once more for good measure, then, his expression thunderous, turned and, propelling the hapless valet before him, marched the man out of the stable and toward the house.

Julian nodded to Hockey and the other men. "Thank you. It seems he, too, has been up to no good."

Hockey—indeed all the men—looked worried.

Hockey approached and fell in beside Julian as he rejoined Melissa, and in Damian's wake, with Felix, they headed for the castle.

"That's two of them." At the entrance to the stable yard, Hockey halted and met Julian's eyes. "I don't like the looks of this."

"No more do I," Julian assured him. "Let's hope this is the end of it."

The look Melissa cast him said she wasn't sure of that, and in truth, neither was he.

They parted from Hockey and caught up with Damian by the steps to the terrace. He continued to hold Manning by the collar, his unforgiving grip a fraction of an inch away from choking the man.

"What do you want to do with him?" Damian growled.

On impulse, Julian halted and studied Manning, then simply asked, "Who put you up to this?"

That was the one question he most wanted answered.

But as he'd expected, after one wide-eyed glance at his face, Manning fractionally shook his head, looked down again, and said not a word.

Stifling a sigh, Julian met Damian's gaze. "Take him to the dungeon and put him in with Mitchell. Perhaps by talking to each other, they can reach a better appreciation of their position and realize that the only way forward for them is to tell me all they know."

That speech, of course, was for Manning's benefit. Julian saw enough reaction to know the man had heard every word. All he could hope was that, having had more time to think things through, when Mitchell saw that Manning, too, had been apprehended, Mitchell might be more amenable to telling Julian what he needed to know.

Until then…

Julian nodded to Damian, and his brother propelled Manning toward the kitchen door, the fastest route to the cell in the old dungeon.

Still holding Melissa's hand, feeling her fingers curl in his, Julian stood and watched Damian and Manning disappear.

On his other side, Felix shifted restlessly. "He's not going to talk, is he? Like Mitchell, for some benighted reason, he feels compelled to keep his mouth shut."

Julian nodded. "That's how I read him."

In a tone of exasperated bewilderment, Melissa put their thoughts into words. "What the devil is going on?"

CHAPTER 13

*T*he next morning, after they'd breakfasted and Melissa and Julian had dealt with their immediate daily duties, they gathered with Felix and Damian in the library to discuss what to do with Mitchell and Manning.

"We've just come from seeing them." Felix dropped into one of the armchairs before the desk.

Damian drew up another armchair, positioning it between the one Melissa occupied and the one Felix had claimed. "And as we all expected"—gracefully, Damian fell into the chair—"neither of them will open their lips. Not to utter so much as a peep."

Felix shook his head. "I've never seen accused men so totally silent. What are they going to do at their trial? Just sit mum?"

Seated in his usual position behind the desk, Julian frowned. "This entire situation—first attack to last—has been increasingly strange, but this refusal to speak, even in their own defense, is another level of oddness."

He paused, then admitted, "I went down to see them first thing this morning, hoping that after spending the night in the same cell, they would have discussed their predicament and seen the sense in adopting a more helpful attitude—at least a bargaining one—but no." His expression grew more puzzled. "While the prospect of being hanged frightens them—they clearly have that much sense—it does absolutely nothing to loosen their tongues."

After a moment, more reluctantly, he went on, "The impression I received was something I've encountered before, in Ireland, when captives from one side would simply wait to be liberated by their leaders. That's the sense I received from Mitchell and Manning—they're waiting for their master to"—he gestured vaguely—"I'm not sure what. Rescue them? Somehow relieve them of any charge?" Perplexed, he shook his head. "It doesn't make any sense."

Along with the men, Melissa was frowning, as puzzled as they. "Does that tell us anything about their master?"

"Well," Felix said, "it suggests that they, at least, believe their master is somehow able to overrule an earl."

"That," Damian said, "or make some sort of deal with you, as I assume was what happened in Ireland."

Julian shook his head. "I can't see any reason that would force me to make a deal with anyone. We're not under threat on any front." He grimaced in frustration and sat back, tapping a single finger on the desk. "As for their master overruling me, in a case such as this, with crimes committed on my principal estate...I can't see how, much less who could accomplish that. Not unless I died, and their master—not Felix or you —inherits."

Damian blinked. His expression blanked. "You don't think Felix or I—"

Julian held up a hand. "No, I don't." After a moment, he confessed, "I'm honestly not sure what I think. We go around and around, yet underneath it all..."

"Underneath it all," Melissa said, eyes narrowed in thought, "there is a hint, a shadow, of a pattern." She looked at Julian. "I mentioned it before, how with the earlier attacks—the thorn in your saddle, the shot in the park, the urn falling—it could be argued that Felix was implicated." She flung Felix an appeasing glance. "Purely through you being there, more or less on the spot, when those incidents occurred. You were also here when the mantrap was planted, and as for the spring gun—someone might suggest you were planting it when it unexpectedly went off."

Stunned, Felix stared at her, then understanding flooded his expression. "You think someone's trying to make me a scapegoat for Julian's murder?" His voice had risen in horror.

Damian was frowning. "You were here for the punt accident, too."

"So were you." When Damian looked at Melissa, she caught his eye. "And Manning was introduced into the household through you."

"But"—Damian looked at Julian, openly horrified—"it's not me!"

Julian waved dismissively. "We know it's not you. What Melissa is demonstrating is that, when viewed by others who don't know us, had any of these attacks succeeded, then both you and Felix might have been thought to have had a hand in my demise."

"And," Felix said, "if that got serious enough to lead to a conviction, aside from any sentence we received, we'd be barred from inheriting." He looked at Melissa, then at Julian. "Could this somehow be about the earldom's succession?"

"I don't know." Julian sat forward, clasping his hands on the desk. "But in some ways, this is starting to feel like someone's long game."

"What's that?" Damian asked. "Is it a strategy thing?"

Julian nodded. "It's an approach that political manipulators employ—a succession of individual events that in themselves appear minor and often unconnected, but in the long run, those events build on each other to achieve a particular goal while, along the way, obscuring the hand of the one pulling the strings and playing the game."

At last, he felt he had a recognizable framework into which all the strange events might fit. "Finally," he breathed, "this might make sense."

Felix remained puzzled. "How?"

"I can't see the end goal yet," Julian admitted. "That's usually the case and, at this point, is to be expected. But equally, once we identify the end goal, the chances are we'll know who wants it and who, therefore, is behind the game."

Feeling increasingly on surer ground, he said, "Let's see what we can make of what we already know. If Mitchell and Manning were both put in place by whoever's behind this—"

"Let's call him X," Melissa suggested.

Julian dipped his head her way. "By X, then Mitchell joined the household twenty months ago. That definitely qualifies as long-term planning. On the other hand, Manning is a recent addition and introduced via Damian, so at the castle, but not formally part of the castle staff. That tells us that X is still actively weaving his plans and moving his pawns into position." He paused, then glanced at Melissa. "Until this ends, we need to be wary of adding anyone to the household in any capacity at all."

She nodded. "I'll speak with the Phelpses and Hockey and Edgerton, but hopefully, it won't be that long before we can find our way to X."

"We can but hope," Julian replied.

"I just remembered," Damian said. "Manning was at Carsely House when the bookcase fell on you."

Julian nodded. "Very true. And as with the punt, a familiarity with tools was required, so perhaps he was behind that attempt, too."

"But"—Felix shifted in his chair—"Manning wasn't at Carsely House when the urn fell."

"He wasn't," Damian agreed. "I hadn't hired him then." Damian looked at Julian. "Are you thinking X might be Gordon? I mean, if you were to die and, for whatever reason, Felix and I were out of contention, the title passes to Frederick."

"And Frederick is old," Felix said. "If soon after inheriting, he dies, no one would think anything of it, and Gordon is next in line."

"Gordon, who recommended Manning to me." Damian's jaw set, and he looked at Julian. "It has to be Gordon."

Julian met Damian's gaze and grimaced. "I'm not so sure of that. I find it difficult to imagine Gordon in the role of X. Gordon's never struck me as being long headed over anything. He's not the sort to think of, much less meticulously execute long-range, complicated, and careful plans. X's game has required all of that plus a cautious yet relentless focus."

When Melissa, Felix, and Damian continued to frown, Julian asked, "Is there anyone else—someone we're overlooking entirely—who fits X's bill?"

They all glanced at him, but no one volunteered any name.

Felix shifted. "Let's come at X from another angle. He's someone who wants to see you—and me and most likely now Melissa as well—dead. And ultimately to remove Damian as well. And if we're entertaining the possibility that, through Mitchell, he arranged for Papa to have his accident and Campbell to hang himself, and there's now been how many attempts on your life that could have harmed others…well, clearly X isn't bothered by how many innocents he murders on his way to achieving his goal."

Julian nodded. "X has a callous disregard for human life—he has no feeling for others. Again, I wouldn't have said such a description fits Gordon."

Melissa grimaced. "Even I'm having trouble putting Gordon into X's shoes."

"However," Julian said, "we all know that Gordon's reckless and easily led. For someone of the ilk of X, manipulating Gordon would be child's play."

"And it would be easy enough to engineer an accident to remove Gordon later," Damian put in. "A carriage accident would be believed without question by everyone."

Melissa frowned. "But if we're working on the theory that this is ultimately about the earldom—that somehow seizing the title, the estate, and the Delamere wealth is X's end goal—then who inherits after Gordon?"

"After Gordon..." Julian frowned, then looked at his brothers. "I've no idea who's next in line."

Felix grunted. "You'll have to consult old Hennessy to be sure."

Julian picked up a pencil and scribbled a note to remind him to write to the family's solicitor. "I'll do that, just in case the answer means something to us, but it occurs to me that inheriting the title isn't necessary to gain access to the estate and the family coffers." Looking up, he met his brothers' eyes. "Having an earl who's a lord in name only—who is nothing more than someone else's puppet—might be the goal X is aiming for."

Melissa had been pondering how their hypothesis of X connected with Mitchell and Manning. "I think there's something we're overlooking."

She raised her gaze to find the three brothers gazing questioningly at her. "Given what we now think is X's goal and his plan to secure it, what is it that's keeping Mitchell and Manning from speaking of him?" She met Damian's, then Felix's and, lastly, Julian's eyes. "They can't possibly be imagining they'll be rescued and pardoned by a new earl. There's too many of you in line for that to be even remotely feasible. Quite aside from the fact that you're still alive, they'll be tried, convicted, and executed long before any new earl could be installed, and regardless, why would the new earl—whichever of you it happens to be—feel moved to pardon them anyway?"

Frowning, she shook her head. "Their refusal to speak makes no sense—not if it derives from hope of rescue and pardon by some future successor."

"I have to agree." Julian studied her face. "So...?"

"I think," she offered, "that their silence must be due to the nature of the hold X has over them. It's something powerful enough to convince them that, regardless of any punishment, it's in their best interests not to offer him up."

"Considering what's at stake for them," Felix said, "'powerful' is the operative word."

She looked at Felix and Damian. "You saw them last. How did they seem?"

Felix arched his brows. "In a word? Weary."

Damian nodded. "Weary. Defeated. And resigned." He looked at Felix. "Didn't you get that impression? That they'd accepted their lot and were resigned to their fate?" He swung his gaze to Melissa. "There was no resistance—no fight—in them. They've given up."

Melissa glanced at Julian. "That fits with what I'm thinking—that it's not that they don't want to talk but that they believe they *can't*. That they absolutely cannot name X. I don't think it's anything to do with loyalty, either." She spread her hands. "It would be a rare loyalty that stretches to murdering an earl you don't even know, one you feel no personal animosity toward."

Julian nodded. "And I'm absolutely certain I've never previously crossed paths or had any interaction with either man."

"Precisely." She went on. "So X has convinced them of something— who knows what—and whatever it is, it's powerful enough to ensure their silence, even, it seems, all the way to the gallows."

After a moment digesting that, Julian said, "That means that no matter what we threaten them with, no matter what approaches or appeals to their better selves I make, nothing's going to work. They won't talk— they won't name X."

The silence stretched as they contemplated that.

Eventually, Melissa stirred. When Julian glanced at her, she met his gaze, then said, "Setting aside all that, I believe we have another, more immediate concern."

All three brothers looked at her, brows rising in question.

She drew in a breath and said, "We've found two of X's henchmen. Mitchell's been here for twenty months, so we have proof of just how long and deep X's plans run. We now know he doesn't appear himself but acts through those he's put in place over time—his pawns, as you called them." She looked around the circle of faces—Damian's, Felix's, and finally, Julian's. "How do we know he doesn't have more pawns planted among the staff?"

Julian grimaced, Felix looked tired, and Damian looked faintly disgusted.

"That's...an appalling, but unfortunately valid question." Damian frowned. "Is there any way we can tell?"

Julian looked at Melissa.

From her pocket, she drew out the list she'd made of the recently hired staff and held it out to him.

He took it, unfolded the sheet, spread it on the desk, and scanned it. "We still have nine possibilities and no reason we know of to suspect any are X's pawns."

Felix sat up. "The names?"

"Biggins and Walter, both stablemen, Carter, the groundsman, Richards and Cantrell, two footmen, Benton, a senior housemaid, Polly Fisher and Enid Wise, junior maids, and last but possibly not least, the scullery boy, Billy." Julian looked up. "I'm sure Edgerton will be keeping an eye on Carter, and Hockey will be doing the same with Biggins and Walter."

Melissa added, "The Phelpses will watch the others as well as they can, but with that number and given the sort of work the indoor staff do, spread all over the house, it'll be harder for the Phelpses to ensure that none of those six indoor staff have a chance to set one of X's schemes in motion."

Grim once more, Julian said, "How X communicates with his pawns is another avenue we ought to pursue, but until we identify X and put a stop to this madness, I suggest we all remain very much on guard."

The others nodded, and Felix somewhat morosely observed, "Sadly, this isn't over yet."

❧

The following afternoon, Melissa and Julian went for a postprandial stroll in the gardens. They ambled across the lawns hand in hand, paused to admire the loggia, currently dripping with white and blue and mauve wisteria blossoms, then walked on, avoiding the shrubbery in favor of making for the bucolic peace of the orchard beyond.

Melissa tipped her head back, allowing the sun to find her face beneath the brim of her favorite straw hat. After the dip in the lake, Jolene had worked wonders, steaming the hat until it was close to its original shape.

Since waking, Melissa had made a conscious effort not to allude to the metaphorical sword hanging over their heads. She'd just opened her lips to inquire about local festivals when the sound of striding footsteps drew her and Julian's heads around.

Felix was walking swiftly toward them. He saw them watching him and waved. "No crisis," he called.

They waited, and when he was close enough to converse, he explained, "I wanted to get some air myself, and in light of the promise we all made over the breakfast table to go nowhere alone, I've come to tag along." He halted before them, looked from one to the other, and belatedly added, "If you don't mind?"

Melissa laughed, and Julian smiled and waved at Felix to join them.

He fell in on Melissa's other side and matched her pace—essentially screening her from that direction, just as Julian was blocking any attack from the other side. She hid a grin. While Julian was increasingly and demonstrably protective of her, so, too, was Felix—he was just a trifle more cautious about showing it.

They left the high hedges of the shrubbery behind, crossed a garden lane, and reached the low stone wall that surrounded the orchard. It was the first time she'd had a chance to study the trees. Resting both hands on the waist-high wall, she scanned the enclosure. "I hadn't realized the orchard was so large." There were dozens and dozens of trees.

"There're over fifty trees," Felix informed her. "Apples, pears, cherries, quinces, greengage, damson, and there's nut trees, too."

Smiling, Julian leaned a hip against the wall. "Felix was always the fruit-mad one. Cook preserves the greengages just for him."

"Well"—Felix shot him a superior look—"I appreciate them. You and Damian were always philistines when it came to fruit."

Melissa laughed.

A high-pitched whine cut through the summer stillness.

She stepped back from the wall and looked toward an old barn that stood twenty yards past the side of the orchard. "Did you hear that?"

A volley of frantic yips answered her.

Felix had turned to look that way. "That's coming from inside the barn."

Frowning, Julian glanced at Melissa. "That sounds like Ulysses—a young dog and not one of our hounds, either. As far as I know, Ulysses is the only dog at the castle likely to yelp like that."

"Ulysses?" Melissa called.

Another round of yips, this time more excited, replied.

"That does sound like him." Mystified, she started toward the barn.

"But when I went upstairs to get my hat, he was fast asleep on his blanket in my room, and I left him there. Jolene said she'd fetch him later and take him for a walk."

The brothers kept pace on either side.

"Perhaps," Felix said, "we have a stray?"

"Generally, strays avoid attracting attention," Julian pointed out.

They reached the barn, and the yips and yelps rose in a crescendo. The heavy doors were barred by a wooden beam supported on iron brackets.

Felix lifted the beam clear and stood it against the side of the barn, and Julian hauled open one of the wide doors.

A dim, cavernous space, illuminated by the sunshine streaming in through the open door, greeted them. Dust motes danced in the air as Melissa walked in, looking around. "Ulysses?" She turned, searching, expecting the golden puppy to come streaking to her as he usually did.

Instead, the frantic barking escalated in both pitch and fervency.

"Where are you?" The frantic yelps were echoing off the tin roof and bouncing around the largely empty space, making tracking the actual source near impossible.

"He's obviously here somewhere." Julian was turning this way and that, trying to decide in which direction to search.

Felix was doing the same. "The echoes are confusing."

Julian waved him toward the far end of the large barn. "Go that way. We'll try this way."

They separated, with Felix walking to the right and Julian to Melissa's left, while she went directly forward, trying to discern in which direction the barks were loudest.

The barn was largely empty, with just a few bales of straw stacked here and there. She'd nearly reached the back wall before she felt confident in turning to her left. "He's this way!" she called.

A stack of bales partially filled the left rear corner of the barn. The bales seemed to be solidly stacked, yet the closer she drew the more certain she became that Ulysses was somehow trapped behind them.

She reached the bales as Julian approached; they rose to her waist. "I think he's trapped behind them. He must have wriggled in and not been able to find his way out again." She hiked up her skirts. "Help me up."

Julian closed his hands about her waist and lifted her up, then scrambled up as well.

Felix jogged up. "Is he there?"

"Sounds like it," Julian said.

It was too difficult to walk on the straw. On her hands and knees, Melissa crawled to the corner of the building. "There's a gap here, between the bales. Right in the corner." She reached the hole and peered in and saw Ulysses leaping up, frantic and overjoyed to see her.

She slumped down and reached into the hole, but although she could touch the leaping pup, she couldn't get a firm grip on his wriggling body.

Julian reached her, and she drew back her arm and turned to him. "My arms aren't long enough. I can't catch hold of him."

Julian looked into the hole, saw the problem, sighed, and stretched out full length on the prickly straw. He reached into the hole. Ignoring the puppy's furious licking, he stretched and felt around with his fingers and managed to curl them into the pup's ruff. "Got him."

Gripping firmly, he started to carefully hoist the squirming puppy up.

The light started to fade.

"What?" Felix swung around. "Damn it—we're in here!" He strode for the door, then Julian heard his brother swear and break into a run.

Julian hauled Ulysses clear of the hole and rolled onto his side.

Melissa grabbed the puppy, and Julian scrambled back across the bales to where he could look toward the front of the barn.

By then, the door had shut.

The beam rattled into its brackets an instant before Felix rammed his shoulder into the door.

The door didn't budge.

Felix stepped back. "Hey! We're in here. The earl and countess are here!"

When no reply came, Felix yelled, "What the devil do you think you're playing at?"

Silence stretched.

With the door closed, the barn was gloomy, lit only by the thin beams that managed to seep between the old boards and around the edges of the door. Julian reached the edge of the bales and scrambled off. When, clutching the ecstatic puppy to her chest, Melissa reached him, he lifted her, puppy and all, to the ground. Then he took her free hand, and they walked to where Felix was examining the door's hinges.

As they joined him, he shook his head. "I can't see any way to open the doors." He glanced around. "And there's nothing here we can use to break through them."

Julian huffed. "You know what they say—they don't build things like they used to. This place is old, well-seasoned, sound, and solid. The only way to get through the door is to have someone open it."

Felix frowned. "We're a fair way from the stable or even the horse paddocks. If we yell, do you think they'll hear us?"

Julian was about to reply when he smelled smoke. He looked down and saw tendrils start to waft beneath the door.

He felt his face turn to stone. "Don't waste your breath." He gripped Felix's arm and, as his brother stared at him, nodded at the smoke. "They're firing the barn."

Felix looked down and goggled at the smoke. "For God's sake!"

Julian slashed a hand through the air, and Felix shut his lips and looked at him questioningly. Julian turned to Melissa and put a finger to his lips, then retook her hand. Tugging Felix along as well, he drew them deeper into the barn. When they were some way from the door, he released Felix and murmured to them both, "There is another way out, as long as whoever it is hasn't realized it's there. If they do know of it, we'll be sitting ducks as we leave, but it is our only way out of here."

Felix's expression cleared as he realized what Julian meant. He waved Julian on.

Julian met Melissa's eyes, then closed his hand more firmly about hers and quickly walked on. He led them around a dividing wall to where a wooden ladder stood anchored on the ground, giving access to the barn's loft.

From around the door, flames were starting to spread across the ground, leaping from wisps of straw to the stacked bales. Denser smoke wafted to them, and Felix coughed. "This place is going to go up like a bonfire."

Julian halted at the base of the ladder and turned to Melissa. "I'll take the pup."

Apparently exhausted by his ordeal, the puppy had fallen asleep in Melissa's arms. Gently, she transferred the sleepy bundle to Julian, and he cradled the small beast against his chest.

"Wait." Melissa stripped off the sash that circled her raised waistline. "Do up your jacket and sit Ulysses inside."

Felix helped, then Melissa wound the sash about Julian's chest, cinching it tight over Ulysses, holding him firmly in place.

Satisfied, she stepped back. "Now we've all got two hands for climbing."

Trying to breathe shallowly, Julian waved her up the ladder. She hiked up her skirt and petticoat at the front and, holding the muslin in her teeth, quickly climbed up.

"You next," Felix gasped through the neckerchief he was knotting about his face.

Julian didn't wait to be told twice. He went up as fast as he dared, careful not to jar Ulysses, who thankfully remained asleep.

Julian stepped off the top of the ladder, relieved to see the loft much as he remembered it. He glanced back down, confirming that Felix was on his way up, then waved Melissa before him to the end of the loft, where the hay doors were closed tight.

He worked quickly to release the latch, then warily eased one door open and peered through the gap. The doors were set high in the back wall of the barn. Unless their would-be murderer had studied the barn, there was no reason he would have known they were there. Julian carefully scanned, but on seeing no one, eased the door wider.

Felix and Melissa joined him as he pushed both doors wide. "I don't think our attacker knows of this, but let's keep as quiet as possible."

Felix nodded and helped ready the winch used to move hay bales up and down. "You two go first. I'll follow," Felix whispered, struggling not to cough as more smoke billowed up from below. The insidious *whoosh* of hungry flames swelled, punctuated by loud cracks and pops.

Julian nodded. After checking that Ulysses, who had woken, was still secure, he stepped onto the plate above the winch's hook, took a firm grip on the rope, and beckoned Melissa to him. "Stand on my boots and hold on to the rope."

She did, and he wrapped one arm around her waist, locking her against him. As soon as he judged she was steady, he nodded to Felix, and his brother used the winch's arm to swing them out into the open air.

Melissa smothered a shriek, but hung on and kept her feet planted on his as Felix rapidly wound out the rope, and they sailed down.

The winch's hook thudded into the ground and tipped them off, but Julian had been ready for that and leapt clear, taking Melissa with him. They staggered, then straightened.

Julian turned and looked up, ready to send the hook back up, but he couldn't see Felix.

He could see flames leaping and flickering farther back in the loft.

Then Felix reappeared and flung down one bale, then another, then he leapt from the ledge and fell—and landed on the bales.

Julian and Melissa rushed over, but Felix was already struggling up.

He grinned through the soot streaking his face. "That was even more fun than I remembered."

Julian bit back his response. He held out a hand and, when Felix grasped it, hauled his brother off the bales. "Let's see if our attacker has hung around to admire his handiwork."

He grasped Melissa's hand, and with Felix following, they headed around the barn.

Even before they reached the front, over the escalating roar of the flames, the sounds of a crowd—of shouted orders, responses, and exclamations—reached them. Julian sighed and glanced at Melissa and Felix. "Sadly, I fear we're too late."

They were. The area before the barn was teeming with people. If the man who had locked them inside and lit the fire was there, he would be indistinguishable from the many others rushing about, ferrying water from the river to douse the area around the barn.

The barn itself was past saving.

"My lord!" Several of those helping spotted them. "My lady! Mr. Felix!"

Hockey and Edgerton, both in full flight directing the response, turned and, shocked at seeing them, lumbered their way.

Julian waved the pair back and, with Melissa, strode across to them. He met their wide eyes. "Someone locked us in and torched the place. We escaped through the hay doors." He turned to survey the old barn.

Edgerton and Hockey did the same.

Grim-faced, Edgerton shook his head. "We can't save it, my lord."

"No"—Julian tugged and undid the knot securing the sash about his chest—"but we need to stop the flames from spreading any farther." He handed the sash, then Ulysses to Melissa, exchanged a swift look with Felix, then said, "Come on. We'll help."

Julian and Felix rapidly liaised with Hockey and Edgerton, then the four men separated, each going to direct the men battling the fire along one of the barn's walls. Determined to do her part, Melissa tucked Ulysses under one arm and strode to where a line of staff were ferrying buckets of water from the river.

She quickly reorganized the system so that the empty buckets were run back along the line by the youngest stable boys, leaving their elders to pass the full buckets along the line of willing hands. That nearly doubled the rate of water being delivered to those working around the burning barn.

When more staff came running from the house, she brushed aside their exclamations and set up a second line, passing buckets to the crew at the rear of the barn, where the breeze was making beating back the flames extra difficult.

Together, led by Julian, Melissa, Felix, and the senior staff, the assembled company worked tirelessly as the sun slowly sank.

It was dusk before the fire had been sufficiently doused for everyone to stand down.

By then, too many people had realized why she, Julian, and Felix had been so immediately on the scene, why they'd suddenly come running from the back of the barn, and word quickly spread that they'd been locked in the barn by the person who had subsequently lit the fire. Dark mutters rose, and there was little they could do about that.

When, with Ulysses gamboling at her heels, Melissa finally returned to the area before the blackened husk of the barn, she found Julian—his clothes soot streaked and his dark hair liberally ash bedecked—standing with Hockey, Edgerton, and Felix and surveying the smoldering ruin.

Ulysses pranced around Julian's feet, then plonked his rear on Julian's boot, as was his wont. Thus alerted to her approach, Julian turned his head, then held out his arm.

She walked within it and all but slumped against him. He curled his arm about her and held her close, then uncaring of who saw, pressed a kiss to her temple. "Are you all right?"

She nodded, then raised her head and met his gray eyes. "You?"

He sighed. "Tired. Of all of this."

She looked past him at Felix, who looked as darkly angry as the majority of the staff.

His hands on his hips, Hockey turned and pinned Julian with a direct look. "Tell us straight—was this another attempt to kill you?"

Julian looked at the destruction before them. "Me, the countess, and Felix as well. And before you ask, we didn't get so much as a glimpse. There's no saying who they were."

Hockey's and Edgerton's expressions darkened. They bit their lips and looked away, unwilling to swear in front of Melissa.

She wouldn't have blamed them.

But others, loosely grouped behind them, had heard, and the mutters grew deeper and darker.

After a moment, Edgerton drew in a long breath. "You'd better get up to the castle—they'll have started to fret over what's happened and where you are. Leave this"—he nodded at the blackened ruin—"to Hockey and me. We'll see all made safe."

Knowing he could trust them and accepting that he had to, Julian nodded and turned away, dislodging Ulysses, who happily followed as Julian urged Melissa around, then took her hand and started toward the castle. Felix came up on his other side.

Julian glanced at his brother, then at his wife and murmured, "Evidently, we have another pawn of X's to unmask."

Both simply nodded, too tired to do more.

Weary to the bone, Julian tightened his hold on Melissa's hand and walked slowly toward the castle.

CHAPTER 14

$\mathcal{M}$ ore worn out—literally exhausted—than she'd ever felt, Melissa retired to her bedchamber earlier than usual that evening. After insisting that the others, still talking in the drawing room, did not need to escort her up, she climbed the stairs alone.

The events of the day had left her shaken, more than she'd initially realized; the need to act and help put out the fire had forced her to focus on that and nothing else. But later, when, over a subdued dinner, she, Julian, and Felix had related to Veronica, Frederick, and Damian—who had been out riding and had missed the excitement entirely—all that had happened, the reality of what had almost occurred had come crashing down upon her.

On returning to the house, the three of them, plus Ulysses, who had refused to allow her out of his sight, had gone straight upstairs to change out of their ruined clothes and bathe. Their hair had stunk of smoke, and fine ash had got everywhere.

Even after they were clean and had donned fresh clothes, the scent of smoke lingered.

Ulysses, of course, had followed her to her room. He'd watched with interest while she'd bathed, and once she'd stepped from the tub, she'd had Jolene dunk the puppy and wash him, too, which he'd decided was a great game. His antics had left them laughing, which had brought some small relief.

We survived. None of us are even hurt.

She'd kept repeating that mantra throughout the evening.

It hadn't really helped.

None of the previous attacks had been so frightening. So real. All those previous attempts, while variously shocking, frustrating, or irritating, had somehow seemed more like a badly designed game, albeit one in poor taste. Although each incident had been potentially dangerous, in the aftermath, all those previous attacks had seemed almost clownish.

This time, the knowledge that she could very easily have died a horrible death remained front and center in her mind. Even more distressing and disquieting was the realization of just how close she'd come to losing Julian. Yes, she would have died with him, and some part of her fully comprehended that, but it was the prospect of his death that most exercised her emotions. That tied them into painful knots and left her confronting a reality she hadn't seen until then.

He is my future.

But not just in the simple, obvious way.

Through the hours she'd spent with him in London, all those enforced hours strolling among the social and political elite of the ton, bolstered by what she'd learned of him here, at the castle—all she'd seen of how central he was to the well-being of such a wide swath of people and how well he filled all his various roles—had opened her eyes to how important he was to so many people and how critically important he might become on a far wider stage.

She hadn't forgotten just how many senior politicians had come to their wedding.

She was coming to understand that Fate had cast her as his helpmate for a reason. She was, after all, her parents' daughter, her grandparents' granddaughter. Few young ladies—possibly no other lady—could claim to be better groomed to be the wife of a lord of such great social and political potential.

He was a good man with a good heart, a man with the status to make political and social changes, with the ability to pull that off and the determination and stubbornness to do it.

Losing him to the fire—to any of these senseless attacks—would have been a shattering blow, not just to her and his family but to the future of the country itself.

Her higher role in life—her duty to the wider good—was increasingly clear.

He might be protective of her, but she would move the heavens to ensure he lived and prospered.

The day had definitely taken a toll, and on reaching her bedchamber, she sighed feelingly, opened the door, and walked in.

The lamps were lit, and a welcoming glow spread through the room.

Jolene was waiting to help her prepare for bed. "I thought you'd be up early." She went to the door, waited for Ulysses, who had paused to sniff the furniture in the sitting room, to gallop in, then shut the door.

Melissa crossed to her dressing table and sat on the padded stool. "Hair first. Perhaps if you brush it, that last hint of smoke will vanish."

"We can but try." Jolene set to, pulling out the pins she'd set in place only a few hours before.

Ulysses came to investigate Melissa's hems. Nosing beneath them, he found the toe of her slipper, gripped it between his teeth, and tugged. "Grr." He tugged and waggled his head. "Grr!"

Melissa laughed, and Jolene smiled. "He really is a character."

Sobering as the events of the afternoon replayed yet again in her mind, Melissa looked down at the puppy, then raised her gaze to the mirror. "I can't understand how he came to be in the barn. It was locked when we reached it, and he was in a spot he couldn't get out of."

Jolene glanced down at the puppy. "No way would he have been silent while someone left him in a barn. I've seen how well the farm buildings are kept here, so I wouldn't imagine there was any hole for him to have wriggled in."

"He couldn't have climbed the bales and got to where he was by himself."

"Well, then." With Melissa's long locks free, Jolene reached for the brush. "Shutting him in there had to be deliberate. Presumably to get you to go in and rescue him. You wouldn't have gone into the barn otherwise, would you? And his lordship and Mr. Felix with you?"

"No," Melissa agreed.

As Jolene drew the brush slowly through her hair, Melissa closed her eyes. "When I left here after lunch, Ulysses was asleep on his blanket in the corner. I shut him in, then I met you downstairs."

Jolene continued plying the brush. "I meant to come and fetch him later, but before I could, the Phelpses had us rushing down to help with the fire." Melissa opened her eyes to see Jolene glance at Ulysses. "I thought the bundle of fur would be safer here."

"He would have been."

After several moments of brushing, Jolene frowned. "Even if one of the maids had let the little terror out of these rooms, he would have scampered after you. It's you he makes a beeline for."

"Hmm." Melissa's brain felt sluggish; she closed her eyes again. "Someone must have come up almost as soon as I left and taken him outside."

The point was a potential avenue to be pursued. Shortly after lunch, there should have been staff around upstairs, tending to this and that. Some maid or footman might have seen whoever had taken the puppy.

"There." Jolene set down the brush. "Your hair's had as much brushing as it can take."

Melissa opened her eyes and considered her long tresses. "If the smoke is still lingering tomorrow, perhaps we can wash it again." She looked down, then around for Ulysses. After losing interest in her slipper, he'd ambled off. She spotted him worrying a knotted rope half hidden beneath her bed.

As if feeling her gaze, he fixed a big brown eye on her, then picked up the rope and came trotting over to offer it. Laughing softly, she bent and obligingly caught one end, and Ulysses launched into an energetic game of tug. "He, at least, seems to have recovered completely from his ordeal."

Jolene was bustling about, laying out Melissa's nightgown. "Well, he was rescued by you and his lordship, his favorite people, so by his lights, all is well in his world."

Melissa grinned. She ended up slipping from the dressing stool to sit on the rug and was engrossed in her tug-of-war with Ulysses, with Jolene indulgently looking on, when a tap fell on the door.

Absentmindedly, Melissa called, "Come in."

The door opened, and Benton, the senior maid, walked in, bearing a salver on which reposed a mug of something steaming.

Melissa had noticed that Benton rarely smiled—indeed, rarely raised her gaze from what she was doing—and the maid did the same now as she carried the mug to the dressing table and placed it carefully on the glass surface.

"What's that?" Melissa asked.

Benton turned her way and, eyes downcast, bobbed a curtsy. "His lordship ordered it brought up for you, my lady. It's a mug of warm milk. He said he thought as you'd benefit from it."

Melissa couldn't stop her eyes widening in surprise. "I see."

Benton bobbed again and made for the door.

His teeth anchored in the rope, Ulysses watched her go, growling and tugging all the while.

The instant the door shut, Jolene declared, "It just shows." Her smile was the epitome of indulgent approval. "Head over ears in love with you he is." She put a hand to her chest. "*Such* a sweet gesture."

Melissa sighed. "Except that I really don't like warm milk—as you well know."

"Yes, well." Jolene waved her to the dressing table. "You'll just have to hold your nose and drink it, won't you? You can't refuse such an offering." She looked at the mug, steaming on the dresser. "It's so romantic that he's thinking of you."

Melissa released the rope, and surprised in mid-tug, Ulysses rolled paws over ears backward. Smiling, Melissa climbed to her feet. She glanced at the mug, only to feel a thump on her foot. She looked down. Ulysses had raced in and dropped the rope invitingly.

She looked at the puppy. Tongue lolling out, he yapped at her, all but daring her to pick up the rope again.

She grinned, swooped, and grabbed one end just as Ulysses darted in and grabbed the other. She tugged, expecting him to pull back. Instead, the pup released his hold, and she was the one tripping backward. Flailing to keep her balance, she released the rope, sending it wildly flying.

Clack!

Jolene had rushed in and steadied her. They both turned to see the mug tipped over, and the milk cascading across the dressing table's top to drip off the edge and pool on the polished floor.

"Drat that puppy." Jolene cast the pup a dark look.

Unrepentant, he grinned and wagged his tail at her.

"I encouraged him. You can't scold him without scolding me as well, and you know you won't do that." Melissa walked to the dressing table and reached out to right the mug. Her hand froze, hovering over the pottery as her eyes took in the gritty residue that the spill of milk had left on the glass of the dressing table's surface, just beyond the lip of the mug.

She couldn't drag her gaze from the sight. "Jolene?"

"What?" The maid had gone to retrieve the rope. She straightened and looked at Melissa.

Melissa felt Ulysses nudging at her skirts, attempting to find a way past to the milk pooling on the floor. Fear streaked through her, and she bent and caught him before he could reach the white puddle. "That's not for you." She lifted him into her arms and straightened, then looked at the tipped mug. "And I don't think I want any of it, either." She caught Jolene's gaze and, with her head, directed the maid to the mess on the table. "What do you think that is?"

Puzzled, Jolene came to the dressing table, then she saw what Melissa had and, frowning more definitely, bent closer to study the powdery pieces.

Cuddling Ulysses, Melissa asked, "What are you thinking?"

Jolene straightened. Her usual rosy color had fled, and with her gaze, like Melissa's, fixed on the residue, she swallowed before saying, "It's not laudanum, that's for certain. If I had to guess...it looks like the poison gardeners put out for rats."

"Arsenic." Melissa glanced at Ulysses, and her features set. She looked at Jolene. "Don't touch anything. Ring for a footman and send them to ask his lordship to join me here as a matter of urgency."

"Yes, my lady." Jolene went to the wall by the dressing room door and tugged the bellpull that hung there.

While the maid went out to the sitting room to intercept whichever of the footmen answered and pass on Melissa's summons, Melissa turned her back on the dressing table and walked across to stand before the fireplace. She stared into the empty grate, hugged Ulysses close, and while she waited, buried her face in his now-sweet-smelling fur.

Five minutes later, Julian burst into the room, already on high alert. "What's wrong?"

Having had time to think, Melissa asked, "You didn't order Benton to bring me hot milk, did you?"

He frowned. "No." His hands rising to his hips, he added, "I would be more likely to send you a brandy. Perhaps Mama?"

"I doubt it." She pointed to the spilt milk. "Look carefully at what's been left behind on the glass."

He crossed to the table and stared down. When he raised his head and met her gaze, his eyes were bleak, and his face had set in forbidding lines. "Benton brought this up?"

Racked by a maelstrom of emotions, fear and fury the foremost, Julian watched Melissa nod. "She said you'd ordered it for me, that you thought I would benefit from it."

Fury surged and roared through him. "Did she, indeed?"

He swung on his heel and strode for the door. "Let's see what she has to say for herself."

He crossed the sitting room, vaguely aware that Melissa, still carrying Ulysses, started to follow, but stopped and turned back, presumably to hand over the puppy and instruct Jolene regarding the spill. He didn't slow; he had to—needed to—seize the moment and Benton, too.

Once out of their apartments, he headed for the main stairs; he was almost running when he reached the gallery and saw Felix and Damian stepping up from the stairs.

His brothers took one look at his face and straightened. "What?" Felix asked.

"Another attack?" Damian guessed.

Grimly, Julian nodded. "Benton delivered poisoned milk to Melissa. Luckily, it spilled—she didn't drink it."

"Thank God!" Felix frowned and fell in beside Julian as he strode for the servants' stairs. "Benton's that older maid, isn't she?"

Julian nodded. "Another recent addition to the household." He'd intended to get Phelps to go with him, but his brothers would do. "The milk was still warm, so I doubt she's had time to run yet. Let's see if she's in her room."

The three of them clattered up the narrow stairs to the servants' quarters in the attic. At the head of the stairs, they ran into Thornley, about to start down. Masking his surprise, the footman stood back to allow them to enter the narrow foyer.

"We're looking for the older maid—Benton." Julian managed to keep his voice low. "Which is her room?"

Thornley's eyes widened, and he looked down the corridor. "All the maids are in the east corridor, m'lord." Thornley pointed. "Go to the end and turn right. Benton hasn't been with us long, so her room's liable to be closer to the corridor's end."

Jaw set, Julian nodded and stalked forward.

Behind him, he heard Damian ask, "Is there any other way down from the other end of the east wing?"

"No, Mr. Delamere," Thornley replied. "The back stairs lead straight down to the kitchen, but they're to the left along that corridor there."

Interpreting that to mean that, once he reached the intersection before him, there would be no escape for Benton, Julian allowed his lips to curve coldly.

He reached the intersection, turned right, and saw a door standing half open toward the corridor's end. Stepping silently along the thin runner, he signaled to Felix and Damian to do the same.

They crept up to the door, and he peeked around the doorjamb.

Benton had her bag sitting open on the narrow cot and was busily cramming her belongings into it.

Julian smiled and, pushing the door wide, stepped fully into the doorway.

Benton looked up and, startled, stepped away from the bed.

She stared at him—her rounding eyes taking in Felix and Damian, who ranged at his back—and every vestige of color left her face.

Julian arched a brow. "Going somewhere?"

Benton swallowed and didn't answer.

Thornley had informed Phelps that Julian was searching for Benton, and Phelps, with a sober Thornley following, came hurrying up to assist.

With his temper barely leashed, Julian, his gaze still locked with Benton's, stepped aside and instructed Phelps to incarcerate the maid in the dungeon, in another of the old cells-cum-storeroom opposite the one presently occupied by Mitchell and Manning.

After Thornley and Phelps removed Benton from the room and marched her off toward the back stairs, Julian retraced his steps to the stairs leading down to the gallery.

Felix and Damian fell in behind him, and Felix murmured, "Is that wise?" Julian glanced back, and Felix caught his gaze. "Putting them all in the same area where they can speak with each other?"

Julian huffed and started down the narrow stairs. "I'm *hoping* they'll talk to each other. Perhaps one of them will see reason and persuade the other two that they need to tell us what they know."

They reached the gallery as Melissa walked into it. She waved behind her, toward the back stairs. "I saw them take Benton down. She wouldn't look at me. Thinking back, I'm not sure she's ever looked me in the eye."

He grunted, took her hand, and with Felix and Damian, they went downstairs to the library. Luckily, his mother and uncle had already retired.

After fortifying themselves with glasses of brandy—even Melissa— they made their way to the kitchens and on to the door to the cellars.

Julian, Felix, and Damian lifted lanterns from a nearby shelf. They lit all three, then carrying one, Julian led the way down the stairs to the main cellar and around into the corridor that sloped down to what was originally the castle dungeon.

Melissa followed close behind him. She shivered and drew the shawl she'd wound about her shoulders tighter. He reached back, caught her hand, squeezed it reassuringly, then released her.

On reaching the cell occupied by Mitchell and Manning, Julian turned to the door opposite and, using the key Phelps had delivered to him in the library, unlocked the heavy door and pushed it wide.

Facing the door, Benton sat on a low bench created from full sacks of flour. She raised a hand to shade her eyes against the lanterns' glare.

Once again, Julian caught and held Melissa's hand. Letting his thumb gently stroke her palm, he studied Benton, then somewhat wearily asked, "Who sent you here?"

He caught the glint of her eyes beneath her raised hand, but her lips remained set in a thin line.

He let several seconds tick past in silence, then almost conversationally inquired, "Were you ordered to poison the countess, or was that your own idea?"

Her lips compressed as if she was battling an impulse to reply, yet the moment passed, the impulse clearly faded, and she continued to say nothing at all.

Just like the other two. Julian thought the words, but didn't voice them.

Felix gave vent to a frustrated sound. "You could at least tell us how many of you there are."

Benton frowned at that, then wonder of wonders, said, "We don't know, do we?" She jutted her chin in the direction of the cell where Mitchell and Manning languished. "They didn't know about each other or about me, and I didn't know about them. We were only told what we were supposed to do and when—in what order things were to happen."

Julian frowned. "So there could be others we haven't yet caught?"

Having grown accustomed to the light, Benton lowered her hand and shrugged. "I honestly don't know."

Now she could see Benton's face clearly, Melissa studied it. She also heard what seemed to be candor in the other woman's voice.

Gently, Melissa nudged Julian aside. He glanced at her, but deigned to shift so she wasn't peering around him. Facing Benton, she finally succeeded in catching the maid's gaze. "Why won't any of you name the man who has put you up to this?"

Benton regarded her steadily, if guardedly, for several seconds, then sighed. "At least you're asking the right question."

"And the answer?" Melissa prompted.

Benton continued to look at Melissa. It was plain Benton, as much as Mitchell and Manning, felt constrained by some powerful compulsion from uttering their master's name. Equally obviously, unlike Mitchell and Manning, Benton was trying to find some way out of the bind.

Eventually, she drew breath and, her head and shoulders lowering in defeat, sighed. "All I can tell you is that, if the other two are like me, then it's because the man pulling our strings has each of us over a barrel. We can't save ourselves for the same reason we had to do what he ordered us to do. If we talk and tell you who he is, he has the power to ruin..." Melissa expected her to say "us," but instead, Benton continued, "Things we hold very dear. More dear than our lives. So if we talk, we lose everything, guaranteed. If we don't talk? Well, then, it all depends, doesn't it?"

Confused, Melissa asked, "Depends on what?"

Benton's head tipped as if she was considering an outcome the rest of them couldn't see. Then she softly said, "On whether he succeeds, I suppose."

She stopped speaking after that, and no matter what questions they posed, they got no more from her.

～

It was late when, with Felix and Damian, Melissa and Julian trooped back up the main stairs.

With weary goodnights, Damian and Felix peeled off to their own rooms, leaving Melissa and Julian walking hand in hand down the corridor to the earl's apartments.

Julian opened the door, and they went in.

No wriggling golden body came to greet them. Melissa glanced at Ulysses's empty blanket. "I told Jolene to take him down to the kitchens."

Julian grunted. "I'll have to remember to tell Cook to reward him with the juiciest bone she can find."

Melissa had told them of the pup's insistence on playing with her and how his rope had knocked over the mug of milk she might otherwise have drunk.

He considered that fact and how close they'd sailed to disaster, then pushed such thoughts aside. He was in no mood to dwell on what might have been.

He followed Melissa into her room. Jolene, he was pleased to note, had made herself scarce.

Good.

He shut the door, and halfway across the room, Melissa paused and looked back at him. They'd fallen into the habit of him going to his room and disrobing, then waiting until Jolene left before he joined Melissa in her big bed.

Tonight, however…he couldn't find that much patience.

All the emotions he'd held back, held in, erupted inside him and pounded like a drumbeat through his veins.

The dangers of the day, the shocks, the fears—the terrifying prospect that they might lose their chance at making this, their marriage, work and the even more petrifying thought of losing her—all rose and swamped his mind.

He forced himself to lean back against the door and try to find some semblance of control.

But something had shifted inside him; something had escaped. He met her gaze, saw the faint lift of her eyebrow in unspoken question, and help-less to do otherwise, responded.

He pushed away from the door and stalked across the room to her.

As he approached, he reached for her, but she was already moving toward him to plaster herself to him, to clutch his head and haul his lips to hers.

That was all the encouragement the prowling need within him required.

He fell into the kiss, claimed her mouth, and devoured. He cinched his arm around her waist and crushed her to him. Splayed, his hands roved her back, then slid down, cupped the delectable globes of her bottom, and molded her hips to his thighs, the softness of her belly easing the sharp ache of his already rampant erection.

She was more than willing. With her hands, her lips, her tongue—with the seductive, sensuous pressure of her body against his—she urged him on. More, she demanded, and he was entirely ready to meet her every need.

Passion welled and swelled, and the heat of their hunger, heightened and escalated by the events of the day, infused and drove them. Their lips demanding, their hands greedy and grasping, in a flurry of urgent, desperate need, they stripped each other of every last stitch. The instant he flung her chemise aside, he seized her and hoisted her up, and she wrapped her arms about his shoulders, wound her long legs about his hips, and with one powerful thrust, he filled her.

And they froze and clung.

Suspended in that moment of infinite awareness, they struggled to catch their breaths, battled to find their mental feet in the face of a tsunami of incomparable sensation as intimacy battered their senses.

Then she levered up in his arms, flicked her hair from her face, framed his between her hands, and met his eyes. "I love you. Now and forever. I will not lose you." The last statement was a promise, a vow.

"Nor I you." His instinctive response came in a guttural growl.

She barely waited to hear it before sealing her lips to his again, then in blatant incitement, she shifted in his arms, using her inner muscles to caress him, and need roared back and crashed over them.

What followed was an education for them both. Years ago, they'd tumbled into love so easily, neither had really questioned what that meant. More recently, when they'd allowed that nascent love to finally blossom as an adult connection, while the feeling had clearly matured, their acceptance of it had remained straightforward, an acknowledgment that the connection existed, that it was there.

Now, as the fires of mutual passion raged and the flames of desire seared, they started to glimpse what such a love—one that had lasted for years and never waned—truly was.

What a force, what a power it could be.

While they'd spent the weeks since their wedding exploring this side of marriage and love, nothing had prepared either of them for the sheer, compulsive power the threats to their lives had unleashed. It went beyond hunger, far beyond mere need.

What gripped them and overwhelmed their minds held echoes of an unrelenting desperation that could only be assuaged by their complete and utter surrender.

To each other, but even more to the compulsive force that needed so powerfully it wouldn't let either of them go.

Buried to the hilt within her scalding softness, repeatedly, compulsively, he lifted her, and gasping, eyes shut the better to savor each sensation, she slid down as he thrust deep. Their breaths, heated and panting, mingled, as together, they strove, hearts pounding, skins slick, then she tightened that last fraction and, on a softly keening cry, came apart in his arms.

Hanging on to his own impulses with an iron grip, he buried his face in the lustrous bounty of her disarranged hair and locked his arms about her, determined to revel in each and every second of her release.

As it faded, he eased his hold enough to fill his lungs with a much-needed breath, then holding her against him, walked to the side of her bed.

Halting there, he eased her now-limp arms from his shoulders and lowered her until she lay back on the silk counterpane. Her pale skin glowed, pearlescent against the midnight-blue expanse.

Boneless, her legs slid from his hips to lie over the side of the bed. He set his palms flat on either side of her shoulders, nudged her thighs wide, settling his hips between, then leaned over her and, once more, pushed deep.

He flexed his spine, withdrew a little way, then thrust deep again.

As he repeated the exercise, she stirred and raised her heavy lids enough to look up at him from beneath the dark fringe of her lashes.

With his features passion set, he couldn't manage a smile. "Again." He thrust into her, and her breath hitched, and her lids fell, but her hands rose to grip his forearms, and she joined him.

Joined him and matched him, and together, they urged each other on, through this new landscape that had opened between them. A place of heat, of raw need, of a furnace forging something finer, harder, more enduring.

In recognition of what each truly yearned for in this, their shared life.

Freed, unrestrained, the compulsion—that unrelenting force—grew, built, and consumed them.

He'd never let go like this, never totally relinquished the reins and let his inner self free.

Free to claim her with all—every last drop—of the intensity that lived in his soul.

Free to claim, with her, all that they could be.

Then the moment was upon them, and she shattered, arching beneath him and taking him with her, and he tipped back his head and, on a long guttural groan, surrendered and let the power take him. Claim him and consume him.

Finally, wracked and spent, he collapsed upon her, and she wrapped her arms around him. Boneless, still reeling, they slumped as the aftermath rolled over them, submerging them in satiated peace.

Their desires satisfied, their needs met.

Love in all its power and glory acknowledged and given its due.

Uncounted minutes later, they disengaged, crawled beneath the covers, and secure in each other's arms, slept.

CHAPTER 15

$\mathscr{E}$ight hours later, Julian, Melissa, Felix, and Damian met over the breakfast table. They were relieved to learn via Phelps that the dowager and Frederick had elected to breakfast in their rooms.

"Good." Damian spoke for them all. "That means we can discuss this wretched situation without having to watch what we say."

Melissa reached for the toast rack Phelps had just set on the table. "I hope your mother can rein in her anxieties until we get to the bottom of this."

Felix grimaced. "Uncle Frederick, too. They're nearly as bad as each other."

"I think it's that they feel helpless." Julian attacked a sausage. "We, at least, can actively do something while both of them are relegated to watching."

"And"—Melissa waved a fork—"learning of things well after the event. That always predisposes one to imagine the worst."

"Speaking of the worst." Julian looked around the table, his gaze briefly touching each face. "What do you think are the odds of Benton being the one who trapped us in the barn and then set fire to it?"

Melissa pointed out, "As one of the upstairs maids, she would have known where to find Ulysses, and he might have recognized her well enough to let her take him without creating a fuss."

Felix frowned. "I would have said lifting the beam on the barn door would have been beyond a female, but Benton's a good size, and she does seem strong. I rather think she could have managed it."

"But did she?" Damian looked from Melissa to Felix to Julian. "We know she tried to poison Melissa, but trapping you three in the barn and setting it alight seems a"—he gestured—"different sort of attack."

Grimly, Julian nodded. "I feel much the same. And that means we have yet another of X's pawns to ferret out."

"Why not start by seeing which of the staff can't be accounted for around three o'clock yesterday afternoon?" Melissa looked at the others. "Whoever trapped us in the barn and set it on fire had to have been down there at that time rather than being busy with their work."

"An excellent point." Julian nodded at Damian. "Ring for Phelps."

The butler had tactfully withdrawn, leaving them free to talk unrestrainedly. When Phelps arrived, Julian explained their need to know who was where at the crucial time when whoever had trapped them in the barn was there rather than in the castle.

Phelps nodded. "Yes, my lord. I see." He paused, then suggested, "Perhaps we might consult with Mrs. Phelps?"

Melissa tipped her head in agreement. "An excellent idea."

Mrs. Phelps was duly fetched, and when Melissa asked if, on the previous afternoon, Benton could have slipped away to the barn around three o'clock, Mrs. Phelps pursed her lips, her gaze growing distant as she appeared to consult some mental timetable, then she refocused on Melissa and shook her head. "I seriously doubt Benton could have been down there, my lady. She was helping neaten the upstairs rooms at that time."

"Are you certain she was there?" Felix asked.

Melissa specified, "Could she have slipped away for about half an hour without anyone else knowing?"

Mrs. Phelps's expression wasn't encouraging, but she said, "Let me check with the other maid, my lady. She would know."

Melissa signaled her agreement, and Mrs. Phelps departed.

They'd finished eating and were sipping coffee or, in Melissa's case, tea when Mrs. Phelps returned.

Her expression the epitome of certainty, the housekeeper reported, "Amber was the other maid on room duty yesterday. She's been with us since she was a slip of a thing and has no reason to lie, and what with Benton trying to poison you, my lady, I can assure you there's no one below stairs with any love for her, either. Yet Amber says Benton was with her the entire time they were doing the rooms. They started about two and didn't finish until after four. They were airing the sheets, which meant they were working together."

Melissa nodded in understanding, then met Julian's eyes. "It wasn't Benton."

Julian thanked the Phelpses and allowed them to return to their duties. He looked at the others. "Let's go to the library and let the staff clear up in here."

They rose and, all plainly cogitating, walked down the corridor to the library.

As soon as all four had sat in the armchairs before the fireplace, Melissa said, "None of the other women on our potential suspects list or the scullery boy would be able to lift the beam across the barn doors."

Julian nodded. "That leaves us with Biggins, Walter, Richards, Cantrell, and Carter."

"So," Felix said, "our question now is which one of those five can't account for his time around three o'clock yesterday afternoon."

They decided to start with Carter, who, aside from being one of the outdoor staff, was one of the most recently employed.

Julian sent for Edgerton and, when the burly head groundsman arrived, explained their reasoning and therefore their need to know where Carter was around three o'clock the previous afternoon.

"Ah, that's easy," Edgerton replied. "He was with me." He shifted his weight. "What with all the uncertainty going around, I decided to keep the lad close, and with all the cutting back we have to do on the borders at this time of year, that was easy enough." He met Julian's gaze. "So Carter was working right alongside me from lunchtime until we saw the smoke and heard the alarm raised and went running down to the barn."

Julian sighed and inclined his head. "Thank you. And I'm glad you thought to keep Carter close. It helps to be able to feel certain in crossing people off our suspects list."

"Aye. That was my thinking, too." At Julian's dismissal, Edgerton bowed and withdrew.

Once the door had shut, Julian said, "On the grounds our unknown attacker is more likely to be someone who had reason to be outside, let's get Hockey in and see what he can tell us about where Biggins and Walter were at the critical time."

Hockey was duly summoned, but like Edgerton, he, too, had been keeping a close eye on Biggins and Walter. "From soon after lunch, I had them with a group of others in the long field, exercising the carriage horses. I'd just come away and left them there when I saw the smoke rising and heard the fire bell start to ring. Then we were all running, and they were there with the others, bringing the horses in before we rushed to the barn." He paused, eyes narrowing in thought, but then his expression cleared, and he shook his head. "I can't see any way either of them could have set the fire. They were with me and the others at the time it had to've been done."

Julian thanked Hockey and dismissed him.

As soon as the door shut, Damian said, "That's Biggins and Walter struck off our list and in a comfortingly definite manner."

"Indeed." Lips thinning, Julian met Melissa's gaze. "That leaves us with the footmen, Richards and Cantrell."

"From what I've learned from the Phelpses," Melissa said, "Cantrell is from one of the tenant families, one that's been on the estate for generations. I went with Veronica when she visited old Mrs. Cantrell—our footman's grandmother. I met his mother and sisters, as well. The idea that the son might put all the family at risk seems not just unlikely but farfetched."

"Hmm," Felix said. "I can also add that yesterday morning, Cantrell brought up my shaving water. Hicks referred to him by name, so I got a good look at our youngest footman." He met the others' eyes. "Remember Phelps refers to Cantrell as a 'junior' footman? Well, there's a reason for that. He's young for the post and not yet fully grown. He's tall and thin and weedy. I seriously doubt he'd have managed lifting that beam to bar the barn doors—not without a great deal of grunting and shuffling and staggering about." He met Julian's eyes. "But I was almost at the doors when the blighter dropped the beam into place. I was close enough to hear any hints of effort, but there weren't any—the action was smoothly and efficiently done."

Julian glanced at Damian and Melissa. "I haven't come across Richards—or I might have, but didn't know who he was. What does he look like?"

Damian promptly replied, "Like he's more than capable of lifting that beam."

Felix was nodding. "He'd manage that easily. He looks quite strong."

"He does," Melissa agreed.

His jaw firming, Julian nodded. "Right, then. Let's have him in and ask him to tell us how he spent yesterday afternoon and who can vouch for that."

Damian sprang up and tugged the bellpull.

Another footman, not Cantrell or Richards but an older man, Martin, arrived in short order, and Julian sent him off to ask Richards to present himself.

They waited, increasingly impatiently, but when a tap fell on the door, it heralded not Richard but Phelps.

An unusually ruffled Phelps. "My lord, you sent for Richards, but I regret to say that it seems the man has…well, scarpered in the middle of the night. His things are gone, and no one has seen him since yesterday evening, when he retired with everyone else. Today was his day off, and no one noticed he wasn't about until Martin went looking just now."

"I see." Julian looked at his brothers and arched a brow.

"Just to be sure"—Felix looked at Phelps—"Richards is the tall one, mid-thirties, squarish face, medium build, with dark, slightly wavy hair and a pale complexion?"

When Phelps nodded, Felix looked at Julian. "I saw Richards hanging back in the shadows of the kitchen corridor when we came up from the cellar after speaking with Benton. I wondered what he was doing there—he didn't seem on his way to anywhere at the time."

Melissa said, "He must have been watching, listening if he could, to see if we blamed Benton for the fire. But we didn't say anything to anyone to suggest we had."

His features setting, Julian nodded. "He must have reasoned that we would work out that she wasn't responsible sooner rather than later and cast our net more widely and, eventually, look at him."

Damian pushed out of his chair, straightened, and stretched. "Well, I, for one, am in the mood for a chase." He met the others' eyes. "There are only so many ways Richards could have gone, and even if he set out late last night, he can't have got that far." He glanced at the clock on the mantelpiece. "It's only half past nine."

Julian mused, "Ashbourne and Ripley are too small to get lost in, and Buxton's the same and also too far away."

Felix got to his feet. "That leaves Chesterfield or Derby—"

"And"—Julian also rose—"if he wants to lose himself and win free of any pursuit, he'll make for London, so Derby it is."

"He's on foot," Felix said, rising excitement in his voice, "so he'll have to go via Kirk Ireton, but from there?"

Julian smiled in cool anticipation. "He'll stay away from the main roads and keep to the byways, not knowing how difficult that will make it for him. He'll almost certainly end on the lane past Kedleston Hall, and that will only slow him further." Glancing at the clock, he rapidly calculated. "Chances are we'll come up with him somewhere along that stretch."

He turned to Phelps, who immediately straightened to attention. Julian gave crisp orders for their horses to be saddled, then glanced at Melissa and arched his brows in question.

Melissa met his gaze. "I've been thinking that it might be as well to interview the remaining recent hires, excepting Cantrell, who is the only local among them and whom we all feel is highly unlikely to be anyone's pawn. That still leaves us with Carter, Biggins, Walter, the two younger maids, and the scullery boy."

She rose and shook out her skirts. "Given how active X has been in recruiting people and placing them on our staff, it would be silly of us not to use the current situation to reassure ourselves we have no other pawns of his lurking as yet undetected."

Felix looked puzzled. "How will you know?"

Quietly confident, she smiled every bit as coolly as her husband. "If there are any others, then I suspect they'll be getting rather nervous by now. We've got three of their number locked up downstairs, and you three are about to ride Richards down." She met Julian's gray gaze and raised her chin. "I'm fairly certain that, if I interview them now and any are X's pawns, it'll be easy to further rattle them—I can't see any maintaining a sufficiently innocent façade—and then we'll know, which, regardless of the outcome, will be something of a relief."

Julian nodded. "You're right. That's an excellent idea, and if I might suggest it, getting Mama and Uncle Frederick to help might kill two birds with one stone."

She squeezed his arm. "That's a brilliant notion. Your mother has a wealth of experience dealing with staff in all sorts of situations, which will undoubtedly be useful in this case."

She understood the need to feel one was contributing, and if she could help ease Veronica's and Frederick's feelings of impotence, so much the better.

Damian was already eagerly striding toward the door. As Julian escorted her in Felix's wake, Melissa met her husband's eyes. "Meanwhile, do take care." She looked at Felix and Damian as they paused at the door and glanced back. "That goes for all of you."

Damian flashed her an insouciant grin. "Yes, ma'am!" He saluted her, then opened the door and strode out.

Felix grinned at her and followed.

Julian paused at the door and drew her to him for a swift yet quite definite kiss. Raising his head, he met her eyes. "We'll be back as soon as we can—hopefully with Richards in tow."

She nodded. "Good hunting."

He, too, grinned, and then he was gone, striding purposefully after his brothers.

Following him into the corridor, Melissa watched him go, then made for the front hall. She found Phelps there. "Phelps, do you know where the dowager and Mr. Frederick are?"

"I believe they're in the family parlor, my lady."

"Thank you." With a nod, she turned and, already planning how best to proceed, headed that way.

$\sim$

Julian held Argus to a ground-eating canter as, flanked by Felix and Damian, he headed down the road toward Derby.

On foot, Derby was a good thirty-five or more miles from the castle, and the way wasn't at all direct. Even if Richards had already plotted his course and wasn't having to check his direction, even if he'd left the castle soon after midnight, he couldn't have reached Derby yet.

In contrast, Julian and his brothers had ridden across country, a very much shorter journey.

They passed the village of Kedleston and continued on. The lane swung almost northeast as it followed the border of the park of Kedleston Hall, the seat of the recently created Earl Howe, one of the Delameres' aristocratic neighbors. Finally, they reached the bend where the lane swung southeast again, onto a more direct line for Derby, still some miles away.

Ahead, they spied a lonely figure, shoulders drooping as he trudged along. He was carrying a worn traveling bag, which hung from one hand.

Damian drew in a breath as if to call out.

"Quiet," Julian warned. "No need to be melodramatic."

Damian huffed, but otherwise kept silent, and Julian urged Argus on, leaving his brothers a few yards behind.

Richards had to have heard the hoofbeats approaching, but he gave no sign; head down, he continued to slog along.

Julian drew level with the weary figure and reined Argus to a walk.

When Richards finally looked up and startled, Julian smiled. "Good morning, Richards." He glanced pointedly at the stone wall bordering the park on Richards's other side. "A fine morning, but I'm sure you're tired after walking all this way. A pity you didn't remain for breakfast—we could have saved you the journey."

Still staring, Richards slowed, then his surprise was overtaken by resignation, and he heaved a massive sigh and halted. He looked around as Felix rode up, followed by Damian with the horse they'd brought for Richards on a leading rein.

Dejectedly, Richards sighed again. His shoulders slumped, and he hung his head.

～

With Felix and Damian, who had Richards in tow, Julian returned to the castle just before noon.

As per the plan he, Felix, and Damian had discussed on their ride down, they'd said very little to Richards. At Julian's direction, he'd mounted the horse and, not being any sort of horseman, had grimly hung on to the saddle throughout the return journey.

They'd debated the point, but had decided to place Richards in the same cell as the other two men. The cell could hold four at a pinch, and Julian had reasoned that Richards learning how the other two had been treated—meaning well enough—might make him more amenable to what Julian later intended to suggest.

They locked Richards in, then climbed the stairs.

Once they'd stepped into the kitchen corridor and Damian had shut the cellar door, Julian said, "I'm going to have to decide what to do with them soon."

"Not until we have X by the heels," Felix said. "They're our only link to him, and we can't go on not knowing who he is and not putting a stop to his game."

Damian agreed, and Julian didn't argue. He couldn't. They needed to unearth some clue to X's identity, which was why he planned to treat Richards rather differently to those they'd previously caught.

When Julian was faced with an impasse, his instinct was to find a way around it.

They came upon Phelps in the front hall.

Before Julian could ask, Phelps informed him, "The countess, the dowager, and Mr. Frederick are in the family parlor, my lord."

"Thank you, Phelps." Julian redirected his footsteps in that direction, and Felix and Damian followed. They were all keen to learn what Melissa, aided by their mother and uncle, had uncovered.

Melissa saw them first. "Did you catch him?" She rose and held out her hands in welcome.

Feeling something in his chest loosen, Julian walked forward, took her hands in his, and raised one to his lips and kissed her fingers. "We did." He released one hand, but settled the other in his grasp as he turned to his mother and uncle. "We came up with him beside Kedleston Hall park."

His mother and his uncle looked relieved.

"So what has he to say for himself?" Frederick asked as Damian and Felix drew up a pair of chairs.

Urging Melissa to sit again, Julian claimed the spot on the love seat beside her. "I decided not to question him yet. Not only were we on horseback, but having a little time to dwell on his position might help loosen his tongue." He glanced at Melissa and met her gaze. "Not that I'm expecting to get any more information than what little we've already got from Benton." Unwilling to dwell on that, he asked, "How did your interviews go? What's your verdict?" He included his mother and uncle with his gaze.

Veronica and Melissa proceeded to describe their encounters with the other recently hired staff. Frederick sat back and left it to the ladies, although Julian noted his uncle agreed with their ultimate declaration.

"So," Veronica stated, "we're very confident that none of the other recently employed staff are under the sway of anyone."

"And that," Melissa concluded, catching Julian's eyes, "should mean that we are, finally, free of X's attacks."

She smiled, and Julian read her relief in the gesture. That she and his mother were both convinced went a very long way to convincing him that they could relax their vigilance.

Veronica was plainly relieved and reassured, but Frederick had always been one to remain concerned long after all danger had passed. He still looked grave, but Julian was grateful that his uncle didn't give voice to any lingering doubts.

Phelps arrived to announce that luncheon was served, and they rose and headed for the family dining room.

Melissa urged Veronica and Frederick to lead the way and fell in with Julian and his brothers.

When she arched a brow at him, he didn't pretend not to understand. "I thought to leave Richards to talk to the others and dwell on their collective fate for a while before speaking to him. And I've decided to change the setting for my interrogation to the library."

When she looked her question, he explained, "I'm hoping that I might be better able to convince him to loosen his tongue in a more civilized setting."

"Ah." She nodded. "I see."

After lunch, leaving Veronica to further soothe Frederick, who was not quite ready to accept that the threat had passed, Melissa went with Julian, Felix, and Damian to the library.

Under Julian's direction, they moved chairs around until he was satisfied, then Damian went with Thornley to fetch Richards from the dungeon cell.

As instructed, Melissa sat in an armchair to one side of the desk, angled to face the upright chair—with its comfortably padded seat, back, and armrests—that Julian had placed directly before the desk.

Felix took an armchair set off to the desk's other side and a little behind it.

Julian sat in his customary chair behind the desk and surveyed the scene. "I don't want to intimidate or to make this into an inquisition."

Melissa wasn't sure he would succeed in that, but she was willing to play whatever role he assigned her. She wanted X's game to end, and the only way they would accomplish that was to identify the villain.

The door opened, and Damian ushered Richards inside. Previously, Melissa would have said Richards was in his mid-thirties. Now, he looked ten years older. At least. The erstwhile footman looked somewhat the worse for wear, but had plainly attempted to make himself presentable; his dark hair had been smoothed, and his clothes were neat and straight.

Julian nodded to the obviously trepidatious man and waved him to the chair before the desk.

Hesitantly, Richards came forward, his gaze flicking about the room. He took note of the rest of them seated and waiting, then glanced at Damian, who had followed him inside and retreated to lean, arms folded, against the bookshelves not far from Melissa's chair.

Rounding the upright chair, Richards glanced at the door just as Thornley, who had remained in the corridor, drew it shut. Richards swallowed and turned to face Julian and, at his encouraging nod, sank gingerly onto the chair.

Julian clasped his hands on the desk and, with his expression giving no clue whatsoever to his thoughts, evenly stated, "We understand that you've been recruited by a gentleman to carry out an attack or attacks on me and my family."

He paused, looking at Richards expectantly, and uncertainly, Richards nodded and croaked, "Aye, my lord."

Melissa blinked. So X was a gentleman? She suddenly understood the rationale behind Julian's approach.

"Before we discuss that further," Julian smoothly went on, "let's set the record straight. You were the one who took the puppy, Ulysses, to the barn?"

This time, when Julian paused, Richards said, "Yes."

"You saw us head for the orchard, so you set a trap and locked us in the barn." Again, Julian paused.

Looking rather ill, Richards merely nodded.

"And then you set fire to the building. Is that correct?"

Richards cleared his throat and raised his head, not defiantly but as if staunchly determined to own up to his misdeeds. "Yes, my lord."

Julian studied the man, not in any threatening way but instead exuding the impression of wanting to understand. "Phelps informs me that your references are sound. They're genuine, although not recent. Apparently until now, you've led a blameless, honest life. Yet you came here and attempted to commit what, had you succeeded, would have amounted to multiple murders." His expression showing nothing but puzzlement, Julian asked, "Why?"

Richards stared at him. That he wanted to answer was written all over his face. His lips even parted, but then his shoulders sagged, and he looked down.

His tone more gentle, Julian asked, "I take it the gentleman who put you up to this is blackmailing you into doing as he wishes?"

Richards's head came up, and the startled look in his eyes was all the answer anyone needed.

Julian leaned forward. "That's the only sensible conclusion. Not only with you but with the others, too. He's blackmailing you all, but what I want you to know is that whatever he's blackmailing you about isn't of any interest to us. All we want is his name. Under duress, he's forced the four of you to attempt dastardly crimes—that wasn't a choice any of you made. You had no choice. Is that correct?"

Richards's expression as he nodded was almost painfully hopeful.

His entire focus on Richards, Julian spread his hands. "All we want is the man's name."

Richards stared at him, clearly thinking, and Julian went on, "You and the others, your attempted crimes pale into insignificance when compared to his. He is the true villain here."

All Julian's years of experience told him Richards was close to taking the final step and telling them what they wanted to know, but he needed more—another push—to tip him over the line.

Drawing in a careful breath, his eyes never leaving Richards's face, Julian shot off a quick prayer that the others wouldn't react and said, "If you will give us your blackmailer's name, I will do all I can to see you and the others free of all charges."

It was within his power to do that; he was fairly certain that Richards, at least, would know it. Melissa didn't move a finger, and neither did Felix. Damian shifted, but kept his mouth shut.

Richards was sorely tempted; that much was plain in his face. His gaze growing distant, he stared unseeing past Julian, then his shoulders straightened, his features firmed, and he shifted in the chair. He licked his lips and leaned forward, as if about to speak, then froze.

A second later, his features crumpled, and his posture sagged. He refocused on Julian, and there was no doubt of the depth of his regret as he said, "Thank you for the offer, my lord, and I'm truly sorry to be disobliging but"—he gestured in helpless fashion—"I daren't." He met Julian's eyes, and Julian would have sworn he saw desperation in Richards's gaze. Sorrowfully, Richards shook his head. "I just can't."

He looked down.

In that moment, Richards was at his weakest. Instinct prodded, and Julian asked, "Tell us this, then. Regarding your attempt to kill us, did you think of the details on your own, or did he, your blackmailer, give you directions and you merely followed them?"

Richards's head came up, but his gaze remained bleak and hopeless. "The latter. He told me to use the puppy as bait, to wait for the right time and get you and preferably your lady, too, into the barn, then lock you in and set the place alight."

His features crumpled, and he dropped his head. "God help me, but I did what he told me."

Julian studied his downbent head. He'd heard the ring of truth and of deep remorse in Richards's words, and from what he sensed emanating from Melissa, Felix, and even Damian, they had, too.

From experience, he knew there was no point pressing at this stage. Richards had tried to throw off the hold X had on him and had failed. More time might help. Time with the three others in similar straits would certainly not hurt.

Evenly, Julian said, "I'm not going to rush into initiating proceedings against you or the others. My offer to you and them stands. If you or any of the others change your mind and are willing to give me the name of the gentleman behind the attacks, all you need do is tell whoever comes with your food to let me know you wish to talk to me."

Richards glanced up, then dipped his head. "Thank you for your forbearance, my lord." He paused, then more quietly said, "I don't know that it will help but..."

The inference was that it might.

Julian nodded at Damian, who pushed away from the bookshelf and went to the door.

Thornley and Phelps arrived, and Richards rose and went with the pair.

As the door closed behind the trio, Julian exhaled and sat back. "At least as far as our prisoners go, now, we wait and see."

Later that night, ready for bed in her nightgown with a shawl wrapped about her shoulders and her hair brushed and hanging free, Melissa stood staring out of her uncurtained bedroom window at the rolling woodland canopies lit by the rising moon.

Jolene had just left, and as Melissa waited for Julian to join her, her mind retrod the events of the day, dwelling especially on the strange interview with Richards and on all she'd sensed rippling beneath the surface, not just Richards's surface but that of the entire situation.

Immediately after the interview, they'd tossed around their various observations, but had ended agreeing to each think through all they'd absorbed and to confer tomorrow and compare their conclusions.

When the connecting door opened and Julian, wearing a gray-silk robe and with his feet bare, came padding in, she drank in the sight, but resisted the distraction long enough to say, "I've been trying to imagine what sort of secret X holds over his four pawns. Not only does his grip on them seem unbreakable, but given they each seem entirely separate, there must be four unconnected secrets, not just one."

Julian reached her and drew her into his arms, and she went readily. Gently, he settled her body flush with his, and something inside her sighed, and she softened against him.

His gray eyes, faintly troubled, met hers. "I've been wondering much the same thing. I can't conceive of what is holding all of them back—and as you rightly point out, the secret has to be different in all four cases. Whatever those four secrets are, they're powerful. So strong, none of them will risk speaking, even though, at the very least, they're facing transportation. They have to know that—and know I can make the charges vanish—yet they still won't speak to save themselves. They won't name the bastard." He frowned and shook his head. "Why?"

Sensing how deeply the situation troubled him—especially as, effectively, he held all four lives in his hands—Melissa raised her arms, draped them over his shoulders, pressed her body more firmly to his, and when his attention refocused on her, said, "Let's forget about X for the next ten hours. Nothing's going to change in that time."

His lips curved, and his gaze warmed. As he bent his head, he murmured, "That's a suggestion—a challenge—I'll accept with pleasure."

His lips met hers, and she smiled under the gentle kiss, then set about suitably distracting them both.

∿

The following morning, Melissa battled to contain her impatience as Mrs. Phelps painstakingly went through the menus for the upcoming week. It was a task they completed every Thursday, and there was little point trying to curtail the discussion.

But the instant the housekeeper signaled that her questions were at an end, Melissa rose. Leaving Mrs. Phelps gathering her notes, over her shoulder, Melissa called, "I must join his lordship," and hurried from her private parlor and headed for the library.

She walked into the large room and found Julian, Felix, and Damian lounging in the armchairs before the fireplace and chatting about horses.

Julian smiled. "As ordered, we've waited for you."

Pleased, she inclined her head gracefully and claimed her usual chair. "So where are we? What do we all think? Specifically, can we draw any conclusions regarding X?"

Julian accepted the challenge. "It's clear X knows something damning about each of his four pawns—damning enough to ensure that even the threat of hanging or transportation isn't enough to loosen their tongues." He glanced at the others' faces. "At this point, we have to accept that they won't speak. They won't give us his name."

"Not because they don't want to," Melissa clarified, "but because they feel they can't."

Julian nodded. "Melissa pointed out that the four secrets must be different—a separate secret for each of them, given they apparently didn't know each other prior to joining the staff here. The Phelpses, Hockey, and Edgerton—and the rest of the staff—have confirmed that." He leaned back and narrowed his eyes. "So not only is X playing a very long game —one going back at least twenty months to when Mitchell arrived—but he's also put a lot of effort into finding four complete but useful strangers with secrets he can exploit. That's...not a small thing." He glanced at his brothers. "How many people with those sorts of secrets do you know?"

"As far as I know," Felix replied, "not a single one."

"Me, either," Damian said.

Julian tapped a finger on the arm of his chair. "That X knew of four... that says something about him, but I can't at the moment see what."

He fell silent for a few seconds, then shook off the distraction. "Let's leave that for now, although I feel it's a point to ponder. To go on, whatever X's aim is, it isn't directly connected to me marrying Melissa, because the attacks started before I'd even decided to go to London and look for a bride."

"But"—Felix raised a finger—"your marriage might have made his game more urgent." He looked at Melissa, then at Julian. "The attacks became more frequent, more deadly, and more included Melissa after your engagement was announced."

"He wouldn't have expected it," Damian pointed out. "None of us did.

He might have thought he had plenty of time to remove you, but then he had to bring forward his plans."

Reluctantly, Julian conceded the point with a tip of his head. "Sadly, that fits, and the possibility remains that X's ultimate goal has something to do with the succession."

Melissa, along with Felix and Damian, nodded.

"Something we haven't yet discussed," Julian went on, "is that X has to be someone who knows the family well. Far better than any casual acquaintance. Let's accept Richards's word on the detail of X's instructions and assume the same was the case for the others. X's directions mean he knows this place and in some detail."

"He couldn't have known about me going to the fishpond," Felix said, "but he plainly knows about the gardens and the paths and the shrubbery and how often we all go walking around, especially in summertime."

Julian nodded. "He's known enough to give orders contingent on us, for example, going to visit the outlying farms in the gig."

"He knew about the boathouse and the punt," Melissa added. "And most telling"—she met Julian's eyes—"he knew about Ulysses."

"Ah, yes!" Julian's expression cleared. "How could he have known about the dog? Who knew about Ulysses?"

"Anyone who came to the wedding," Felix replied, "but only them. No one knew Melissa's grandmother was going to bring her the pup as a bridal gift from the Dowager Duchess of St. Ives. No one could possibly have predicted that."

"No, indeed," Melissa agreed. "And while none of the wedding guests saw Ulysses, the news of his existence was doing the rounds at the wedding breakfast."

Damian had been frowning, almost absentmindedly. Now, he waved his hands. "Wait, wait, wait!" When the other three looked at him, he said, "Richards told us that X *told* him to use the puppy. When? After the wedding guests left, no one else has been here to stay. Did X come into the area and meet up with his pawns to give them their instructions?"

"Or," Felix said, "did he come to the wedding prepared and simply seize on the new puppy as a likely useful bait?"

Julian narrowed his eyes. "Coming up here and staying anywhere local would have been a colossal risk. In order to speak with each of his pawns separately, he would have had to remain for a few days at least, and we're all out and about, even Mama and Frederick and the Phelpses.

If anyone had spotted him, they'd have noted him as an unexpected visitor to the area."

"He didn't write," Melissa added. "Phelps collects and distributes the mail, and I asked, and he doesn't recall any of the four receiving any letters over the weeks since the wedding."

Julian looked at Felix. "I think your idea is the right one. He was here for the wedding and used the opportunity to prime his agents."

Damian was nodding. "We know he has to be someone close to the family, and many relatives and close connections stayed overnight, both before and after the wedding."

"But," Melissa said, "he must be one of those who stayed afterward. Ulysses was only spoken of on the morning of the wedding."

"True." Julian paused, then looked at his brothers. "We haven't yet discussed Gordon recommending Manning to Damian, and Manning proving to be one of X's pawns."

Grimly, Felix met Julian's gaze. "And Gordon otherwise fits our deduced description of X."

"Except," Julian said, "in one vital way."

Damian shook his head. "Can any of you see Gordon searching for and learning four damning secrets of four different people and holding those secrets over those four people's heads to force them to do his bidding—namely, to commit multiple murders?" Lips compressed, Damian shook his head decisively. "I know Gordon's an ass sometimes, but he's not a cold-blooded killer, and that's another thing X definitely is —cold-blooded."

"And calculating." Julian tipped his head to Damian. "That's the point on which I stumble. No matter how hard I try, I just can't see Gordon formulating this plan, much less organizing and activating it."

Julian noticed Melissa was frowning, not as if she disagreed but as if she was thinking of something else. He caught her eye. "What is it?"

She grimaced. "I was just thinking..." She paused, then with renewed determination, went on, "Correct me if I'm wrong, but if both you and Felix are killed, as nearly occurred in the barn fire, then Damian inherits, and if Damian is also removed, then Frederick inherits, with Gordon as his heir."

When she looked at them expectantly, they all nodded.

"That," Julian confirmed, "is the succession as it currently stands."

"All right," she said. "Let's back up one step. Damian is earl. Frederick is his heir, but Frederick is old, much older than Damian or Gordon.

Couldn't it be said that, at least until Damian marries and sires a son, Gordon is the effective heir to the Delamere estates?"

Along with Felix and Damian, Julian stared at her, then slowly inclined his head. "I could see that argument being made—by Gordon, if no one else."

"And that," Melissa stated, "is precisely my point. He could borrow on the expectation, couldn't he?"

"Damn," Felix muttered. "Yes, he could."

"And he would." Damian didn't sound happy to have to admit that.

Julian concluded, "As much as we don't believe that Gordon is X, it's Gordon we need to concentrate on."

But Melissa waved her hands as if to hold them back. "I haven't finished," she stated and, when they looked at her, continued. "No more than any of you can I see Gordon as X, much less Gordon managing all that X has done. What we've established is that if Julian and Felix are removed, Gordon will be in a position to borrow funds against his expectations." She looked at Damian, then Felix, and finally met Julian's eyes. "What we haven't asked ourselves is who is in a position to borrow from Gordon?"

They stared at her, then Julian asked, "You think someone else is behind this, and his plan is to put Gordon in a position to borrow on his expectations?"

Melissa looked at Damian. "If you were the earl, and Frederick was your heir, and Gordon got into serious debt—scandalous debt—wouldn't you bail him out?"

Damian passed his hands over his face, then nodded. "Very likely." He glanced at Julian. "You've bailed him out once already, haven't you?"

Curtly, Julian nodded. "I hoped I'd put the fear of God into him over ever going to the cents-per-cents again, but..."

Melissa said, "We know Gordon is easily led, and we have no idea who's whispering in his ear or what they're saying."

Felix looked at Damian. "You're closest to our dear cousin. Do you have any idea who he might be persuaded to funnel money to?"

Damian shook his head. "But Gordon as a dupe? That, I can believe. Sadly, as to who intends to pull his strings, of that, I have no clue. We're not, in fact, that close. I have no idea who his other friends are."

"But it doesn't matter, does it?" Melissa looked around the circle. "Gordon must know who X is."

Damian frowned. "You mean Gordon is in league with X?"

"No." Julian felt the first inklings of clarity seep into his mind. "But Gordon must know who recommended Manning to him as a suitable candidate for Damian's valet, and that man is X." He met Melissa's increasingly bright gaze. "That's what you meant, wasn't it?"

She nodded. "So we need to contact Gordon, but specifically to ask who suggested Manning as Damian's valet."

"Well," Damian said. "We'll be able to do that in two days' time."

"Indeed." Julian could finally see the way forward. He looked at Melissa and explained, "Gordon will be here for the Wirksworth Ride."

Melissa had been told of the event—something of a pagan ritual, it involved a mock hunt chasing not a fox but a runner dressed as the god Herne, all in pursuit of a good harvest. "Your mother said guests might start arriving from late this afternoon."

Julian nodded. "From this afternoon to Saturday morning. Most will arrive just before the hunt."

"We never know when Gordon will show," Damian said, "but he'll definitely be here. We've all ridden the hunt since we were children—he won't miss it."

A scarifying thought occurred to Melissa, and she caught Julian's gaze. "We're hosting the Midsummer Ball next Thursday. Will Gordon and the others who come for the hunt expect to stay until then?"

Julian smiled, but it was Felix who answered. "No. The Ride is held on the Saturday before the solstice, and generally, those who come leave later in the day or, if they stay over, on the following morning."

"The ball," Julian added, "is strictly local. Our family and the other families who live in the area. It's the one annual event we reserve solely for the gentry from around about."

"Ah. I see." Relieved, she sat back.

Looking enthused, Damian clapped his hands. "Regardless, whenever Gordon gets here, once the hunt starts, we can cut him from the pack and pin him in place long enough to put our questions to him."

"And," Felix added, "wring the answers from him as well."

Rising certainty gripped them all.

Julian summed it up. "At last, we have a clear pathway that will lead us to X."

CHAPTER 16

$\mathcal{B}$y Saturday morning, all four of them were in a state of high alert.

With those who had arrived on Thursday and Friday to stay at the castle as well as the locals who had ridden in over the past hour congregating in the forecourt, Julian, with Melissa on his arm, both dressed to participate, walked out onto the front porch and, smiling affably, descended the steps to mingle with their guests.

While they moved through the crowd, fulfilling their roles as gracious hosts, Julian found it difficult not to overtly scan the throng. The previous evening, with Gordon yet to arrive, Julian, Melissa, Felix, and Damian had discussed the ride at length and made their plans. They'd agreed not to mention their intentions to anyone, not until they'd succeeded in extracting the critical name from Gordon. Although they felt confident that Gordon wasn't X, they'd agreed that exercising a degree of circumspection would be wise. Gordon was a Delamere, and if there was an outside chance that he was an accomplice in any way, they owed it to the wider family to minimize the risk of a scandal engulfing the family name. Julian had no intention of allowing the family to be harmed in any way.

As he introduced Melissa to those she hadn't previously met, he noted the appreciative glances she drew from many of the males as well as the approving looks she received from their spouses. His heart swelled with pride and also amusement as she glibly steered conversations and, in general, took control of their social interactions, saving him from having to deflect overly inquisitive queries. She was very skilled at that, something he recognized as a true gift in that arena.

Even over the few weeks since their wedding, he'd noted how much more passionate in her protectiveness of him and his family—their family now—she'd become. Of the household as a whole, in fact. She'd taken them all under her wing, and he felt rather humbled by her devotion to his cause.

As she smiled at a lady who would have claimed their attention for the next hour had she been able and deftly excused them and nudged him on, he squeezed her hand and, when she glanced up at him questioningly, smiled, raised her gloved fingers to his lips, and brushed a kiss over her knuckles.

She arched a warning brow at him. "Has Gordon arrived yet?"

He shook his head. "But he'll be here soon. He won't miss the Ride."

Of that, he felt certain, although he was surprised Gordon hadn't turned up the previous evening.

Melissa continued to smile welcomingly and engage with the visitors milling in the forecourt. Many had traveled from towns around about and from summer estates and great houses dotted about the district, while still others had come from as far afield as Lincoln and London. The Wirksworth Ride was considered an eccentric pastime, a convivial gathering purely for fun. Most of those present had participated many times before.

She seized the chance to ask Lord Keldale, another local landowner, "Has the hunt always started from the castle?"

A heavy man, his lordship stroked his luxuriant moustache and rumbled, "Certainly in living memory. I've heard it said that the castle has hosted the Ride since medieval times." He looked at her earnestly. "The castle was here even then, you know."

"I had heard." Smiling, she patted his lordship's arm and excused herself, then turned to extract Julian, who had been buttonholed by a rather pompous older gentleman from Derby. Seizing a fractional break in the conversation, she blithely declared, "My lord, we have some new arrivals who we should welcome. I'm sure Lord Abersythe will excuse us."

His lordship was transparently partial to pretty females; he grew quite gallant in expressing his understanding.

As she drew Julian toward the steps where several new arrivals had, indeed, appeared, he dipped his head and murmured, "Thank you. I never know how to break away from him without giving offense."

They duly welcomed the newcomers, ensuring they had everything they needed. The castle grooms and stablemen were helping riders check over their mounts and tack in preparation for getting under way.

As Julian and Melissa turned from handing the latest arrival into Hockey's care, Damian materialized beside them. He cast them a puzzled look. "He's still not here."

They didn't need to ask to whom he referred.

Felix joined them, also looking concerned. "If he's in some way involved in what's been going on, perhaps he won't show."

Julian murmured, "Missing the Ride would be the equivalent of waving a big red flag with 'I'm guilty' blazoned on it. Not even Gordon would be so stupid."

Felix waggled his head. "Possibly."

"Trust me," Julian said. "He'll be here."

"He needs to get moving, then," Damian observed. "We've less than twenty minutes before Herne's appearance."

They were all about to move back into the milling throng when, through a gap in the crowd, Melissa saw a flashy phaeton-and-four—the carriage obviously new with a gleaming bright-yellow body—come bowling up the drive. She focused on the driver's face and clutched Julian's arm. "Here's Gordon now, in what looks like a new phaeton."

"What?" Damian stepped up onto the castle steps and stared over the heads. "Lord above," he breathed, reverence in his tone. "Not only a new phaeton but four new high-steppers as well."

Felix flicked a frowning look at Julian. "Where the devil did he get the money?"

Others had noticed the approaching carriage and turned to look. Murmurs, snide comments, as well as exclamations of appreciation flowed through the crowd, but as the equipage was forced to halt to one side of the drive, unable to go farther because of the crowd, most returned to their conversations and largely ignored the newcomers.

Julian, with Melissa on his arm and flanked by Felix and Damian, strode around the crowd. It took effort to keep his genial host's smile in place. Felix had asked the most pertinent question. Where had Gordon got the money for the carriage, let alone the four horses, plus, Julian noted, a showy hunter trailing on a rein behind? As far as any of them knew, Gordon was perennially pressed for cash.

Sitting beside Gordon on the high seat of the phaeton was Captain Findlay-Wright. His presence didn't surprise anyone; over the past years, he'd often come up for the Ride, usually accompanying Gordon, who, after all, lived in the same house.

After exchanging nods with the occupants of the phaeton, Felix and Damian fell to examining the horses and carriage, while smiling, Julian and Melissa welcomed the captain and Gordon.

Findlay-Wright climbed down from the high seat and bowed over Melissa's hand. "It's always a pleasure to return to Carsington, Countess." Smiling, he nodded affably to Julian. "Carsely, well met." He glanced at the crowd. "It should be an excellent day. I'm looking forward to it."

"Indeed," Julian replied.

Hockey came up, and Findlay-Wright indicated which of the two horses trailing the carriage was whose. Naturally, the showy mount was Gordon's, and the steadier, solid-looking hunter was the captain's mount. The saddles had been placed in the phaeton's boot, and Hockey and a groom hoisted them out and led the horses aside to be saddled.

Gordon, meanwhile, had climbed down on the phaeton's other side and was proudly showing off the finer points of his new equipage to Damian and Felix.

After glancing that way, Findlay-Wright half bowed to Julian and Melissa and followed Hockey.

With Julian, Melissa rounded the carriage in time to hear Gordon proudly say, "I would have been up yesterday, but we took the trip in easy stages to baby my beauties." He patted the glossy hide of the nearest horse.

Their family group was screened from the crowd by the body of the carriage.

Damian noted that, looked at Gordon, and bluntly stated, "What I want to know is where you got the blunt for all of this." He waved at the phaeton-and-four.

Gordon grinned and, with one finger, tapped the side of his nose. "Being a part of this family, even if distant from the title, has its benefits."

Felix and Damian blinked, and their expressions blanked, while Julian's expression became utterly impassive. Melissa managed not to react, but Gordon seemed oblivious to the rigidity that had gripped his cousins. Beneath her hand on his sleeve, Julian's muscles had tensed until they felt like unforgiving steel.

Far from noticing the impact his words had had on his relatives,

Gordon was looking over his horses' backs at the assembled crowd. "Heigh-ho! It looks like it's almost time to get started. Some are mounting. Truth to tell, I'm relieved we got here in time."

He glanced at Julian and Melissa, then smiling genially, looked at Damian and Felix; by then, they'd all fixed mild expressions on their faces. "I take it we'll all be riding. Excellent! It'll be another grand ride, I'm sure. I'd best go and check on my new hunter—it's the first time I'll be out on him." He winked at Damian. "I'll leave you in the dust."

Damian managed a scoffing noise, but it sounded half choked.

Melissa, Julian, Felix, and Damian watched Gordon walk to where Hockey had got Gordon's new hunter—a pale dappled-gray gelding —saddled.

Julian shook his head. "Am I the only one unable to decide what to make of any of that?"

"No," Felix said. "He's obviously involved in some way, but he seems entirely unaware of what he's involved in."

"Is he a willing participant in X's schemes, or is he an utterly unwitting pawn?" Damian snorted. "This is Gordon—I know which one I favor."

"He wasn't at all surprised to see us hale and whole," Melissa mused. "If he knew anything of the attacks, wouldn't he at least have been looking to see if we'd been harmed in any way?"

Transparently as bewildered as she, Felix and Damian shrugged.

"Regardless," Julian said, his features hardening, "we need to mount up." He met Felix's and Damian's gazes, then looked at Melissa. "We stick to our plan, get Gordon alone, and extract all he knows, including what he doesn't know he knows."

And then I'll decide just how complicit our distant cousin is in the attacks aimed at me, my brother, and most importantly of all, my wife.

That, Julian silently vowed, would be one outcome of the day.

He steered Melissa to the castle steps, where grooms were holding their mounts, and lifted her to her saddle. After swinging up and settling in his saddle, today on his own heavy hunter, a steady bay with a huge heart, he glanced around, noting that Felix and Damian had mounted as well, then looked out over the forecourt. Virtually all the guests were mounted and ready to ride, and Phelps and the footmen were circulating with the stirrup cup, which, given the season, was a light summer wine.

Phelps approached and offered Julian and Melissa two small silver tankards. They took them and drank. As Julian returned the empty tankard to the salver, he asked, "Is Herne ready?"

"Yes, my lord. He's waiting just around the west corner."

"Right, then." Julian stood in his stirrups, waved his riding glove over his head, and yelled, "To me!" and all those gathered shifted excitedly and looked his way. "Are we ready?" he shouted.

"Yes!" the crowd roared back.

Into the expectant hush that followed, the sound of small bells tinkling drew everyone's attention to the castle's raised front porch, onto which stalked a tall, lanky, gangling figure. Dressed in a strange conglomeration of clothes—leggings and a ragged tabard with odd bits of braid and feathers attached, trailing wispy scarves and wearing a horned mask—he leapt high in the air, whirled, and danced.

With long paddles covered in small bells in each hand, he cavorted and twirled, scarves flaring out around him.

He was grotesque yet strangely graceful, and the dance and his posturing were openly taunting.

Finally, the Herne halted abruptly, as if only just noticing them all gathered below him. Hands lowering to his hips, the paddles sticking out at an angle on either side, he surveyed them, turning his masked face slowly from west to east and back again.

Then in an explosion of motion, he flung the paddles away, whirled once, and bounded off the porch, leaping down and racing off across the lawn, then veering along the drive before plunging toward the woods.

Excited chatter erupted. Horses shifted, and people jockeyed for position, bringing their mounts around ready to ride in the direction Herne had taken.

"Time starts now!" Hockey bellowed and climbed the steps to stand on the porch where everyone could see him.

Phelps and the footmen went around again. People drained the cups and absentmindedly handed them back, their gazes returning to where Herne had vanished around a distant stand of trees.

Julian caught Melissa's eye. "We give him a quarter-hour start, then Hockey will give the signal to hunt." They were close to the steps and, therefore, now at the rear of the pack. Julian's gaze settled on Gordon, a few horses ahead of them in the scrum. "Once we start off, we'll put our plan into action."

∼

Finally, the moment came when Hockey, now mounted himself and stationed at the mouth of the forecourt, raised the hunting horn to his lips and blew a long, rousing blast.

The assembled hunters cheered, and the hunt set off, with the riders in the front falling in behind Hockey as he led them out, initially down the castle drive, then veering across the fields, more or less following the line the Herne avatar had taken.

Gradually, as they left the park and advanced across the pastures, the riders spread out, and the steady drumbeat of hooves filled the air and fired the blood.

It had been some time since Melissa had ridden in any hunt; she'd forgotten the welling excitement and the sense of exhilaration fed by the power of the galloping horses, all strong, heavy, muscular beasts.

As per their plan, Felix and Damian steered their mounts to either side of Gordon's, Damian appearing to assess Gordon's new mount's action and trading barbs and comments.

Riding alongside Julian, just a little behind him and more or less at the rear of the pack, Melissa could appreciate how Felix and Damian used the pace of their own horses to slow Gordon's, gradually edging to the left, subtly separating Gordon from the bulk of the riders, who were streaming ahead in laughing and joyous pursuit of Herne.

She glimpsed the carroty-headed figure of the captain racing ahead. He was clearly caught up in the exuberance of the hunt and, helpfully, wasn't hanging back with Gordon.

Then the hunting horn sounded again, signaling that the quarry had been sighted, and the chase was on. With whoops and shouts, the hunt surged forward.

Damian used his horse to check Gordon's mount. When Gordon, wrestling with his flighty beast, remonstrated, Damian pointed to their left with his crop.

Melissa didn't hear what Damian said, but Gordon looked and willingly turned aside, following Damian onto a little-used bridle path. Felix followed.

Julian slowed, and Melissa slowed with him, allowing the last stragglers—two older couples—to forge ahead. The instant the foursome was far enough in front not to notice, Julian veered after Felix, and Melissa fell in alongside.

With all the riding the three brothers did—it was almost a religion in their family—they knew every foot of the estate, every byway and bridle path, every clearing.

Damian led Gordon through woodland and, ultimately, into a clearing that must, at one time, have been used by charcoal makers. Closely growing trees ringed the area, and a large pile of old charred logs stacked in a rectangular pattern squatted in the middle of the oval space. Other than the path along which they'd ridden in, there was no other way in or out. As a place of ambush, the clearing was an excellent choice.

Damian circled the pile of logs, then halted, fluidly dismounted, and tied his horse to a convenient branch.

Following and increasingly puzzled, Gordon reined in. "What?" He looked around. "How do we get out?" Frowning, he looked at Damian as he strode up. "I thought you said this was a shortcut."

"For our purposes, it is." Damian caught the bridle of Gordon's horse. "Get down."

Gordon glared belligerently and made no move to comply.

Having halted his horse so that it blocked Gordon from riding forward, Felix rolled his eyes. "Come on, Gordon." Felix dismounted as well. "We just want a little chat. Don't make us pull you down."

That had the ring of a threat that had been acted on in the past.

Gordon glanced behind him, only to discover that Julian and Melissa had followed him around the woodpile and now blocked his retreat. Gordon scowled at them, then Julian caught his eye, and after a second, Gordon's scowl vanished, and his face fell into sulky lines. He muttered a half-smothered oath, then grumpily said, "Oh, very well."

He dismounted, and Damian led the horse aside and tied it alongside his.

Julian swung gracefully down and loosely tied his reins to a tree. Returning to lift Melissa from her saddle, he said to Gordon, "We just need a few words, and once you hear them, I'm sure you'll agree that they would be better exchanged in absolute privacy."

Looking dejected—like a schoolboy caught doing something forbidden—Gordon grimaced. "I suppose you've heard, although how, I can't imagine."

What? Frowning, Julian gripped Melissa's waist and helped her slide to the ground. "Heard what?"

"You know what." Disgruntledly, Gordon waved at their surroundings. "Why else are we here? Although why it should concern you, I don't know. It's not as if it caused you any harm! I was totally within my rights, and while it might be stretching fairness a bit, I can't see that I did anything all that wrong!"

Gordon's color had risen, and he ended what was clearly the ravings of a guilty conscience with, "And besides, you might be the head of the house, but you're not my keeper to be riding rein on me."

Julian had not just listened to Gordon's words but had also taken in every other nuance of Gordon's reaction. Sifting through it all... Frowning, Julian pinned Gordon with an unrelenting gaze— one that wouldn't let him look away—and baldly asked, "What do you know about the spate of accidents that have been occurring at the castle?"

Gordon blinked, and his expression blanked. "Huh?" He stared at Julian. After a moment, he ventured, "That's what you wanted to speak with me about? Some accidents here?"

From that first blink, Julian knew Gordon didn't have a clue—not about the accidents, much less their target or their intent. Damian had guessed correctly; Gordon was X's utterly unwitting pawn.

Gordon was shaking his head. "I don't know anything about any accidents here." He glanced over his shoulder at Felix, then at Damian on his other side.

"What about in London?" Felix asked, his tone almost conversational. "Someone shot at Julian in Hyde Park. And then someone tried to smash his head in by dropping an urn off the parapet of Carsely House during the engagement ball."

"*What?*" The horror in Gordon's face could not be doubted.

From significant past experience, Julian knew Gordon to be a poor actor and an even worse liar.

"There was an early attempt made here, before I went down to London." Julian studied Gordon's face as his cousin refocused on him. "Then after the wedding, the accidents here resumed." Succinctly, he ran through the list, aided by dry and pointed comments from Felix and Damian.

From her position at Julian's side, half a pace behind him, with her arms crossed, Melissa watched Gordon. The more he heard of the accidents, the more color drained from his face. She saw the instant he realized that the stories were real, the attacks serious and potentially lethal, and that his most powerful relatives were questioning his involvement in them.

When Julian reached the end of the list, Gordon croaked, "I had nothing to do with any of that. You can't think..." He glanced at Damian, then Felix.

"Where did you get the money for your new phaeton-and-four?" Damian demanded.

Felix asked, "It wasn't from some cent-per-cent who you managed to convince that you would soon be the next best thing to the heir to the earl-dom, was it?"

"No!" Gordon looked truly horrified.

In that moment, Melissa accepted he wasn't in any way a knowing accomplice in X's scheme.

"Well," Julian said in a reasonable tone, "how did you come by the money?" When Gordon hesitated, Julian arched a brow. "I assume that's what you thought we'd heard about."

Gordon eyed Julian as if searching for a way out.

Julian simply waited.

Damian huffed. "You know that comment of yours about how being a part of the family has its benefits?" When Gordon frowned and, puzzled, nodded, Damian continued, "Taken in the context of the accidents, it doesn't sound good, does it? I'm sure you can see how it appears from our point of view—indeed, the point of view of anyone who hears those words and knows of the current situation."

Gordon grimaced. "It isn't that—what Felix said—I swear." He looked at the brothers, and they looked back. With not an ounce of soft-ness between them, Julian and Felix remained silent and immovable, while Damian had planted his hands on his hips and was leaning forward on the balls of his feet, as if debating whether or not to launch himself at Gordon and beat the answers from him.

Gordon sighed and surrendered. "If you must know, I placed a wager on Melissa marrying Julian before the engagement was announced." Color flooded his face as he darted a glance at Melissa, and his expres-sion turned wary. "There was a book—a long-standing wager—on you marrying, you see. On who would finally win you."

He fixed his eyes on her face rather than look at the three men. "The wager had been registered years back—must've been in your second Season—and the sums ventured had accumulated over the years. I even thought to back myself, the return would be that huge. But when I left you and Julian in Lady Connaught's gazebo, well, I knew that the old ladies would turn up, and knowing Julian, what would likely happen then." He shrugged. "So I thought it was worth putting in a bet. I left

Connaught House and went straight to the club holding the book and entered a wager that Julian would be the one to marry you." His expression still wary, Gordon glanced at Julian. "And you did marry, so I won."

When Gordon looked back at Melissa, bemused, she slowly shook her head. "I have no idea how I feel about being the subject of such a wager, but I gather you weren't the one to start it?"

Adamantly, Gordon shook his head. "No, no. I don't even know who did."

"How much did you win?" Damian asked.

Gordon met his gaze, and his face lit. "Over four thousand pounds."

"Good Lord." Damian looked as if he was wishing he had known about the wager.

"Back to the accidents." Julian's dry tone reclaimed everyone's attention. His gaze once more pinning Gordon, Julian asked, "Do you know anything at all about them?"

Gordon sobered and straightened, and for quite the first time, Melissa saw some resemblance to the other Delamere men. Unflinchingly, Gordon met Julian's gaze. "This is the first time I've heard anything about these accidents, and I swear I have no idea who's behind them."

"Hmm." Damian grimaced. "Well, you see, cuz, the problem we have with that is that the person who was responsible for the bookcase falling in the Carsely House study and the punt springing a leak on the lake here is none other than Manning, the valet you recommended to me, who, incidentally, doesn't know how to iron a shirt."

Gordon blanched. "What?"

"You heard me." Damian glowered at Gordon. "You were responsible for planting one of the attackers into my service and, through that, into the Carsely House household and also the household here. You were instrumental in putting him in a position to harm Julian, Melissa, and Felix, too." Damian jutted his chin aggressively. "So what do you have to say about that?"

His expression blank again, Gordon blinked and blinked, then finally said, "Oh."

He lowered his gaze, and from his expression, it was clear the situation was clarifying in his brain.

"Now you understand why we wanted a word," Julian smoothly—and faintly menacingly—said.

"But"—Gordon looked up and met Julian's gaze, then glanced at Felix and Damian—"it wasn't me." He grimaced. "I mean, it was me who told Damian about Manning, but it was Findlay-Wright who mentioned Manning to me. I happened to let fall that Damian was looking for a man, and Findlay-Wright said he might know someone suitable, then a few days later, he told me about Manning, and I passed the information on to Damian."

"Findlay-Wright." Julian stared unseeing at Gordon as, in his mental jigsaw, several new pieces clicked into place.

"Oh, God!"

Julian refocused to see Gordon looking paler and sicker than he had at any point previously.

His eyes wide, Gordon locked his gaze with Julian's. "He—Findlay-Wright—brought two brace of pistols with him. I couldn't understand why, and when I asked, he fobbed me off, but I think—"

Crack!

Wood splintered behind Julian, and he whirled to see Melissa, shocked and stunned, staring at her elbow.

Drawn in by Gordon's urgency, she'd stepped closer at the crucial instant. Instead of hitting her, the ball had scorched the velvet covering the back of her arm, then gone on to hit a tree.

"Get down!" Julian reached her in one stride, swept her into his arms, and hauled her down beside him to hunker in the lee of the old woodpile.

She gulped and whispered, "I'm all right. He missed." Her voice quavered slightly, but when he met her eyes, he saw an anger to match his rising in the midnight depths.

Reassured, he glanced around. Gordon was hunched on his other side, and Felix and Damian had taken cover in the trees.

Julian looked at Gordon. "Four pistols?"

Gordon nodded. "Six-inch barrels, all of them."

"We need to make sure he doesn't have time to reload." Julian was looking at his brothers as he spoke.

"I glimpsed movement just before the shot." Melissa also spoke loudly enough for Felix and Damian to hear. "I think he's behind the largest tree over there." She pointed over her head toward the other side of the clearing, beyond the woodpile at their backs.

Damian and Felix were searching. "Yes, he's there," Felix reported.

"Whatever happens," Julian said to Melissa, "stay here." He made the words more like an order than he ever had. He caught his brothers' gazes and nodded, then raised his head and called, "Really, Captain, how on earth do you think you'll get out of this? We've seen you, and you don't have enough pistols to kill all of us, even if you could shoot true."

"Who says I need pistols to kill?"

"Correct me if I err, but thus far, despite all your attempts, including that effort just minutes ago, you've singularly failed to kill anyone. Am I right?"

The man laughed, a chilling sound. "You might lead a damned charmed life, Carsely, but luck runs out for everyone eventually."

"Really? In that case, I suppose the question we face at this juncture is whose luck will run out first, yours or ours?"

"Funny. I believe I'm the man with the pistols, and you're all cowering."

Julian didn't correct him. As he'd hoped, in focusing on verbally sparring with him, Findlay-Wright hadn't noticed Felix and Damian slipping away through the trees. Felix had gone one way, Damian the other.

Julian laughed. His years of experience negotiating allowed him to make the sound convincingly contemptuous. "You fool yourself, Captain. After all, how many attempts have you made? All have failed."

Julian looked at Melissa, put his finger to his lips, then waved that finger, indicating that they should swap places.

She frowned, but did as he asked.

In a crouch, he crept toward the end of the woodpile. Resuming his contemptuous taunting, he snidely said, "On what grounds do you imagine your luck will change?"

"Show yourself, and we'll see, shall we?"

Julian leapt up. "All right." Immediately, he ducked.

Crack!

As he'd hoped, the unexpected movement, not quite where Findlay-Wright had been focusing, had made him squeeze off another shot. This one had gone winging into the woods.

Melissa had scrabbled closer. She fisted both hands in his lapels and, with surprising strength, hauled him to her. "Have you lost your mind!" she hissed.

He smiled reassuringly and patted her shoulder. "He missed me, too."

She held his gaze for an instant, then let out an explosive sigh and buried her head in his shoulder. He wrapped his arms around her, lifted his head, and called, "What happened then, Captain? Dust in your eye?"

From the corner of his eye, Julian saw movement farther around the clearing. Silently, Felix stepped out from the tree line, hurled a large pine cone toward Findlay-Wright, then smartly stepped back into the cover of the trees.

Crack!

Julian stared, then saw Felix moving stealthily deeper into the wood. He exhaled. "Felix wasn't hit, either."

Melissa had lifted her head at the sounds. She looked at him. "That's three shots. Are we sure he has only one left?"

On her other side, Gordon muttered, "Only one way to find out." With no further warning, he hurled himself out from behind the pile in a headlong dash for the woods.

Crack!

Gordon dove into the bushes. A second later, Julian saw him lift his head and look toward where Findlay-Wright was hiding. Slowly, Gordon rose to his feet, an expression of determination stamped over his features. Eyes narrowed, he stared into the trees.

Then Gordon yelled, "He's out of guns!" and charged across the clearing.

"I'm impressed." Julian pushed to his feet.

Melissa scrambled to hers.

With Julian, she studied the melee that had erupted, with both Gordon and Damian flinging themselves at the captain, who was endeavoring to flee through the woods.

Then Julian laid his hand on her arm and pressed lightly. "Please, stay here." Briefly, he met her eyes. "Please."

With that, he took off. Felix had already crossed the clearing and plunged into the woods. Julian glanced that way, but instead of heading in the same direction, he ran hard along the track leading out of the clearing.

She frowned, then mumbled, "I can't." She scooped up the train of her riding skirt and set off after him.

Julian knew every inch of his land and proved it by veering onto a deer trail that cut through the woods. Trusting that he knew what he was doing, she ran as fast as she could in his wake.

The trail ended on the other side of the woods, where the trees gave way to pasture.

She halted, panting, where the trail met grass. Sounds drew her attention left, and she saw Julian running flat out along the edge of the wood toward a horse left grazing—the captain's horse.

Beyond the horse, approaching from the other side, arms pumping in a desperate run, was Findlay-Wright. Plainly, he'd broken free of the three younger men and escaped.

Melissa turned that way and kicked something. Glancing down, she saw a thick branch lying on the ground. She stooped, picked up the branch with her free hand, and, lips setting, chased after her husband.

Findlay-Wright reached his horse first, ripped the reins from the branch they'd been tied to, then swore viciously and swung the beast so his hindquarters cut Julian off.

Julian leapt back, then slapped the hunter's rump, and the horse side-stepped out of his way.

Melissa had expected Findlay-Wright to use those seconds to remount. But as the horse skittered from between the men, she saw that instead, the captain had freed a saber from his saddle.

Before he could draw the sword back enough to swing it, Julian flung himself on Findlay-Wright.

Julian's fist connected with the captain's jaw, and Findlay-Wright staggered. Fighting to keep hold of his reins, he heaved and pitched Julian off, reversed his hold, and before Julian could regain his balance, struck out viciously, bashing the saber's hilt into the side of Julian's head.

Julian crumpled and fell.

A cry lodged in Melissa's throat, but she swallowed it down and forged on.

His expression one of outright gloating, focused entirely on Julian, Findlay-Wright reversed his sword once more, then with his lips stretching wide in a triumphant grin, raised the blade, clearly intending to plunge it into Julian's chest.

Melissa dropped her train, gripped the branch with both hands, and skidding to a halt beside Julian, swung the branch with all her might at the captain's head.

He saw her a second before she struck, but too late to avoid her blow. The branch cracked across his jaw and sent him reeling.

He dropped the sword and staggered drunkenly back, but managed to keep his feet.

The spooked horse shied away, and Melissa stepped over Julian's body. Gripping the branch, holding it before her like a sword, she glared at Findlay-Wright as, blinking rapidly, he refocused and narrowed his eyes on her.

His sword lay on the ground, midway between them. With her eyes, with her whole expression, she dared him to bend and reach for it.

Behind her, Julian groaned and shifted. She didn't dare look, didn't dare take her eyes from the captain.

Then the thud of running feet reached them. Findlay-Wright glanced along the wood's edge, swore foully, then lunged for his horse, swung up to his saddle, and was off.

Melissa dropped the branch, whirled around, and crouched beside Julian, who had managed to sit up. Careful not to touch where Findlay-Wright had struck, she cradled Julian's face and searched his gray eyes. "Are you all right?"

His eyes looked surprisingly clear.

He huffed. "I wasn't completely senseless. He just rattled my brain." Proving he hadn't lost track of things, he looked at Damian and Gordon, who were standing watching the captain vanish. "Get the horses."

"Felix has gone to fetch them." Damian didn't take his eyes from the captain's vanishing figure. "What's the bet he thinks he'll get away?"

Accepting Melissa's offered hand, Julian got to his feet. "That's not a wager any of us will take."

He turned to Melissa and, squeezing her fingers, brushed his lips to her temple. "I'm still reeling, but not from Findlay-Wright's blow. What in 'Please stay here' didn't you understand?"

She met his gaze and arched her brows haughtily. "And what in 'until death do us part' don't you remember?"

He studied her for a second, then sighed and hung his head. Quietly, so only she could hear, he whispered, "I don't know how to deal with this —with everything you make me feel."

She whispered back, "You don't have to deal with it." She squeezed his hand reassuringly. "Let's concentrate on catching the captain. I assume from your comment you think that's still possible?"

He turned and looked in the direction the captain had gone, and a cold, ruthless smile curved his lips. "Oh yes. We'll catch him yet."

Felix came riding up, leading all the other horses.

Julian looked, then shook his head. "You should have left hers."

Felix regarded him as if he were mad and handed over his reins. "She's your countess, and I'm unmarried, remember? I wouldn't dare."

Already at her horse's side, Melissa favored Felix with a regal nod. "Very wise." She turned to Damian, who had just collected his reins from Felix. "Lift me up, or I'll make your life a misery."

Damian glanced at Julian as he swung up to his saddle and shrugged.

"See." He gripped Melissa's waist and hoisted her up. The instant she was steady, Damian released her and mounted.

After one last shake of his head, Julian started off in pursuit, and the others—Melissa included—followed.

During the ensuing chase, Melissa came to fully appreciate just how well her husband could ride. Stretching low over his horse's neck, he became one with the powerful beast, and the pair flew over the turf and the pastures, leaping across a stream and surging up the low hills.

His brothers weren't far behind him.

Findlay-Wright had had a head start of several minutes, but Melissa realized Julian and his brothers hadn't been indulging in unrealistic optimism in thinking they would catch him. The captain might be riding hard—indeed, as if the hounds of hell were on his horse's heels—but his horse wasn't of the same caliber as the hunter Julian rode or even the horses his brothers were riding.

They all closed the distance. Gordon was having trouble managing his new mount and fell back to ride with her. Nevertheless, whether the captain was pushing his horse too hard or it was simply an inferior beast, even they had him in sight soon enough.

Then Julian's knowledge of the land came into play. While the captain, having noticed his pursuers, desperately flogged his horse down a track following a small stream along a shallow valley, Julian took to the ridge above, riding hard along the crest before rocketing down the slope at the other end and leaping across the stream to land almost on the captain's horse's heels.

High on the ridge, Melissa watched the scene unfold. Julian paced the captain's horse for several strides, then urged his mount forward, almost alongside the captain's flagging steed, and launched himself across. He hit Findlay-Wright and carried him out of his saddle and onto the ground.

The pair rolled in the thick grass.

Felix and Damian were thundering closer, but were still some yards away when Julian and the captain stopped rolling.

Julian had heard Findlay-Wright's breath leave him when they'd hit the ground and knew the man was almost spent. But the bastard was a fighter and would keep clawing and fighting to the end. Before Findlay-Wright could get his breath back enough to come at him again, Julian reared up, pinned the bastard down, and smashed his fist into Findlay-Wright's face.

The man's eyes rolled up, and he slumped in the grass.

Not entirely sure he trusted the faint, Julian rolled to his feet. He stood over the captain and absentmindedly massaged his knuckles as the others rode up.

Damian slowed his horse, then walked it forward and leaned over to study Findlay-Wright's face. Damian smiled, then grinned at Julian. "Despite the pain, that must have felt good."

Julian nodded. "It did." He looked around as Gordon and Melissa followed Felix toward him.

Noting Findlay-Wright's horse waiting with Julian's farther along the stream, Gordon offered, "I'll fetch the horses."

Julian nodded his thanks. As Gordon rode past, to Felix and Damian, Julian said, "Let's tie him up, lash him to his saddle, and take him back to the castle."

Melissa had halted a yard away. She looked down at Findlay-Wright with a degree of satisfaction, then she looked at Julian. "Your hand?"

He wiggled his fingers at her. "Bruised, but not broken."

The look she bent on him informed him that was just as well.

Gordon returned with the horses.

Damian had dismounted and used a rope from his saddlebag to bind the captain's hands and feet. Leaving the horses with Felix and Melissa, Gordon got down and assisted Damian in hoisting Findlay-Wright up and over his saddle, then they tied him securely to the saddle.

"There." Damian slapped the still-unconscious man on the back. "That should hold you."

They mounted up and turned toward the castle, walking their tired horses.

They hadn't gone far before the reality of the situation impinged on Julian. He looked searchingly around, then called to the others, riding just ahead, "Hold up."

They obediently halted and waited for him and Melissa to reach them.

Julian drew rein and folded his hands over his saddle bow. "The hunt. We can't run into it, and at least Melissa and I"—he glanced her way—"can't simply vanish. We'll need to be there, in the forecourt, to greet the riders when they return."

Felix agreed. "The last thing we want is to set tongues wagging."

"Especially," Damian added, "when we've yet to get to the bottom of this."

"Indeed." Melissa looked at Julian. "If possible, you and I should fall in with the returning riders. Do you know where they'll be?"

"If we swing north from here, we should meet up with them on their way back." He looked at Felix. "It would be better if you were there, too. The locals at least will expect to see you at the end."

Felix grimaced, but dipped his head in agreement.

"Meanwhile," Damian said, exchanging a look with Gordon, "Gordon and I will ferry Findlay-Wright to the dungeon."

"Don't put him in with his henchmen," Julian said. "Use the last cell at the end of the corridor."

Damian saluted. "I will. I'm sure Hockey, Edgerton, and their men will be only too happy to provide any assistance we might need."

Julian's lips quirked. "Just make sure they don't drop him on his head."

Damian grinned.

Gordon's horse shifted. When the others glanced his way, he said, "After we reach the castle and Damian has help with him"—he tipped his head toward Findlay-Wright—"I'll ride out and fetch those four pistols."

"And the sword," Melissa said. "Don't forget that."

"Thank you," Julian said. "I'd rather those weapons weren't left lying around for others to find."

With that, Julian, Melissa, and Felix headed north across the pastures, while Damian and Gordon, leading Findlay-Wright's horse with the captain draped over the saddle, apparently still unconscious, made directly for the castle, which lay to the northeast.

When, flanked by Julian and Felix, Melissa came within sight of the returning riders, walking their horses after their hard run, Julian informed her, "If you'd been present at the culmination of the hunt, you would have seen the riders approach our Herne, who would have been kneeling on the grass, his arms drooping and head hanging. The first dozen riders form up in a line and circle him three times clockwise, then three times widdershins. After that, they draw back, bow to him, and let him go. He leaps up, dances a shorter version of his earlier dance, then he flees into the trees, and it's over."

Felix added, "Their compassion in letting the god go, despite having him at their mercy, is supposed to guarantee a good harvest."

"Ah, I see." After a moment of imagining it, Melissa said, "That's a rather nice custom."

"Hmm." Julian's gaze was on the hunters, some of whom had noticed them rejoining the pack from a different direction. "If any ask where we've been"—briefly, he met Melissa's eyes—"we'll say that you got distracted by a deer and rode off on a tangent, and Felix and I followed to steer you back."

Felix nodded. "It has to be you who went off track. They'd never believe it of either of us."

Melissa chuckled. "Very well. I'll play the helpless female you had to rescue." She glanced at Julian and met his gaze. "Just this once."

His smile bloomed—the one that turned him into a stunningly handsome man.

After letting her eyes feast, entirely content, she faced forward.

With practiced ease, the three of them fell into their roles as co-hosts of the Wirksworth Ride. Melissa threw herself into the task of preserving their façade of unrelieved serenity as if nothing dramatic, much less life threatening had occurred. Luckily, the bruise on Julian's head was concealed beneath his hair, and he'd dusted off his clothes before remounting.

By the time they reached the forecourt, most of the riders were wilting. Phelps was waiting with a round of ale and cider to quench the riders' thirsts, plus slices of Mrs. Phelps's seed cake, an offering that was gladly accepted by all.

Still mounted, Melissa circulated, chatting and graciously congratulating those who had reached Herne in time to claim a place among the dozen ceremonial riders. With genuine sincerity, she assured several neighbors that she would never forget her first Wirksworth Ride.

From the corner of her eye, she saw Hockey step to Julian's stirrup and report. From the expression on the grizzled stableman's face, he was delightedly conveying the news that the captain had been secured.

Later, when Julian and Felix joined her on the steps to wave their guests on their way, Julian confirmed that.

Finally, as the last rider disappeared down the drive, Julian met Melissa's gaze, and she sensed an easing in his stance as if a weight had slid from his shoulders.

"No one seemed to suspect anything," he said.

She nodded. "I kept an ear out, but I didn't hear so much as a single whisper."

"Everyone was caught up in the day. Most knew what to expect, and that's what they got." Felix grinned at Melissa. "The only unusual comments I received were commiserations over having missed the finale while rescuing you."

She humphed. "I suspect, at least with those who attended today, I'll never live down missing the finale of my first Wirksworth Ride."

Julian caught her eye. "But it's over now, in many more ways than one. Or so I hope." He tipped his head indoors. "Let's see if we can get some answers to our most pressing questions."

CHAPTER 17

hey went straight to the corridor off the kitchen and down the steps to the cellars and the old dungeon. Julian was grateful that they didn't encounter his mother or his uncle along the way.

With Melissa and Felix, he walked past the cell holding Mitchell, Manning, and Richards. He noted all three were hovering close to the open grille in the heavy door, as best they could listening to and watching what was happening in the cell at the end of the short corridor.

Benton also stood at the grille in the door of her cell, directly opposite that of the three men.

Damian and Gordon were slouched against the wall on either side of the door to the third cell. They straightened as Julian, Melissa, and Felix neared.

Julian halted before the cell door and, through the grille, studied Findlay-Wright.

In an undertone, Damian reported, "He came around as we got him into the cell. If his arrogance is anything to judge by, he's perfectly certain he's going to walk away from all this unscathed."

Gordon looked troubled. "I don't understand it. He seems totally unconcerned. I would have said he's demented, only I know he's as sharp as a tack."

Damian lowered his voice still further. "I got the distinct impression he knows something we don't. He's smug as can be."

Julian drew in a long breath, then nodded. "Let's see."

They'd left the key in the door. Julian turned it, then opened the door and set it wide.

The cell hadn't housed a felon in decades and was normally used as a storage room. Sacks of grain were piled against all three walls, and several barrels stood to one side.

Findlay-Wright had fashioned a bench of sorts on which he sat facing the door—rather reminiscent of a king on his throne, holding court for his subjects. As Damian had warned, the dastardly captain appeared remarkably relaxed.

Julian decided to play along with the king-and-subject theme, at least to begin with; people like the captain often let down their guard when they believed themselves in control. He stepped into the cell and halted just inside the door. The cell was about three yards deep, which meant the captain had to look up to meet his eyes—possibly not what the man had had in mind with his staging. Julian waited impassively as the others filed in. Melissa paused by his left shoulder, a half step behind him, while Felix took up a position to his right and Damian and Gordon ranged behind them.

"The first question I have," Julian evenly said, "is what you hoped to gain by this campaign of yours against me. You'll never be able to claim the title, so what was the point?"

Findlay-Wright's slow smile was the epitome of contemptuous, with just a hint of the derisive. "You haven't worked it out, have you?" He made a show of being struck by a sudden insight and widened his eyes. "Could it be that you don't actually know?"

Julian sensed both his brothers shift restlessly, reacting to the captain's taunting.

But it was Melissa who moved, stepping up to stand beside him. She fixed the captain with an openly inquiring, overtly curious gaze. "Your campaign has been so exquisitely planned and stretches over such a long time." Her tone bordered on the admiring. "You clearly thought through every move very carefully."

Findlay-Wright's gaze had deflected to her. He studied her for a moment, then smiled and, almost preening under her supposed recognition of his abilities, replied, "Indeed, I did. I worked to have multiple agents in place before I made the first move." His pale-blue gaze returned to Julian, and a smirk touched his lips. "I've long observed that careful planning wins out every time."

Melissa folded her arms and nodded understandingly. "In hindsight, your plan is really rather amazing." She frowned, faintly puzzled. "How far back did you start?"

Julian had seen ladies pander to gentlemen's vanities in pursuit of information before. He knew that approach frequently worked and prayed his brothers and Gordon would follow his lead and remain silent.

Sure enough, Findlay-Wright relaxed on his improvised throne and happily revealed, "As it happened, I had my epiphany when I was here for the late earl's funeral. That's when it occurred to me how unexpected accidents could move control of a major estate on down the line of succession, and I started hypothesizing about removing Julian and making Felix appear guilty."

Melissa nodded. "Two birds with one stone."

"Exactly. And that would advance my potential cause in a leap and a bound. And *then*"—Findlay-Wright was clearly warming to Melissa's implied understanding and her subtext of flattery—"I recognized Mitchell and realized who he was, and he became my first pawn on the board, as it were. I took that—finding Mitchell already ensconced and in place—as a sign that the plan crystalizing in my mind was worthy and that if I pursued it carefully, it would work."

His gaze had grown distant, his expression unconcerned as he grew consumed with his tale. "And given that older groom had suicided, Mitchell was reasonably secure."

Julian couldn't resist confirming, "So you had no hand in my father's death?"

Findlay-Wright refocused on him and smiled condescendingly. "No, indeed. You won't catch me with that. By all accounts, it was pure accident that took your father off." The captain's eyes twinkled. "And gave me my grand idea."

"I'm curious." Melissa edged forward, recapturing Findlay-Wright's attention. "I take it all the strange accidents were dictated by you and put into action by your pawns. Was the first the thorn Mitchell put in Julian's saddle?"

The captain nodded. "Another idea sparked by the late earl's death." He shrugged. "It was worth a try."

"But next came the shot in Hyde Park." Puzzled, Melissa frowned. "Who was that?"

"Ah." Findlay-Wright looked faintly chastened. "I fear that was me. I was at that family dinner a few nights previously when you announced your wedding date. That, I admit, unsettled me. Until that moment, I had hoped the engagement, coming about as it had, would prove more bluff than substance. Then while riding in the park, I saw you and Julian riding, too, and I'd seen Felix out as well, and I couldn't resist seizing the opportunity and trying for a hit." He grimaced. "Sadly, nothing came of that, and I really should have learned the lesson that planning always pays, but..."

When he didn't go on, Melissa prompted, "The urn falling during our engagement ball was the next incident."

Findlay-Wright sighed. "As I said, I really should have learned my lesson, but when you both went out onto that side terrace, it was simply too good a chance to squander, or so I thought. But then I came within a whisker of being caught." His gaze shifted, rising past Julian's shoulder to Damian, and Findlay-Wright smiled. "If it hadn't been for young Master Damian"—the way he said Damian's name was openly disparaging —"and his band of merry men, I would have been hard-pressed to explain why I was in that rear corridor at that time. But several of the men were so well oiled they didn't notice that, although I walked back to the ballroom with them, I hadn't been with them when they'd left nor yet been to the water closets." He returned his attention to Melissa. "After that near miss, I truly did learn my lesson and left the actual acting to my pawns." He smiled gently. "That is, after all, why I put them in place."

Melissa nodded, her expression suggesting Findlay-Wright's tale was an eye-opening revelation.

That wasn't all that far from the truth.

"And then," he confirmed, "your wedding gave me the perfect opportunity to escort dear Helen here and spend a few days contacting my pawns, reminding each of them of what they had at stake and giving them their orders."

From the corner of his eye, Julian watched as his wife's expression once again grew puzzled. "We know who did what after the incident with the urn—Manning rigging the bookcase to fall, then once we were here, Mitchell with the mantrap, the spring gun, the line across the bridle path, and the gig's axle breaking, followed by Manning with the punt, Richards trapping us in the barn and setting it on fire, and Benton trying to poison me."

How she managed to keep her tone so even, so merely curious, Julian didn't know; he would have battled to do the same.

"What I don't understand," she went on, "is how you managed to recruit your pawns. We know Mitchell really is a groom, and at some time in his past, Richards was a footman, but the other two aren't all that well-trained in the roles they were hired to fill."

Findlay-Wright tipped his head in mild approval. "Noticed that, did you? Clever of you, and yes. Benton is a highly regarded seamstress in London, and Manning is an engineer, while more recently, Richards was a solicitor's secretary. But each of them knew enough to play the roles I had in mind for them, well enough to pass muster for a while."

Still puzzled, Melissa tipped her head. "But what did you offer them to secure their services?"

This time Findlay-Wright's smile was patronizing in the extreme. "My dear countess, if there's one thing I've learned over the years, it's that in order to get people to commit murder for you, you need much more than 'something to offer them.' You need a lever—a truth, a fact— that will destroy them. Or even better"—Findlay-Wright's expression grew chilling—"destroy someone they hold very dear. I assure you that, once you have such a lever in your hand, you can be certain people will do whatever you say in order to stop you from pulling it."

Sensing that Melissa was struggling to hold back, to hide her disgust, Julian said, his voice flat, uninflected, and low, "So with these four pawns…"

"Well…" Findlay-Wright tipped his head as if inwardly debating, then his chilling smile returned. "As they've all failed, and you've caught them, I suppose there's no reason I shouldn't tell you all. So, let's see. Mitchell's younger brother, who looks sufficiently like Mitchell that I realized the relationship as soon as I set eyes on him, was in a regiment fighting alongside mine during a skirmish in India. He subsequently deserted and made it back to England, so on my word, I could have him charged not only with desertion but also for murdering an officer." The captain's smile grew positively evil. "Not that the boy had anything to do with the murder, of course, but the added threat lent heft to my leverage over Mitchell." If anything, his smile grew. "And then there was Richards, whose young nephew works in the War Office and has a sad and provable preference for men. Quite aside from the activity being illegal, the government takes a dim view of such things and, given the young man's role, might even consider the matter a treasonable offence. Manning, I stumbled over by sheer luck. His eldest son recently won a prized scholarship to Winchester, with the only fly in their ointment being that the family is secretly Catholic—not something the Winchester board would be pleased to learn. And lastly, there's Benton, whose younger sister was known to some as being no better than she should be, but is now married to an upright deacon who is entirely unaware of his wife's past."

Findlay-Wright leaned against the sacks of wheat at his back. His smile as he regarded Julian and the others brimmed with confidence and assurance. "It really was a hell of a plan. A pity I didn't think to hide my guiding hand sufficiently well with Gordon."

"The final point I don't understand," Melissa said, and her tone was no longer admiring but direct and to the point, "is what you hoped to gain from all of this. You can't inherit, so how did you think to benefit from Julian's death?"

Findlay-Wright studied her, then surveyed them all. "Not just Julian's death, but in one way or another, I intended removing Felix as well." His taunting smile returned. "Once they were gone…"

He paused, then in almost philosophical vein, went on, "That, you see, is one mistake the aristocracy frequently make, an entrenched weakness in their system, if you will. They don't promote their strongest and most capable but rather the one who is next in line, and that"—he held up a hand to stay any protest—"bear with me, would be Frederick. He would be earl, and Gordon would be heir, and that, of course, would give me the keys to the Delamere coffers."

Findlay-Wright met Julian's gaze, and for once, there was neither pretense nor boasting in his words. "I never cared about the title or anything else to do with the earldom. I wanted access to the money, and with Frederick so old and not really all that able, and Gordon as he is, it would have been child's play to promote myself—Helen's faithful savior —into the role of trusted advisor. Over time, both Frederick and Gordon would have handed the financial reins to me—so much easier than trying to manage them themselves—and then I would have achieved my goal. To have unfettered access to the Delamere wealth and no one in a position to stop me bleeding the family dry."

There was enough malignant triumph in his tone to make Julian ask, "Why the Delameres? As far as I know, prior to you returning from India with Helen and Maurice's body, you and the family hadn't crossed paths."

Findlay-Wright's smile flashed briefly. "Well, there was India, after all. But as it happened, I returned to England with a vague notion of sponging off the family in one way or another for some time. Until I found a better target, at least. But then, through escorting Helen to family gatherings—she does talk so very freely, you know—I learned of the situation here, the true facts, and then your father died, and I realized the possibilities." The captain leaned forward, adopting a patently false, confiding manner. "And in large part, realizing those possibilities hinged on the one fact none of you in this room seem yet to have learned." He caught Damian's gaze. "Namely, that Damian is not in the line of succession. He's illegitimate."

Julian felt the shock that rippled through them all, heard the indrawn breaths. But they all contained their reaction, and not one gave Findlay-Wright the joy of seeing how much he'd shaken them.

Could it be true?

Julian fought not to look at Felix or at Damian.

With his taunting smile blooming anew, Findlay-Wright sat back and returned his gaze to Julian. "And that, my lord earl, is the lever I hold over *you*. If you put me on trial, I will destroy your little brother and your mother, too. Just imagine what that will do to your own prospects, let alone those of the rest of the family."

He paused to let his words sink in, then went on, "And that's why, after you've retreated and thought matters through, you and all your family are going to let me walk out of here a free man. More, you're going to guarantee me safe passage out of England. Although I would prefer to remain in the land of my birth, sadly, I suspect I would fear for my continuing health." His smile deepened. "Especially knowing how easy it is for accidents to occur. All in all, the Continent will, I feel, be safer, at least for a time." He fell silent and looked at Julian expectantly.

Holding Findlay-Wright's gaze, Julian drew in a slow breath. He suspected they were all mentally reeling, trying to absorb the bombshell the man had let fall.

"Ah." Findlay-Wright held up a finger. "Before we descend into a futile round of what-ifs, I should perhaps lay all my cards on the table." He dropped all lighthearted pretense, his expression hardened, and his voice grew steely. "I have proof. Irrefutable proof. In my possession, but not here. Indeed, that proof—my insurance, as it were—is secreted in a very safe place, one you will never find."

"Who's my father?" Damian sounded as if he was barely holding in his fury.

Findlay-Wright arched a condescending brow. "Haven't you worked it out yet?" He sighed. "I'll give you a clue. The three of you look like brothers, yet you aren't. You're half brothers, yet there is a reason you look so alike."

His expression turned openly taunting again. "Surely you can work it out from that?"

Julian felt sure all of them had. Indeed, the obvious had been staring them in the face—not that Damian was illegitimate but that if he was, who his father had to be.

And if that was true and proven, and the knowledge became widely known…Findlay-Wright was correct in thinking the family, root and branch, would be ruined socially and politically, too. Julian and Melissa's future would be nothing like the one they'd started to frame and build. And all the hopes they and the elite of the ton had been nurturing would turn to ashes.

With a thoroughly satisfied smile, Findlay-Wright leaned back on his throne, crossed a leg over his knee, and in an easy manner, swung his booted foot.

Julian fisted his hands. He needed to get out of there before he gave in to the urge to throttle the man.

As if sensing that, Findlay-Wright waved them back. "Go. Think. I'm happy to wait here while you do."

"Good." Damian turned and marched out of the cell. Gordon quickly followed.

Julian gave Melissa his arm. With one last, severe look at the captain, she turned and, with Julian, swept from the room.

Felix was the last to leave. He swung the door shut behind him, turned the key in the lock, then handed it to Julian. "Now what?" Felix whispered.

Julian took the key, slid it into his pocket, and murmured back, "Now we do as he suggested and figure out our best way forward."

～

They took refuge in the library. Despite the mental trauma of the past hour, it wasn't yet six o'clock.

Gordon slumped into one of the armchairs and gratefully accepted the glass of brandy Julian offered him. He took a gulp, then exhaled. "My God—if he'd ever succeeded in making me heir, my life would not have been my own."

As the others settled in the armchairs gathered before the fireplace, Gordon looked around the circle and admitted, "As the dear captain intimated, he's been sponging off Mama ever since he returned from India with her and the pater's body. Whenever I've tried to broach the matter with her"—he grimaced, sipped again, then mumbled—"she defends him as if he's, quite literally, her savior. And as soon as he heard of my recent windfall, he started making plans to 'borrow' most of it from me, which is why I went out and bought the phaeton-and-four. I didn't want him to get Mama to put me in a bind to hand over the money to him."

Felix frowned. "Would she have done that?"

"Oh yes." Gordon nodded emphatically. "He has her wrapped around his little finger. He has a large suite in the house and pays nothing in room and board. Mama wouldn't hear of it, of course."

Damian had already drained the glass of brandy Julian had given him. "What I want to know is what his 'irrefutable proof' of my illegitimacy is."

Julian grimaced, but before he could respond, the door opened, and his mother came in, followed by her devoted shadow, his uncle Frederick.

As those seated all rose, his mother swept up, paused to touch cheeks with Melissa, then turned to grip Julian's sleeve. "My dear, Frederick heard that you have that wretched creature, Findlay-Wright, locked up in the dungeon." Glancing around, she saw Gordon, and her eyes widened. "And Gordon's here, too." She returned her gaze to Julian's face. "What on earth's going on?"

At Julian's signal, Felix and Gordon had moved back their armchairs. Together, they fetched the sofa from farther down the room and set it so that it faced the fireplace. Julian waved his mother and his uncle to the sofa. "It's a long story. You'd better sit down."

His mother and Melissa sat, and the men followed suit.

Where on earth do I begin? Julian glanced at Melissa and drew strength from her understanding look. Transferring his gaze to his mother and uncle, he said, "We've learned that Findlay-Wright is the person behind the attacks. He's the one who's been pulling the strings of the people he'd planted in our household. He tried to murder us again today, while we were out on the Ride, but we turned the tables and caught him instead."

"Oh!" His mother shook herself. "I always knew he was a rotten apple. There was something dark and unhealthy inside him, even when he first came back to England with Helen and we all felt we had to be grateful for what he'd done for her. I've never felt entirely comfortable with him, although Helen still thinks he can do no wrong."

Frowning, Frederick asked, "But why?" When everyone looked his way, he elaborated, "I can't see what Findlay-Wright would gain by killing you. Any of you."

Succinctly, Julian outlined the captain's plan to remove him, preferably implicating Felix. "But in one way or another, he was determined to remove Felix as well." Julian exchanged a swift glance with Felix and Damian, then looked back at his mother and uncle. "At that point, the situation became rather more convoluted than we'd anticipated." He paused, but there really was no way to edge around the point. He drew breath and said, "Findlay-Wright maintains that, after Felix, the title moves directly to you, Frederick, bypassing Damian and making Gordon the heir."

His mother's expression blanked, then she paled. Her hand blindly reached for Frederick's, and in a gesture Julian realized he'd seen a thousand times and never really thought about, Frederick—also without looking—gripped her fingers. She glanced swiftly at him, at his sober, set features, then looked across at Damian, sitting back in his chair, his features impassive and his eyes locked on her. "Oh, my dear, sweet boy—we hoped you'd never learn. That you'd never have reason to learn."

"That I'm illegitimate?" Damian asked in a voice that was eerily calm.

"No." Frederick's voice carried a strength Julian couldn't remember ever hearing from his usually quiet uncle. His gaze capturing and holding Damian's, he stated, "You are a Delamere. Never doubt that. But you're my son, not Vernon's."

"Did Papa know?" Felix asked, more, Julian sensed, as a diversion.

"We assume so," their mother replied. "He and I hadn't been together for over a year before Damian was born. But between us, we never referred to or discussed Damian's paternity."

Frederick sighed, but there was no sadness in the sound. He seemed almost relieved to be able to discuss the issue openly. "If you cast your minds back not all that long ago, you'll recall that Vernon and I were always close. Closer than either of us were to our other brothers. Vernon married Veronica and brought her home to the castle, but"—still holding her hand, he turned his head and caught her gaze—"I was the Delamere who fell in love with her."

Melissa watched Veronica faintly smile.

As if satisfied that she was all right, Frederick turned to the rest of them. "Vernon saw and...he understood. He recognized that I loved Veronica in a way he did not. He came to accept that, and once the two of you"—he nodded at Julian and Felix—"and your sisters were born, he stepped back and let love have its way. Vernon was an honorable man. He loved me, and he loved Veronica, too, in his own way. He was never heartless and unfeeling. He wanted us to be happy, and so we were. We all were."

"But was Findlay-Wright correct in thinking that after Felix, the succession bypasses Damian and goes to you?" Julian asked.

Veronica and Frederick exchanged a look, then Frederick said, "I know of no reason why that would be so. As far as I'm aware, Vernon never did anything that in any way whatsoever threw doubt on Damian's paternity." Frederick met Julian's gaze. "You've read your father's will. There's no codicil or amendment that bars Damian from his expected position in the succession."

Julian inclined his head. "You're right. I've not heard or seen anything on that point, which is why Findlay-Wright's assertion so blindsided me." He looked at his brothers. "Blindsided us."

"What about the irrefutable proof he spoke of?" Felix looked questioningly at Frederick and Veronica. "He seemed very sure he had something that the family would move heaven and earth to keep hidden."

Veronica and Frederick frowned. After a moment, still frowning, Veronica shook her head. "I can't imagine what proof he might mean." She looked at Frederick. "Can you?"

Frederick started to shake his head, but stopped. Then he grimaced. "He must mean the letters."

"Letters?" Julian asked.

Frederick glanced almost guiltily at Veronica. "I didn't tell you because I didn't want to worry you, but sometime around Vernon's funeral, your letters to me—all those I'd kept—vanished from the secret drawer in which I'd hidden them." He looked at Julian. "Findlay-Wright was here for the funeral. He stayed in the castle for those three days, remember? He could have found time to search my room."

Julian nodded. "I've a feeling he's the sort to know all about secret drawers."

"What was in the letters?" Melissa asked. "Was there enough in them to prove irrefutably that Damian isn't Vernon's son?"

Veronica met Frederick's eye. "Those were my letters to you, so no." She glanced at Damian, then focused on Julian. "As I said, we three—your father, Frederick, and I—were always careful never to do or say or even imply anything that would bring Damian's paternity into question.

So even if the letters were made public—read out in open court, even—there's nothing in them that can't be attributed to a lady informing a doting uncle about her latest baby's progress."

"This was when I was called to London to assist with organizing supplies for the war effort," Frederick said. "But both before and after, as usual, I was here, so the letters only spanned a matter of months."

"Outside that period," Veronica said, "there was no need to put anything on paper. We could stroll in the gardens or in the conservatory if we wanted to talk privately, and Frederick often went up to the nursery and played with you all."

Julian nodded. "That, I remember." He blew out a breath, then frowned. "But if Findlay-Wright couldn't have learned of Damian's paternity via the letters or, it seems, any other document, how did he come to know...something all the rest of us didn't?"

Veronica waved. "That's easy. He got the idea from Helen. And no, she doesn't actually *know* anything, but she was here when Damian was born. She was expecting Gordon and was living with Maurice in quarters, so I invited her to see out her confinement here." Veronica paused, her gaze resting, not unkindly, on Gordon. "Most people think your mother chatters incessantly and tend not to listen to all she says, but although she does talk far too much because she's very shy, she's also one of the most observant people I've ever met." Veronica looked at Damian. "When you were born, Frederick was frantic—far more frantic than Vernon."

Frederick passed a hand over his face. "I still remember that day vividly. I've never felt so terrified in my life."

Veronica patted his arm. "I heard Vernon explain to Helen that the difference was due to him—Vernon—being an old hand and that Frederick had simply got an attack of nerves. But I always thought Helen saw through that. So in her mind, she knows, but that's solely based on her instincts on witnessing Frederick's reaction. She has no actual proof to support her conjecture." Veronica tipped her head consideringly. "That said, I can readily imagine Helen babbling on and including Damian being Frederick's son as a known fact in her ramble. If Findlay-Wright picked that up, then went looking for proof, found the letters, and read them with the idea already in his head..." She looked at Julian. "Then yes, I can imagine he might *think* he has proof, but I assure you on your father's grave that he doesn't have anything that would withstand even the most cursory scrutiny."

Julian's eyes narrowed. "So if Findlay-Wright tried to publish the letters, thinking to shame the family—"

"Oh, slander would be the very least of it," Veronica assured him. She caught his gaze. "But will he, do you think? Publish the letters, thinking to harm the family?"

"I think," Julian said, "that your revelations significantly alter the board on which the captain thinks he's been playing his game." He looked at Damian. "It appears that, no matter what bombshell Findlay-Wright thinks he has, we're in a position to call his bluff."

Damian met Julian's gaze, then his jaw firmed. "There's only one way to deal with scum like Findlay-Wright."

Melissa wholeheartedly agreed.

"Be that as it may"—Julian swept the gathering with his gaze—"I'm very much in favor of honoring Papa's stance on this matter. As head of the Delamere family, I never ever wish to hear of Damian's paternity being questioned in any way whatsoever."

Veronica smiled in approval, and Frederick looked relieved. "Obviously, that's what your father wanted."

Everyone looked at Gordon.

Abruptly realizing he'd become the center of attention, looking faintly alarmed, he held up his hands, palms out. "No argument from me. I assure you I won't say a word." Then his features hardened. "And I especially won't say a word or lift a finger to help Findlay-Wright. I don't want anything to do with the man. I'm going to put my foot down and turf him out of the London house. It is mine, after all. And even if I have to sit her down and explain in words of no more than two syllables, I'll make sure Mama understands that he's a very bad man and that she shouldn't indulge in sympathy for him because he most definitely doesn't deserve it."

Julian inclined his head. "Well, it'll be up to you to break the news to her that your lodger, for want of a better description, is going to be put on trial for attempting to murder me, Melissa, and Felix."

Gordon almost demurred—they all saw it in his eyes—but then he squared his shoulders and nodded. "All in all, it's the least I can do. Mama was the one who introduced Findlay-Wright into the family circle, so to speak. Only reasonable I do my part to put things right."

Melissa studied Gordon. She'd seen more signs of maturity in him over that day than at any time before.

"So," Veronica asked, addressing Julian, "how do you plan to proceed with that horrible man?"

"And," Melissa hurried to say, "his pawns." She caught Julian's gaze. "Given what he told us, regardless of what they tried to do, I can't help but think they're his victims, too."

He held her gaze for several seconds, then raised a hand and looked around the circle. "It's been a long day, and it's almost time for dinner. I vote we leave our prisoners where they are for tonight, safe in the cells. We can meet over breakfast tomorrow and decide on our next steps, and then we can tell Findlay-Wright that, contrary to his arrogant belief, he will be tried for all his attempted crimes. All in favor?"

"Aye, aye!" rang out around the room. With the motion carried unanimously, the entire company determinedly turned their minds to less-fraught subjects.

~

Later, as the moon rode the sky and the castle settled to sleep, swathed in his silk robe, Julian walked into Melissa's bedchamber.

She was standing before the window, her arms crossed beneath her breasts. Clad only in a single layer of delicate silk, she was absentmindedly surveying the night-dark landscape.

The lamps were already doused, and the moonlight limned her face and her figure.

The sight caused something in him to clutch and tighten, and he slowed.

An inexorable, irresistible wave of yearning—of need and hunger and something so much more—rose and crashed over him.

It washed through him, scouring away all pretense, all ability not to recognize and own to the power of what he felt for her.

His step had hitched, the realization sharp enough to momentarily shake him.

Resuming his steady pace, he approached her.

She sensed him and half turned his way. Through the dimness, her shadowed eyes, dark as midnight, met his.

He sensed more than saw her knowledge reflected in the star-laden depths of her eyes—her newfound understanding of him, of herself, of what they had become, each to the other.

He halted, but before he could speak, she did, her voice low, husky.

"Today, when I saw him fell you, then raise that sword to strike you dead..." She paused, then drawing in a breath, tilted her chin upward and went on, "Until that moment, I hadn't known I could feel what I did. I hadn't had any inkling that the full gamut of emotions encompassed so much more or that the power emotion can wield could compel so utterly."

They were, it seemed, consumed by the same realization, dwelling on that single revelatory moment.

"I wasn't entirely unconscious," he replied, his own voice low and uncharacteristically rough. "I saw you strike him with that branch...then you stepped over me and faced him, and I nearly died, drowned by my panic."

Even the memory jarred him to the core.

Moving slowly, he gripped her upper arms and drew her to face him, then he forced his fingers to gentle and soothingly stroke her bare skin. "I couldn't protect you." He could barely get the words out. "I couldn't even help you."

"In that moment, that role wasn't yours." Melissa waited for his gaze to rise and meet hers, then forthrightly declared, "In that moment, it was mine."

For several steady heartbeats, their gazes remained locked, their senses communing. In that moment, so much hung in the balance. A final acceptance by them both of the true meaning of their love.

An acknowledgement of what, between them, love in all its glory truly meant.

Then he let out a shuddering sigh. His gaze remained leveled on hers as in a hoarse whisper, he admitted, "Yes. It was."

He looked down, caught her hand, raised her fingers to his lips, and pressed a long, lingering kiss to her fingertips. "Thank you." The words reached her on a breath. "For saving me. For marrying me. For loving me."

He lowered her hand, and his eyes rose to meet hers again, and even in the poor light, she could sense the roiling storm within him.

"I need you tonight. Now."

Her lips faintly curved. "I'm yours. Take me." A deliberately brazen response, but she wanted him, too. She stepped closer, set her body to his, and raised her hands to his nape to draw him to her. "Hold me."

She didn't have to ask twice. The steely bands of his arms cinched about her, and his lips found hers in a searing kiss.

Between them, the flames of desire sparked, ignited, rose, and raged, and the exchange grew ever hotter, ever more fiery. Ever more demanding.

Silk slid and *shushed* to the floor, and skin met skin and burned.

Breathless, near mindless, she broke from the kiss to exhort, "Love me," and felt his lips curve as they ruthlessly reclaimed hers.

His hands sculpted, his fingers teased, and finally, he lifted her, and she wrapped her arms and legs around him and welcomed him into her body on a long, shuddering, exultant sigh.

She clamped around him, and he groaned.

He lifted her, and she rose and slid down, and they fell into the age-old dance, one they'd rehearsed and no longer needed to think to perform.

Exquisitely.

Their senses expanded, and they clung, their conscious minds awash in pleasure and delight.

Overwhelmed, overpowered, they gasped and strove and, somehow, found their way to the bed and fell full length upon it.

They came together in passion and in love, with a desperately greedy need to claim the other.

To seize and hold, to demand and surrender, to glory in their burgeoning understanding.

For this was love—the power that rose to their call.

The power that, in extremis, would always rule them. Now and forever.

For them, love had become the determining force in their lives, and together, they embraced it and held on with everything in them.

Never to let go, never to be parted. Through the thundering in their veins and the frantic beat that drove them up to ecstasy's peak, they opened their hearts and let the glory flood in.

Until they shattered, and the ultimate eruption of mind-numbing brilliance blanked their minds and welded their souls.

All awareness hung suspended in that moment of indescribable joy, that moment of scintillating crystal-clear exultation.

Until ecstasy faded, and with their wits long gone and their senses beyond recall, holding tight to the other, they spiraled together into the soothing satiation of oblivion's sea.

CHAPTER 18

$\mathcal{T}$hey all met about the breakfast table the following morning. Everyone was down punctually, even Veronica and Frederick, whose appearance at that hour underscored the gravity of what was to come.

It wasn't simply a matter of dealing with Findlay-Wright. The fate of his pawns hung in the balance, and what to do with them wasn't nearly as clear as deciding what to do about their master.

Melissa sipped her tea and looked around the table. Everyone appeared reasonably well rested, yet all seemed to harbor an underlying tension. She glanced at Julian, who was finishing a plate of kedgeree alongside her, and inwardly admitted that despite the catharsis of their past hours, she, too, shared that same wariness, and she knew he did, too. She doubted any of them would feel completely safe, secure enough to drop their guard and truly relax, until this entire saga was over and Findlay-Wright and his machinations were no longer a threat in any way, shape, or form.

Formally charging Findlay-Wright and binding him over to face the next assizes, while undoubtedly the correct thing to do, still carried an element of risk.

What if he did have some real evidence—evidence no one else realized existed—that plunged the family into scandal?

She glanced around the table again and decided she wasn't going to borrow trouble. They would go forward, all of them united, and together, to the best of their abilities, they would deal with whatever came.

When all was said and done, their combined abilities weren't anything to sneeze at.

Reassured and recommitted, she looked up as the door opened, and Phelps—a plainly agitated Phelps—quickly came in.

"My lord." When Julian and everyone else looked at him in surprise, Phelps made a visible effort to pull himself together, hauled in a breath, and raised his head. "I regret to inform you, my lord, that the captain is dead."

"What?" Along with everyone else, Julian stared. "Dead?" He set down his fork and started to push back his chair. "How?"

As if he'd got the worst out, Phelps seemed to calm. "He hanged himself, my lord."

Julian stood, and the others around the table followed suit.

Felix frowned. "I can't recall there being any rope in that storeroom."

"He fashioned one from his own clothes." Having regained his composure, Phelps faced Julian. "We checked all the doors, my lord. None of the cells were unlocked. It does not appear that those in the other cells could have had anything to do with the captain's death. We also found no unexpected marks on the body, and there was nothing in the cell to suggest that anyone else had been inside."

Damian was shaking his head. "This doesn't make any sense—he was so damned arrogantly sure of himself when we left him yesterday."

"He seemed in excellent spirits when we took him his dinner tray," Phelps confirmed. "And when Thornley and Carmichael fetched the trays later, they mentioned that the captain was making himself comfortable and seemed very confident he would be riding off tomorrow, meaning today. He—the captain—asked Thornley to check on his horse."

"That doesn't sound like a man contemplating taking his own life," Frederick remarked.

"No, indeed." Feeling blindsided again, Julian asked, "So what changed?"

"As to that, my lord," Phelps said, "the other prisoners have asked to speak with you. They claim they had nothing to do with the captain being hanged. They are adamant about that, and it's difficult to see how they might have managed it. However, they say they have something to tell you, and that they believe they know or at least can suggest why the captain killed himself."

"Is that so?" Julian glanced around at his family and saw the same interest that he felt reflected in every face. "I find I'm keen to hear what they have to say." He met Melissa's eyes, then looked at the others. "Should we go down there? Or…?"

"The library," Melissa stated. "We want their cooperation in solving this riddle, so let's make them comfortable rather than intimidate them." She met Julian's eyes and faintly smiled. "They'll be intimidated enough as it is."

Everyone agreed.

Julian looked at Phelps. "Give us ten minutes to get settled in the library, then bring all four up together. Use Thornley and two other footmen as guards." Recalling that the household knew of the attacks and would have a very real interest in the outcome, he added, "We'll set chairs for our prisoners in the library. Knock and bring them in, see them to the chairs, then I want you and the footmen to remain, standing against the bookcases."

"Yes, my lord." With his master taking charge and clear orders to follow, Phelps had regained his butlerish demeanor. He bowed and silently left the room.

Julian glanced around at the assembled Delameres, then waved to the door. "Shall we?"

En masse, they repaired to the library and, between them, set their stage. Under Julian and Melissa's joint direction, they rearranged the armchairs and sofa in a curve with their backs to the fireplace and set four upright chairs, placed an arm's length apart, in a line five yards away, facing the armchairs and sofa.

After some discussion, Julian and Melissa sat on the sofa, in the center of the curve and directly opposite the line of chairs. Felix sat in the armchair on Melissa's left, with Damian in the next chair along, while Veronica was ensconced in the chair on Julian's right, with Frederick in the next armchair and Gordon in the chair at that end of the curve.

They'd just settled in their appointed seats when a tap fell on the door. Julian took in everyone's now-eager expressions and called, "Come."

Phelps opened the door and led the prisoners in. Phelps paused to bow, and the four ex-staff did the same, then Phelps directed them to the chairs. After a momentary hesitation—they'd clearly not expected to be offered seats—they sorted themselves out and sat, with Mitchell at one end, then Manning and Richards, with Benton sinking onto the final chair.

Once they were settled, Phelps shut the door and with the three foot-men, who had followed the prisoners into the room, retreated to stand before the bookcases as instructed.

Mitchell, Manning, Richards, and Benton all took note of the arrange-ments, then all four looked at Julian.

Mildly, he said, "I understand you have something to tell us regarding Findlay-Wright's suicide."

The four exchanged glances, with Richards being the focal point for the other three.

Then all four returned their gazes to Julian, and Richards cleared his throat and said, "My lord, we couldn't help but overhear all that was said between you and the others of your family"—he dipped his head to indi-cate Melissa, Felix, and Damian—"and the captain yesterday, down in the dungeon. Well, we couldn't not hear. So we know the captain told you our secrets—the secrets he used to make us do his bidding in return for him not telling. Even though we did as he ordered, he told anyway." Self-disgust colored Richards's expression and touched the other prisoners' faces, too. "We might have guessed he wouldn't honor our bargain, but then, he had us over a barrel, as it were." Richards refocused on Julian. "But of course, we also heard what he said about your family and the threats he made against you. Before we tell you what else we know of him, we wanted to make plain that..."

When he paused, clearly searching for words, Benton gruffly said, "That we know what it's like being threatened like that, and you can be sure that not a word of what we heard will ever pass any of our lips."

Richards glanced at her, and her chin firmed, and she nodded. "There."

"Yes, well." Richards looked back at Julian. "We wanted to be clear that despite all that we did, we never had any wish—not of our own—to harm you or your family."

Reminded of Melissa's comment that these four were Findlay-Wright's victims, too—and if he had forgotten, she'd just squeezed his hand meaningfully—Julian inclined his head. "Duly noted." He paused, then added, "We're starting to understand your situation."

Richards nodded. "So that's that. Now, as to what we believe might have caused the captain to hang himself, it's like this." He glanced along the line. "Mitchell?"

The groom straightened on his chair and looked directly at Julian. "The captain told you that my brother was fighting in a regiment alongside his during a skirmish in India, and that my brother subsequently deserted. What he didn't tell you was what came in between. As my brother tells it, the regiments were fighting in parallel along the sides of a ravine. My brother and two of his mates were scouting to the rear flank, right along the edge of the ravine, looking for enemy stragglers, when they spotted two Englishmen who walked out into a space on the ravine's other side. Two officers from the other regiment. The senior officer turned to the junior one, and it was clear he was giving the man a dressing-down. The wind shifted, and they heard the senior officer say the words 'court martial.' Soon after, the senior officer dismissed the other man and started to walk off. The junior officer stood there a moment, then he pulled a pistol from his jacket, turned, and called to the senior officer, and when the officer paused and turned back, the junior officer shot him. A clean shot. The senior officer was dead before he hit the ground."

Mitchell paused, and Julian realized they were all sunk in the tale. No one moved so much as a finger, let alone looked away.

After drawing in a breath, Mitchell went on, "One of my brother's mates had called out, thinking to warn the senior officer, and in shock, they'd all sprung to their feet. The junior officer—and my brother and his friends recognized the man—saw them. He looked at them—took careful note of them—then he turned, picked up his dead senior officer's body, and carried it away." Mitchell blew out a breath. "The thing is, my brother and his mates didn't know either officer's name. But they did recognize the one who pulled the trigger. Carrot-Top Captain was his nickname, and the warnings in the camps were that you never got on his wrong side, or else you might get shot when next you were in the field, and who was to say it wouldn't be by an enemy sniper?

"My brother and his mates were in a panic. Given what they'd seen— given who they knew pulled the trigger—they didn't like their chances of surviving even another night in the camp. The enemy sometimes crept in, and men died. They were sure they'd be next. So they left—then and there, they struck out for the coast. They didn't go back for their things. They just left. Of course, they were said to have deserted, but they figured that was better than being dead. They found places on a ship's crew and made it back to England."

Julian was already connecting the facts and was increasingly stunned by the mental picture he was assembling. "All three of them?" he asked.

Mitchell nodded. He met Julian's gaze and held it. "My little brother is a carpenter now. He has a shop in Derby, and he's worked hard and made something of himself. He's married, and he and his wife have a little boy and another on the way. When I first saw Findlay-Wright here, I didn't think anything of it. I heard he was an ex-captain, but there're a lot of them about. But then he came and found me while I was exercising horses in the paddock, and he leaned on the fence and smiled and told me that if I didn't do as he said, exactly as he said, he'd report my little brother to the War Office as a deserter and also say that he was responsible for the death of that officer. That he and his mates—and I know them all, and they're all married with little ones—were the snipers that killed that man."

"You were coerced into being his agent," Melissa said.

"Yes." Mitchell nodded. "I'm not proud of giving in, and I'm ashamed of what I've done thanks to him, but I couldn't let him ruin my brother and his family—they're all the family I have."

Julian heard himself say, "I can't fault you for that," and knew it was the truth.

Mitchell looked faintly taken aback. Then he gathered himself and said, "That's all I knew of what happened in India, until last night."

Mitchell looked at Richards, who nodded, then straightened on his chair and looked at Julian. "The captain told you of my nephew. His father died when he was just a babe, and my sister and the boy came to live with me. I gave up being a footman and got a job with a solicitor so we could get a house and I'd be around more, and my sister cooked and kept the place neat. The lad's my nephew, but more like a son to me, and he's my sister's whole life. She and I scrimped and saved and put him through grammar school. He's bright and did well. Like Mitchell's brother, he's made something of himself, and we were all going along nicely until one evening, the captain came up to me as I was leaving work and told me he had evidence of my nephew's...preferences, and if I wanted to keep him out of jail, I would have to do as he said." He paused, then went on, "I knew he was evil, but I couldn't bring myself to ruin my nephew's and sister's lives. I did what he—the captain—told me. I regret it, but..."

Julian nodded. "You felt you had no choice."

Without meeting his eyes, Richards bobbed his head. "But I couldn't figure out why the captain had singled out Ronald—my nephew. To have the evidence the captain had, he had to have followed Ronald for days. So without letting on as to why I wanted to know, I asked my nephew if he'd ever come across a tall man with carroty-red hair. He had to think for a while, but then he remembered. The only such man he'd ever met was the captain who accompanied Colonel Maurice Delamere's body from India back to England. Ronald is the clerk at the War Office who deals with such matters, and he'd met the captain on several occasions while registering the details of Colonel Delamere's death and arranging the pension for his widow, who the captain knew well and was advising."

Richards's words set every Delamere in the room stirring. They all exchanged glances. They'd all seen the light.

With his gaze on the rug, unaware, Richards went on, "Ronald's a sympathetic soul, which is why he has that job. Dealing sensitively with the bereaved is something he's good at. I think Findlay-Wright saw enough at those meetings to guess about Ronald, and that's why he followed him. By the time Findlay-Wright spoke to me, he'd learned all about our family and knew I was the one to approach to blackmail to do his dirty work."

Richards glanced sidelong at Manning.

Manning straightened and took up the tale. "We saw you bring the captain in yesterday and put him in the cell. Until then, until after you spoke with him, we hadn't shared our stories with each other." He grimaced. "I suppose we were all clinging to the hope that, somehow, the secrets we'd sold our souls to conceal would remain buried. But then we heard him tell you of them anyway, and after you left, we got to talking." He glanced at Mitchell on his right and at Richards on his left. "Until then, neither Mitchell nor Richards had realized what your family's name —the name of the family holding the earldom of Carsely—is."

Mitchell pointed out, "We in the stables always hear you referred to as the earl, the countess, the dowager, and your brothers are Mr. Felix and Master Damian, and your uncle is Mr. Frederick."

"And for me," Richards put in, "it's always the earl, the countess, the dowager, and Mr. Frederick, or his lordship, her ladyship, and so on. I haven't been here long enough to realize that you're Delameres. Or that Mrs. Helen is the widow Ronald met."

Mitchell dragged in a breath. "But once we realized that…what I didn't mention in my earlier story was that the ravine was narrow, and my brother and his friends saw the senior officer more than well enough to describe him. When they first got home, they told me the story one night over several pints—I remember it clearly. They said the senior officer wore a colonel's uniform and was tall, dark-haired, and distinguished looking. All of them agree he had a scar across his jaw on the left side—

he was angry, and when he clenched his jaw, it stood out like a small white stripe."

Gordon made a choking sound. He pushed to his feet, spun blindly around, stalked behind the chairs to the window behind the desk, and with his feet braced apart, stood looking out. His arms were rigid by his sides, his hands tightly fisted.

Everyone's attention had been caught by the movement, but when Gordon didn't turn back or say anything, Julian looked once more at their erstwhile prisoners. "You figured it out—that Findlay-Wright was the captain who Mitchell's brother and his friends saw murder Colonel Maurice Delamere on the lip of an Indian ravine."

With something akin to sympathy in his eyes, Manning drew his gaze from Gordon, refocused on Julian, and nodded. "We put it together between us. We whispered—we didn't want him to hear. Not at first. Then later, once we'd had our suppers and they'd taken the lanterns and the place was dark for the night, we told Benton our story."

"I knew he was evil," Benton said. "Years ago, before he went to India, his regiment was stationed near the village where I lived with my mother and sister. My sister's a sweet, pretty thing. One afternoon, he and a couple of his friends raped her and left her for dead. I found her, and my mother and I put it about that she'd caught a debilitating fever, and I nursed her back to health. It took months, and often I feared she'd never recover, but eventually, she did. And then she met the local deacon. He's a kind, gentle man, and they fell in love and married, and I could finally stop worrying about Dolly."

Her face hardened. "But late last year, Findlay-Wright came back to the village. He saw Dolly and her husband, and from the way Dolly fainted away at the sight of him, the evil man realized the deacon didn't know what had happened to Dolly all those years ago. But he didn't approach Dolly—she wouldn't have been much use to him. He found me instead. He said he'd tell not just her husband but the whole village that Dolly had whored herself to him and his friends. It wasn't true, but of course, he'd be believed, and Dolly's life, and my mother's and mine as well, would be ruined." Her face darkened. "Or worse. Dolly was bad enough the first time. With it all brought back and made public, her marriage destroyed...she'd be like to end herself." Benton looked at Melissa. "I didn't want that to happen."

Melissa hadn't expected to feel sorry for Benton. Hadn't expected to find tears in her eyes. But they were there, and she nodded. "I understand."

Benton blinked, then drew in a breath and looked at Julian. "It was the first time I'd heard their tale, but I knew what it meant. Between us all, we explained to Findlay-Wright that we knew he'd killed Colonel Delamere. Manning and I knew the colonel was Mr. Gordon's father. We told Findlay-Wright we could prove that he did the deed, that we knew where the three witnesses were, and that we'd be telling you everything we knew first thing in the morning—as we are."

"Of course," Manning said, "we'd no idea he would take his life rather than face justice."

"But," Benton went on, "last night, we spelled out for him just what that justice would be. Not only had he murdered your relative in cold blood, but he'd then tried to kill several of you as well. He'd be convicted, and it was likely the Army would also take an interest. There was no way he would escape the hangman."

"As soon as we mentioned India," Richards said, "he fell silent. We didn't know how he was reacting, so to make sure he understood, we went on and on. It was a case of the worm turning. We'd been under his thumb for months, but now, we'd turned the tables."

"And as we pointed out to him," Mitchell said, "if it hadn't been for his grand scheme that had landed me, Richards, and Manning in the same cell at the Delamere principal estate, so we learned who the family was and could share our stories and understand what they meant, he'd never have been caught."

"But now that you—the family—would soon learn the truth from us," Manning said, "there would be no escape for him. While it was him against us, he would always win, but once it was him against the Delamere family, he would lose. He would hang, and he knew it."

"He didn't say a word," Benton said. "Didn't make a peep. We eventually settled down for the night—it was the first night I slept easily since he came back into my and my family's lives."

The three men nodded.

"Then we woke this morning"—Benton straightened in her chair —"and when the staff came with our breakfasts, we discovered he'd taken the coward's way out."

Silence descended.

The four simply sat there, staring vacantly as if they were looking back on the past months and barely daring to believe their ordeal was over and they were free of Findlay-Wright's yoke. Melissa saw the moment when they realized that was true. The tension that, until then, had gripped them eased, and animation returned to their features. Almost in unison, they drew in deep breaths, squared their shoulders, raised their heads, and looked at Julian.

All his family also looked at Julian. Even Gordon, still at the window, turned so he could glance sidelong and watch Julian's reaction. Everyone waited to learn what he would decide.

Julian studied the four people lined up before him, then formally inclined his head to them. "Thank you for telling us all you have. I commend your honesty and, indeed, your bravery. In our society, reacting as you did to threats to weaker family members would be judged a mark of honor. That doesn't excuse what you did, but it does make your actions much more understandable."

Much more relatable.

He paused. Knowing full well that, had he been in their shoes, he would almost certainly have done as they had, evenly, he said, "I wish to consult with the countess and other members of my family before deciding what should be done regarding you." He glanced at Phelps. "Please take Mitchell, Richards, Manning, and Benton to the small parlor and wait with them there. One of us will fetch you and them when I've made my decision."

Phelps bowed. "Yes, my lord." He turned, and the four ex-members of staff came to their feet. They also bowed, then preceded by the footmen, filed out of the room under Phelps's direction.

When the door shut behind the procession, Damian blew out a gusty breath and leaned forward, his elbows on his thighs. "My God! What a turn-up!" He looked across at Gordon. "Gordon?"

Gordon drew in a breath and, his expression set, walked back to the armchair he'd earlier occupied and sat. Stony-faced, he looked at Julian. "I vote we let all four of them go. I know they did terrible things, but none of them actually killed anyone, and they were in thrall to the monster who killed my father. I've seen how he works. He gets into people's heads, finds a weakness, and exploits it. He sows doubts and makes them unsure of their own minds, then he takes control. He does it —did it—with Mama constantly."

Frederick gave vent to a disaffected sound. "They might not have managed to kill anyone, but it wasn't for lack of trying."

Veronica turned her head to look at him, then reached out and grasped his hand. "They acted out of love. Love for their families." She looked at Damian, Felix, and lastly at Julian and Melissa. "How can any of us blame them for that?"

That was an unanswerable question. Julian glanced at Melissa. She'd been quiet, clearly thinking. He waited until, sensing his regard, she glanced at him and, trapping her gaze, arched his brows in silent question.

She held his gaze for several seconds, then said, "I was thinking of the Ride and of Herne, and of how the blessing of the gods is bestowed in return for compassion. I wonder if this is one of those situations when compassion is called for—when it's the right response in a difficult situation."

"So I should let them go?"

"I think you should. They've already paid a price, one that should never have been demanded of them. They've sacrificed some of their humanity in order to protect their loved ones, and as we've all admitted, we can't fault them for that. They were inherently good people forced to behave as the agents of an evil man, and I judge that what each was forced to do has left a scar on their souls that they will carry for the rest of their lives." She paused, her gaze steady on his, then concluded, "Like Gordon, I don't think it would be fair to add to their punishment. I, too, vote to let them go."

Felix stirred and, when Julian looked at him, inviting his comment, his brother offered, "If you think about it, in pushing Findlay-Wright into committing suicide, the four of them have saved us, the whole Delamere family, considerable anguish and distress. A trial of any sort would have created a furor, no matter how much we tried to keep things quiet. Just think of Helen, let alone our aunts. Hysteria would have been the least of it."

Julian inclined his head. "That's true." He looked at Damian.

Damian nodded. "I'm with Felix. Yes, they nearly harmed some of us, but they didn't, and in the end, they've done us a good turn. We haven't lost through what they've done—what they were forced to do." He paused, then amended, "Well, aside from the punt being holed and the gig disintegrating and the old barn burning down, but those are such minor things against the benefits of having Findlay-Wright exposed and removed from this earth, by his own hand, no less." He glanced at Gordon. "And we've learned the truth about Maurice. That's important, too."

Gordon dipped his head in acknowledgment.

Julian looked around the small gathering, studying all the faces. They'd made up their minds, and he had, too. He nodded. "Right, let's have them in and inform them of their fate."

Damian volunteered to fetch the group. He returned, followed by the procession of the prisoners, Phelps, and the footmen. At Julian's wave, the four returned to stand before their chairs.

He took in their resigned expressions. They were all expecting him to send them to trial.

"We've discussed your activities while under the control of the late Findlay-Wright. Your actions were very wrong, but you did not make them of your own free will." He glanced once more at his family and felt both grateful for their support and proud of their collective decision. Looking back at the four, he stated, "We've determined to allow you to leave Carsington free of all charges. It's early enough in the day—if you gather your belongings, we'll have Hockey drive you into Derby."

The stunned looks that overtook their expressions were almost enough to make him smile. Those looks also assured him that the decision to free the four was the right one. They looked like people waking from a nightmare and finally understanding it truly was over.

He looked at Phelps. "Please make sure they have all the wages due to them and add two pounds to each sum, so that they can travel to their homes in reasonable comfort."

Looking back at the now-incredulous four, he met their gazes. "I hope you'll seize this chance with both hands and get back to leading blameless lives. You've escaped unscathed from the crucible Findlay-Wright dragged you into. Don't squander this chance."

"No, my lord," came from all four throats.

"I'll never set a foot wrong again," Mitchell said, his heartfelt tone making the vow transparently sincere.

Julian nodded a dismissal, and with steps much lighter than when they'd entered, the four made for the door.

It was Benton who paused in the doorway, glanced back, and with a more relaxed expression than they'd previously seen on her heavy-featured face, observed, "He's dead and gone, and we're all free of him now."

Julian, Melissa, and all the Delameres inclined their heads in agreement.

The footmen trooped after the four, and Phelps followed on their heels and shut the door.

The sudden dissipation of tension affected all those remaining. As if they were puppets whose strings had been cut, they slumped in their chairs.

A second later, Damian sprang to his feet and headed for the tantalus. "I know it's early, but after that, we all need a drink."

No one demurred, and Damian poured libations for them all, which Gordon helped ferry around.

Accepting a glass of his best brandy, Julian looked around the faces of his nearest and dearest and found a smile curving his lips. He sipped, then as Damian and Gordon returned to their chairs, held up his glass. "Here's to a future free of Findlay-Wright and his murderous machinations. As the head of the family, I hereby decree that we should put his works behind us and go forward as if he'd never been."

"Hear, hear!" resonated through the room, and everyone drank.

That night, after sating their continuing need for the physical and emotional reassurance that lovemaking bestowed, Melissa settled beside Julian in her bed and, with her head pillowed on his chest, idly played with the crisp hair adorning the sleekly muscled expanse while her mind retrod the events of the day.

His hand closed over hers, and he lifted her fingers and kissed them before returning them to his chest and anchoring her hand beneath his. "What are you thinking about? I can hear your mind whirring."

She chuckled, but when he pointedly waited, as patient as ever, she replied, "I was just thinking of the lessons one learns during our journey through life, if one is wise and opens one's eyes."

"And what have you deduced from our recent travails?"

"That love is so much more than I'd thought." She paused, searching for the right way to phrase her musings. Eventually, she settled for, "We've been wrestling, you and I, with the meaning of love, of what love means to us. Yesterday, in learning of Veronica and Frederick and your father, we saw another, albeit similar aspect, and today, with our four would-be attackers, we saw love in yet another form."

He shifted his head and brushed his lips over her temple. "One thing I've learned is that love is a powerful force. I hadn't truly understood that before, but it's a force to be reckoned with."

"It's a force that should never be underestimated." She glanced up and, through the shadows, met his eyes. "And if properly appreciated and harnessed, love can achieve so very much."

Julian held her gaze and smiled. "I'm willing to give it our best shot. Are you?"

She laughed, and her smile was the most glorious sight he had ever thought to see.

"I'll take that challenge, my lord, and make sure you live up to your side of our bargain."

He grinned at her. "Please do."

$\sim$

Four evenings later, Julian and Melissa stood at the head of the ballroom stairs and welcomed their guests to the Midsummer Ball.

The surrounding gentry had turned out in force, eager to meet the new Countess of Carsely. As the stalwarts of the county rolled in, it was plain as a pikestaff that their expectations of the evening, and of Julian and his new bride, had been not just met but exceeded. Compliments rained down on their heads as the guests admired the handsome couple, so gracious, so assured, then in moving on, took in the greenery-bedecked ballroom already aswirl with color and life as the early comers milled and sipped the champagne dispensed by footmen in full livery.

This was their new mistress's first major event, and the staff had pulled out all stops. The ballroom had been transformed into a woodland glade, and the ladies in their bright finery were the butterflies flitting through it. As befitted the occasion, the evening was almost balmy, allowing the long doors to the terrace to be propped wide, affording views over the lawns, fields, and woods to the black, star-spangled sky.

By the time the receiving line dwindled and Julian and Melissa quit their post to circulate among their guests, an air of unrelieved gaiety had taken hold. Good cheer abounded, and laughter rose in waves, then the musicians set bow to string, and the dancing began, and everyone threw themselves into enjoying the unfettered pleasure.

Everyone seemed to think it appropriate that Julian and Melissa should lead the company in the first waltz, and they didn't demur. With his wife in his arms, Julian swept down the floor, the smile on his face a banner of proud happiness.

Melissa drank in the sight, then smiling herself, murmured, "I never expected to feel like this—so unreservedly happy, literally without a care in the world. I didn't know reaching such a state was possible."

His smile deepened, and he whirled her through the turn, then drew her closer. "Me, either."

She glanced aside to exchange a pleased smile with Veronica, circling in Frederick's arms, then turned back to Julian. "Dealing with Findlay-Wright's machinations distracted me and diverted my attention from what's been growing between us and around us, with your family and this household." She met his eyes. "We've somehow meshed together, all of us. We've reached an accord with each other, and it all feels so very comfortable."

While his smile didn't waver, the expression in his gray eyes grew more serious. "Me, you, all those here, this place, and this time. It's all clicked together in interlocking pieces, ultimately forming a lock and key."

Her smile deepened. "And now we turn that key and see what comes?"

His grin flashed. "More or less."

They whirled on, then he said, "We go forward—together and with everyone who supports us, and they are legion—and see what we can make of the chance Fate has handed us." He looked into her eyes. "You and me—politically, socially—we know we can be a force for change. For good, for right. If we choose to be so."

Equally committed, she replied. "If we choose, and we do so choose."

He nodded. "Agreed."

Felix whirled his partner close, and Damian, also circling, lightly bumped Julian's shoulder.

Insouciantly grinning, Damian ducked closer and said, "Just a warning, brother and sister dear, that Felix and I have arranged a little something extra in honor of our new countess. All will be revealed half an hour after supper is over."

Julian and Melissa came alert, but before they could speak and question, Damian and Felix whirled their partners away and kept their gazes and their attentions focused on the young ladies.

"What on earth have they done?" Melissa asked.

Julian sighed. "I doubt it will be dangerous, and I'm sure they won't surrender and say no matter how much we badger them, so I suggest we forget that Damian even spoke." He caught Melissa's gaze, and his confident, assured expression returned. "Besides, given all we've been through, whatever it is, we'll be able to handle it."

She laughed and agreed, and they let the last phrases of the waltz reclaim them.

The evening rolled on, and they moved among their guests, with many eager to speak with them regarding local events and concerns, but here and there, they encountered those wanting to engage on wider-ranging subjects, allowing them to gain an informed view of attitudes to and opinions on the issues they felt would soon be addressed in Parliament.

Supper came and went. Engrossed in interacting with their guests, Melissa and Julian had largely forgotten Damian's warning until shouts went up.

"To the terrace! To the terrace!"

Melissa and Julian recognized the initial voices, but the call was taken up by many others, and the guests dutifully streamed through the wide-open doors to spread along and across the flagstone terrace.

Exchanging amused but wary glances, Julian and Melissa were among the last to leave the lights of the ballroom and step into the cooler air. They paused just outside, taking advantage of a space by the castle wall. As they settled and looked around, a rocket streaked into the sky and exploded in a fiery burst of bright red stars.

A collective "Ooh!" rose from the crowd, and every head rose to stare at the heavens.

Melissa smiled as a second rocket exploded in a cascade of silvery stars. She leaned against Julian, and he wrapped his arms about her, holding her there. As more fireworks lit up the sky, still smiling, she sighed. "I do like your brothers."

"I'm passingly fond of them myself."

Heads raised, they watched as the display continued, then Julian looked down at Melissa's profile. "Here we are, and for my money, life in this moment is perfect."

"Hmm." She glanced up and, with her lips irrepressibly curved, met his eyes. "I can't disagree."

He tightened his arms and gently squeezed her. "As I recall, you didn't approve when the grandes dames and so many others dubbed ours the perfect match." His gaze teasing, he arched his brows. "Yet here we are."

Melissa allowed her smile to bloom, then faced forward and pressed her head back against his shoulder. "I'll tell you a secret," she whispered. "Sometimes—just sometimes—the grandes dames are right."

Dear Reader,

This is one of those books that was always going to be written. The instant Julian, Viscount Dagenham, appeared as a brash young nobleman in the first of Lady Osbaldestone's Christmas Chronicles, *Lady Osbaldestone's Christmas Goose*, I suspected that, one day, he would feature in his own book. He was that sort of character. And when, in the second of the Christmas Chronicles, he met one of Lady Osbaldestone's granddaughters, Miss Melissa North, it was obvious—I'm sure to all—that one day...

So finally, Melissa and Dagenham have had their romance, and we can now leave them to enjoy their happily-ever-after. I had fun creating Carsington Castle (it doesn't exist) but also incorporating some of the actual local customs, such as the early June "dressing of the wells" with flowers, that in that period, occurred in Wirksworth and the surrounding district. Much of the details of Julian's Irish political background are based on fact—Gregory was the Under-Secretary for Ireland at the time, and the Ribbonmen were an Irish political group. The Wirksworth Ride, however, is entirely fictitious! And when it came to the puppy, well, who could resist including Ulysses in the tale?

I hope you enjoyed reading of Julian and Melissa's journey into love and marriage.

Next up, as flagged in the last pages of my previous novel, *The Secrets of Lord Grayson Child*, we return to the Cynsters Next Generation novels, following Gregory Cynster, who has, as his sister Therese informs his younger brother Martin, gone to claim his inheritance, namely Bellamy Hall. As Therese foreshadows, Gregory is in for a surprise.

That book, *Foes, Friends, and Lovers*, will be with you on March 17, 2022.

With my best wishes for continued happy reading!

Stephanie.

For alerts as new books are released, plus information on upcoming books, exclusive sweepstakes and sneak peeks into upcoming novels, sign up for Stephanie's Private Email Newsletter http://www.stephanielaurens.com/newsletter-signup/

Or if you don't have time to chat and want a quick email alert, sign up and follow me at BookBub https://www.bookbub.com/authors/stephanie-laurens

The ultimate source for detailed information on all Stephanie's published books, including covers, descriptions, and excerpts, is Stephanie's Website www.stephanielaurens.com

You can also follow Stephanie via her Amazon Author Page at http://tinyurl.com/zc3e9mp

Goodreads members can follow Stephanie via her author page https://www.goodreads.com/author/show/9241.Stephanie_Laurens

You can email Stephanie at stephanie@stephanielaurens.com

Or find her on Facebook
https://www.facebook.com/AuthorStephanieLaurens/

COMING NEXT:

FOES, FRIENDS, AND LOVERS
Cynster Next Generation Novel #10
To be released on March 17, 2022.

Gregory Cynster arrives at Bellamy Hall believing that, in taking up the reins, he'll be able to fashion the house and estate into a typical country gentleman's residence. Instead, he discovers that the previous owners have filled the house and the estate with people he'd had no idea were there and created a situation entirely beyond his imagining. And then there's the Hall's chatelaine, who is an attractive, distracting mystery in her own right. Just who is Miss Caitlin Fergusson, why is she hiding, essentially in isolation in Northamptonshire, and most importantly, what is she hiding from?

Available for pre-order from January, 2022.

RECENTLY RELEASED:

THE SECRETS OF LORD GRAYSON CHILD
Cynster Next Generation-Connected Novel
(following on from The Games Lovers Play)

#1 New York Times *bestselling author Stephanie Laurens returns to the world of the Cynsters' next generation with the tale of an unconventional nobleman and an equally unconventional noblewoman learning to love and trust again.*

A jilted noblewoman forced into a dual existence half in and half out of the ton is unexpectedly confronted by the nobleman who left her behind ten years ago, but before either can catch their breaths, they trip over a murder and into a race to capture a killer.

Lord Grayson Child is horrified to discover that *The London Crier*, a popular gossip rag, is proposing to expose his extraordinary wealth to the ton's matchmakers, not to mention London's shysters and Captain Sharps. He hies to London and corners *The Crier's* proprietor—only to discover the paper's owner is the last person he'd expected to see.

Izzy—Lady Isadora Descartes—is flabbergasted when Gray appears in her printing works' office. He's the very last person she wants to meet while in her role as owner of *The Crier*, but there he is, as large as life, and she has to deal with him without giving herself away! She manages—just—and seizes on the late hour to put him off so she can work out what to do.

But before leaving the printing works, she and he stumble across a murder, and all hell breaks loose.

Izzy can only be grateful for Gray's support as, to free them both of suspicion, they embark on a joint campaign to find the killer.

Yet working side by side opens their eyes to who they each are now —both quite different to the youthful would-be lovers of ten years before. Mutual respect, affection, and appreciation grow, and amid the chaos of hunting a ruthless killer, they find themselves facing the question of whether what they'd deemed wrecked ten years before can be resurrected.

Then the killer's motive proves to be a treasonous plot, and with others, Gray and Izzy race to prevent a catastrophe, a task that ultimately falls to them alone in a situation in which the only way out is through selfless togetherness—only by relying on each other will they survive.

A classic historical romance laced with crime and intrigue. A Cynster Next Generation-connected novel—a full-length historical romance of 115,000 words.

RECENTLY RELEASED:

THE GAMES LOVERS PLAY
Cynster Next Generation Novel #9

#1 New York Times *bestselling author Stephanie Laurens returns to the Cynsters' next generation with an evocative tale of two people striving to overcome unusual hurdles in order to claim true love.*

A nobleman wedded to the lady he loves strives to overwrite five years of masterful pretence and open his wife's eyes to the fact that he loves her as much as she loves him.

Lord Devlin Cader, Earl of Alverton, married Therese Cynster five years ago. What he didn't tell her then and has assiduously hidden ever since—for what seemed excellent reasons at the time—is that he loves her every bit as much as she loves him.

For her own misguided reasons, Therese had decided that the adage that Cynsters always marry for love did not necessarily mean said Cynsters were loved in return. She accepted that was usually so, but being universally viewed by gentlemen as too managing, bossy, and opinionated, she believed she would never be loved for herself. Consequently, after falling irrevocably in love with Devlin, when he made it plain he didn't love her yet wanted her to wife, she accepted the half love-match he offered, and once they were wed, set about organizing to make their marriage the very best it could be.

Now, five years later, they are an established couple within the haut ton, have three young children, and Devlin is making a name for himself in business and political circles. There's only one problem. Having attended numerous Cynster weddings and family gatherings and spent time with Therese's increasingly married cousins, who with their spouses all embrace the Cynster ideal of marriage based on mutually acknowledged love, Devlin is no longer content with the half love-match he himself engineered. No fool, he sees and comprehends what the craven act of denying his love is costing both him and Therese and feels compelled to rectify his fault. He wants for them what all Therese's married cousins enjoy—the rich and myriad benefits of marriages based on acknowledged mutual love.

Love, he's discovered, is too powerful a force to deny, leaving him wrestling with the conundrum of finding a way to convincingly reveal to Therese that he loves her without wrecking everything—especially the mutual trust—they've built over the past five years.

A classic historical romance set amid the glittering world of the London haut ton. A Cynster Next Generation novel—a full-length historical romance of 110,000 words.

And if you haven't already indulged:
PREVIOUS VOLUMES IN LADY OSBALDESTONE'S CHRISTMAS CHRONICLES

The first volume in Lady Osbaldestone's Christmas Chronicles
LADY OSBALDESTONE'S CHRISTMAS GOOSE

#1 New York Times bestselling author Stephanie Laurens brings you a lighthearted tale of Christmas long ago with a grandmother and three of her grandchildren, one lost soul, a lady driven to distraction, a recalcitrant donkey, and a flock of determined geese.

Three years after being widowed, Therese, Lady Osbaldestone finally settles into her dower property of Hartington Manor in the village of Little Moseley in Hampshire. She is in two minds as to whether life in the small village will generate sufficient interest to keep her amused over the months when she is not in London or visiting friends around the country. But she will see.

It's December, 1810, and Therese is looking forward to her usual

Christmas with her family at Winslow Abbey, her youngest daughter, Celia's home. But then a carriage rolls up and disgorges Celia's three oldest children. Their father has contracted mumps, and their mother has sent the three—Jamie, George, and Lottie—to spend this Christmas with their grandmama in Little Moseley.

Therese has never had to manage small children, not even her own. She assumes the children will keep themselves amused, but quickly learns that what amuses three inquisitive, curious, and confident youngsters isn't compatible with village peace. Just when it seems she will have to set her mind to inventing something, she and the children learn that with only twelve days to go before Christmas, the village flock of geese has vanished.

Every household in the village is now missing the centerpiece of their Christmas feast. But how could an entire flock go missing without the slightest trace? The children are as mystified and as curious as Therese—and she seizes on the mystery as the perfect distraction for the three children as well as herself.

But while searching for the geese, she and her three helpers stumble on two locals who, it is clear, are in dire need of assistance in sorting out their lives. Never one to shy from a little matchmaking, Therese undertakes to guide Miss Eugenia Fitzgibbon into the arms of the determinedly reclusive Lord Longfellow. To her considerable surprise, she discovers that her grandchildren have inherited skills and talents from both her late husband as well as herself. And with all the customary village events held in the lead up to Christmas, she and her three helpers have opportunities galore in which to subtly nudge and steer.

Yet while their matchmaking appears to be succeeding, neither they nor anyone else have found so much as a feather from the village's geese. Larceny is ruled out; a flock of that size could not have been taken from the area without someone noticing. So where could the birds be? And with the days passing and Christmas inexorably approaching, will they find the blasted birds in time?

First in series. A novel of 60,000 words. A Christmas tale of romance and geese.

The second volume in Lady Osbaldestone's Christmas Chronicles
LADY OSBALDESTONE AND THE MISSING CHRISTMAS CAROLS

#1 New York Times *bestselling author Stephanie Laurens brings you a heart-warming tale of a long-ago country-village Christmas, a grandmother, three eager grandchildren, one moody teenage granddaughter, an earnest young lady, a gentleman in hiding, and an elusive book of Christmas carols.*

Therese, Lady Osbaldestone, and her household are quietly delighted when her younger daughter's three children, Jamie, George, and Lottie, insist on returning to Therese's house, Hartington Manor in the village Little Moseley, to spend the three weeks leading up to Christmas participating in the village's traditional events.

Then out of the blue, one of Therese's older granddaughters, Melissa, arrives on the doorstep. Her mother, Therese's older daughter, begs Therese to take Melissa in until the family gathering at Christmas—otherwise, Melissa has nowhere else to go.

Despite having no experience dealing with moody, reticent teenagers like Melissa, Therese welcomes Melissa warmly. The younger children are happy to include their cousin in their plans—and despite her initial aloofness, Melissa discovers she's not too old to enjoy the simple delights of a village Christmas.

The previous year, Therese learned the trick to keeping her unexpected guests out of mischief. She casts around and discovers that the new organist, who plays superbly, has a strange failing. He requires the written music in front of him before he can play a piece, and the church's book of Christmas carols has gone missing.

Therese immediately volunteers the services of her grandchildren, who are only too happy to fling themselves into the search to find the missing book of carols. Its disappearance threatens one of the village's most-valued Christmas traditions—the Carol Service—yet as the book has always been freely loaned within the village, no one imagines that it won't be found with a little application.

But as Therese's intrepid four follow the trail of the book from house to house, the mystery of where the book has vanished to only deepens. Then the organist hears the children singing and invites them to form a special guest choir. The children love singing, and provided they find the book in time, they'll be able to put on an extra-special service for the village.

While the urgency and their desire to finding the missing book escalates, the children—being Therese's grandchildren—get distracted by the potential for romance that buds, burgeons, and blooms before them.

Yet as Christmas nears, the questions remain: Will the four unravel the twisted trail of the missing book in time to save the village's Carol Service? And will they succeed in nudging the organist and the harpist they've found to play alongside him into seizing the happy-ever-after that hovers before the pair's noses?

Second in series. A novel of 62,000 words. A Christmas tale full of music and romance.

The third volume in Lady Osbaldestone's Christmas Chronicles
LADY OSBALDESTONE'S PLUM PUDDINGS

#1 New York Times bestselling author Stephanie Laurens brings you the delights of a long-ago country-village Christmas, featuring a grandmother, her grandchildren, an artifact hunter, the lady who catches his eye, and three ancient coins that draw them all together in a Christmas treasure hunt.

Therese, Lady Osbaldestone, and her household again welcome her younger daughter's children, Jamie, George, and Lottie, plus their cousins Melissa and Mandy, all of whom have insisted on spending the three weeks prior to Christmas at Therese's house, Hartington Manor, in the village of Little Moseley.

The children are looking forward to the village's traditional events, and this year, Therese has arranged a new distraction—the plum puddings she and her staff are making for the entire village. But while cleaning the coins donated as the puddings' good-luck tokens, the children discover that three aren't coins of the realm. When consulted, Reverend Colebatch summons a friend, an archeological scholar from Oxford, who confirms the coins are Roman, raising the possibility of a Roman treasure buried somewhere near. Unfortunately, Professor Webster is facing a deadline and cannot assist in the search, but along with his niece Honor, he will stay in the village, writing, remaining available for consultation should the children and their helpers uncover more treasure.

It soon becomes clear that discovering the source of the coins—or even which villager donated them—isn't a straightforward matter. Then the children come across a personable gentleman who knows a great deal about Roman antiquities. He introduces himself as Callum Harris, and they agree to allow him to help, and he gets their search back on track.

But while the manor five, assisted by the gentlemen from Fulsom Hall, scour the village for who had the coins and search the countryside for signs of excavation and Harris combs through the village's country-house libraries, amassing evidence of a Roman compound somewhere near, the site from which the coins actually came remains a frustrating mystery.

Then Therese recognizes Harris, who is more than he's pretending to be. She also notes the romance burgeoning between Harris and Honor Webster, and given the girl doesn't know Harris's full name, let alone his fraught relationship with her uncle, Therese steps in. But while she can engineer a successful resolution to one romance-of-the-season, as well a reconciliation long overdue, another romance that strikes much closer to home is beyond her ability to manipulate.

Meanwhile, the search for the source of the coins goes on, but time is running out. Will Therese's grandchildren and their Fulsom Hall helpers locate the Roman merchant's villa Harris is sure lies near before they all must leave the village for Christmas with their families?

Third in series. A novel of 70,000 words. A Christmas tale of antiquities, reconciliation, romance, and requited love.

The fourth instalment in Lady Osbaldestone's Christmas Chronicles
LADY OSBALDESTONE'S CHRISTMAS INTRIGUE

#1 New York Times bestselling author Stephanie Laurens immerses you in the simple joys of a long-ago country-village Christmas, featuring a grandmother, her grandchildren, her unwed son, a determined not-so-young lady, foreign diplomats, undercover guards, and agents of Napoleon!

At Hartington Manor in the village of Little Moseley, Therese, Lady Osbaldestone, and her household are once again enjoying the company of her intrepid grandchildren, Jamie, George, and Lottie, when they are unexpectedly joined by her ladyship's youngest and still-unwed son, also the children's favorite uncle, Christopher.

As the Foreign Office's master intelligencer, Christopher has been ordered into hiding until the department can appropriately deal with the

French agent spotted following him in London. Christopher chose to seek refuge in Little Moseley because it's such a tiny village that anyone without a reason to be there stands out. Neither he nor his office-appointed bodyguard expect to encounter any dramas.

Then Christopher spots a lady from London he believes has been hunting him with matrimonial intent. He can't understand how she tracked him to the village, but determined to avoid her, he enlists the children's help. The children discover their information-gathering skills are in high demand, and while engaging with the villagers as they usually do and taking part in the village's traditional events, they do their best to learn what Miss Marion Sewell is up to.

But upon reflection, Christopher realizes it's unlikely the Marion he was so attracted to years before has changed all that much, and he starts to wonder if what she wants to tell him is actually something he might want to hear. Unfortunately, he has set wheels in motion that are not easy to redirect. Although Marion tries to approach him several times, he and she fail to make contact.

Then just when it seems they will finally connect, a dangerous stranger lures Marion away. Fearing the worst, Christopher gives chase—trailed by his bodyguard, the children, and a small troop of helpful younger gentlemen.

What they discover at nearby Parteger Hall is not at all what anyone expected, and as the action unfolds, the assembled company band together to protect a secret vital to the resolution of the war against Napoleon.

Fourth in series. A novel of 81,000 words. A Christmas tale of intrigue, personal evolution, and love.

ABOUT THE AUTHOR

#1 *New York Times* bestselling author Stephanie Laurens began writing romances as an escape from the dry world of professional science. Her hobby quickly became a career when her first novel was accepted for publication, and with entirely becoming alacrity, she gave up writing about facts in favor of writing fiction.

All Laurens's works to date are historical romances, ranging from medieval times to the mid-1800s, and her settings range from Scotland to India. The majority of her works are set in the period of the British Regency. Laurens has published over 80 works of historical romance, including 40 *New York Times* bestsellers. Laurens has sold more than 20 million print, audio, and e-books globally. All her works are continuously available in print and e-book formats in English worldwide, and have been translated into many other languages. An international bestseller, among other accolades, Laurens has received the Romance Writers of America® prestigious RITA® Award for Best Romance Novella 2008 for *The Fall of Rogue Gerrard.*

Laurens's continuing novels featuring the Cynster family are widely regarded as classics of the historical romance genre. Other series include the *Bastion Club Novels*, the *Black Cobra Quartet*, the *Adventurers Quartet,* and the *Casebook of Barnaby Adair Novels.*

For information on all published novels and on upcoming releases and updates on novels yet to come, visit Stephanie's website: www. stephanielaurens.com

To sign up for Stephanie's Email Newsletter (a private list) for heads-up alerts as new books are released, exclusive sneak peeks into upcoming books, and exclusive sweepstakes contests, follow the prompts at http:// www.stephanielaurens.com/newsletter-signup/

To follow Stephanie on BookBub, head to her BookBub Author Page: https://www.bookbub.com/authors/stephanie-laurens

Stephanie lives with her husband and a goofy black labradoodle in the hills outside Melbourne, Australia. When she isn't writing, she's reading, and if she isn't reading, she'll be tending her garden.

www.stephanielaurens.com
stephanie@stephanielaurens.com

CPSIA information can be obtained
at www.ICGtesting.com
Printed in the USA
LVHW021038211021
701060LV00009B/136

9 781925 559507